Bright Dead Things

Bitter Legacies I

Hailey Turner

To Lily Morton.
We need to go back to York together.

Come away, O human child!
*   To the waters and the wild*
*   With a faery, hand in hand,*
*   For the world's more full of weeping than you can understand*

— W. B. YEATS

Content Warnings

This book contains the following:

Implied sexual slavery
Implied rape

The Otherworld
Tech Duinn
Winter Court
Gorias
Mag Mell
Spring Court
Falias
Murias
Tír na nÓg
Summer Court
Emain Ablach
Autumn Court
Findias

Chapter One

There was a body in the woods.

Park ranger Cillian Dunne grimaced as he drove his government-issued Ford truck down the dirt road within the Quabbin Reservoir wilderness. Vehicles weren't typically allowed in this part of the state-owned land in order to keep the water clean, but his supervisor was turning a blind eye to that particular law after the 10-65 had been called in. Cillian was glad Captain Henry MacIntyre—*call me Mac*—had waived the no-driving rule for the moment. The early July heat meant hauling a corpse out of the forest on foot wouldn't have been pleasant.

Cillian didn't know what to expect when he finally pulled off to the side of the dirt road and parked behind Mac's truck. He turned off the engine and picked up his wide-brimmed hat from the passenger seat, putting it on once he got out. He left his rifle secured in the truck cab, but his duty-issued Glock was holstered to his belt. Its presence was a comfort in the quiet of the forest.

At twenty-five, Cillian had always preferred the slow pace of the outdoors over the hustle and bustle of a city. He'd grown up in Pelham, Massachusetts, busing to school in Amherst with his childhood best friend for years. Small-town life was all Cillian had known before going to university to get a degree that would let him become a park ranger. He liked Pelham better than Boston, liked the quiet and the seemingly endless stretch of forest he'd spent hours playing in during daylight hours as a kid, but never at night. No one went into the forest at night if they could help it.

The Quabbin Reservoir was acres of wilderness surrounding a man-made body of water where the only recreation allowed was fishing, biking, and hiking in designated areas. Because it served as drinking water for over two million people, swimming, boating, and anything that required an engine were prohibited. Which meant the unfortunate hiker who'd died within the tree line hadn't had an easy way to escape.

From what, Cillian didn't know for sure.

"Over here," Mac called out from where he stood beneath the shade of a white oak tree.

Cillian stepped off the dirt road into the sparse grass, the tread of his work boots catching on loose pebbles. The black cloud of buzzing flies swarming over a body sprawled on the ground was impossible to miss. Cillian could smell the decomposition in the air, like meat that had sat out in the sun for too long, spoiled and rotten. "So it's definitely a body, not a possible one like you radioed."

"Unfortunately," Mac said with a grimace, looking at the corpse rather than at Cillian. His graying brown hair was shaved close to his skull and mostly hidden beneath the wide-brimmed hat he wore. His tan shirt with the ranger badge insignia patch sewn onto the left shirt sleeve, dark green pants, and black work boots that were good for hiking, was the same uniform Cillian wore. Cillian's hair wasn't quite regulation, falling a little past his shoulders when it wasn't tied back while on duty, but Mac had never complained.

Mac had been a park ranger for almost twenty-seven years now, having lived in Pelham most of his life. He was older than Cillian, a good man, a great mentor, and a pillar of their small town's community for as long as Cillian could remember. Mac was rarely fazed by the calls they all found themselves on, but today, the most senior ranger in the Division of Water Supply Protection Rangers assigned to patrol the Quabbin Reservoir appeared tight-lipped and worried.

Cillian stopped a few feet from the corpse, knowing better than to get any closer. He didn't want to disturb the crime scene. But no matter how far away he stood, Cillian knew he wouldn't be able to get the image out of his mind of the ravaged body with its ripped-open torso and last bits of intestines and other organs hanging out from the cavity. It was as if some vicious animal had clawed the man open and feasted on his insides.

Despite the sun overhead making the air heavy with summer heat, a chill ran through Cillian's body. His teeth clacked together faintly for a moment, jaw twitching. "Was it a bear?"

Mac raised a hand to rub at his mouth, eyes on the body. "Best if it was."

That wasn't an answer. "Mac."

"I had to call it in to the police. They're sending a couple of patrolmen out to take over, but the county's Crime Scene Unit and medical examiner are coming from outside Pelham. They won't get here and be done with two crime scenes in time before sunset."

Cillian jerked his head around. "Two? Where's the other body?"

Mac finally raised his gaze and looked at him, something like grief in the older man's eyes for a split second that disappeared so quickly Cillian questioned if he'd even seen it in the first place. "This is Ray Carroll. Patrolmen went to his home after I called in my report. They found it ransacked and Juliana dead. I wanted to be the one to tell you. I'm sorry."

Cillian stepped forward without thinking, stopping only when Mac held out an arm to block him from getting any closer. He stared at the body of his childhood best friend's stepfather in disbelief. He couldn't see the man Ray had been in the ragged remains of his face, but Cillian recognized the gold Catholic saint medal the electrician had always worn. Other details clawed their way through the shock, rattling through him, making it difficult to breathe, making it impossible to deny the bloody truth lying at his feet.

Ray Carroll had been Bran Gallagher's stepfather since he was thirteen and Cillian fourteen. Juliana Gallagher had married Ray but hadn't taken his name, even after they had a daughter. Cillian hadn't much liked the man growing up because Bran hadn't, but he'd never wish this kind of death on Ray. He didn't think even Bran would, and Cillian hadn't seen Bran since the night before their high school graduation, when he'd ruined everything by pushing the younger boy away.

Seven years since that fateful night, and Cillian still thought about Bran.

Which meant, in that moment, he thought about Aisling as well.

"Where's Aisling? What happened to her?" Cillian asked, forcing himself to work past the shock and focus on the job at hand, which was worrying about Bran's younger sister. The thought that she might be dead as well made his stomach clench into a horrific little knot.

"She wasn't in the house or on the property. The police are checking with the neighbors. If we can't find signs of her, we'll need to start a search. First places we'll look will be the cabins."

Cillian looked past Mac at the trees stretching deep into the forest and the shadows that existed beneath the leafy canopy. It was instinctive to want to stare, but he knew better than to look for long and so jerked his gaze away from the trees. "Why? You don't really think the stories are true? That it's the lights?"

Mac's lips twisted up at one corner, the grimace looking as if it ached. "Is your iron secured?"

The answer was in the question, and Cillian could only put his hand in his pocket and pull out the small iron disk the size of a quarter he carried with him every hour of every day he was outside his home. He forgot about it most of the time until moments like this. Mac stared at it for a few seconds before nodding curtly, and Cillian returned it to his pocket.

Everyone who grew up in Pelham carried a bit of iron with them wherever they went, admonished by the older generations to do so. Younger generations laughed off the stories that had been around as long as the town, but those who stayed never went without iron. Even those rangers who didn't call Pelham home but were in their division carried iron because Mac made it a mandate, always saying the forest might be beautiful, but it wasn't kind.

Cillian had lived his entire life with those stories whispered as warnings by town folk, but had never seen anything that meant they were real. Still, the unspoken threat was why Cillian didn't leave Mac there alone on that dirt road, waiting with him until the patrolmen from the

Pelham Police Department arrived. They exchanged greetings with the pair closer to the road than the forest, with Mac offering up a brief verbal report to the senior patrolman, a man about a decade older than Mac.

"Hikers found Ray's body when they were coming back from the trails," Mac said.

"Two deaths on the same day," the older patrolman said, staring at where the body lay in the tree line. The name on his badge read *Wilson*. "We'll need to warn for bears."

Cillian frowned, eyeing the forest. He'd been a kid the last time there was a bear attack, and his mother had kept him inside the entire summer. He hadn't even been able to see Bran except for a few times when Juliana had dropped the younger boy off for a sleepover.

Mac only nodded at the patrolman's statement. "That's the plan. I'll have my rangers post signs at the area gates and begin outreach with people coming to the reservoir. It's been years since we've had to discourage people from coming out here. We're lucky the Fourth of July celebrations are over, but school is still out. It'll be tough to convince people to find somewhere else to go for their recreation."

"Better you than us."

Mac snorted. "I'm not the one who needs to talk to the medical examiner about bear attacks."

"The crime scene at the home is worse than this, from what I've heard, but the body looks the same as Ray's. I don't think it should be a problem."

Mac flinched ever so slightly, but the patrolmen either didn't notice or pretended otherwise. Cillian noticed. Cillian knew Mac and his wife had been friends with Juliana and Ray. As for Cillian, he was trying not to think about Bran's mother being dead because that was a grief he couldn't deal with right then.

His right hand started to itch, a faint burning sensation creeping across his palm. Cillian ignored it.

"Those not handling the crime scene at the Gallagher home are looking for Juliana's and Ray's daughter. We're prepared to launch a search if needed. We also have a staff member trying to track down her son," the younger patrolman said.

"Are your people willing to search at night?" Mac asked.

Patrolman Wilson hesitated before shaking his head, gaze flicking toward the trees. "Not in the forest."

Pelham didn't exactly shut down when it got dark, but people tended to stay within the town's perimeter, driving between their homes and Red's Diner or the lone bar if they felt the need to hang out. Stories about lights were still told to children and travelers passing through town, and ingrained superstitious habits were hard to break. People didn't walk alone after dark, and they certainly didn't go traipsing through the forest if they could help it. Rangers did because that was their job.

What the locals knew, and which rangers made sure all visitors were aware of, were the forest paths that led to tiny, one-room cabins dotting the wilderness surrounding the Quabbin Reservoir. The path to each one was designated by what locals called witchmarks carved into trees, carvings that Cillian had memorized as a child during summer camps. The cabins themselves weren't meant for camping but for safety, a long-standing tradition that could be traced back generations, to a time even before the reservoir existed.

Cillian wondered if maybe Aisling had run to one of those cabins in the terror of whatever she might have experienced. He hoped so. It was better than the alternative. Cillian mentally mapped where he knew her home to be against the forest with its hidden cabins. A cabin might have been close enough for her to reach, but he wasn't sure she'd go *into* the forest if the threat had come out of it.

"I'd like to head over to the Gallagher home and coordinate with the patrolmen about Aisling," Cillian said to Mac.

Mac nodded. "I'll go check on the Gallaghers' Shoppe. Reports came back that nothing seemed amiss over there, but we can't rule anything out. If we haven't found signs of Aisling in the next hour, we'll start an official search."

No one asked about Bran, Juliana's oldest child and only son. As far as Cillian knew, Bran had left for Boston after high school, leaving the running of his family's Ye Olde Curiosities Shoppe to his mother. He'd come back to Pelham a few times, but Cillian never heard of his visits until after Bran was gone again. He no longer had Bran's phone number and would have no idea how to locate him without breaking some laws when it came to accessing a search program. Sometimes he thought about trying social media, but never did.

He still missed Bran with an ache that hadn't ever really gone away. Cillian had tried to fill that absence with other friends over the years, but even now, it still felt like he was missing half of himself.

"We'll take it from here and keep you updated. The CSU team was instructed to start with this crime scene first. Don't want to be wasting daylight," Patrolman Wilson said. Cillian and Mac said their goodbyes to the patrolmen before returning to their trucks.

"Cillian," Mac called out.

Cillian paused in climbing into the driver's seat. "Yeah, boss?"

"Be careful. Keep your iron on you."

Cillian nodded and hauled himself the rest of the way inside his truck. He closed the door and buckled up, grimacing at the reddened, raw-looking skin on the palm of his right hand where the iron disk had sat. He flexed his fingers, wincing at how his skin pulled. It looked and felt like a burn, an allergic reaction he had lived with all his life. His fellow rangers didn't know about it, or anyone else for that matter outside medical providers, except his mother. He always forgot to mention it.

Shannon Dunne had raised him as a single mother, and her frustration with doctors when he was younger was what had caused her to become a nurse. Cillian had always been a little sickly growing up, with the doctors saying he might outgrow the allergy someday. He hadn't, even though his immune system had gotten better at fighting off illnesses.

He leaned over to open the glove compartment, pulling out a small, dark jar of the ointment he'd used since he was a child. He stared down at the faded sticker on the lid, the Gallaghers' Shoppe trifecta logo printed on it. It was the only stuff that had ever been able to heal the allergic reactions he experienced. His mother had been skeptical the first time Bran's mother had brought up the healing ointment she sold in her Shoppe. Eventually, Shannon had bought a jar and used it, thinking it wouldn't work, only it had.

Cillian had been five years old at the time, but the warning his mother had told him at such a young age was one she still spoke in the quiet moments just between them, mindful of everything and everyone around them, even the whispers on the air.

Never trust a witch.

She'd allowed his friendship with Bran, mostly because Bran had been his *only* friend growing up. His mother had never softened much around Juliana despite the years of knowing the other woman, even when she gave up on clinical medicine and bought the healing ointment from the only Wiccan in Pelham. Cillian never understood the distance between his mother's words and her actions, but he loved her, and he still used the ointment she'd found to heal his hurts.

He wondered, in that moment, if this was the last jar he'd ever get to buy now that Juliana was dead.

"Fuck," he muttered quietly.

He unscrewed the lid, dabbed a bit of the ointment on his palm, and rubbed it in. Then, he put the jar away, the itch already fading from his mind, started the engine, and turned his truck around to head back to town. The trees on either side of the dirt road rose up like a high wall of greenery, leaving only the sky visible. Cillian could see Mac's truck farther up the dirt road, and the chatter on the radio channel the Rangers used kept him company on the drive out of the forest.

Once he made it to the two-lane US Route 202, he turned left, crossing the double-yellow line to head south. The Gallaghers' home wasn't located in what passed as the center of town. Like their Shoppe, it was on the outskirts. When Juliana had married Ray, she'd moved out of the two-bedroom apartment above the Shoppe into the home she and Ray had bought amid the trees and which everyone had always referred to as hers. The Gallaghers had always had a peculiar reputation in town, regarded with a sort of polite deference by the older genera-tions. There wasn't much of a younger generation these days, what with everyone moving to the cities.

Cillian had stayed. Once, years ago, Bran had promised to stay as well. Considering what had occurred today, it was probably for the best he'd left Pelham. Cillian had mostly survived Bran's leaving. He knew, even now, after seven years of silence, he'd never survive Bran dying.

State Route 202 only had a few turnoffs and a couple of long drives leading to homes set far back from the road, deeper in the forest. Few homes were built directly adjacent to the road. Mostly, it was bordered by trees and the telephone poles stretching down one side, birds perched on the wires every few hundred feet.

Cillian didn't need the GPS to take him to the Gallaghers' home; he still knew the way. Which meant his eyes were on the road, not on the screen of his phone attached to the hands-free cradle on the dash. That was the only reason he saw the flash of white amid the trees to his left.

He slammed on the brakes, seat belt cutting into his shoulder and locking from the force of his stop. Cillian yanked the steering wheel to the right, driving onto the shoulder to get off the road. He pulled up the emergency brake, put his hazards on, and reached for the rifle secured in the rack behind the two front seats before getting out.

The summer sun beat down on him as he stared across the road at the expanse of trees there and the soft shadows that lingered beneath the branches. The greens and browns of summer nearing its peak filled his eyes, that flash of white nowhere to be seen, but Cillian *knew* something had been moving there between the trees.

Not lights—if the stories were true—but someone.

"Aisling?" Cillian called out as he crossed the road, cradling the rifle in both hands, finger resting over the trigger guard. "It's me, Cillian. I promise I don't mean you any harm. You have a lot of people worried about you."

He reached the other side, stepping over the guardrail, careful of the slight incline below it. The only thing in front of him was trees, some ferns, and a few bushes, all of it blocking the view deeper into the forest. The wind blowing through the branches made the leaves rustle, the soft susurration not quite loud enough to hide the delicate sound of a twig breaking.

Cillian raised the rifle, bracing the buttstock against his right shoulder as he stared down the rifle sights into the forest. "Aisling?"

Mac always said one couldn't trust what came from the forest, but Cillian trusted his own eyes. He stayed right where he was, staring into the forest, willing for it to give up the lost. Seconds that felt like hours passed, and that flash of white he'd seen while driving finally resolved itself into the slim figure of a young teenage girl who crept out from behind a tree.

Aisling looked nothing like her mother and father, nothing like her brother, with their dark hair and dark eyes. She stood out and always had with her startling white-blonde hair and deep blue eyes he remembered looking almost black in the shadows, like right now. Aisling's appearance hadn't changed much since the last time Cillian had seen her a few months ago in passing. She was tall for thirteen, skinny and pale, standing before him barefoot in bloody clothes, looking as if she'd seen a ghost.

Or a nightmare.

Cillian lowered his rifle and let out a heavy breath. "Aisling."

She didn't respond, only watched him with those big eyes of hers, body stiff in a way that spoke of being primed to flee. Cillian didn't know how long she'd been out there in the forest, but it had been long enough to make her want to run. Cillian trekked through a bit of vegetation to reach where she stood, going slow so as to not spook her.

"Let's get you out of here," he said quietly, offering her his hand. She stared at it for a long moment, shivering in a way he didn't like. He wiggled his fingers at her, trying to ignore the way his heart beat hard against his ribs. "Come on, Aisling. I'll keep you safe."

She grabbed his hand with shaking fingers, and the moment she touched him, her expression crumpled. Her lips trembled badly as tears welled up, but she didn't make a sound as she cried. Cillian carefully guided her out from the tree line and back toward the road. Once in the sunlight, the cuts and scratches on her legs became more apparent. Her bare feet were dirty and bleeding in areas, and her sleep clothes looked as if she'd rolled down a couple of hills in them.

He needed to get her somewhere safe.

"My truck is right there, and I'm going to take you back into town."

From the time he'd stopped his truck to when he got Aisling situated in the front passenger seat, not a single vehicle had driven by. It was just the two of them out on State Route 202, the next house maybe half a mile down the road, so that didn't explain why the hair on the back of his neck suddenly stood on end.

Aisling finally made a sound, a breaking sort of whimper as her hands gripped his, her ragged fingernails biting into the rash stretched over his palm. He noticed her fingernails were painted robin's-egg blue, but the polish was all chipped now. The beaded bracelet she wore seemed to be intact. She wasn't looking at him but back the way they'd come, face going as white as her hair.

Cillian carefully caught her chin, turning her head around to focus on him. "Look at me, not the forest."

She was breathing so hard her entire body shuddered from it. But her gaze returned to him, no longer lingering on whatever she thought she saw in the trees. Cillian wasn't going to check. He buckled her in, wrapped an emergency foil blanket around her, and then hurried around the front of the truck to get into the driver's seat. He racked his rifle, then started the engine, intent on getting back to Pelham. He didn't reach for the radio receiver until he was already driving down the road well above the speed limit, heading north.

"Dispatch, this is Ranger Seven. Aisling Gallagher has been located alive and in need of medical assistance. I'm bringing her in, over."

Beside him, Aisling tucked her head beneath the edge of the emergency foil blanket and curled up in a ball beneath it, as if she could hide from whatever she had suffered through in the last twenty-four hours.

Cillian watched the road, and he watched Aisling, and he watched the forest out of the corners of his eyes, hoping to see nothing there in the shadows of the woods.

Hoping the stories about lights weren't true.

Chapter Two

Bran Gallagher pulled into the first open parking spot he saw in the lot behind the white building that served as Pelham's town hall, library, police department, and fire station all in one. It sat at the intersection of Amherst Road and South Valley Road, a familiar landmark from his childhood spent riding up and down the small town's roads on his bicycle.

He switched off the headlights and killed the engine on his Honda Civic, which had honestly seen better days, and sat there for a moment, staring blankly at the white-paneled walls of the building. The single streetlight in the parking lot sputtered on, its light reflecting in the rearview mirror.

This was not how he thought he'd come back.

Bran had gotten the call about his mother from the Pelham Police Department maybe two hours ago. He'd left his job at the Massachusetts Historical Society and driven west without even stopping at his apartment. The hour-and-a-half drive from Boston had passed in a blur that Bran barely remembered. Some distant part of him knew that wasn't good, but there was nothing to be done for it.

He'd been called home to Pelham because his mother and stepfather were dead, and his little sister had been missing until she wasn't.

His mother was dead.

Bran still hadn't let go of the steering wheel.

"Fuck," he whispered, eyes filling with tears. "*Fuck.*"

He wiped them away with one hand, sniffing hard enough to pop his ears. Bran blinked his eyes to clear them, his view of the multipurpose community center obscured by the animal perched on the hood of his car. The large raven cocked her head at him, gold-flecked black eyes peering at him worriedly. Jupiter *cawed* softly, took a short hop forward, and pecked lightly at the windshield. She'd followed him out of Boston because she could never leave him, not after he tied them both together through a ritual of magic he'd performed when he was nine years old.

Every witch needed a familiar, after all.

"Okay, okay. I'm going," Bran muttered.

Jupiter *cawed* at him again, seemingly satisfied with his statement. She spread her wings and launched herself off the car and into the air, flying up to the roof of the building. Bran got out and shut the door behind him, not bothering to lock it. He'd triple-click his key fob in Boston every time he left his car behind, but not here. Pelham rarely had break-ins of any sort, which brought him right back to the reason he'd returned to his childhood hometown.

He lengthened his stride, walking up the black asphalt path that led from the parking lot behind the building to the front door facing Amherst Road. The porch light was on, casting a warm yellow glow against the oncoming twilight. The sun hadn't set yet, but it was hidden behind the trees at this hour. The sky overhead was that deepening pale blue mixed with oranges that would darken into purples when the sun set in an hour or so. No clouds meant the stars would be a bright blanket across the sky, something that was nearly impossible to see in Boston with light pollution.

Those random thoughts flitted through Bran's mind in a desperate sort of pondering as he opened the community center's front door. If he could keep the clawing, ugly grief at bay, then perhaps he could get through the next few hours. Maybe even the next few days.

"Bran."

He rocked to a stop past the door, gaze going unerringly to Mac's stiff-shouldered figure as the ranger stood from the wooden bench in the hall, as if the older man had been waiting there for hours to intercept him. Bran swallowed hard, throat clicking painfully with the motion. "Mac."

The man who was both a ranger and a guardian from a tradition only spoken of in whispers pulled off his wide-brimmed hat and bowed his head. "Forgive me your grief. I should have seen the warning signs."

Bran clenched his hands into fists, fingernails digging into his palms for a few seconds. "Did she call you?"

Mac raised his head and shook it, the regret in his eyes something Bran had to look away from. "No, but that doesn't excuse the fact I didn't see the threat first."

Bran crossed his arms over his chest, the tattoo on his right forearm on clear display. The bracelet of evergreen trees that ringed his wrist in black and green ink stretched up his forearm, a mimicry of the forest surrounding them. An unkindness of ravens flew away from the tattooed treetops toward his elbow in a swirl of black ink. His other wrist carried a corded leather bracelet decorated with bone beads that had tiny witchmarks carved into them by his mother and iron beads that didn't, but which still carried magic in them.

Everything came back to her, and Bran had to take a slow, deep breath to help shove down the grief that threatened to choke him. "You did your duty."

Mac flinched, the sadness lining his face something Bran refused to let affect him. Not yet. "It wasn't enough."

At that, Bran kept silent because he knew it wasn't. Still, he wouldn't lay blame at the feet of a man who had allied with his family and coven for decades until he understood more about what had happened. "Where's Aisling?"

"In an office inside the police department. Cillian is with her."

Bran couldn't help the way his entire body stiffened at the name of his former childhood best friend. He shoved down that clawing bit of longing that hadn't left him in years, pretending it didn't exist, lying to himself as he did so. "Why is *he* with her?"

Mac put his hat back on before tucking his thumbs over the top of his belt. "Because he's the one who found her."

Bran glared past Mac at a spot at the end of the hallway. He gritted his teeth against a reflexive mix of hurt and anger that hadn't truly left him since Cillian had shoved him away after a tentative, hopeful kiss the night before their high school graduation. A kiss he hadn't been able to forget. A kiss he'd thought would give him everything he wanted and instead had only left him feeling barren, as if his heart had been carved out of his chest. "Where?"

"In the forest."

Bran's gaze snapped back to Mac, the air catching in his lungs. He had to clear his throat before the words would come. "What was she doing in the forest?"

"We don't know. Aisling isn't talking. We think it's the trauma from —we think she saw your mother get killed."

Bran closed his eyes, dropping his arms down to his sides. Jupiter *cawed* loudly from the eaves over the door outside, clearly agitated, reflecting his mood. After a moment, Bran opened his eyes and met Mac's gaze. "Take me to her."

"We have out-of-towners here," Mac warned. "We needed the crime scenes handled and a medical examiner brought in."

"Bear attack?"

"It's tradition in a situation like this."

A lot of things were tradition in Pelham. Bran's entire life had been built on it, gladly following in his mother's footsteps until she'd married Ray. Bran had never gotten along with his stepfather, and when he finally turned eighteen on Summer Solstice, he'd moved to Boston. Ostensibly, it had been for school. Mostly, it had been to escape Ray's need to assert his authority in a home and town that had always looked to Bran's mother first.

It was the same reason his father had left back when Bran was a toddler, escaping the doldrums of small-town life. Bran had no memory of the man he'd seen only in a handful of pictures. He didn't even carry his father's last name. A witch kept their coven's name, after all, even if his father had never known his mother had been a witch the same way Ray hadn't. Wiccan, yes, but not *witch*, and the distinction was in the duty that had tied their coven to this land for generations.

Few knew that secret, despite his family and coven running the Ye Olde Curiosities Shoppe for the last twenty years or so on land they'd owned for centuries. A witch had always called Pelham home and always would. The Council of Witches had decreed that after Boston had been founded, and the Gallaghers had been forced to answer that call, carrying iron with them from the old country into a forest that wasn't kind.

People went missing in the forest. It was only in modern times that the number of missing was enough to cause outside concern. Those whose bodies were found had their deaths blamed on bears when the people in Pelham who believed in the stories knew it wasn't bears.

It was always the lights.

I'm not ready.

"She should never have moved into that house. It was too close to the edge of the forest," Bran rasped. Not that the Shoppe was much better in terms of location, but at least the Shoppe had a protective circle laid down in it. Ray had never allowed any of their practices in the home he considered his.

Mac tipped his head in silent agreement, but it didn't matter, not anymore.

His mother was dead, and Bran, as the last Gallagher witch in their tiny coven, had a duty—to the town, to its people, and to the creeping threat in the forest that had always existed.

But first, he had to see to his little sister.

Mac led the way to the door marked *Police Department* in black lettering over the frosted glass window. The Pelham Police Department was so small that there wasn't any worry about ever outgrowing the space in the community center. The handful of people inside that open workspace all stopped talking when they entered the room. Bran wouldn't meet anyone's gaze, following Mac to one of the rear offices that still had its lights on. He pushed open the door, waving for Bran to enter first.

Aisling sat on a chair someone must have dragged in from the neighboring library in the same building because the faded upholstery of the cushion didn't match any of the other chairs in the office. She was wrapped up in an emergency foil blanket, feet bandaged, along with her hands, with gauze taped to one cheek and her forehead. Her long, white-blonde hair was tangled and dirty, but someone had at least tied it back in a ponytail to get it out of her face. She held a mug of what looked like hot chocolate, but she hadn't drunk any of it, judging by how full it was.

The man kneeling in front of her was someone who could still, even after all these years, make Bran's heart skip a beat and his breath catch. He'd thought he was over his first love and first heartbreak, but apparently not.

Cillian turned his head at their arrival, those blue-gray eyes of his widening in a too-handsome face with model-sharp features that Bran drank in like he was starving. Cillian's dark blond hair was pulled back in a messy bun at the back of his head beneath the wide brim of his hat. Bran was pretty sure that hairstyle wasn't regulation, but it somehow suited him.

Seven years since Bran had last seen Cillian, and it felt like yesterday in that moment. The emptiness in his life he'd lived with for so long desperately wanted to be filled by the shape of the man before him—a man who had once pushed him away. But Bran wasn't going to risk his heart again, even if everything inside of him was screaming he should.

"Bran," Cillian said, rising to his feet.

Bran had to tilt his head back a little to meet Cillian's gaze. He remembered they used to be the same height in high school, but Cillian must have hit a late growth spurt during their years apart. He was nearly a whole head taller than Bran now, easily over six feet, and broad-shouldered in a way that hinted at defined muscle beneath his drab-looking ranger uniform. His skin was a golden tan color, shades darker than Bran's own fair coloring, no hint of freckles anywhere that Bran could see. He looked *good*, and Bran was acutely aware of the way his stomach clenched at the sight, how his mouth went dry without his permission.

Before Bran could figure out how to respond, he was saved by Aisling dropping her mug on the floor. She ignored the mess and threw herself at him with a rasping sort of sob that made Bran's entire body flinch. He hugged her tightly as she shook through almost soundless sobs. The force of her crying, paired with the lack of words, worried him.

"I'm here," he murmured, voice catching. "I'm here now."

It was a few minutes before he could even think about anything else.

Eventually, he coaxed Aisling back to the chair to get her off her feet, picking up the emergency foil blanket to wrap it around her thin shoulders again. Someone had given her a pair of joggers and a T-shirt that clearly didn't fit her, but better than nothing. Bran crouched in front of Aisling, mindful of the mess on the floor. He gently took her bandaged hands in his, gaze dropping to the bracelet she wore, similar to the one around his wrist. Hers just lacked iron beads. "What happened?"

He thought Aisling would tell him, but she only looked at him with those big, watery, deep blue eyes of hers as her lips trembled and said nothing. It was Cillian who spoke instead.

"I found her along Route 202, in the tree line. She was alone," Cillian said.

"Where?"

"On the way to your house."

"It's not my house."

It hadn't been even when he lived there, angry that his mother had moved them out of the Shoppe's apartment to a place where Ray insisted Bran listen to every rule he laid down and got angry when he didn't. Ray hadn't ever hit him, but Bran always felt he'd wanted to.

"The house is a crime scene. You can't take her back there right now," Mac warned.

Bran's shoulders inched toward his ears. "I still have my key to the Shoppe."

"The Shoppe was locked up tight with no signs of forced entry, according to the police."

"Then we'll stay there."

Better a place with no memories of whatever had occurred that put such a haunted look in his little sister's eyes than anywhere else. Aisling had always been a quiet child growing up, bused to the same schools Bran had gone to in Amherst and forced to deal with the social stigma of where they'd grown up. She had friends, he knew, but none in Pelham. The handful of kids in town who were her age knew of their family and the Shoppe, and that was enough, sometimes, to make locals steer clear.

"Was anyone with you out in the forest?" Bran asked.

Aisling shook her head, still not talking. He was relieved to know he wouldn't have to search for anyone else. It'd been years since he had walked the forest at night, and he wasn't in the right mindset to do so right now.

Just get through this.

"No one else has been reported missing," Cillian said.

Bran didn't care about anyone else. "I'm taking Aisling home."

Mac cleared his throat. "CPS won't come until later. I'll have the police chief talk to them."

Bran worked his jaw but kept his grip on Aisling's hands gentle. "She's my *sister*. What are they going to do? Leave her with someone else when I'm right here?"

"I think if you hadn't come, the chief was going to let her stay with me and my wife. I'll go talk to him."

Mac slipped out of the office, and Bran wished Cillian would follow him. But he stayed, and Bran could feel the weight of Cillian's gaze like an itch between his shoulder blades.

"I would've taken Aisling home so she had somewhere to stay if Mac didn't," Cillian said quietly.

Bran eased up out of his crouch and stood, letting go of one of Aisling's hands so he could turn and look at Cillian. "Thank you for finding Aisling, but she's not your responsibility."

Cillian's lips firmed into a flat line, gaze unreadable. Bran used to be able to read the other man's moods, but that was back when they'd been best friends, before he'd been stupid enough to kiss Cillian on the night before the rest of their lives started.

Coming back here, seeing Cillian for the first time face-to-face in years, dredged up so many memories and emotions that left Bran wishing Cillian hadn't stayed. That he'd moved out of Pelham like Bran had so Bran wouldn't have to deal with the person who'd once unknowingly owned his heart and shattered it while he mourned his mother.

The stupid, fucked-up thing was that Cillian still owned his heart. Would always own it.

Seven years wasn't going to change that.

"Bran," Cillian began, but Bran cut him off.

"I don't have anything to say to you."

Which was a lie, but Bran pretended otherwise because that was the only way to protect his heart. He wasn't going to risk it again, even if some part of him wanted to.

Cillian closed his eyes, a pained expression crossing his face before he opened them again and nodded. "The police are handling the investigation. The rangers won't be involved."

Cillian gave Aisling a nod goodbye before leaving the office. The door clicked shut quietly behind him, and Bran let out a heavy breath. He forced all thoughts of Cillian out of his mind and turned his attention to his little sister. Aisling looked back at him with wide eyes, waved her hand at him, then pointed at her throat.

Bran frowned. "So it's not that you won't talk, it's that you can't?"

Aisling nodded rapidly. He held her other hand higher, eyeing her bracelet. Bran remembered watching his mother create the bracelets in her stillroom, hunched over a table with delicate tools and a pair of jeweler's magnifying glasses on her head. She'd whispered magic into every line she carved to create a witchmark, a spell of protection meant to keep the wearer safe. It should have protected Aisling from whatever had killed their mother and Ray. But she couldn't speak, and that meant *something* had gotten through their mother's legacy.

Something to do with magic.

Bran glanced over his shoulder at the door, calculating the risk of casting magic with so many people outside the office. His mother had always been adamant about making sure their family's secret didn't get out. It had been ingrained in him ever since he was old enough to understand that magic should never be spoken of outside their coven, which had consisted of himself and his mother for years until Aisling came along, even though she wasn't born a witch and had no magic.

He let go of Aisling long enough to lock the office door. The window there was made of frosted glass, but Bran didn't take its opaqueness for granted. Then, he knelt in front of Aisling and raised his right hand between them, fingers slightly curled.

A witch earned the right to carry their coven's witchmark only after they completed their training. Most witches these days made do with pendants or rings, something unobtrusive and easily overlooked. Few carried it on their skin anymore, but the Gallagher coven still adhered to the old tradition. It hadn't broken, even during the terror of the Salem Witch Trials.

The Gallagher coven had always guarded the forest surrounding Pelham, with its long history of bright lights and the creeping edges of the wyrding—that barrier between worlds—in its depths. An itinerant witch had done his mother's tattoo when she was twenty, and a different witch had done Bran's when he turned eighteen. Fine-line needlework meant the witchmarks denoting his family's coven were expertly hidden amid the branches of the pine trees ringing his forearm.

Blood was the oldest form of the earth, and all magic came from the elements that made up Nature. It took belief and a strength of will to master, and Bran had been casting magic since he was a child. It was easy to trace a witchmark in the air between them, glittering golden light following in the wake of his fingertip. He'd memorized all the hundreds of witchmarks used by the Gallagher coven, and the one he cast meant *unveil*.

The glowing witchmark hung in the air for a moment before Bran made a pushing motion with his hand. The witchmark floated toward Aisling's throat and settled on her skin. It pulsed brightly before fading into a different shape that Bran only saw for a couple of seconds, but it was long enough for him to memorize the malevolent black lines that rose to the surface of Aisling's skin. He jerked back at the sight of the geas for *silence* wrapped around his sister's throat. The magic of its making was very much *not* that of a witch.

Aisling touched her throat, the geas fading from sight, and furrowed her brow at him in a silent question. It took a moment for Bran to speak. "They silenced your voice."

Aisling's eyes widened, and she dug her fingers into her throat, as if she could claw the geas out of her body. Bran grabbed her wrist, pulling her hand away. "Don't. You'll hurt yourself."

She smacked her hand against his chest, then gestured at her throat, in clear articulation of what she wanted. He shook his head. "Not here."

He wasn't going to attempt to lift a geas like that unless he researched it in their coven's grimoire first. Aisling's shoulders slumped, but she didn't protest when he stood and helped her out of the chair.

She was careful not to step in the puddle of hot chocolate on the floor, but winced when she put pressure on her feet.

Bran gently tugged on her ponytail. "Want me to carry you?"

Aisling shook her head, and he didn't fight her on it. They left the office, their appearance in the workroom catching everyone's attention. Bran only looked to Mac, jerking his head at the police department's front door. "I'm taking Aisling to the Shoppe."

Home was on the tip of his tongue, but he bit it back at the last second. Aisling sniffled beside him, and he wrapped his arm around her shoulders.

Mac nodded and stepped away from the police chief, someone Bran wasn't familiar with. They must have been a new hire within the last few years. "I'll walk you out."

Cillian wouldn't look at him, and Bran forced himself to turn away from the other man. Mac led them out of the police department and back outside into the encroaching twilight. Jupiter *cawed* from the tree line, a lone cry amid the crickets that were out in force.

Mac walked them around the building and to Bran's car, watching in silence as Bran got Aisling situated in the front passenger seat. Only when he closed the door did the ranger speak. "I know this isn't the time for it, but the medical examiner will need you to identify the bodies at some point."

Bran clenched his teeth and swallowed hard. "You're right. It's not the time for it."

"The medical examiner is an out-of-towner. They won't be around long, but they'll need to finalize their paperwork. The police chief will most likely reach out to you soon about it. I can play intermediary if you want."

"Who is he?"

"The chief? Guy from Hadley. Town voted him in two years ago in the last election. He's a good man. Has a family he wants to raise in a small town."

Bran snorted. "He picked the wrong town."

"He has extended family from here. They've made sure he knows our ways."

Pelham wasn't the kind of place you moved to for an easy life. Yes, it was far from major cities, hidden away in an expanse of forest no one was allowed to drive through, save on designated state routes and locally approved roads. People knew each other and knew their histories, and outsiders were tolerated at best. Some who had moved to Pelham in the past and didn't adhere to the local superstitions went missing, turned into cautionary tales for visitors driving through who stopped at Red's Diner or the only bar in town.

The iron beads on his bracelet felt like a thousand-pound weight. Bran cleared his throat, trying not to hunch his shoulders. "Aisling will need clothes."

Mac's expression was difficult to read in the low light cast by the single streetlight at the other end of the parking lot. "I'll talk with the chief and have him give me access to the house as soon as the CSU team finishes processing it. I'll get whatever she needs."

It was the least he owed them as a guardian, those who were the first line of defense against the wyrding and the lights and everything they represented. Whatever warnings a guardian discovered in the forest, they were supposed to bring to a witch's attention.

There used to be more guardians, old families that had deep roots in Pelham, helping to keep the stories and warnings alive of what walked through the forest. The modern age had enticed many younger people and whole families away to better opportunities not found in a tiny town of barely a thousand people. Mac remained, much as his mother once had. Theirs was the last family of guardians in town. But the stories that had sustained Pelham were dying with the older generations, and maybe that was why the lights were back.

Bran couldn't wait to escape Pelham after high school, under the illusion his mother would be there for years to watch over the forest. He'd been convinced he could live his life in Boston and elsewhere however he liked, regardless of the magic he carried and the witchmarks tattooed into his skin and the duty he'd left behind.

And yet, here he was.

"Go be with your sister," Mac said.

Bran nodded stiffly and went around the car to climb into the driver's seat. Mac watched them drive away, his figure fading into shadows in Bran's rearview mirror.

Chapter Three

Bran's cell phone rang, jerking him out of a fitful sleep and uneasy dreams. He blinked open gritty eyes, staring up at a ceiling that didn't look like his apartment in Boston. It only took a second for the past evening to slam through him, bringing with it the realization of where he was.

The apartment above the Shoppe.

Last night, he'd put Aisling in his old room, which hadn't been updated since he was a preteen. He hadn't been able to bring himself to sleep in his mother's old bed yet and had camped out on the creaky leather couch instead. It was warm enough in the apartment that he hadn't needed the musty throw blanket.

He fumbled his cell phone out from beneath the pillow, wincing at the crick in his neck. He quickly muted it so as not to wake Aisling. Considering the time—well after eight in the morning—they probably should get up. He didn't recognize the number on the screen, but he answered the call anyway.

"Hello?" he asked, trying to sound more awake than he felt.

"Is this Bran? Juliana Gallagher's son?" a woman asked.

Bran immediately lost all sense of sleepiness. "Yeah? Who are you?"

"This is Tina Roberts. I don't know if you remember me?"

Bran knuckled one eye and sat up, slouching on the couch. He tipped his head back and stared up at the mural of the night sky his mother had painted on the ceiling when he was a kid. "My mother's lawyer."

"Yes. I was informed by a park ranger this morning about the unfortunate details of her passing. A Captain MacIntyre? He told me you took custody of Aisling."

"I have her."

"I'm glad to hear that. Listen, it's not my general area of expertise, but I have a partner in my firm here in Boston who handles family law cases. I can put you in touch with them."

"Why would I need to speak with them?"

"Well, Aisling is a minor. She needs a guardian, and that requires paperwork."

Bran pinched his nose, swallowing against the knot in his throat. He'd known—sort of—on the drive to Pelham that he'd be responsible for Aisling. But knowing that and having to talk about it were two different things. The fact that he had to deal with the logistics of legal guardianship for his little sister right after they'd lost their mother and Ray was a hurdle he wasn't sure he could overcome right then.

"Is this something I need to deal with right now? Is the Commonwealth of Massachusetts going to take her away from me?"

"No, not if she's been placed with family. But legally speaking, you'll need to file for guardianship for her."

Bran dragged his hand down his face and then shoved himself to his feet. "Yeah. Fine. Give your partner my number. I'll talk with them later."

"Understood. You should also know your mother had a burial package from the Amherst Funeral Home. I can give you their number. They'll handle your mother's remains for you."

He closed his eyes against the sudden bout of grief that threatened to choke him. Tina seemed to understand his silence and so quietly gave him the number without him needing to prompt her for it. Bran ended the call without saying goodbye and opened his eyes, staring blankly at the wall.

He gave himself a couple of seconds to get his emotions back under control before typing the phone number for the funeral home into his contacts. When he finally looked up, the sight of Aisling hovering in the entrance to the hallway where the bedrooms were startled him.

"Sorry if I woke you." Aisling shrugged and gestured at her throat. Bran sighed. "How about you shower first and use more of the healing ointment on your feet? I'll head downstairs to grab the grimoire. Mac said he'd bring you some clothes as soon as he's able to."

Aisling wrinkled her nose at him before nodding and disappearing back down the hallway. The apartment wasn't all that big, even with two bedrooms. It only had one bathroom, and the living room was right next to the kitchen, a small pass-through the only thing separating the two spaces.

His stomach growled a little. Bran had checked the refrigerator last night, only seeing a Tupperware of leftovers that must have been his mother's lunch from the other day, which had left him crying on the tiled floor after Aisling had gone to bed.

He'd take his chances with the coffeepot downstairs in the Shoppe.

He popped into his old bedroom only long enough to get dressed before heading downstairs, the steps creaking under his passage. When he made it to the bottom landing, he opened the door to the Shoppe and reached around the doorframe to flick the light switch. The vintage-style Edison light bulbs in their ceiling fixtures buzzed on, brightening the space. The Ye Olde Curiosities Shoppe came into view, the sight of it more familiar to him than even his apartment in Boston.

Antique bookshelves were crammed together along the back wall directly to his right, carrying a hoard of items on their shelves. The opposite wall held a smaller window and the wooden front door with its witchmarks carefully carved into the frame amid the flower and vine motif there. To his left was the sales counter that doubled as a display case for jewelry, carved crystals, and other expensive antique pieces. The register, incongruously enough, was an iPad in a stand situated on top of an old-school cash drawer. A side door led to the small utility room where cleaning supplies, a small stacked washer and dryer set, and the boiler were located.

Small wooden tables clustered in the center of the Shoppe were filled with all manner of strange and curious items he'd spent his summers inventorying while growing up. On the opposite side wall to his right, a pair of bookcases bracketed the large circular stained-glass window with its trifecta welded in iron. The glass was a pale sky blue in every pane, easy enough to see out of into the nearby trees.

Bran drifted toward his mother's altar behind the display case. A thin wooden board sat on the back counter, the phases of the moon carved near the top edge. A larger carving of an oak tree inside a circle took up the center. A shallow metal dish sat beside it with a half-burned sage bushel left in it. The three dark purple candles looked new, with barely any wax drippings on them. Quartz and bits of dried flowers were scattered on the counter, his mother's set of tarot cards stacked messily nearby.

Bran touched the wooden board, drawing in the sense of his mother's magic in that altar and all the prayers she had whispered to it over the years. His fingertips tingled as he stood there in the quiet space where his mother had once worshipped. Bran's altar used to sit by hers, filled with carved wood and bone, but he'd taken it with him to Boston. Ray had never wanted their altars in his home, not comfortable with a religion he didn't understand.

Aisling suddenly appeared next to him, startling him back to reality. She stared mournfully at their mother's altar before moving down the counter to where hers sat, a messy thing of wildflowers and agate and thin branches bent and tied into the shape of a pentagram. Her candles were tall and skinny, made of beeswax, and she lit them with a match from the Shoppe's junk drawer.

Bran stood by her, holding his hands like Aisling—raised before him, palms toward the ceiling—and stared into the flickering candle flames. "May the Mother take her home. May the Father steal our tears. May she ever rest."

Aisling mouthed along silently to his prayer, tears glittering in her eyes. They worshipped no gods or goddesses in the Gallagher coven, for those deities carried the names any true witch stood against. But the eddies of the mortal world and the power found in Nature? They would always bow to that.

Bran let his hands drop down to his sides. "Come on. Let's get the grimoire and see what can be done for the geas."

Aisling pulled her phone out of a pair of black skinny jeans that were a little baggy on her. The jeans were his, and she'd taken the string from the joggers to use it as a makeshift belt. She'd found a pair of his old flip-flops that were too big for her but worked for now. He hoped Mac managed to get her clothes from the house.

Aisling rapidly tapped away at her phone before lifting it up for him to see the screen. *I only saw a glimpse of the light before Mom told me to run. The spell hit me when I reached the trees. It hurt, but then Mom's bracelet activated, and I kept running until I reached the cabin. I stayed there overnight.*

"When did it attack?"

After it got dark.

"Was Mom the only one home?"

Aisling shook her head. *Dad was there.*

"Ray was found in the forest. It must have taken him when it went looking for you." Bran didn't know why, unless the light wanted to play with its food. He didn't say that out loud, though. "I'm glad it didn't find you."

Aisling scrubbed at her eyes with the back of her hand, and he pulled her into a hug. She was too young to have gone through such a trauma, and as much as Bran wanted to grieve, he knew he had to be strong for her.

"I swear I'll do everything to keep you safe," Bran confessed into her hair.

Lights could never get through witchmarks, but Bran knew from their coven's history what could, and he had to prepare for that possibility.

He held Aisling for a minute, rubbing her back, before letting go. He urged her out of the way and then crouched to reach the latch made to look like a knot in the wooden floor plank. With a grunt, Bran lifted the wooden door to their mother's basement stillroom that doubled as a storage place for the Shoppe's extra inventory. Bran took the steps one at a time down into the dark, Aisling following at his heels.

He found the switch that would turn on the overhead light without needing to feel for it, the location ingrained in memory. The bare light bulbs down there were soft white, brightening a space no one but the three of them ever entered, and now it would just be him and Aisling.

The concrete walls of the stillroom were painted white to help make the space feel bigger. The floor was painted a dark moss green, while the pentagram circle that touched all four walls was a riot of colors from the flowers designed into it. The witchmarks representing the Gallagher coven were painted bright gold, the magic imbued in the circle glowing softly as Bran and Aisling stepped onto the floor. It recognized and welcomed them, a faint buzz tingling against his skin.

One wall was fitted with a metal shelving unit where the Shoppe's extra inventory was kept. Wooden shelves had been drilled into the rest of the walls, with a tall cabinet centered against one. A rectangular worktable sat in the middle of the stillroom, jars and sachets scattered across it, and a hot plate sitting next to a chopping board. Herbs, plants, and vials of liquid and oil ringed the cutting board, with empty jars and tins stacked at one end of the worktable, filled ones at the other. Lughnasa had recently passed, and the potency of some plants was stronger after that holiday. His mother must have gone foraging in the forest.

He wondered if that was how the lights had found her and followed her home.

It should have been peaceful, being in their mother's favorite space, but Bran only felt broken.

Bran approached the cabinet and opened the wooden doors. He scanned the interior, frowning when his gaze settled on the empty spot between two leather-bound books on the top shelf where their coven's grimoire should have been. The space was wider than his hand, the grimoire holding centuries of his coven's spellwork history, and *it wasn't there*.

Aisling tugged fiercely on his shirt, trying to get his attention. Bran glanced at her, not liking how wide her eyes were as she pointed at where the grimoire was always stored when their mother wasn't using it.

"Did Mom take it back to the house with her?" Bran asked, thinking of the worst-case scenario. That whatever had followed her home had done so to deprive their coven of power.

Aisling shook her head before writing out another text on her phone. *You know Dad never liked it staying there.*

Fear left Bran cold, more than the air in the stillroom could. He turned away from the cabinet and knelt over a line on the pentagram's circle. He pressed his palm flat over a gold-painted witchmark, seeking out the magic embedded in it. He blinked back tears at the touch of magic, the last remnants of his mother's power there in the space she'd built and maintained. He sent a pulse of magic through it, watching as the gold shimmered against the floor in a wave, washing through every painted line until it returned.

"The circle is intact. No one broke through the spells," Bran said slowly. He made a fist with his hand, letting the protective magic in the pentagram fade away. Aisling patted his shoulder, but he didn't need to look at her to know what she wanted to say, but couldn't. "I know that doesn't mean anything if Mom left with the grimoire."

Which meant the grimoire could be *anywhere*.

Including in the hands of the enemy.

Bran strangled the urge to panic the same way he'd strangled his grief, shoving it down into a hard little knot that sat heavy in his chest. "Maybe she left it upstairs."

Maybe it was tucked away behind the sales counter or somewhere in the apartment. Maybe, if they were lucky, the police had taken it as evidence, and he could get Mac to retrieve it for them somehow.

Maybe the history of the Gallagher coven wasn't missing, only temporarily misplaced.

Bran glanced up at the ceiling as the sound of someone knocking loudly on the front door echoed down to them. He shared a look with Aisling before they hurried back upstairs. Bran lowered the basement door and reset the latch before straightening. Aisling popped up beside him, both of them staring at the front door. Through the front window, he could make out the black truck of a ranger parked out front next to his car.

"I think it's Mac," Bran said.

Neither of them moved.

It was daylight, but that didn't mean the threats from the forest wouldn't come out and make themselves known when the sun was in the sky. They just preferred the cover of night.

Bran curled his fingers, but before he could call up his magic, Jupiter *cawed* a greeting from the porch. Bran let out a breath and went to open the door, squinting at where Mac stood on the porch, a backpack slung over his shoulder. His hat shielded his face from the sun, but it couldn't hide the dark circles under his eyes. "I brought Aisling some clothes."

Jupiter *cawed* again, and Bran looked up at the roof. The raven hopped along the rain gutters, flapping her wings, but otherwise appearing unbothered. "Thanks."

Bran stepped back, allowing Mac to enter. He came inside, glancing around the Shoppe. "The police said the Shoppe hadn't been broken into."

Bran held his tongue for the moment about the missing grimoire. "No. The door was locked when we got here last night, and nothing was out of place."

Mac slid the backpack off his shoulder. It looked as if it might have belonged to one of his kids before they'd gone off to college. The fabric was a little worn and stretched near to bursting at the seams. Bran wondered how he'd managed to get the zipper closed. "I packed as much as I could. The house is still a crime scene. When it is finally released into your hands, you'll need to do some deep cleaning."

"Police still aren't paid enough to do it for us?"

"No."

Aisling took the backpack from Mac and clutched it to her chest with both hands. Mac looked at Bran, grimacing a bit. "The medical examiner is coming back today. The bodies are being held in cold storage at the morgue in the ranger's station. You need to name them before the medical examiner arrives."

Bran couldn't help the way he flinched at that demand. "You kept the bodies?"

"You know why."

Pelham didn't have the resources for a medical examiner's office, which meant the police department didn't have anywhere to store the bodies the forest sometimes gave up. The rangers always handled the dead. Federal funding gave them the ability to have a morgue in their station located midway between Pelham and Belchertown on State Route 202.

Mac's shoulders slumped a little. "I know it's not what you want to do, but it should have been done last night when the bodies came to us for holding."

"Why didn't you call?" Bran asked.

"Would you have come out last night after everything?"

Bran looked away, staring at the rack of antlers on the nearest display table. The antlers still had their velvet lining, and the price tag neatly written out in his mother's handwriting accounted for that. "Aisling needs to get dressed."

"I can wait."

Bran didn't want to bring Aisling with him, but neither was he willing to leave her behind. "Fine."

Aisling hefted the backpack onto her shoulder and scurried upstairs, presumably to get dressed. Her footsteps were loud on the stairs, and the ceiling squeaked overhead with her passage through the apartment. Bran crossed his arms over his chest and shifted on his feet, nausea roiling his stomach at the thought of what he had to do.

"How is she doing?" Mac asked.

Bran shrugged one shoulder. "How do you think?"

"Has she spoken yet?"

"No."

Mac grimaced. "And you? Have you taken up the mantle yet?"

"My mother isn't even in the ground yet. Don't talk to me about the mantle."

Pelham had a cemetery on the north side of town, a bit of land with graves that held dates on headstones going back to the town's founding. A corner of the cemetery was reserved for Gallaghers, and Bran wasn't sure how he'd be able to get through his mother's funeral, much less the identification of her body.

"I'm sorry," Mac said gruffly, eyes kind rather than accusing. "But if the lights are back, then the town needs you."

Bran looked away, staring out the trifecta stained-glass window at the trees beyond. "I know."

Being a witch meant doing one's duty, and right now, that duty was to tend to the dead. The grief clawing at his ribs, at his heart, would have to wait.

Aisling clattered back downstairs a few minutes later and barreled into the Shoppe, dressed in her own clothes. She reached for his hand and put his car keys and wallet in his palm, saving him a trip back upstairs. "Thanks."

"You can follow me to the station," Mac said, turning and heading for the front door.

They left the Shoppe, Bran pausing only long enough to lock up behind them. He touched a finger to the witchmark etched into the door above the knob, the magic there warming the wood for a split second. Then, he headed for the car with Aisling, getting in and starting the engine. "Do you have your iron?"

Aisling nodded. Knowing he couldn't stall any longer, Bran put the car in reverse and pulled away from the Shoppe, turning the car around to get on the road.

Mac escorted them south, thankfully without running his lights and sirens. Bran let Aisling destroy his music app's algorithm by playing whatever her heart desired for the half hour it took to get to the ranger's station. It kept her distracted, and that was all that mattered. When they finally pulled off the road and into the parking lot adjacent to the one-story building, Bran had a whole new playlist consisting of pop songs he wasn't familiar with on his phone.

Two other black ranger trucks were parked in the lot, and Mac pulled in next to one. Bran parked a few spots away, setting the brake and turning the engine off. Aisling undid her seat belt but didn't immediately open the door. Bran reached across the console to tweak her ponytail. "You can stay in the work area inside while I go with Mac."

Aisling nodded and got out of the car. Bran followed suit, watching as Jupiter flew past to settle on the edge of the station's roof. The radio tower built on top of the station offered a higher perch, but Jupiter didn't seem enticed by it. Aisling immediately darted to his side, wrapping one skinny arm around his waist and tucking herself close. Bran draped his arm around her shoulders as they walked to where Mac waited.

Mac gestured for them to follow him inside. "It won't take long."

Bran wouldn't know. He'd never had to identify a body the forest gave up before.

He'd never dreamed he'd have to do it for his mother.

The ranger's station encompassed the whole squat building, more modern-looking inside than Pelham's police station. He couldn't remember the last time he'd been inside it—maybe when he was a kid—but only a handful of people were working, one of whom was at the dispatch desk in the corner, judging by the number of screens. Mac greeted the receptionist, an older woman who smiled kindly at Aisling but didn't ask how she was doing. "She can stay with me while you handle your meeting, Mac."

"Thanks, Doris," Mac said as he pushed open the wooden swing gate that separated the work area from the public area. "Bran? The morgue is this way."

Bran steeled himself and followed Mac through the work area to a rear hallway. It led farther into the building, past some interior offices, and finally to an elevator that was large enough to handle a gurney. Mac hit the button for the basement, and the elevator slowly descended. The doors pinged open on a hallway that led to a single door at the end. When they reached it, Mac opened it, but Bran couldn't quite get his feet to move.

"Bran?" Mac asked, looking back.

He swallowed, blinking through the burn of tears. "Sorry."

"Don't be. I know this is a difficult time and an even more difficult request."

Bran nodded jerkily. Everyone always had his family name the dead in Pelham. Bran was the only one left to name his because he'd never lay that at Aisling's feet.

Mac led him into the small, cold room meant to hold the dead until arrangements to be taken to a funeral home could be made. Bran knew he should call the one Tina had given him, but he couldn't bring himself to do so. Not yet.

"Ready?" Mac asked quietly.

"No," Bran said with a watery, strangled little laugh. "Let's get it over with."

"All right. We'll do Ray first."

Mac opened up one of the three cold storage doors set into the wall and rolled out the gurney. The body was in a black bag that he unzipped, revealing the ravaged mess of Ray's face, throat, and chest.

Bran could only look for a few seconds before he wrenched his gaze away from the horror. He hadn't ever cared for his stepfather, and the feeling had always been mutual. But he'd never wanted the man to suffer how he obviously had.

Mac zipped the bag closed and stepped away from the gurney. Bran mentally shook himself before letting his right hand hover over the body, fingers spread wide. "I name you Ray Carroll. May your soul rest in our world and never haunt the wyrding. May your body and bones return to the earth."

He drew a witchmark in the air above Ray's broken body with his magic, the shape of it *named*. He drew a second, this one for *rest*. He cast both into the dead, glowing lines passing through the black body bag to settle in flesh that lived no more. Mac nodded and pushed the gurney back into cold storage. When he opened the second door and drew out that gurney, Bran nearly lost it.

"I need a minute alone," Bran rasped.

Mac hesitated before bowing his head. "You should know it's only her. We couldn't find Talon. I'll be right outside."

Bran only hoped his mother's familiar—a house cat who never aged —hadn't suffered when he died.

It probably went against some protocol to leave Bran alone with the bodies, but guardians had never stood in the way of witches. Mac didn't start now and took himself out of the morgue. The door clicked shut behind him, sounding overly loud to Bran's ears. Scrubbing a hand over his face, Bran stared at the body bag that held his mother's remains and told himself it had to be done. She wouldn't be the first of their coven targeted by what crawled out of the forest.

Bran wondered, distantly, if he'd have been in the third cold storage drawer if he had been home for a visit.

He unzipped the bag down to her navel with shaking fingers, revealing his mother's cold, lifeless face. She didn't look how he remembered her, and Bran couldn't stop the sob that ripped its way out of him. He covered his mouth with one hand, hunching over as everything blurred from tears, jostling the gurney. His mother's hand slipped out of the bag, bloated fingers dangling off the side. Something fluttered free of them, drifting to the floor.

Bran wiped away a couple of tears, breathing in deep a couple of times to try to get himself back under control. He crouched to retrieve what had fallen, peering at the crumpled flower in his palm. The bruised petals were a color blue he'd never seen before, its pollen a startling, vibrant pink. Even the one smelled like a dozen, a sweetly floral scent reminding him strongly of spring.

His lips trembled—from rage or grief, he couldn't tell—as he stared at a flower that didn't belong in this world.

"Fuck," he rasped, fingers folding around the delicate petals.

The lights were back.

Shoving the flower into his pocket, Bran zipped the bag back up over his mother's body, gaze averted. He hesitated before settling his fingertips on her covered forehead. "I name you Juliana Gallagher, witch of the Gallagher coven. May your mantle be mine in the shroud of your passing. May your soul rest in our world and never haunt the wyrding. May your body and bones return to the earth."

Bran drew the same witchmarks he had with Ray's body over his mother's, pushing his magic into the memory of her, for she was gone from this mortal world now. As the last glitter of magic faded at his fingertips, an impossible breeze that came from nowhere blew past him, rattling everything not bolted down in the morgue. It carried the smell of earth and a hint of his mother's favorite perfume with it. Bran breathed it in, trying to commit it to memory, as the witchmarks inked into his right forearm burned with power.

He bit back a cry, gripping his forearm with his other hand as the coven's broken generational circle closed there in the morgue, with Bran the last witch of their line to carry a duty, a mantle, in the face of a threat that would see them dead. All the knowledge his mother once held had died with her, and Bran ached for that loss, for the grimoire that was missing, too. He didn't know how he was supposed to stand against the horror found in the depths of the forest when it had been strong enough to take his mother from them.

The strange breeze faded to nothing, leaving Bran aching to see sunlight. The circle had closed, and the Gallagher coven was his to lead. It was just him and his sister, and his sister carried a geas on her throat that proved she was a target as much as their mother had been.

The lights had certainly whittled his coven down to nearly nothing.

Bran gripped the gurney and rolled it back into cold storage, closing the square door behind it. He headed for the exit, stepping back into the hallway where Mac waited. Bran nodded stiffly at the other man, not up for speaking just yet as he tried to swallow around the knot of grief stuck in his throat.

"Let's get back upstairs," Mac said quietly.

Bran finally found his voice. "The grimoire is missing."

Mac froze, panic flashing across his face. "What?"

"It's missing. It wasn't in the Shoppe. Can you check with the police to see if it was at the house?"

Mac closed his eyes. "Yeah, I will."

"Great. Thanks. I need to get the hell out of here."

Mac didn't argue his request. They returned to the work area on the first floor, and Aisling stood from the chair she'd been curled up in at the receptionist desk, hurrying over to him. Bran hugged her tight, refusing to cry in front of her.

"Mac?" the woman manning the dispatch desk called out worriedly. "We got another 10-65."

Mac swore, leaving them with a hasty goodbye. Bran tracked his passage, wondering what that was all about. Aisling tugged on his hand, and Bran jerked his attention back to her. "Yeah, I know. Let's go get breakfast."

Red's Diner was the only place in town that offered milkshakes, something he knew Aisling loved. While it wasn't Dunkin' Donuts, it would do.

Chapter Four

Cillian circled the tiny, one-room cabin hemmed in on all sides by trees with their lower branches broken and trampled bushes. He watched where he stepped, not wanting to disturb the impressions in the dirt that could have been animal tracks. He reached the front of the cabin again, grip on his rifle tight as he peered at the front door and the claw marks gouged deep into the wood. The door had held up to whatever had tried to get in, as had the walls. The cabin, like all the others scattered through the forest, didn't have any windows.

What they did have were iron nails used in its build and tiny witch-marks etched into the doorframe and along the top of the walls, beneath the eaves of the roof. The markings were difficult to see, but they matched the ones he'd passed on some trees along the path leading to the cabin. Growing up, he'd never known what the witchmarks meant other than *this way to safety*. Everyone in Pelham knew to follow them to a cabin in the woods if you were out too late and got caught in the twilight, home too far away.

Some early morning hikers had found a body down the forest path. Maybe the victim had been trying to reach the cabin, hoping it could save him from whatever he'd been running from. Cillian was good at tracking, and the dead man's footprints had ended where he'd fallen, but a second set had made it to the cabin, and the door was locked when he tested the knob.

He stepped back and off to the side of the narrow dirt path, the sole of one hiking boot catching on a knot of grass. Something caught his eye by the foundation, and he knelt in the dirt, reaching for the blue blossom of a flower he'd never seen before, and he knew plenty of the local flora.

Cillian picked it up, careful to keep his fingers away from the broken stem. The brilliant, almost electrifying blue petals weren't a color he'd ever seen any plant come in, pollen a bright pink that seemed out of place. The petals weren't a shape he was familiar with. The flower was strange-looking, and it had a strong, sweet smell that he couldn't place. Frowning, he stood and carefully tucked the flower into his pocket.

He knocked on the door loudly, calling out as he did so. "Ranger Dunne out here. Anyone inside? Hello?"

Cillian canted his head toward the cabin wall. It sounded as if someone was moving around inside, but no one answered his query. He knocked again, glancing around the trees, keeping an eye on the woods. "If anyone is inside, you can come out. It's daylight. I'm a park ranger, and I can escort you back to town."

He strained his hearing, listening for that noise inside. It sounded like footsteps. Cillian adjusted his grip on his rifle, finger resting over the trigger guard as he focused on the door. A creak sounded inside before a tentative voice called out, "Hello?"

"Hey there, ma'am. I'm Ranger Dunne. Could you open the door, please?"

It took a few minutes before she did so, and Cillian couldn't fault her hesitancy, not with the damage done to the door and the walls of the cabin. When the door finally cracked open, a woman's pale face peered out at him, blue eyes bloodshot with dark circles beneath them. She had a scrape on her cheek that could've been from a fall or a branch, scabbed over now in the hours since she obtained it. Cillian did a quick once-over, not seeing any other wounds on her, but he needed to be sure.

"Are you hurt?" Cillian asked.

The way her expression crumpled into immediate tears made him wince. She sobbed as she stumbled out of the cabin, her entire body shaking, but she seemed to be moving all right. Cillian wrapped an arm around her shoulders and drew her away from the cabin door.

"Where's Jack?" she gasped out.

Cillian thought of the torn-up body Mac had radioed he was handling farther down the path and ignored her question. "What's your name? Can you tell me what happened?"

"Samantha." Her lips quivered as she spoke. Her hair had bits of leaves and small twigs stuck in it from her run through the forest. "We were hiking, and it was getting late, so we headed back to the car. Jack thought he saw someone in the woods coming toward us. Only it was—and he told me to run—"

She broke off with a ragged sob, covering her mouth with her hand. She shook so violently that Cillian worried she'd break a tooth. "Come on, let's get you out of here."

He made sure the cabin door was shut but not locked before guiding her down the dirt path through the trees. Sunlight filtered through the branches, but they passed through more shade than brightness. Samantha's grip on him was tight in a desperate way. Cillian had to be careful with how he carried his rifle on the walk back to the road. Halfway there, he radioed ahead. "Ranger Seven to Ranger One, do you copy, over?"

Static crackled for a second before Mac responded. "Ranger One copies, over."

"I'm on my way back with a hiker who was in the cabin. We're half a mile out, over."

"Copy that. We'll be ready, out."

Cillian let go of the receiver hooked to his shoulder strap and focused on getting Samantha out of the woods. Letting her huddle close meant he couldn't hold his rifle with both hands, but if anything approached, he'd still be able to aim and fire quickly. Luckily, nothing hunted them on their retreat back to the road, which now held more than just his truck. Mac's was parked there as well, along with a patrol car.

Mac and the patrolman stood off the dirt path, in the underbrush, and Cillian knew not to let Samantha see whatever they were looking at.

Beyond them, waiting on the road by the patrol car, were the two hikers who had called in the body and who Cillian had told to stay behind while he went into the woods.

"Let's get you seen to." Cillian steered Samantha toward his truck and let her sit in the front passenger seat. Now that they weren't on the move, he could see some of the scrapes and cuts on her arms were pretty deep. "I have a first aid kit in the back of the truck."

He stepped back, and she reached for him, panic filling her face. "Don't leave me."

"I won't." He pointed at the truck bed. "I'll be right there."

Cillian went to get what he needed and wasn't surprised to see Mac walking toward him. He unhooked the tailgate and folded it down, resting his rifle on it. "Sorry, I wasn't able to stay with the body, but a second set of footprints led toward the cabin. I had to check it out."

Mac nodded, resting his elbows on the side of the truck. "Your instincts were right. She's alive, at least."

Cillian reached for the first aid kit and pulled it closer to him. He drummed his fingers over the top, staring at the bright red cross painted on the rugged case. "She said they saw something in the woods, and she ran for the cabin. She made it, but the cabin has claw marks all around the walls. Looks like it could've been a bear."

Mac's expression was shuttered when Cillian looked up. "Lee radioed for backup, so the police will handle the body and the survivor. The ME hasn't left Pelham yet. I called dispatch and got who's on station duty to have her come out here to handle the scene so she doesn't have to make a second trip. You and I should take another look at the cabin before she gets here."

Cillian looked past Mac at the forest, listening to the rustle of leaves moved by the summer breeze. "All right. Lee can see to Samantha."

"Is that her name?"

"Yeah. The dead guy is Jack. I think he saved her life. He knew she needed to get to the cabin."

Mac pushed away from the truck. "If he's local, I don't envy that conversation with the family."

As park rangers, it wasn't their duty to notify the living of the dead. That fell on the police, and Cillian was glad for it in that moment.

Lee came back to the road, meeting them at the truck. He was an older man, weathered a bit from time spent outdoors, and of a generation who didn't question Mac when Cillian's captain said they were going to check on the cabin.

"Better you than me," Lee said, fingers worrying at a dark, coin-shaped object in one hand. "I'll be here when you get back."

Cillian handed over his first aid kit and left Samantha's care to Lee. He took his rifle with him back into the forest, past the body, following Mac down that shadowy, tree-lined path. Occasionally, Mac would pause next to a tree, studying its bark and the witchmark carved into it, the edges of each one a little dull from overgrowth. Like sign markers, each witchmark led the way through the twisting dirt path to the small cabin.

Mac stood in front of that refuge, frowning at the ground and the imprints Cillian had been careful not to disturb—Samantha's footsteps, but something else as well. Mac knelt, touching the dirt outside the strange imprint that no shoe had made. "Do you have your iron on you?"

Birds chirped nearby, and insects buzzed in the air, all the normal sounds Cillian was used to. The forest wasn't quiet, not in the way it would be if a threat were nearby. "Yes, but I think my rifle will be of better use if we're attacked."

He followed Mac around the cabin, treading carefully around crushed shrubbery and scuffed dirt, both of them studying the gouges in the walls. When they circled back to the front, Mac studied the cabin for a few moments more before turning to stare into the forest. "The report will say it was a bear."

"This is the third body in less than two days," Cillian said quietly.

"A rabid bear. It happens at least once a decade."

Cillian tightened his grip on the rifle, thinking about what Samantha had said and the furious evidence of a terrifying night she'd somehow survived. "We don't have any proof."

Mac looked back at him, eyes narrowed beneath the brim of his hat. "You grew up here. It's always a bear when it comes to outsiders."

"And what are we supposed to believe? That it was the lights?"

"*Don't*," Mac said sharply, stepping closer. "Don't name them."

Cillian frowned, uncertainty crawling beneath his skin. "They're just stories, aren't they?"

"What do you think?"

"Sometimes I think I don't know the forest, and I grew up here."

Mac's mouth twisted into a hard little smile. "Good. You might survive it, then."

Cillian looked back at the cabin, at the marks of something that had tried desperately to get inside but ultimately was denied. The reports would say it was a bear, but Cillian wasn't so sure now.

Mac clapped him on the shoulder before nodding back the way they'd come. "You're overdue for lunch. Let's head back to the road. I'll help Lee handle the medical examiner when she makes it out here. We're going to be patrolling in pairs after this."

"Going to let her drive in the forest?" Cillian asked.

"Emergencies mean paperwork, but it's paperwork the higher-ups can accept for vehicles near the reservoir."

They trudged back down the path to the road, and Cillian didn't let go of his rifle until they met up with everyone else. The medical examiner hadn't arrived yet, but another patrolman had. Samantha sat in the back of his patrol car now, and Cillian was fine with that.

Cillian racked his rifle and drove away from the scene of the crime, not hungry after such a stressful morning, to say nothing of yesterday. Rather than turn on the radio, he called his mom.

"Hey, Mom," Cillian said when she picked up. "Are you in Amherst?"

"My vacation isn't until next week. I had to get through the drunken stupidness of the Fourth of July first, so yes, I'm still home," his mother replied cheerfully enough.

"Was the emergency room that bad again?"

"I feel like people get stupider about fireworks every year."

"Packed for your cruise yet?"

"Not yet. Did you want to come for a visit and help me out?"

"Probably not a good idea right now."

Her tone changed from loving and welcoming to worried in a nanosecond. "Why? What's wrong?"

What Cillian always called her *mom radar* seemed to be working fine. "I don't know if you've heard the news yet, but Juliana and Ray were killed yesterday. It was a bear attack."

The line was silent for long enough that Cillian thought he'd lost the connection. When his mom finally spoke up, her voice was quiet and flat, a thread of worry running through it. "A bear?"

Cillian glanced out the side window at the trees rushing past and the shadows beneath the branches before wrenching his gaze back to the road he was driving down. "That's what Mac says."

"That's what the rangers always say during times like this."

"What do you mean?"

His mother ignored the question. "What about Aisling?"

"She's okay." Cillian paused before saying, "Bran came back for her."

"Ah." His mother paused to clear her throat. "Have you spoken to him?"

"I kind of had to since I was the one who found Aisling."

"So he's back in Pelham. Will he stay?"

Cillian frowned, grip tightening on the steering wheel. "I don't know. Why do you ask?"

"Perhaps I shouldn't go on my cruise."

"What? Mom, no! You've been looking forward to it for months. There's no reason for you to stay."

"It's not safe in Pelham if there's a rabid bear."

"All the more reason for you to go on your cruise. There are no forests out in the middle of the sea near the Bahamas."

"You're in Pelham."

"I'll be fine. I know the forest."

"I'd feel better if you left."

"I'm not going to abandon my job for something like this."

"Even if it meant you'd be safe?"

"Mom," Cillian sighed. "I won't leave Pelham. It's just bears. I've been trained to handle those kinds of encounters."

He wasn't going to let Mac and his fellow rangers patrol alone. Then there was Bran.

He couldn't stop thinking of Bran.

It was his mother's turn to sigh. "Fine. Stay in town. But Cillian?"

"Yes, Mom?"

"Remember what I've always told you. No matter what, never trust a witch."

It'd been his mantra as a child, whispered admonishments that were almost like a prayer when his mother spoke in the quiet corners of the town they found themselves in. Cillian hadn't understood the warning as a kid or a teenager because the only witches in town were the Gallaghers, and they'd never been anything but kind.

"Cillian?" his mother pressed.

"I won't," Cillian dutifully promised. "Have fun on your cruise."

"Love you."

"Love you, too."

He ended the call, letting the thrum of the engine fill the cab for a few minutes before he switched on the radio. Music kept him company all the way to Red's Diner because even if he didn't eat, he still needed to take a break. Mac would supervise the handover of the crime scene to the police, and the medical examiner would hopefully finish her job in a few hours. Cillian's report could wait.

Half a dozen cars were parked in the lot adjacent to Red's Diner. The start of the lunch crowd wasn't that terrible, and when Cillian pushed open the glass door, bell jingling overhead, he knew he'd have his pick of empty booths or tables, but the booth taken in the corner caught his eye first.

His heart rate sped up a little as he locked eyes with Bran, the sounds of the diner fading out to nothing in that moment, as if they were the only two people there. It felt like a sucker punch to the gut, same as last night when he'd seen Bran for the first time in seven years. The ache of Bran's absence that he'd lived with since the end of high school dug itself deeper, reminding him of what he'd been missing and which his memory refused to give up. Now that Bran was back, Cillian didn't want to let go again, even though he knew he didn't have the right to hold on anymore.

There was just something inside him demanding that he try.

Cillian swallowed hard, making a split-second decision he hoped he wouldn't regret. He nodded at Lottie as he passed by the register, giving her a quiet hello before he reached Bran's booth. The younger man was holding on to a mug of coffee with a white-knuckled grip, table empty of plates.

"Mind if I join you?" Cillian asked.

"Yes," Bran said with the same clipped ruthlessness he'd greeted Cillian with last night. It left a sour taste in Cillian's mouth, one he was determined to wash away with some company.

"It's been a while."

"I haven't been counting."

Cillian bit the inside of his cheek. "I just want to talk."

Bran's fingers flexed around the coffee mug, gaze dropping. "I don't have anything to say to you."

"Well, I do, so you can listen while I take my lunch break." Cillian took a seat before he could second-guess his decision, staring defiantly across the table at Bran.

Bran scowled at him. "I don't know why anyone ever thought you were a pushover when we were kids."

"I had you to fight for me."

"You don't have me anymore."

The words cut like a knife, and Cillian would've bled out from them if the wound had been real. He clenched his teeth, refusing to look away. Bran had changed; of course he had. Cillian knew he was still the same height as when they'd graduated high school, but that was the only thing that hadn't changed. He'd grown out his dark brown hair a bit, the faint wave to it much more prominent now. Those hazel eyes that had always caught Cillian's gaze with silent mirth in homeroom and other classes when they were younger now looked at him with a wealth of emotion he didn't think was meant for only him.

Lottie bustled up to the table, notepad in her apron and pencil tucked behind one ear as she set a glass of soda in front of Cillian. She was an older woman in her fifties and co-owner of Red's Diner. Her graying red hair was the signature look for the women in her family and the reason for the name of the diner that had existed since the early 1900s. The crow's feet at the corners of her eyes deepened when she smiled at them. "Well, doesn't this feel familiar? I remember serving you boys as kids, and now look at you, such handsome young men. Your usual, Cillian?"

"Thanks, Lottie," Cillian said, deciding he was hungry after all.

"Coming right up, sweetheart." She turned her attention to Bran, expression softening. "And for you and your sister? You both finally ready for lunch?"

Bran shook his head, letting go of his coffee mug. "We'll be leaving as soon as Aisling finishes up her game."

Cillian looked past him at the far corner of the diner, where Lottie's mother and father had built a small arcade nearly forty years ago. Aisling's distinctive white-blonde hair was barely visible over the top of a seat in the racing car game he and Bran had always played when they were kids.

"All right, then. Let me know if you want anything to go."

Lottie bustled off to put in Cillian's order, and he knew he only had a short window of time to convince Bran to stick around. He'd never been any good at small talk, but he tried. Cillian cleared his throat and pointed at the tattoo covering Bran's right forearm. "That's new."

Bran wrapped his left hand around his tattooed forearm. "Let's not pretend you're interested in me."

Some curl of anger crept into Cillian's voice, despite how hard he tried to push it back. "How about you don't put words in my mouth? I wasn't the one who changed my phone number before running off to college."

Bran's lips pressed together into a hard line as his expression shuttered. As seemingly good as he was at closing himself off, he couldn't hide the redness in his eyes from a grief Cillian shared. He sighed, leaning back and meeting Bran's gaze, shoving aside whatever lingering animosity he felt for the other man. "I'm sorry. I don't want to fight with you."

"And I don't want to talk," Bran ground out.

"Bran." Cillian tried to think of what to say, but everything that came to mind sounded so trite. He settled for a truth that couldn't be denied. "I miss your mother, too."

Bran's expression broke, twisting into something that was all grief for a split second before it disappeared. "I *don't* want to talk about it."

Cillian nodded, wishing he had the right to hold Bran, to comfort him. "Okay. But would you please listen?"

Bran looked as if he wanted to argue, and maybe he would have if Aisling hadn't run up to the table and leaned into Cillian's side of the booth to throw her arms around his neck and hug him. She nearly knocked off his hat, but Cillian didn't care as he hugged her back. "Hey, there. How are you doing?"

Aisling squeezed him tight before pulling back and shrugging, her expression sad.

"Still not talking?"

She shrugged again before looking over at her brother and mimed eating. They were like day and night in appearance, but they were both Gallaghers. Bran sighed and slid out of the booth. "Fine. I'll let Lottie know you want a burger and fries. Go play for now."

Aisling ran off back to the arcade corner, Cillian watching her go. "How's she doing?"

"She just lost her mother and father to a violent attack and refuses to speak. How do you think she's doing?"

It was on the tip of his tongue for Cillian to ask how Bran felt, but he knew the question would be met with more than a little hostility. Bran had always been like a cat with its hackles raised when he got angry and defensive. "There's another body."

Bran rocked to a halt barely a foot away from the table. He turned around and stared at Cillian, eyes wide, hands clenched into fists. "What?"

The question came out low and disbelieving. Cillian turned on the bench so he could better see Bran. "Some hikers called it in this morning. I got to the scene first and radioed for backup. One body and one survivor."

"Someone survived?"

Cillian nodded. "She made it to a cabin."

Bran slowly retook his seat, staring at Cillian, all that prickliness gone. "Should you be telling me this?"

Cillian raised an eyebrow. "Mac said we probably have a rabid bear in the forest again. That's not a secret anyone is keeping."

Bran pulled out his phone and checked the screen, frowning slightly. "Mac hasn't called me."

"Why would he need to?"

Lottie came by their booth right then, delaying Bran's answer as she poured him another cup of coffee before wagging her notepad at him. "I saw you getting up, but you know you don't need to come to the counter to order. What would you like?"

"Aisling wants a burger and fries and another milkshake," Bran said.

"And for yourself?"

"I'm not hungry."

"You weren't hungry this morning either when you came in for a late breakfast. You need to eat something, sweetheart."

Her voice was soft and cajoling, but Cillian knew Bran could be stubborn. He'd always been the one to stand his ground against the bullies at school, coming home with bruised knuckles and black eyes that healed faster than the other kids' broken noses.

Cillian caught her eye. "I'll take another basket of fries, Lottie."

She nodded and put her notepad away. "I'll go put that in for you."

She left, and Cillian focused on Bran. "You realize she's putting together a whole box of food for you to take with you, right?"

Bran slumped in his seat and lifted a hand to rub at his forehead. "I'm not hungry."

Cillian didn't fight him on that, knowing it was pretty impossible to force Bran to do anything. Once upon a time, he'd been adept at knowing how to be friends with Bran, but that seemed like a lifetime ago. "I meant it, you know. The whole town is going to miss your mom."

Bran tipped his head back and stared up at the ceiling, anger replaced with a tiredness that Cillian couldn't fix. "I know."

His voice was tight, sounding almost as if he were going to cry despite his dry eyes, which refused to look at Cillian. The silence that settled between them wasn't as antagonistic as it could have been, and Cillian was reluctant to break it, but he was more reluctant to leave things unsaid between them. "Can we talk?"

Bran finally looked at him, face pale from weariness and grief that was impossible to hide. "Why?"

"Because..." His voice trailed off as he struggled to put into words all the tangled-up feelings that had roiled in him since seeing Bran for the first time in years last night. He'd never truly been able to let Bran go, still wanting him now as he had back then with a smoldering need that burned and burned, like those fires in abandoned mine shafts that eventually burst forth to swallow an entire town. "Because I think we need to."

Bran didn't say anything—not then, and not through lunch when their orders were finally brought to the table and Aisling was called to join them. None of them spoke, and the silence stopped being awkward when Cillian shoved the extra basket of fries across the table to Bran, arching an eyebrow at the faintly irritated look the other man gave him. Cillian stared right back at him, daring Bran to say no. He'd always stolen Cillian's fries when they were younger. Buying an extra basket had been the only surefire way to keep Bran's fingers from his plate.

When Bran reached for the fries, Cillian considered it a victory.

Cillian finished his lunch and knew he couldn't linger even if he wanted to. What finally drew him out of the booth was the sound of his phone ringing, Mac's name on the screen when Cillian pulled it out of his pocket. "I have to get back to work."

Bran worried his bottom lip between his teeth. Cillian fought the urge to reach over the table and touch his fingers to Bran's mouth. "Come by the Shoppe tomorrow."

Cillian didn't know who was more surprised at the offer, Bran or himself. He nodded hastily as he stood. "I will."

He finally answered the call, pressing the phone to his ear and holding it there with his shoulder so he could dig out his wallet and leave enough cash on the table to cover his lunch and theirs. He left before Bran figured it out.

"Dunne speaking," Cillian said.

"The medical examiner made it to the scene, and the police have taken it over. I need you back at the station for your report," Mac said.

"I'm on my way."

He didn't want to leave, but at least he left knowing Bran had invited him around tomorrow, and maybe they could work past the ache of impulsive, painful teenage decisions. It felt like a long shot, but Cillian was willing to try. He left the diner and was halfway to his truck when Bran called out to him. "Cillian!"

He jerked around, as if strings were tied to his body and leading back to Bran. "Yeah?"

Bran stood outside the door, arms crossed over his chest. He didn't speak right away, and Cillian found himself returning to the diner, coming to a stop in front of Bran. With Bran on the porch, they were at eye level, and Cillian could see how Bran was biting his lower lip. "Do you have your iron on you?"

It was the same question Mac had asked, and he shouldn't have been surprised Bran would ask it, too. Juliana always had. Cillian was always so forgetful of the iron in his pocket, and he was beginning to think all the stories he'd grown up on were more than just superstition. "Always."

Bran's shoulders slumped a little. "Good."

They stared at each other for a few moments, the air hot between them, and Cillian wasn't sure he could blame the summer sun. His fingers twitched with the urge to reach for Bran, but he didn't have that right, not now.

Maybe not ever.

Finally, Bran stepped back, and Cillian had to fight not to reel him close. "See you tomorrow."

"Tomorrow," Cillian promised. He forced his feet to move because he had a job to do, but he couldn't stop himself from looking over his shoulder when he was halfway across the parking lot, seeing Bran looking back at him.

Bran was the first to turn away, retreating into the diner. Cillian tucked away all the messy emotions tangled around the man he'd never forgotten and headed for his truck, focusing on the job ahead and not the past behind him.

Chapter Five

"Listen," Bran said as he opened yet another cupboard in the Shoppe and started moving items around, making sure to get eyes on every inch of the space. "How long does it take to become a legal guardian? Will the government come and take Aisling from me if I don't have anything filed on time?"

"You're her immediate family, and DCF prefers those kinds of placements. My understanding is the police in Pelham notified them, and a counselor spoke with you yesterday?" Thomas said. The lawyer Tina had put him in touch with seemed all right so far and hadn't sounded condescending or anything.

"Someone came by yesterday afternoon."

The woman had driven in from Amherst, spent less than an hour with him after their lunch at Red's Diner, and left Aisling in his care. Bran was glad he hadn't needed to use magic to change her mind. Compulsion wasn't something he liked to use, and his mother had always frowned on the spells that took away someone else's autonomy. Just this once, though, if it had been necessary, Bran would have done it.

"You have a job, and you have somewhere to live. That's more than some people can give their kids." The sound of rustling papers filtered over the line. "I can have the paperwork drawn up, and we can get it filed within the week. It'll necessitate you driving into Boston to meet with me. Unfortunately, Pelham doesn't have a courthouse, but we can file online in the one in Hampshire."

Bran closed the cupboard door and settled back on his heels. He ran a hand through his hair, yanking on it lightly out of frustration. "Does it need to be this week? I have a funeral to plan."

"I understand. The sooner, the better would be preferred, but Aisling won't be displaced from your care if we take a few weeks to get everything in order."

"Great."

"Give me a call in a week or two, whenever you're ready."

"Thanks."

Bran ended the call, not in the mood to deal with legal things, but knew he needed to if he wanted to keep Aisling and get full control of his mother's business and bank accounts. The short call he'd had with Tina that morning to set up a more in-depth meeting indicated they had a lot to go over. Part of Bran didn't want to have that meeting because it would truly mean his mother was gone. Denial was a creeping sort of insanity Bran knew he couldn't succumb to, even if part of him desperately wanted someone else to take over being the adult. But at newly twenty-five, he *was* the adult.

He stood, eyeing the next set of cupboard doors in the cabinet set against the wall. Bran wasn't doing inventory so much as looking for any sort of hidden space his mother could have stashed the grimoire. So far, he was coming up empty-handed, and the panic he'd managed to shove aside was back, skittering through his bones. Mac hadn't located the grimoire in the house, which Bran still hadn't set foot in. The ranger had handed off another load of clothes and shoes when Bran returned to the station yesterday afternoon to name and put to rest the latest body taken from the woods.

It was strange performing a duty his mother had handled for decades. It felt a lot like playing dress-up, as if he were some character in a play on a stage he had no right to stand on. He'd taken over the mantle to guard and fight against the wyrding and all it entailed, and he liked to think he had his mother's blessing for it.

He still wished she was there to do it for him.

Bran clenched his teeth against the knot in his throat and the ready burn of tears in his eyes. He'd done his best not to cry around Aisling, trying to be strong for her. Right now, she was upstairs watching television while Bran tried not to fall apart.

Someone knocked on the door at the same time Jupiter *cawed* outside, his familiar's tone a warning only Bran would recognize. He froze, head snapping around to stare at the door. The lights in the Shoppe were on, and his car was out front. It probably looked as if they were open, but he'd turned the hand-painted little wooden sign hanging on the door outside to *closed* the first night they'd stayed in the apartment.

Everyone in town knew of his mother's death. While he'd accepted quite a few casseroles and other easy-to-store and cook meals in the last twenty-four hours for him and Aisling to eat, Jupiter wouldn't have cawed like that if the person knocking was local.

Another knock finally got Bran moving. He stood and approached the door, settling one hand on the knob. "We're closed."

"Yes, but it's past the opening time, and I had an appointment," a woman called back.

Another *caw* from Jupiter, this one almost angry-sounding, and Bran's grip tightened on the cool metal pressed against his palm. After a moment of hesitation, he finally undid the deadbolt and the regular lock, pulling open the door but fitting his body in the space it created to block the way inside. "I said we're closed."

The woman standing on his porch was taller than him, even in the pointed pair of flats she wore. Her cream dress with black polka dots was sleeveless, buttoned down the front, with a neatly folded down collar. Her eyes were hidden by oversized sunglasses, and the silk scarf she wore over her red hair was as fashionable as it was useful, judging by the sleek convertible Porsche parked next to his run-down Honda Civic. Her makeup was flawless; so were her neatly manicured nails. Everything about her was eerily perfect, and the hair on the back of Bran's neck stood on end at that uncomfortable realization.

The woman cocked a hand on one hip, her other hand adjusting the strap of the pristine Chanel purse she carried. "And as I said, I have an appointment. I didn't drive all the way from Boston just to be turned away. I'm here to see Ms. Gallagher about a return. It's important that I meet with her."

Her accent was the genteel sort of old money that belonged to the kind of person who summered at Martha's Vineyard and wintered in Aspen or the French Alps. Bran didn't know why someone like her was in Pelham, looking to browse the Shoppe.

"Ms. Gallagher is dead," Bran said flatly, not caring about politeness when grief tasted like acid in his mouth. "The Shoppe is closed."

The woman drew back slightly, one hand coming up to press over her chest. "I didn't know."

"It was sudden. She was the only one in charge of the business."

The woman frowned prettily. "Are you taking over for her?"

"I'm her son." Which wasn't an answer, even if the answer was *yes*. The woman didn't need to know that.

"Well, then. It's nice to meet you. Bran, is it? Ms. Gallagher spoke lovingly of you over the years. I'm Meghan."

Bran gritted his teeth against the desire to tell Meghan to shut up. He settled for one better. "Like I said before, the Shoppe is closed."

He stepped back, intent on closing the door, when Meghan put her hand out, palm against the wood, and halted the swing of it with surprising strength. Jupiter *cawed* again from the roof, and Bran stared at Meghan, some instinct telling him that turning his back on her would be a terrible mistake.

Letting her inside would be worse.

She smiled, her eyes difficult to make out through the lenses of her sunglasses. "I'm sorry to press the issue, but I did have an appointment with your mother this morning on an urgent matter. She was meant to finalize a return for me, and I came to bring it to her. If you're here, perhaps you could handle it for me? I'm sure it shouldn't take long."

"Come back some other day. Some other week, even. My mother is dead, the Shoppe is closed, and I'm not taking any customers."

He spat the words out like they were bullets, wishing she'd take a hint. The edge of the door dug into his shoulder from the strength of her hand, her body refusing to give an inch when she had no right. Bran wanted her gone. He'd trusted Jupiter's opinion of people for years, and she'd never led him astray. That his familiar was perched overhead, still cawing out a warning, told Bran he couldn't trust who—or *what*—stood on the porch.

Their staring contest was broken by the sound of a truck engine getting louder from down the road. Moments later, a black truck favored by park rangers pulled in alongside Bran's Honda Civic. The engine cut off, and Cillian got out of the truck, hat left behind, but wearing the uniform favored by rangers. Bran stared at Cillian, stomach swooping a little as he watched the other man approach with a confident stride.

He wore a short-sleeved shirt today as an acknowledgment of the heat, the fabric pulled tight over his broad shoulders, showing off the muscles in his arms. Bran didn't realize his gaze was drifting downward to the bulge that not even the loose uniform pants could hide until he had to jerk his eyes back up to meet Cillian's.

"I didn't know you had opened the Shoppe to customers," Cillian said slowly.

"I didn't. She was leaving," Bran said.

Bran glanced at Meghan and realized she was no longer looking at him but at Cillian, focused in a way Bran didn't care for at all. He'd almost take a flirty look over the predatory sense he got off her in that moment. It made him want to put himself between the woman and Cillian, to call up a witchmark for a spell that would cast her out of Pelham and send her back to Boston.

If she even was from Boston.

Meghan moved away from the door, and Bran nearly pitched face-first to the ground, stumbling badly now that she wasn't forcing it open. Cillian eyed him worriedly, but Bran ignored him.

"Fancy meeting a ranger all the way out here," Meghan said. She held out her hand to Cillian, expecting him to reciprocate, which he did.

"Ma'am," Cillian said politely, shaking her hand before letting her go. "Do you need directions?"

"I came for an appointment. I didn't realize it was a bad time."

"I'd suggest setting up another one later on. If you've no other errands in Pelham, it might be best to head back home. Woods aren't safe right now."

"Oh?" Meghan crossed her arms over her chest, and Bran was a little surprised to realize she and Cillian were the same height. "Has something happened?"

"Rabid bear. The rangers are putting out a notice."

Bran bit the inside of his cheek at the lie Cillian so easily told. The tried-and-true warning was one that had been in rotation for decades. He wondered when people would start realizing it wasn't bears.

Meghan gasped, covering her mouth with her hand. "A rabid *bear*?"

"Yes, ma'am."

She shook her head, long ponytail swaying with the motion. "Well, you don't see that in Boston."

She stepped away from them both, but all of her attention was still on Cillian. It was as if Bran no longer existed, and he'd be glad of that if he could trust her appearance. Jupiter *cawed* again, and Meghan tilted her head back, searching the eaves of the roof. Bran leaned out farther and looked up as well, but he couldn't see Jupiter.

"A friend of yours?" Meghan asked, finally looking at Bran. The sunglasses made her face appear as if they were black holes where her eyes should be.

"Bye," Bran said pointedly.

She quirked another little smile at him, and Bran would never see it as friendly. Meghan opened her purse and rummaged through it before coming up with a narrow metal tin that apparently held business cards. She passed one over, and Bran had to force himself to take it from her. "My contact information for the return I still need to process. I'll call the Shoppe in a few days."

Bran held the business card between his thumb and index finger as if it would bite, glancing at the name. Meghan Teague. "Sure."

Meghan's smile directed at Cillian was friendlier. Inviting, even. Cillian, for his part, only nodded a polite goodbye. They both watched Meghan saunter back to her Porsche and get behind the steering wheel. The sound of her car's engine was a purr compared to Cillian's truck or the sometimes rattling wheeze of Bran's Honda Civic. She backed out of her spot and zipped off down the road, heading north rather than south, a route Bran knew wouldn't take her to Boston.

"What was that all about?" Cillian asked.

"Nothing." Bran shook his head, pocketing the business card and looking anywhere but at Cillian. "I didn't think you'd stop by so early."

"My shift isn't for another hour, so I thought now would be a good time to visit. It's not that early, and you did invite me, remember?"

"Only because you probably would've caused a scene at Red's if I didn't."

"Causing a scene was always your specialty, not mine."

Which was true. Cillian had always been the quiet one, holding himself back out of shyness, sickly through elementary school, and relegated to the sidelines during recess. His anger ran deep and cold, with a long fuse before his temper ignited, which was rarely. Bran's could be set off with a single spark if the situation called for it. Any of the scrapes Bran had gotten into as a kid had almost always been in defense of Cillian. The handful of times the fights escalated to being suspension-worthy, his mother had always talked the principal down. When he'd gotten older, he always wondered if it was magic that had let him stay in school when others might have been expelled.

They'd been inseparable as children, though. Then Cillian had pushed him away after Bran had offered up his heart, and coming back from that wasn't easy. First loves always hurt, but losing Cillian had felt like carving out his heart and soul. Now, with Cillian standing before him—taller than in memory, those blue-gray eyes staring at him so intently, beautiful in a way that made Bran's mouth water and had him wanting to sink to his knees—that ache took root in his chest once more as if it had never been forgotten.

Bran sighed. "Yeah, fine. Come in."

Bran kicked the door open wider and gestured for Cillian to step inside. He went, and as soon as he was off the porch, Jupiter flew down from the eaves and settled on the wooden planks, out of sight of the door. Bran glanced at her and then in the direction Meghan had driven off in. Pursing his lips, he jerked his head at the road, speaking in a low voice and hoping Cillian wouldn't hear him. "Follow her. I don't trust her skin."

Jupiter *cawed* an affirmative, hopped to the edge of the porch, spread her massive wings, and launched herself into the air. She flapped hard to gain altitude before winging into the sky, flying north. Bran withdrew into the Shoppe and closed the door behind him, locking it to keep anyone else out. He brushed his fingers over some of the witch-marks carved into the door frame to soothe his nerves a little.

"Are you sure nothing was taken from the Shoppe? Place looks messier than how your mother always kept it," Cillian said, looking around.

Bran went behind the display case that doubled as the sales counter rather than to the next cupboard he'd been about to dig through before being interrupted by Meghan. "I'm trying to do inventory."

He didn't say he was looking for something, especially not the grimoire, because Cillian wasn't a guardian, and he wasn't a witch, and the most important secret that Pelham kept could never be turned into a superstitious legend.

Cillian stepped up to the counter, and Bran braced himself—both physically and mentally—before meeting Cillian's gaze. "I was rude to you the other night. You got Aisling out of the woods, and I'm grateful for that. So, thank you."

Cillian's eyebrows crept toward his hairline. "That's the only thing you wanted to say to me?"

"What else is there?"

A flash of anger flickered in Cillian's eyes, something that had rarely been directed at Bran when they were younger. "I think there's plenty. Starting with why you ran off after graduation before I could talk to you."

"I didn't run."

Cillian laughed, the sound sharp and angry as he leaned forward. "Bullshit, Bran. You changed your number and told your mom not to give it or your new address to me. I'd always hear you were in Pelham for a visit only after you'd left again. I haven't seen you in seven years, and this isn't the reunion I wanted."

"We didn't need a reunion."

"I wanted one."

Bran's gaze skittered away from Cillian's face, looking at the Shoppe instead. "And if I didn't?"

Before Cillian could respond, the door to the stairs opened, and Aisling popped her head out. Her expression brightened when she caught sight of Cillian, and Bran wasn't surprised when she made a beeline for him. Cillian opened his arms for a hug, and Aisling readily gave him one. "Still not talking?"

It seemed to be everyone's refrain over the last few days, usually followed by pity and sometimes a promise to feed her and Bran, as if food could fill the emptiness in them both. Cillian didn't look at Aisling with pity, though, only a sadness that made Bran clench his teeth.

"She'll talk when she's ready," he said. *After I've found the grimoire and I've removed the damn geas on her.*

Becoming a pseudo-parent hadn't been in the cards—tarot or otherwise—but Bran wasn't going to walk away from his sister and leave her to the whims of foster care. There might be a twelve-year age gap between them, but that didn't matter. She was all the family he had left, and he would protect her.

"Do you want me to make breakfast, or did you want to go to Red's?" Bran asked. Aisling pulled away from Cillian and frowned before pointing at the ceiling. "All right. Head upstairs. I'll join you in a few minutes."

Aisling nodded and left the Shoppe on quiet feet. Bran watched her go because it was easier to follow her passage than to look Cillian in the eye.

"She's a good kid," Cillian said softly, his anger seemingly gone.

"She's been through a lot."

"You both have."

Grief welled up, sudden and deep. Bran squeezed his eyes shut for a moment, getting himself back under control. "I think you should go."

"Bran—"

"I only wanted to thank you for helping Aisling."

"You don't ever have to thank me for that."

"Yeah, well." Bran let out a heavy breath and opened his eyes. "I'm still glad you found her."

Cillian nodded slowly. "Are you staying in Pelham?"

"What?"

Cillian's sharp-eyed focus was impossible to escape. He felt pinned like a scarab beetle in a frame. "You heard me."

It wasn't like he could *leave*, even if Cillian didn't know that. Bran was hit with the uncomfortable realization that staying meant escaping the other man would be impossible. "You're going to be late."

Cillian stepped back from the display case, a look in his eyes that Bran couldn't read. "See you around, Bran."

He left, and Bran stood there alone in his mother's Shoppe, trying to decide if Cillian's parting words were a promise or a threat and whether or not he minded either way.

CHAPTER SIX

Jupiter pecked the crouton out of the salad bowl before Bran could shoo her off. "No! That's not for birds!"

His familiar *cawed* at him with a smug look in her starry eyes before swallowing the crouton. He waved the metal tongs at her, causing Jupiter to hop off the table and onto the back of one chair before winging her way back to where Aisling sat on the couch, watching television. Jupiter *cawed* at her, and Aisling lifted one arm without looking, letting the large raven snuggle close.

"Thief," Bran grumbled.

Jupiter tossed her head back and *cawed* at the ceiling, the tone mocking even if no one else could parse it. His familiar had always been a brat and reveled in it. Bran loved her, though, and couldn't imagine life without her.

The timer on the oven went off, and Bran returned to the small kitchen to pull out the lasagna someone in town had dropped off for them the other day. The refrigerator was packed with food, and Bran didn't know how they'd eat all of it before the dishes went bad. "Aisling, dinner is ready."

He missed the sound of her voice—viscerally and suddenly—right then. Only hearing his own was lonely when she was right there with him. Aisling still smiled at him as she approached the table, holding Jupiter in her arms. His familiar gently pecked her cheek in a facsimile of a kiss. Bran set the lasagna pan on the trivet in the middle of the small table, then took off his oven mitts.

"Here, let me have her," Bran said.

He raised his arm, elbow bent, bracing himself. Aisling set Jupiter on the back of a chair, giving the raven somewhere to balance and stretch her wings before she flew across the table with an easy flap of her long wingspan to land on Bran's tattooed forearm. He grunted at her weight, giving her another crouton. "Been eating too many mice."

She blinked and ruffled her feathers before *cawing* at him. Bran snorted and carried her to the nearest window. He undid the latch and pushed it open so he could extend his arm outside. Unlike the other windows in the apartment, save the one with the air conditioner attached, this one didn't have a screen. Jupiter launched herself off his arm and into the darkening sky, winging off into the sunset. She'd come back at some point and find a spot to sleep on the roof or one of the trees near the Shoppe.

Bran closed the window and locked it again, absently touching the witchmarks etched into the window frame. The warmth of the magic layered into them over the years buzzed softly against his fingertips. He joined Aisling at the table, serving them both pieces of lasagna and the salad he'd prepared. He made sure to cut a slice from the middle for Aisling.

"I know you still don't like the edges," he said, sliding the center piece onto her plate.

She huffed out a laugh and nodded, the soft noise all she could make right now. Bran sat beside her, watching as she filled half her plate with salad, spilling a few lettuce leaves because most of her attention was on her show. He was content to eat dinner in silence, with only the sound of the television to fill the air. Aisling would need her phone in order to text back answers, and he didn't want her dinner to go cold. It'd been a few months since he'd seen his little sister, and it was nice to sit beside her after everything that had happened.

Only toward the end of dinner did he speak, broaching a subject he hadn't talked with her about yet. "I'm going to file for guardianship of you."

Aisling's head snapped around so she could look at him. She paused mid-chew, food making one cheek bulge like a chipmunk. She chewed furiously to swallow it, even as she reached for her phone to type out a question.

I won't have to go somewhere else?

"You're my sister. I'm not letting you go into foster care."

Where will we live?

Bran hesitated, thinking of his job and apartment back in Boston, bits of a life he wouldn't get to have anymore. "Here, in Pelham."

Aisling frowned and angrily shook her head. Her next text wasn't a surprise. *Not at the house.*

Bran touched her shoulder with a gentle hand. "I know. We can stay here until I sort out the title of the house. I was thinking we can rent it out or sell it. Renting might be better, but I'm not sure we'd find anyone local to move in after what happened."

You think outsiders would be better?

"Easier to sell to. Maybe it could be someone's summer home."

In Pelham? Aisling rolled her eyes.

Bran managed a laugh. "Yeah, we aren't the Hamptons."

Aisling stuck her tongue out of the corner of her mouth as she tapped away at her phone. *Could we stay here?*

Bran glanced around the small apartment that had been the only home he'd ever known before his mother met Ray. "That's what I was thinking. I'm going to need a place in order to take over legal guardianship for you. I'll have to quit my job in Boston, but Mom left me the Shoppe. I can run it."

The learning curve might be a little steep. There was a difference between helping out during the summers as a kid and teenager and actually running a business, but he'd figure it out. If it meant he kept Aisling, then he'd do anything.

Okay. I won't have to change schools?

"No. That's part of why we're staying."

Aisling blinked at him before dropping her gaze back to her phone.

More typing ended with another question. *WILL YOU DO WHAT MOM DID?*

He didn't say *I took up the mantle*. He didn't say *it's what I was born to do*. He didn't say *I don't want to*.

Witches weren't given the option of walking away from the wyrding they stood guard against. If they tried, they were inevitably tracked down and their magic stolen from them by order of the Council. It wasn't fair to lose your sense of self like that, but letting the wyrding spread was far worse. Bran didn't want to ever know what it would be like to live without the heat of magic he could call up from the elements. The iron beads on his bracelet felt heavy, but what they helped protect against made it easy to answer. "Yes."

Aisling's bottom lip trembled, and her next question had Bran getting up from his chair so he could hug her. *WILL YOU DIE LIKE HER?*

"No one else is dying," Bran said fiercely, holding her tight. "I won't let it happen."

Three people were dead already, and he'd named them all. Bran vowed those would be the only names he'd have to speak for the ritual this summer. Aisling sniffled a little but only scrubbed at her eyes rather than fall apart crying. Both of them had experienced their fair share of crying jags over the last few days. Bran tried to do his where she couldn't see, but the apartment was small, and Aisling seemed not to want to leave his side, even here in their new home.

He rubbed at her back before straightening. "Come on. If you're finished, let's put everything away. I think there's a berry pie someone brought that we can eat."

Aisling nodded and put away her phone before helping him clean up. The apartment didn't have a dishwasher, so Bran hand-washed them, and Aisling dried. Afterward, he pulled a whole pie from the fridge, its lattice-work top sprinkled liberally with sugar. He didn't bother with plates, carrying it and two forks back to the couch. They sat and ate the pie from the middle out to the crust while watching a show he'd never seen before but which Aisling was invested in, and that was all that mattered.

Summer meant no school for her, and Bran didn't need to work at the moment, so they both stayed up until almost midnight before he turned off the television. Aisling went into his old room that was now hers to get ready for bed. At some point, they'd need to redecorate it, but it could wait until he moved stuff from her room in the house to the Shoppe.

Bran went into the bedroom that had once been their mother's. He turned on the light and closed the door to get ready for bed. Nothing about the room had been changed since their arrival, and all of it reminded him of his mother. Gritting his teeth against the lump in his throat, Bran pulled off his jeans and got into bed in his boxers and T-shirt after turning off the light. Light from the full moon shined through the top portion of the bedroom window, the air-conditioning unit humming along steadily.

Bran curled up on his side, staring at the wall and willing sleep to take him. As stressed-out and tired as he was, sleep was difficult to come by. At some point, though, he slipped into restless dreams, but even those weren't enough to keep him under. He jerked awake however long later, blinking blearily through the shadows of the room, surprised to see Aisling standing by his bed.

He opened his mouth to speak, but she put her hand over his mouth and frantically shook her head. The moonlight had shifted over the hours, but it was still bright enough to see how big her eyes were, the way her bottom lip trembled, and how her shoulders and chest moved like a hummingbird's wings as she breathed. Terror had a look, and it was his little sister as she twisted to point at the window, stabbing her finger in that direction over and over again.

Bran pried her hand off his mouth and sat up, staring at the window. Nothing had blocked the light coming through over the air-conditioning unit, and they were upstairs from the Shoppe, which didn't have any security system because it didn't need any when the entire building was covered in witchmarks. But then he heard it—the heavy, harsh breathing of *something* outside their home.

Bran scrambled out of bed as quietly as he could and grabbed his jeans off the floor, yanking them on in a matter of seconds. He shoved his feet into his sneakers and hastily tied them, glancing at Aisling, glad to see she wore a pair of sneakers as well, even if she was only wearing shorts and a tank top. The air-conditioning units weren't the best, and it was still warm in the apartment despite the early morning hour. Bran reached for his awareness of Jupiter and couldn't sense his familiar anywhere nearby. He still tugged on their bond, sending a burst of desperate emotion best translated as *help* down that magical connection.

He crept toward the window, ignoring the frantic tugging on his shirt and arm by Aisling. He made a shushing gesture at her, stayed low, and put his back up against the wall. The bedroom looked out onto the back of the property, facing the forest instead of the local road. He angled his head to look out the glass, and in the moonlit forest, floating gently through the trees and coming closer, were small glowing lights. Bran jerked back, horror washing through him like ice water, making his skin prickle. He reached for Aisling without looking, her hand sliding into his as she pressed close.

Whatever was out there, he knew why they had come—they wanted Aisling.

He leaned down and whispered into her ear so softly it was barely sound. "We need to get into the circle."

The Shoppe was surrounded by witchmarks, the same way their other home had been. The magic embedded in the walls should have been enough to keep out what was hunting them, but the nightmare outside had broken through their mother's defenses. Whatever was out there was more powerful than what typically haunted the forest.

Witchmarks should have been enough to keep them safe.

That they hadn't been meant the only thing Bran trusted right then was the coven's circle, a barrier of magic stronger than any combination of witchmarks. Reaching it meant getting downstairs on creaking steps and into the basement, all while something hunted them from outside.

Aisling nodded agreement, her breathing ragged. Bran tugged on her ponytail, wishing he had time to comfort her, but they had to survive this night first. He gripped her hand tight in his and bent low, pulling her with him as they passed the window, hoping nothing outside would see them. Bran led her out of the bedroom and down the hallway, heartbeat thrumming in his ears like a drum. Panic was a band around his ribs, making it difficult to breathe, and the only thing that quieted it was the memory of his mother's voice.

Never let them see fear. Your magic can hurt them just as surely as iron can.

Bran had walked the forest plenty of times before and set witch-marks into the trees to guard the paths that led to the cabins made of ash wood. He'd only seen the lights a handful of times over the years, the first when he was newly thirteen and foraging during the light of the harvest moon with his mother. He'd frozen back then, fear anchoring his body to the earth, and Bran knew he couldn't freeze now. Aisling would die if he did.

He led her to the stairs and gestured at her to look at where he stepped, a lifetime of knowing where the steps creaked from pressure enabling him to descend without making a sound. Aisling literally followed in his footsteps, fingers of her other hand clenched tightly around the fabric of his T-shirt. They reached the bottom landing, and Bran wrapped his free hand around the doorknob, turning it slowly. He held his breath at the faint squeak of metal as the latch retracted and carefully pushed it open.

Through the crack, he could see the Shoppe was dark, nothing seemingly out of place. But the urgent need to run still clawed at the back of his mind, and for all that the Shoppe appeared safe, he couldn't trust the emptiness, not when he knew what hunted beyond the walls.

He flexed his fingers around Aisling's hand and carefully pushed the door open wider. The hinges squeaked from the motion, and he froze, Aisling whimpering at his back. Bran gritted his teeth and opened the door wider, stepping into the Shoppe and tugging Aisling along with him. He didn't turn on the lights because they couldn't risk whatever was outside knowing they were awake.

But then a shadow blocked the moonlight streaming through the trifecta stained-glass window, and Bran knew he shouldn't look—he *knew*—but he did so anyway.

What stared back was a horror from the depths of a hellish nightmare.

The gray face was eyeless, mouth a slit full of teeth in a Cheshire cat grin. Large horns grew from its skull on either side, arcing overhead into tapering points that almost touched, giving the illusion of a crescent moon crown. Narrow palms with elongated fingers were splayed against the stained-glass window. When it curled its fingers, the claws at the tips made a terrible sound against the glass. Then it opened its mouth, its head nearly splitting in two, and the animalistic scream it let out was a sound Bran would never be able to forget. It slammed its horned head against the window, the blow rattling the stained-glass in the frame but not breaking it.

The creature screamed again, and when it lifted its head, Bran saw burns on its face from the welded iron connecting the stained-glass panels to each other and the frame. Witchmarks sizzled into being across every stained-glass panel, magic keeping what had come from the forest at bay.

For now.

Aisling crashed into him, arms wrapping around his body as she buried her face against his back while hyperventilating. The creature screamed again, and all the witchmarks their coven had etched into the wood of the walls and floor and ceiling of the Shoppe burned to life in the wake of that sound.

"There goes our chance at hiding," Bran said. "Hurry! Get to the basement!"

He twisted around, herding Aisling toward the space behind the register, keeping his eyes on the creature through the window. Movement out of the corner of his eyes made his head jerk a little to the left. Another horrible face pressed itself against the glass of the front window that looked out on the road. Lights floated in the distance beyond it, drawing closer, bringing with them shadows of things that shouldn't exist but did.

We're surrounded.

The thought made his stomach sink, but despair wasn't going to save them. Bran raised his right hand and called up his magic. It burned through him, coalescing against his palm in a brilliant golden light because he had nothing to hide here. With his other hand, he drew a witchmark in the air, holding his fingers against the last two points of the glittering lines that meant *shield*, readying it for any attack. Both creatures at the windows kept banging their clawed hands and strangely shaped heads against glass that wouldn't break because of the magic that anchored the foundation of his coven's home.

Then something slammed against the front door, rattling the hinges and making the wood creak badly. The heavy breathing he'd heard while upstairs grew louder, as if whatever had been circling the Shoppe was now on the other side of the door, wanting to get in. He swallowed hard, attention torn between the windows and the door. The creatures had broken through their mother's witchmarks at the house. Bran knew he had to expect the same here.

A loud thud from behind him made Bran jump. He looked over his shoulder at the register area where Aisling had gone. The door to the basement had been flung open, and she smacked her hand a couple of times against the top of the glass display case, trying to get his attention.

"Get—"

Bran never finished the sentence.

The door bowed in the frame before exploding inward, hinges shattering and the witchmarks with it in a glittering spray of damaged magic that filled the Shoppe. Something large hunkered down in the doorway and began forcing its way inside. The way it crouched spoke of it being tall, cloven feet visible in the glow of approaching lights. Its thick fingers gripped the doorframe and *shoved*, cracking the wood there as it made space to enter. Glowing threads of green magic crawled away from its fingers, carving through the witchmarks in the wall and strangling the magic there.

Its deer-shaped head came through, followed by broad, furred shoulders, looking nothing like any deer that roamed the forest. The creature's head tapered outward from the elongated nose into a broad shape, three glowing eyes lined up across its face. Antlers with leaves sprouting from it like branches protruded from its skull, bits of them scraping over the ceiling as it clawed its way into the Shoppe.

It opened its mouth, revealing sharp teeth that would never be found on any deer, and roared. The sound ripped through the air with a ferocity that probably echoed for miles. If anyone heard it, Bran doubted they would come looking for the noise or to help. That's not what people did in Pelham when they knew the lights were out hunting.

"Get down to the basement!" Bran yelled.

Aisling dropped out of sight, and he cast the witchmark in the direction of the display case, desperately wanting to build a shield between his sister and the creatures after her. Bran thought he was fast enough, that Aisling would get below in time and he could follow, but even as the shield anchored itself to the floor in a glittering wall of light, the creatures at the windows broke through the barrier, helped by way of insidious magic not of this world.

Glass shattered, the screaming nightmares writhing their way into the Shoppe, and Bran swore, heart beating loud enough to make his ears ring. More of the creatures forced their way into the Shoppe behind the first two, the magic in the walls bleeding out faster than he'd ever be able to replenish it. He didn't know why the witchmarks were being subverted now when they never had before.

Bran backed up toward the display case, wrenching one arm around to expand the shield around his position and connect it to the back wall. He got it up just in time as the creature who'd come through the trifecta stained-glass window lunged at him, knocking over tables with its many spindly legs. It reminded him of a spider—if a spider resembled a demon-like creature that had dragged itself out of the hell that was the wyrding.

It crashed into his shield, clawing at the magic, and Bran reared back, nearly tripping over his own feet. The creature at the door abruptly pulled back, its antlers breaking through the top part of the doorframe as it did so. What streaked through the damaged opening was a flock of things shaped like bats, but nothing about them would ever be mistaken for that animal. These were things that were little more than teeth and wings, more mouth than anything, meant to rend flesh from bone.

Bran wondered which of these creatures had murdered his mother —which one deserved magic shot through whatever passed as their heart, beating or otherwise—but the thought was a fleeting thing, there and gone. He drew a pair of witchmarks in the air using both hands, the last finger curl tying it together with a burning knot of magic. He threw it forward with all the intent he could muster, *return to the earth* heavy in the making of it. The witchmark slammed into the creature with the crescent moon–shaped horns, throwing it backward through the Shoppe. The creature crashed into a bookcase, destroying the furniture and sending all the antiques to the ground.

The way it screamed and writhed from the attack told him at least some of his magic was working.

Bran was halfway through sketching out another witchmark in the air when a hum vibrated through the air, like an oncoming freight train. He only got one more line twisted into place before a force unlike anything he'd experienced before slammed through the Shoppe and shattered his shield, picking him up off his feet and tossing him backward. He slammed against the back wall near the utility room door, head cracking against wood hard enough that everything spun. In that moment where the world tipped sideways and magic flowed just out of reach, something stepped into the Shoppe.

Its presence was ancient, filling the Shoppe with a malevolence that told Bran *this* was a thing humans had once hidden from during the night before their iron cities grew into a bedrock of defense that rarely could be crossed. But out here, in the forest far from a city, where the trees seemed to stretch forever if you looked just right, this was where the wyrding slipped through.

Where the Fae hunted.

And Bran was nothing but prey in that moment, the only witch for miles around, his mother not even buried yet. He struggled to get an elbow underneath him, to get back on his feet as the entire room seemed to lurch with the motion, stomach roiling like he was on a rickety roller coaster. He lifted his head, wincing from the harsh glow of magic gathered around the Fae like a halo.

"I had thought all the witches of Pelham were dead," the Fae said, ancient voice like the rumble of an earthquake.

He was beautiful in the way all the stories said the Fae were, tall and broad-shouldered, the antlers that protruded from his head adding to his height. His face was perfectly handsome in its symmetry, eyes honey-gold in color and reflecting the light from magic, framed by long brown hair. Bran half wondered if the Fae was the thing that had tried to get through the Shoppe door, but he couldn't be sure. This Fae didn't look like a nightmare with its deer head and strange eyes, more like an uncannily beautiful man dressed in elegant dark green pants and a brocade tunic picked through with shining gold thread. A small glass sphere hung from a gold necklace, shining from sparks held within its delicate casing.

The iron beads on Bran's bracelet would keep the Fae from reading his mind and the intent there, whether a lord or not. Only Bran couldn't count on that right then, not after the Fae had broken through the witchmarks in the Shoppe. Not with the antlers on his head he'd seen on a monster and the insidious magic that pressed against Bran's own. No, this Fae might be a lord, but they were dangerous, and Bran knew better than to name him, to give him power. He had enough already.

Bran's attention snapped to the blue flowers tangled like a garland through the Fae's antlers, and he knew, in that moment, this was the Fae responsible for his mother's murder.

"You bastard," Bran ground out, fingers moving against the hardwood floor, magic filling the witchmark with nothing but *force*.

Before he could release it, the bat-like creatures dived through the entrance of the basement, and Bran cried out wordlessly, trying to get to his feet, even as his head wanted the rest of him to lie still. He scraped the witchmark off the floor and tossed it in the direction of the Fae who'd come through the door, but like with his shield, the Fae broke that, too.

The backlash was like getting shocked with an electric jolt over and over again. Bran's teeth clacked together as he forced himself to his feet. He'd barely made it upright before the bat-like creatures returned from below in a swirl of wings and teeth and talons, Aisling held in their many-clawed grips. She struggled, but they held her fast by her clothes and arms and hair. She kicked against them, mouth open in a silent scream as she tried to reach for Bran with desperate fingers, and he would always remember that moment when he couldn't save her.

"No!" Bran yelled, lunging for her, feet sliding on broken glass and jagged bits of wood and other broken things. But he was too far away, and the creatures were too many. They flew for the door, out into the dangerous night, taking his sister with them.

Bran let out a guttural yell of denial, fury and fear leaving an acidic aftertaste on his tongue, fingers clenched around glittering motes of magic as he faced off with the Fae. "Give her back!"

"She was never yours to begin with," the Fae said in that rumbling voice of his.

"Bullshit. She's my *sister*." He'd lost his mother. He would not lose Aisling, not like this.

The Fae smirked at him, a terrible expression for a beautiful nightmare. "You know nothing of the Fae, witch."

The witchmark burned against Bran's palm, a *force* filled with all his rage and grief. "And you don't know witches. This is not your land."

"It was, once. It will be again. You witches cannot hold us back forever."

The Fae resided in the Otherworld, the way to it found at the end of forest paths, in the fringe of the wyrding, through hidden mounds the stories taught people never to approach. The mortal world wasn't theirs to claim, not anymore. Witches had stood against their encroachment since the Fae were banished from Ireland millennia ago, magic cultivated amid a history of fighting.

Iron would always hurt the Fae, but witch magic could be just as damaging. Except it usually took an entire coven to eradicate the Fae and the lights when an incursion happened upon a town, and here, it was only Bran.

Somehow, he would have to be enough.

He cast the witchmark with furious intent. Magic exploded away from him in a concussive blast that drew on the remnants of witchmarks carved into the Shoppe's foundation and the circle in the basement, all of it anchored in iron, and channeled it like he was a river. Bran focused on the Fae lord—for the antlered Fae could be nothing else—wanting the bastard *out* and *gone* from his home.

The Fae lord skidded back from the force of the attack, his own magic deflecting Bran's with an ease that made his fear deepen. The creatures that had followed the Fae into the Shoppe fought against the force of his magic, screaming all the while in hideous voices.

Then a sound cut through it all, high and angry, Jupiter's *caw* echoed by the sound of others. His familiar flew into the Shoppe, followed by dozens of ravens and crows, awake outside their normal daylight hours, their eyes glowing the same glittering gold as his familiar's.

Never before had he seen other corvids afflicted with magic in such a way. It wasn't Bran's doing. For a moment, Bran thought it was the Fae. Then Jupiter opened up the bond between them, her presence awash with the power of Nature and something else that lurked deep he'd never felt before.

Bran didn't have time to question it, and in the end, it wouldn't matter. There wasn't a world where he could repudiate her, not now, not after they were bound. So Bran took the support offered, took the power of Nature and that thread of something darker, and clawed another witchmark in the air, this one a mix of *trespass* and *hearth*. When he cast it, he let it tap his reserves with no restrictions.

This was his home, and he didn't want the Fae in it.

The Fae lord retreated before the spell could take effect. Magic ripped away from Bran, but it didn't touch Jupiter or the corvids, the essence of Nature passing harmlessly through them. Bran stumbled from the effort, witchmarks burning in the air before disintegrating in seconds.

The lights outside suddenly vanished, and he let out a wordless, frantic cry of protest and scrambled toward the door through the debris in the Shoppe. Bran staggered outside into the warm summer night, finding the road empty and the forest dark, the only light to be seen that of the full moon in the black, starry sky.

Chapter Seven

Bran shifted where he sat, the porch step creaking under the movement. He raised his head at the sound of a motor growing louder from down the road, two black trucks in the distance coming closer. He barely noticed the soft light of dawn hitting his skin, numb in a way even the encroaching summer day couldn't warm. Moving his head didn't hurt as badly as it had before he'd choked down a healing potion from his mother's stores and called Mac.

The trucks eventually pulled off the road and parked in the dirt space in front of the Shoppe. Cillian was the first one out of his truck, his presence making Bran dig his fingers into the muscle of his thighs. Cillian wasn't in uniform, and Bran wondered if it was Cillian's day off. His jeans and T-shirt looked rumpled, as if he'd pulled on the first thing that had come to hand. His hair wasn't even tied back, falling loose past his shoulders, and his wide-brimmed hat was nowhere to be seen.

"Bran!" Cillian called out, his long legs eating up the distance between them. The concern in his voice made Bran flinch. He steeled himself against the urge to turn away. "Bran, are you all right? Where's Aisling?"

Bran didn't answer Cillian. Instead, he watched Mac get out of his truck and slowly approach. Bran licked his lips, mouth still so utterly dry as he stared at Mac. "I need to talk to you."

Cillian drew up short, glancing between them. "What's going on? What happened to the Shoppe?"

Bran wrapped his fingers around his left wrist, grinding the beads against his bone, wondering what use iron was to hide his thoughts when the Fae and the lights already knew he was in Pelham. Mac seemed to understand that Bran was holding on to his sanity by sheer goddamn luck and said, "Can Cillian take a look inside?"

Bran nodded tightly, not moving from his spot on the porch. "Nothing will harm him."

"Bran," Cillian said, stepping closer, raising a hand as if he were going to try to comfort him.

He turned his head, hunching his shoulders, refusing to meet Cillian's gaze. His jaw worked, and he only half listened to Mac urging Cillian to get eyes on the crime scene inside. Bran bit back a hysterical laugh at the words *crime scene* because that seemed to be the only thing his life was these days.

After a moment, Cillian stepped past where Bran sat on the porch, carefully picking his way into the wreckage of the Shoppe. The door was a hopeless cause, so there was no way to keep the conversation private. Mac still tried, crouching in front of Bran, anguish bleeding into his eyes. He opened his mouth to speak, but Bran cut him off, getting the words out first. He didn't feel like being the star in an interrogation, no matter how well-meaning. "The lights came last night. They took Aisling. I couldn't—they had a Fae lord with them. He wanted her."

Mac flinched with his entire body, face losing all its color. "Bran..."

"He went back to the Otherworld. I'm going there to get Aisling back."

Mac reeled back as if Bran had punched him. "*What*?"

"The Fae lord would have killed me, but he wanted her alive. I'm not letting the bastard keep her."

"But you can't—"

Mac broke off as a floorboard squeaked behind Bran. A blanket was draped over his shoulders, the feel of it the same one that had been folded over the back of the couch last night. "You look cold, despite the weather."

Bran plucked at the edges of the blanket, refusing to turn and look at Cillian. "I'm going into the forest."

"You shouldn't," Mac said.

"Are you crazy?" Cillian asked. "The Shoppe is basically ruined, and you want to hunt whatever did that?"

A tired *caw* made him look up. Jupiter circled overhead before folding her wings back and diving toward them. She landed beside him on the porch, hopping close and *cawing* loudly. She fluttered her wings, the gold flecks in her eyes catching the sunlight. If it were anyone else but Mac and Cillian with him, her eyes would be pure black, no hint of magic in them. But Mac was a guardian, and Cillian had been his best friend once upon a time, and she knew them.

It'd been Cillian's mother who had brought Jupiter to the Shoppe years ago, explaining she'd found the raven injured on the side of the road. She hadn't known she'd brought the animal that would become Bran's familiar, and Cillian had only ever known Jupiter as she was— gold-flecked eyes and smarter than she should be.

Jupiter leaned in and pecked Bran lightly on his thigh, sadness echoing through their bond. She missed Aisling, too, but she was willing to guide him however she needed to.

"I'm going," Bran said again, fingers tightening on the edges of the blanket, gaze drawn to the trees across the road.

"Then I'm going with you," Cillian said.

That finally got Bran to jerk around, head twisting so he could look up at Cillian. "What? No."

Cillian's mouth firmed in a way Bran remembered when they were kids and the older boy was determined to get his way. Everyone always thought that just because he was quiet, Cillian wasn't willing to fight, but he dug his heels in when it was important for him. "You haven't lived in Pelham for years. You need someone who knows the forest to go with you."

It took everything Bran had not to laugh in his face. "You don't think I know the forest? *Me*?" A witch not knowing the forest they were made to guard. He'd find it funny if the situation wasn't so fraught. "You're not coming with me. I don't have time to babysit you."

Cillian arched an eyebrow, the look pure condescension that made Bran bristle. "I'm a ranger. I don't need babysitting in the forest. We're patrolling in pairs right now because of the threat out there. I'm off today, and you shouldn't be in the forest alone. I'm going with you."

"No, you're not."

"I'm leaving with you, or I'm following you. Take your pick."

Bran opened his mouth to argue, but Mac put his hand on Bran's shoulder, prompting him to hold his tongue. Bran turned his head back around, feeling as if he were the ball in a tennis match. Mac's expression was grim, his grip a little desperate, but his voice, at least, was steady. "He's right. The forest isn't safe, even for you. Let Cillian go with you. He can be trusted. I'll stay behind to put the Shoppe to rights so it's ready for your return."

Bran swallowed tightly, shrugging off Mac's hand. Guardians were meant to track the encroachment of the wyrding and warn the witches in the covens. They had no magic, no way to tap the eddies of power that moved through Nature, not the way a witch could. But they were stalwart in a way Bran's coven remembered well, and he knew he could leave all his worldly belongings in Mac's care and the other man would keep them safe.

"And I'll keep looking," Mac said, not speaking of the grimoire, but the inference was plain between them.

Bran gritted his teeth and finally nodded. The last thing he wanted was someone tagging along who didn't know he was a witch, but Cillian had always known Bran had weird habits.

He'd thought about it when they were younger—telling Cillian his secrets. That he was a witch. That magic was real. That the lights were more than a superstitious legend. But he hadn't because he knew better. Because his mother had taught him better. Yet here they were, forced to work together because Bran knew Cillian wouldn't leave him now that Mac had made his wishes known. No matter everything between them, he'd never leave Cillian to wander the forest alone.

The thought of doing so left him terrified and sick to his stomach.

"Fine," Bran said through gritted teeth. He got to his feet, dragging the blanket off his shoulders and handing it back to Cillian. "Take this back upstairs."

Cillian glanced from Bran to Mac before snorting. "If you wanted a private conversation, you could just ask."

He still went into the Shoppe, giving them the privacy Bran wanted. Bran leaned down and offered his arm to Jupiter, who hopped on it before jumping to his shoulder. Her talons pricked his skin through his thin T-shirt, but she'd never hurt him, and the weight of her was comforting after last night.

"Going to the Otherworld is a death sentence, especially for witches," Mac said quietly before glancing over his shoulder at the forest, as if even speaking the name of the Fae's homeland risked bringing them forth.

"Covens have done it before when incursions got bad. I can't leave Aisling with them. She's all I have left, and I won't lose her," Bran said.

"If you go, it'll be weeks for us until your return. Maybe even months. What do you want me to tell the town?"

Bran glanced back at the ruined Shoppe, stroking a finger down Jupiter's beak. "I'll lay a witchmark to keep people away from the Shoppe except you. Tell them I took Aisling to Boston, or don't tell anyone at all. It's not their business."

"And the Council of Witches? What do I tell them if you're gone and they come asking for your coven when they can't get in touch with you?"

"Tell them I did my duty."

It wouldn't even be a lie.

Footsteps heralded Cillian's return. Jupiter *cawed* at him and shamelessly fluttered her wings. Cillian scratched gently at her head through the small feathers there, smiling a little. "You haven't changed one bit."

She wouldn't, but he didn't need to know that. Bran dipped his arm before thrusting it upward, tossing Jupiter into the sky. She flapped her wings to gain altitude, banking on a wingtip to circle the Shoppe, clearly waiting on them.

"I need to get dressed, and then we can go. Wait here," Bran said.

He retreated into the Shoppe, picking his way through the debris, hating to leave everything a mess. But he'd lost hours already, and staying behind wasn't an option. Bran hadn't gone after the Fae last night because of his head injury. It had taken time to heal it, and leaving without letting Mac know what was going on wasn't how his mother would have done it. As witches, they couldn't just up and leave their town without a warning, and the night hadn't been safe to travel through while wounded. Even daylight wouldn't be once they got deep enough into the woods, but that was what magic was for.

Once upstairs in his old bedroom, Bran dressed for the forest, pulling on an old pair of hiking pants and a T-shirt from the closet. He had to shove aside some of Aisling's clothes to sort through his own, and the sight of the neatly folded and hung-up clothing had him pounding a fist against the wall. "I'm getting you back."

Bran dug up an old pair of hiking boots from a box at the top of the closet and grabbed a sweatshirt from a dresser drawer that he tied around his waist. He left the apartment, stepping lightly down the stairs back to the Shoppe, where he ducked behind the register. His boots crunched through glass on the floor and bits that had tumbled onto the stairs leading to the basement. It was cool below, his skin prickling from the chill.

Bran opened up one of the storage cabinet drawers along the wall, pulling out a small leather backpack that had witchmarks branded on the inside. He proceeded to fill it with soft leather cases that held satchels of dried herb mixtures, small iron boxes that contained vials of liquids, and tiny glass jars of strange ingredients. A witch's field pack held all manner of things one would need to brew potions and mix poisons. Not all magic was held in a witchmark, and the practical aspects of spellcasting were just as important as intent. Bran couldn't take the entire inventory of his mother's carefully cultivated store of ingredients, but he could take some and hope it would be enough.

The last thing he took with him from the basement was a pair of railroad spike knives, the curved handles and blades etched with witchmarks, both weapons expertly crafted back in the 1800s. The knives were made entirely of iron—deadly to the Fae. His mother had taught him knife-work since he was a boy. Bran wasn't an expert by any means, but he could defend himself well enough when it mattered.

Bran climbed the stairs once he was finished, switching off the lights on his way out before lowering the door and letting it settle into the grooves of the floor once more. Then he knelt and traced a witchmark over the center of it, one meant to *lock*. The golden twisting lines of the witchmark spread over the door before sinking into the wood, ensuring no one but himself would be able to open it.

Satisfied, Bran turned around to face the two altars that somehow hadn't been destroyed during the attack. With careful motions, he wrote out a witchmark in the center of the tree carved into the wood. Glittering motes of magic rose into the air, a faint hum filling Bran's ears.

He pushed his magic outward, lining the Shoppe with a subtly layered spell powered by a witchmark that would *hide* the building from curious eyes. *Move along* and *forget* were added, with a singular carveout in the shape of Cillian, Mac, and Marisol—Mac's wife—at the heart of it all.

Bran flattened his hand against the altar, murmuring softly, "May the Mother guide me true."

He dragged his fingernails through the witchmark, and it disappeared, even if the magic in the walls didn't. If the lights came back, it wouldn't keep them out, but it would keep everyone in town from stopping by and digging through everything he was leaving behind.

Bran left the Shoppe and headed to where Mac waited by the truck while Cillian rooted through the bed of his. Bran pitched his voice low so only Mac could hear him once he was close. "The Fae know I was here. If you're going to clean the place up while we're gone, only do it during the day, and make sure your other shotgun's buckshot has iron in it. Don't come alone."

Mac nodded, expression grim. "You're sure you want to do this by yourself?"

"You made sure I wouldn't be."

"You know what I mean."

Bran worried his bottom lip between his teeth before letting out a harsh sigh. "Mom didn't much care for the red tape the Council of Witches kept making us jump through. If I notify them about what happened, especially that our coven's grimoire is missing, they'd see it as a reason to remove me."

Mac frowned. "Town won't like that."

"It doesn't matter because neither of us will tell the Council. If they call you, tell them we're on vacation." Bran met Mac's eyes, trying to will the other man to believe him when he said, "I'm coming back with Aisling."

"We'll be waiting."

Bran pulled out his cell phone, turned it off to save the battery, and passed it over to Mac. "It won't work in the Otherworld. None of our technology does."

"I told Cillian to leave his with me, too. He's taking his rifle and as much ammunition as he can carry for use in the forest, at least. Food and water, too."

"I had planned to stock up on supplies at the nearest cabin."

"Might as well." Mac squinted at Bran before reaching out to clap him on the shoulder. "You remember where they all are?"

"Yes." His mother had made sure he did when he was younger, and it wasn't something he'd ever forgotten while living in Boston.

"Good. I'll see you when you return. And...I'll take care of your mother and Ray."

The burn at the back of Bran's throat was hard to swallow around, but he managed. "Thanks, Mac."

It should have been him handling the dead, but he'd named them already, and his mother would've been the first one to go after Aisling if she'd still been alive.

It was up to him now.

Mac stepped back, giving one last nod goodbye before climbing into his truck. He started the engine, the sound loud in the morning quiet. Bran watched him reverse out of the parking spot and turn onto the road, driving off.

The sound of the tailgate closing finally made him look over at Cillian. He had a rifle slung over one shoulder and wore a backpack that appeared laden down with items Bran didn't ask about. He'd tied back his hair but hadn't bothered with a hat. When he turned to face Bran, he looked ready for a fight, as if he expected Bran to tell him to stay behind again.

If Bran was honest, he'd thought about it.

"I gave Mac my keys," Cillian said, sounding almost defiant.

"Don't blame me if your truck gets broken into for being abandoned," Bran retorted. He started across the road, heading determinedly for the trees. Jupiter *cawed* as she flew overhead, leading the way.

Cillian caught up to him in seconds, matching his longer strides to Bran's. "If I had known you were going into the forest, I would have had Mac pick me up instead."

Bran gave him a sidelong glance. "Why did you even come?"

"Rangers don't patrol alone right now."

"This isn't a patrol."

"You called Mac, not the police, and he called me."

Bran wrenched his gaze forward as they reached the other side of the road. He scanned the area, noticing the churned-up dirt, ripped grass and broken shrubbery, as if something large had torn through it. Most people wouldn't have noticed the damage or thought anything of it. Cillian proved he wasn't most people.

He paused there at the side of the road, forcing Bran to stop, too. Cillian's gaze darted around, lingering on the trampled ground. Then he turned slowly and stared back at the Shoppe they were leaving behind, its damage hidden behind magic, but not for Cillian, even if he didn't know.

"Was it really a bear?" Cillian asked in a hushed voice.

"Let's get to the cabin," Bran said, ignoring the question.

He started walking again, passing the first tree with its witchmark carved into the trunk and claw marks cutting through it. Bran clenched his teeth together, anger taking root in his chest as he stepped onto the hiking path hidden from the road but which led from the Shoppe to the first of many cabins in the woods.

Cillian was never more than a step behind him, traversing the slightly overgrown forest path with ease. Bran was glad for the hiking boots he'd found because the streets of Boston weren't like this. He could sense Jupiter flying overhead through their bond, winging from tree to tree in intervals that kept her near but also let her keep watch.

He didn't know what had happened to the other corvids to make them follow Jupiter into the fight at the Shoppe. How she'd summoned them was beyond his knowing. The corvids who hadn't survived he'd buried in the back before calling Mac, as was only right.

The rest had disappeared once the lights were gone, and only Jupiter had stayed.

The only sound for the first thirty minutes or so was their footsteps and the buzz of insects and the chirping of birds waking up for the day. Heat was a heavy blanket that settled in the air, promising another muggy summer day. Sweat was already beading on Bran's skin by the time they made it to the first cabin, the tiny building hidden within a copse of trees that helped it blend into the scenery.

If one didn't know the stories, they'd probably find the cabins scattered through the forest creepy. They certainly looked out of place. The one-room building was smaller than the living room in the apartment over the Shoppe, not meant to camp in but meant as a safe haven if one was lost in the woods at night.

Made entirely of ash wood with a slanted roof, it had no windows to see out and only the one door, which was always unlocked unless the cabin was occupied. Bran approached it, testing the knob, gaze drifting up to where witchmarks were carved over the doorframe and lining the edge of the wall near the eaves. He could pick out the iron nails used to build the cabin, another layer of protection against what hunted in the woods.

The knob turned easily, and Bran pushed the door open. The air inside was hot and stale, but the cabin was empty of occupants. The single twin bed tucked into a corner was the same kind in every cabin. An unused compost toilet was in the other. A low cabinet held packets of energy bars, jerky, and bags of mixed nuts and dried fruit. Jugs and smaller bottles of water were tucked away on the bottom shelf, with plastic cups stacked neatly beside them. None of the seals appeared to be broken.

Bran automatically checked the clipboard hanging on the inside of the cabinet door, throat catching at the sight of his mother's neat handwriting from over the years, interspersed with others. Part of their duties as witches was to make sure the cabins were secured, that the witchmarks were all whole, and that supplies were readily available. The rangers helped as well, with the checks happening every six months, usually in the spring and fall, but it was a witch's duty to ensure the cabins could stand against the lights and what followed them.

"Do you think we'll be in the forest long enough for you to need all that?" Cillian asked.

Bran didn't respond and kept dropping packets of food into his backpack, adding three bottles of water as well before tossing Cillian one. "Here. You'll need some, too. Don't take everything, though."

They still needed to leave enough supplies to aid whoever might end up in the cabin next. Theft wasn't an issue from regular hikers, as all the locals knew never to take unless they were staying in the cabin. Those with ill intentions never found the supplies, courtesy of the witchmarks carved into the shelves, the ones that meant *do not see*.

He ran his fingers over one of them, sensing his mother's magic within the shape of it, and he closed his eyes for a few seconds. Someday in the near future, once they'd returned with Aisling, it would be his duty to trek from cabin to cabin and ensure the witchmarks were all functioning as they should. But not today.

Bran stood, closed the cabinet doors, then slung the backpack over both shoulders. "Come on. Let's go."

"Do you even know where we're going?" Cillian asked.

"Into the forest."

"The Quabbin Reservoir wilderness isn't like Yellowstone or Yosemite. It's not like we're trekking into backcountry. Where are we going?"

Bran headed for the cabin's door. "I said you didn't have to come."

A strong, callused hand wrapped around his arm, jerking him to a stop. It was, Bran realized in a heart-stopping moment, the first time Cillian had touched him since the kiss that had cleaved them apart when they were younger.

Cillian's grip was firm, the strength behind it impossible to ignore as he carefully pulled Bran around to face him. They stood so close that Bran could smell the sweat on the other man, the tang of it hitting his nose. A half-hysterical thought bubbled up through his mind—he didn't want Cillian to stop touching him.

Cillian stared down at him with those blue-gray eyes of his, the color like a winter storm, a shade Bran had never seen in anyone else's eyes. He'd always looked for it over the years and came away wanting. "What do you think you're going to find out here in the forest?"

Bran steeled himself to pull away, and Cillian let him. "Keep your iron with you."

He turned on his feet and hurried out of the cabin, the spot on his arm where Cillian had touched him burning through his awareness. Cillian followed after a moment, his footsteps heavy on the hardwood floor. Bran closed the door to the cabin, and they started down the forest path again. He was acutely aware of Cillian walking beside him, skin still prickling from his touch. Bran resisted the urge to fold his fingers over where Cillian had grabbed him.

They followed the path deeper into the woods, the branches overhead keeping the sunlight at bay but doing nothing for the heat. Bran's shirt was sticking to his skin well before noon, and the hiking pants he wore were damp at the waistband when they finally stopped for a quick lunch of energy bars.

Seated on a fallen tree, Bran looked up at what he could see of the sky through the trees, listening to the sounds of the forest. The rustle of leaves and cries of birds were vastly different from the sounds of Boston. But nothing in Boston wanted to kill him, and he knew what dwelled in the forest.

"You still haven't said where we're heading," Cillian said, the first words he'd spoken in hours.

Jupiter *cawed* nearby, impatience in the sound. She wanted them to keep moving. "I'll know when I find it."

The Quabbin Reservoir wilderness was hilly terrain, and Bran's calves already ached from the hours they'd trekked. He was, admittedly, out of practice, but aching muscles weren't going to stop him.

Bran picked up the last crumb from the energy bar, ate it, then crumpled up the wrapper and shoved it into his backpack. He'd never in his life littered in the woods, the "carry out what you carry in" ethos drilled into him by his mother since he was a kid.

"Mac says it's always bears when we get attacks like this," Cillian said quietly. "It's not, is it?"

"No," Bran agreed after a moment. "It's not."

He didn't say what it was, didn't name them. Nothing good ever came of naming them.

"So the stories are true? About the lights in the woods?"

"What do you think?"

"I think whatever attacked wanted you dead, and I don't know why you aren't, but I'm glad they didn't kill you." Bran startled at the feel of Cillian's hand resting on his shoulder, head jerking around. Cillian stared back at him, looking as sweaty as Bran felt and still so handsome. "I'm sorry about what happened to your mother and Ray and Aisling, but for once, I was happy you were gone. It meant you were alive."

Bran didn't know what to say to that. Cillian patted Bran's shoulder before picking up his rifle and getting to his feet, offering his hand. Bran thought about ignoring it, but he gave in. Cillian's hand was cool, unlike his own warm, slightly sweaty one, but his grip was strong in a way Bran wouldn't have minded if they were in a bedroom and not a forest, if they didn't have seven years of silence stretched between them. Resentment still simmered, low and deep with anger at how Cillian had pushed him away as a teenager, but the pain of losing his best friend still cut deeper.

He'd thought about Cillian almost every day since, even when he didn't want to. It was maddening, sometimes, the absence of the other man while Bran learned to live without him, hating it all the while. It always felt like he was missing his other half. Now, he had Cillian back in his life, and Bran didn't want to let him go again.

"Come on. Lead the way," Cillian said.

Bran picked up his backpack and pulled the straps over both shoulders. He bounced it a couple of times to settle the weight, ignoring the faint tightness of the muscles in his back. It'd been a while since he had to hike with gear. Jupiter *cawed* from up ahead. Bran watched as she launched herself off a branch, flying low beneath the tree canopy.

The path they followed wasn't one most hikers would ever get to enjoy. Most of the wilderness was off-limits, but people still found their way into land they shouldn't trek through. The paths connecting the cabins weren't found on any map handed out to the public. Bran remembered them only because of the years he'd walked every last one with his mother.

The path they were on twisted through the woods from cabin to cabin in the area they were in, the way designated by subtle witchmarks, until the hilly terrain dipped toward the Quabbin Reservoir itself. They arrived on a muddy, rocky shore, the sun more than halfway to the western horizon behind them.

Bran stared across the calm blue water, at the trees on the other side and the distant rising slope of Prescott Hill. The land out here was pristine, restricted in order to keep the water clean. That hadn't stopped his coven from carving out paths to do their duty.

"I didn't know this was here," Cillian said.

Bran looked over at the long wooden storage compartment tucked between two trees, clearly not part of the ecology. Cillian had undone the latches and opened it, revealing the canoe stored inside. Bran stepped close and reached for the tarp that covered the canoe, peeling it off. The fiberglass hull appeared intact, though it looked like it hadn't been used in ages. "It's not for anyone else's use."

"Just your family?" Bran wouldn't look at him. "Right. You know water recreation is restricted."

"You call what we're doing fun? Help me get the canoe into the water."

Cillian sighed heavily and did as he was told. They lifted the canoe out, the paddles in the bottom of the hull rattling as they carried it down the shore. They got it in the water, and Bran held it steady while Cillian climbed in, making sure not to drop his rifle or backpack. Bran followed, and once he was settled on a bench, he passed an oar to Cillian and took the other. With a bit of effort, they pushed off into the water.

"Where to now?" Cillian asked.

Bran pointed with one hand across the water. "East."

They could've hiked north and gone around the reservoir over land to get where Bran was aiming for, but cutting directly across the man-made lake was quicker. The way through the wyrding wouldn't be close to the roads anyway. Part of the land jutted south, nearly bisecting the deep water in two, and it was that area of the forest Bran needed to get to. Rangers always warned hikers away from that area, but not everyone listened. Locals knew to steer clear, though, knew it was where all the superstitions stemmed from and the reason iron was something everyone carried in Pelham.

Bran's arms burned from exertion by the time the canoe slid onto the far shore. He threw down his oar with a groan before shaking out his arms, muscles aching. "I'm used to driving, not paddling."

"It's not that bad," Cillian said mildly.

Bran didn't even dignify that with an answer. He had spent the entire trip across staring at the way Cillian's biceps had flexed. It'd been super distracting.

He scrambled out of the canoe with his backpack, boots sinking into mud on the shore. Cillian followed him out, and Bran paused only long enough to orient himself through Jupiter. She *cawed* from deeper in the woods, *this way* pulsing through their connection. Bran followed where she flew through the birch and oak trees stretching out before them. Cillian stuck beside him as Bran located another path. A witchmark caught Bran's eye, and he came to a sudden stop.

"What is it?" Cillian asked.

Bran crunched his way through fallen leaves and brittle twigs, getting closer to the birch tree in question. The white-washed bark had a witchmark carved in at head height, but cutting through it were long scratches that went deep into the trees, something like sap oozing out of it, but it was too black to be that. He reached for the broken witchmark, fingers hovering over it, sensing no magic in the damaged lines, only something rotten. He tilted his head back, looking up, seeing how the leaves on the branches above were becoming brown and brittle, at odds with the summer greenery on the neighboring trees.

Cillian came up beside him, frowning at the sticky blackness streaking the tree bark. "I've never seen damage like that before in a tree."

Bran made a fist and dropped his hand back down to his side. "Let's go."

"Would you at least tell me where we're going? Sunset is only a couple of hours away. It's too late to head back the way we came. We'll need to find a cabin for the night."

"You wouldn't believe me if I told you," Bran said, regretting the words the moment they left his lips.

"Try me."

Bran moved away from the tree. "Let's keep walking."

"Bran—"

"You wanted to come, but I didn't ask you to. Now, I can't leave you behind, so would you start walking?"

"Are you looking for the lights?"

Bran shook his head, anger leaving him hotter than the weather. "I'm looking for my sister."

Hours later, when the sun was impossible to see through the branches and the soft shadows of twilight crept through the woods, the air went quiet. Still. Birds quit chirping, and the soft sound of crickets that had been background noise in Bran's ears abruptly stopped. A fissure of fear shot through his bond with Jupiter, the raven quiet in the treetops. He rocked to a halt on the forest path, breath suddenly loud in his ears. Cillian stopped beside him, slowly pulling his rifle off his shoulder. For a moment, deep in the darkening forest, it was just the two of them.

Then Bran's eyes caught on something far ahead, off to their left—something bright and glowing as it passed between trees, the stuff of nightmares come out to hunt once more.

"Run," Bran choked out. "*Run!*"

Chapter Eight

Cillian didn't know true terror until he was running through ever-darkening woods, away from the lights that relentlessly followed, trying not to trip on exposed roots or rocks in uneven dirt. Rifle clutched in his hands, breath a rasp in his throat, he stuck close to Bran as the younger man hurtled down a forest path that was getting more difficult to see in the fast-encroaching twilight. Some nights, Cillian thought it took the sun forever to set in summer. Right then, he wished it hadn't been so quick.

Something wailed behind them, the sound nothing like anything he'd heard before. The hair on the back of his neck stood on end, stomach knotting tight in his gut, or maybe that was a cramp. He couldn't tell, and it didn't matter because Cillian wasn't going to stop running.

Bran crashed ahead, running as if he knew where he was going, and Cillian hoped he did. All he could think about in that moment was the claw marks outside the cabin the woman had made it to, how Ray's body had been ripped apart, and the damage in the Shoppe. Whatever had done it was with them in the forest now, and he didn't want to meet them in the glow of the lights that were real.

Another wail, and the forest around them got incrementally

brighter—not from the lights, but from witchmarks carved into tree trunks. Cillian tried to make sense of it, brain thinking up excuses on why they might be *glowing* all on their own, but the impossibility of it seemed insignificant when they were being chased by the lights.

By monsters.

"Hurry!" Bran called over his shoulder. "The cabin is close by!"

Another scream behind them, sounding closer than all the others, and Cillian chanced a look over his shoulder. What he saw would live in his nightmares forever. "*Bran*!"

"Keep running!"

The creature hunting them was limned in ghostly light, thin and tall, with elongated arms and many legs. Horns grew from its head, curved in a way that reminded him of a crescent moon. Even with the rapidly closing distance between them, Cillian could see that its face had no eyes, that the gaping bit of darkness there on its head was its mouth, and what glinted in it was teeth.

How Ray's body had looked flashed through his memory, vivid and horrible. Cillian knew now why Ray's ravaged face had been twisted with such terror in death. The creature screamed again, gaining ground on them as the twilight settling in got darker with every second that passed. Even the light emanating from the witchmarks wasn't enough to offset the darkness.

Something glittered out of the corner of his eye, and Cillian looked to the left, seeing another light cutting its way through the trees. He didn't know what monstrosity followed it, and he didn't want to know. "There's more lights following us."

Bran swore, looking over his shoulder. Cillian didn't like the way his eyes went wide, how he stumbled to a stop and let Cillian run past him. Cillian skidded to a stop and spun around, bringing up his rifle and bracing the buttstock against his shoulder. Before he could even warn Bran to get out of the way, Bran drew his arm back as if he were tossing a baseball and snapped it forward.

Something left his hand—glittering and golden like the witchmarks that surrounded them—and Cillian's finger spasmed hard over the rifle's trigger guard. The creature that was almost upon them shrieked from the ensuing explosion, knocked back by a concussive force that had Cillian gaping for a moment in the fading light. It was odd, he distantly noted, how the force of the explosion had only been one way.

Then Bran turned and grabbed him by the elbow, yanking him back down the path. "That won't stop it for long."

Cillian stumbled into a run again, clutching his rifle close. "Was that a *bomb*?"

He wanted it to be because that would maybe make sense amid everything else that didn't. Bran didn't answer him, just kept running, and Cillian followed in his footsteps because that was the sane thing to do instead of interrogating the other man. His lungs burned from the exertion, but better that sort of pain than death.

Maybe a minute later, Bran let out a cry of relief and pointed ahead. "There!"

Cillian squinted through the dimly lit darkness, catching sight of a shadowy shape looming up from between the trees. The cabin was the best thing he'd ever seen in that moment, worth more than a million-dollar property in Boston. Bran reached it first, slamming against the door and wrenching at the knob. He shouldered it open and stumbled inside, one arm reaching back for Cillian, hand grasping at open air.

Cillian didn't think twice about taking Bran's hand and pitching himself through the doorway into the cabin. He got inside, and then Bran slammed the door shut with a bang. He turned the lock right as something heavy crashed against the door on the outside. They both stepped back, and Cillian brought his rifle up out of instinct, aiming at the door as the monster outside screamed in fury. He braced himself because there was nowhere to run in the tiny cabin, no window to see out of, and he couldn't decide if that was a good thing or not.

Light flickered on, and he flinched, staring around wide-eyed at the space he and Bran huddled in. The single light overhead hummed in time with the tiny generator in the corner that couldn't be drowned out by the creature screaming beyond the cabin's walls. Its furious voice was joined by another, and something heavy slammed against the right side of the cabin. Cillian jerked around, pointing his rifle at the wall, trying to get his breathing under control.

"They can't get inside," Bran said in a low, tight voice.

Cillian could barely hear Bran over the rushing sound in his ears. "They got into your Shoppe."

"They had help."

"Yeah? Is that help out there?" Bran's silence was answer enough to that possibility. Cillian drew in a breath, then another, forcing himself to find a calm that was as elusive as a butterfly in winter.

"You can lower your rifle. We're safe for now in here. I promise."

Bran's words weren't a comfort, and Cillian didn't let go of his rifle. "I'd like to be prepared."

"This will be a better weapon."

He half turned, seeing that Bran held one of his strangely curved knives out like an offering. "I don't exactly want to get up close and personal with whatever is out there."

"And if you lose your rifle? What else do you have on you that you can fight with?"

Nothing, unfortunately. Cillian had hoped his rifle would be enough. Glancing back at the wall, noting how it still stood despite the heavy thumps on the other side, he finally lowered his rifle. He reached for the knife Bran offered, but the second his fingers almost touched it, he jerked his hand back. A warning clawed at his mind out of nowhere, instinct telling him not to touch that cold iron. "Keep it. I'll take my chances with my rifle."

Bran frowned at him, looking like he wanted to argue. Cillian turned his back on the other man and crossed the cabin in two strides to reach the bed. He leaned his rifle against it and sat down.

"Are you sure?" Bran finally asked after a moment.

"Very." Cillian looked past Bran at the cabin wall. "Those things out there are the lights."

He made it a statement, not a question, meeting Bran's gaze. The monsters outside still screamed, and the heavy hits against the cabin walls and door seemed never-ending. He wanted to believe that none of this was real, that the witchmarks he thought were merely superstitious symbols all his life hadn't glowed like beacons in the dark with the same sort of illumination Bran had impossibly held in his hand. Cillian wanted all of what they'd just escaped to be a dream, but it was too much of a horror to ever be anything but a nightmare turned real.

Bran stood in the middle of the cabin, looking like he wanted to hide, but there was nowhere he could go. The cabin was small, meant to hold only the twin-sized bed with its musty-smelling blankets, the cabinet probably filled with long-lasting food supplies and water, and a compost toilet in one corner that smelled like no one had used it in years, thankfully. This cabin, like all the others in the forest, was meant to be a refuge, and Cillian finally knew from what.

Bran dragged a hand over his face. "Do you have your iron with you?"

"Yes. That's not what I asked about."

"It's relevant."

Cillian's heart beat a little faster, and he rested his elbows on his knees, hunching over a little as he stared at Bran. "How?"

Bran glanced reflexively over his shoulder at the door as one of the creatures outside slammed against it. The door didn't even rattle on the hinges. "Iron hurts them."

The only stories Cillian knew where that occurred were just that—stories. Except what circled the cabin outside was far too real to be some long-lived tale passed down through generations. Some part of his mind was still having trouble believing that. "The lights are real."

Bran nodded jerkily, looking at a point over Cillian's shoulder. "They've always been real."

He didn't want to believe that, but the proof had chased them through the woods like they were prey. "They're what killed your mother and Ray and the hiker?"

Bran flinched. "Yes, but they shouldn't have been able to get inside the home or the Shoppe."

"Why not?" Bran's gaze finally met his again, the grimace on his pale face pulling at his lips, but he kept mutinously silent. Cillian dug his fingernails into his palms. "Why not, Bran? Why did the witchmarks glow? What did you do out there?"

Cillian wanted answers, even though he knew he probably wouldn't like them. Bran seemed disinclined to give them. But what battered at the walls of the cabin and kept Cillian's fight-or-flight reflexes on a knife edge meant he'd get them. They weren't going anywhere until dawn at the earliest, and there was no chance either of them was sleeping tonight.

"We were friends once. You used to trust me," Cillian said in a low voice.

"You pushed me away," Bran said heatedly. "After I kissed you, you pushed me away, and I know what rejection looks like when it's standing right in front of me."

Cillian stood, long-leashed temper finally fraying. "You didn't give me a chance to explain."

"You looked pretty pissed when you put your hand over your mouth at the time. Like I was so disgusting you were going to puke."

It'd been seven years, but Bran seemed to remember that moment in high definition just like Cillian. Even after all this time, Cillian remembered that night, remembered what had caused him to live the past seven years with the realization he was missing something vital and integral in his life.

It was a loss he should have been able to get over, but Bran had been his best friend and his first love, even if he hadn't told the other man. He'd meant to—he'd wanted to—but the first and only kiss Bran had given him when they were teenagers had burned like iron against his lips. Cillian had been so startled at the time that he had reacted out of instinct. Bad instinct, he'd come to realize over the years he'd lived without Bran in his life.

"It wasn't disgust, and you never gave me a chance to explain. You changed your number and ran to Boston and never let me know when you visited after I moved back," Cillian argued.

"I wasn't going to be friends with someone who seemed to secretly hate me."

"I never hated you! Stop putting words in my mouth." A heavy thud against the wall and an ear-piercing scream made both of them flinch. Cillian swallowed hard and lowered his voice from the angry shout he'd been trending toward. "You were my best friend, Bran. Losing you was horrible. It was like half of me was gone."

Bran crossed his arms over his chest, shoulders hunching forward. He had a scratch on his right cheek that was coming up red on his pale skin, gained at some point during their mad dash through the forest. He looked chilled, but his sweatshirt was nowhere to be found. Probably lost somewhere in the forest. He was sweaty, T-shirt damp with it, and Cillian knew he probably looked the same, both of them smelling like they'd spent the day outdoors because they had.

Despite all that, Cillian drank in the sight of him because it was only them there in a cabin in the woods, having outrun a nightmare that still desperately wanted in. And while Cillian would think it was possible the horror out there might break down the door, Bran didn't, and he wanted to know why.

"Why did you push me away?" Bran asked.

Cillian didn't know how to answer that, not with his mother's voice whispering a long-lived warning through his mind. *Never trust a witch.*

The Gallaghers were Wiccan, but Cillian's mother had seemed grudgingly okay with them. Cillian hadn't cared either way, but his mother had, and he'd always listened to her as a child. By the time he got older, the habits were too ingrained to break. He'd shared everything he could with Bran as a kid, just not that iron burned him because he always forgot about his allergy. So had Bran's kiss, and Cillian didn't know why. Saying that sounded strange and ridiculous, but then again, they'd been chased through the forest by monsters Bran wasn't surprised to see.

"I wasn't expecting it," Cillian hedged.

They'd been at Cillian's house while his mom had a late shift at the hospital, fighting over who'd won at the latest video game. In the ensuing squabble, Cillian had found himself pinned to the floor with Bran stretched over him, their faces so close their noses brushed. Looking back, the kiss seemed inevitable, but at the time, he hadn't been sure. Bran had kissed him, and Cillian's lips had burned from it, heat streaking through his skin like being branded. He'd shoved Bran off him, scrambling up and back, and Bran had taken it for the rejection it wasn't.

Cillian had spent the last seven years regretting his actions and trying to stop thinking about Bran. He'd dated other men in college, but once he'd moved back to Pelham, it had been slim pickings. There weren't many men close to his age, and of those that were, none liked men. When the urge for something more than his right hand hit him, he spent his day off in Boston, haunting the clubs and bars, kissing people whose lips didn't burn him and wishing they did.

Another crash against one of the walls had Cillian's entire body tensing. He stood, looking past Bran at the door, which hadn't yet caved in. "You seem real sure they can't get in."

Bran wouldn't look him in the eye. "They won't."

"Tell me why. Tell me what you did out there."

Bran went, if anything, paler. "What makes you think I did anything?"

"Don't play stupid. I saw you throw whatever that was at the creature and knock it back."

Bran swallowed audibly. "You wouldn't believe me."

Cillian let out a rough laugh, gesturing furiously at the nearest wall and everything beyond it that shouldn't exist but did and was trying to get in. "I believe in *that*. In the lights."

"You thought they were stories."

"That's not a story out there."

"Can we not do this?"

"We're stuck here until whatever is out there leaves. We might as well start talking. Seven years of silence has to be broken at some point." Cillian dragged a hand through his hair, fingers catching on the hair tie. He yanked it out and redid the ponytail. "Why can't they get in? What do the witchmarks really do?"

Bran was silent for long enough that Cillian thought he wouldn't talk. Scowling, Cillian approached the storage cabinet and yanked open one of the doors to dig through the supplies there. The energy bars weren't expired yet, and he ripped open a fruit and nut one, biting into it.

"They're magic," Bran finally said so quietly that Cillian thought he'd imagined the words.

Cillian turned around, swallowing the food. "What?"

Bran kept his back to him as one of the creatures outside screamed out its frustration. "The witchmarks are magic. My coven has carved them in the forest for generations to mark the paths to the cabins."

"You're Wiccan," Cillian said slowly.

Bran laughed, thick and ugly, as he turned around. "*Witch*. I'm a witch. There's a difference when it comes to guarding against the wyrding and the Fae."

Never trust a witch.

His mother's voice again, ripping through his mind like a knife. The hideous ringing sound in his ears drowned out the creatures and their screams as he stared at Bran like he didn't know him—and he didn't, not seven years out from their last moment together, one burning kiss that was scarred into Cillian's memory the same way this moment was going to be.

He still wanted to.

"You're a what?" he asked in surprise.

Bran shook his head, sliding both hands through his hair to lock his fingers together at the back of his skull. He bounced a couple of times on his heels before lowering his arms and pacing. He wouldn't look at Cillian as he moved, gaze focused inward as the creatures outside moved around the cabin. "Do you believe me?"

He didn't have a choice, not after surviving what they'd barely outrun. "Yes."

Bran startled, head snapping around as he planted his feet. "You do?"

Cillian tipped his head at the door, gaze flicking to it, unable to see what hunted them beyond the cabin's entrance. "I don't have a choice not to."

"You could call me crazy."

"The lights aren't stories. Stands to reason witches aren't either."

"Right." Bran cleared his throat. "You remember the old warnings?"

Cillian nodded shallowly and set the energy bar aside, suddenly not hungry anymore. "Always keep iron with you. If you're lost, follow the witchmarks. If the forest stares back at you, you're already prey."

"My coven has kept those superstitions alive since my ancestors moved out here centuries ago, following the threat. The lights are creatures of the Fae. They come through the wyrding in the forest, hunting humans."

Cillian frowned. "What's the wyrding?"

"A barrier between our world and the Fae's. The lights only ever come out of it. They're used to clear the way, to prepare the land for the

Fae to return by killing humans. Witches are the only ones who can stop them. With magic."

Bran raised his right hand, palm up, fingers slightly curled. In the cage of his fingers, a soft, golden glow sparkled into existence. Cillian didn't know he'd gasped until the sound rang in his ears. He closed the distance between them, eyes locked on the glittering brightness hovering above Bran's palm. The light wasn't like the cold, white flickers of illumination that had hunted them. Instead, it was warm, carrying a softness to it that reminded him of a cozy winter day, when the snow was high and the fire inside was warm.

Cillian let his hand hover over the golden glow held in Bran's hand, unable to look away. "How?"

"We're born with it, along with the duty to stand against the Fae." Bran made a fist, snuffing out his magic, and let his arm drop back to his side. Cillian's hand hovered over empty air for a moment before he finally dropped his arm as well. "The Fae aren't anything like the stories you know. They're powerful and cruel, and they would like nothing more than to return to the world us witches banished them from."

"And you fight them?"

"No one else can."

Cillian met Bran's gaze, cognizant of the wariness in his eyes, the way he held himself so rigid in the wake of his confession. "The Fae killed your mother."

Bran's lips trembled for a second before he pressed them together so hard they went white at the seam of his mouth. When he finally spoke, all Cillian could hear in his voice was grief. "Yes. She died giving Aisling enough time for a head start to make it to the cabin near the house. But the Fae put a geas on Aisling so she can't talk. I don't know why, of all spells, they used that one."

"What's a geas?"

"A type of spell only the Fae use. There are different kinds, and the one on Aisling is for silence."

"So she can't talk or scream." At Bran's look, Cillian grimaced. "If she couldn't scream, no one would come looking for her. You said the Fae tried to kill you, but they took her. Sounds like they wanted her."

If anything, his words made Bran go gray in the face. "She's not a witch. She doesn't have any magic. I don't know why they'd want her."

"So the creatures can't get through witchmarks on their own, but they can if the Fae are with them."

Bran shook his head. "Not every Fae. The witchmarks at the home and Shoppe should have held. But I think the Fae last night was a lord. It would take so much power to rip through my coven's magical defenses, and he tore through it all like wet paper."

The idea that Cillian could have come upon the ruined Shoppe and Bran's dead body yesterday was a nightmare he didn't want to think about. "Do you think the Fae lord will come tonight?"

"I don't know."

Cillian blew out a breath. "All right. We can't leave until dawn at the earliest, right? So we might as well get comfortable."

"You want to sleep? Through this?"

One of the creatures outside snarled furiously, the sound deep and haunting. It made Cillian's skin crawl. "I'd have better luck sleeping near a stack of speakers at a concert. No, I meant let's sit down. I don't think either of us will sleep tonight."

The only place to sit was the bed. Cillian retrieved his rifle, then sat down, laying the long gun over his thighs. After a moment, Bran approached, joining him on the bed, both of them staring at the door that still hadn't been battered down.

"You're taking this awfully well," Bran said however long later.

Cillian laughed, the sound cracking in his throat. "I'm not. But what's out there is real, just like you, and I've always believed in you, even when you left me behind. Believing in the Fae isn't that far-fetched."

Bran didn't need to know about the panicked spiral of his thoughts. He definitely didn't need to know about all the caution Cillian's mother had imparted to him over the years and how all of it meant nothing now that he knew what Bran was.

Cillian would never trust a witch, but he'd always trusted Bran, and seven years of silence wasn't enough to change that for him.

The truth wasn't enough either.

The night passed slowly, oh so slowly. Neither of them slept, remaining where they were on the bed, the wide space between them diminishing as they shifted position every now and then until their bodies finally touched, taking comfort in the closeness. When the world outside had been quiet for more than an hour and Cillian's watch said it was getting close to six in the morning, Bran finally stood, grabbing his backpack. "They're gone."

Cillian grabbed his wrist, causing Bran to look at him. "How do you know?"

Bran licked his lips, the skin there chapped and bleeding a little from him biting at it all night. Cillian wanted to touch his thumb to those ruined lips and keep them from Bran's teeth. "Jupiter told me."

"She talks?" Cillian asked as he stood, hefting up his rifle.

Bran shrugged. "She's my familiar. She thinks and feels at me. It's not words, more like emotions."

Cillian didn't know how that would work. "She always did have strange eyes."

"You're still taking this fairly well." Bran tugged against Cillian's grip, and he belatedly let the other man go. "I thought you would protest."

"I think even if we were kids, I'd have believed you if you'd given me a chance."

Bran opened his mouth, but whatever he was going to say was drowned out by Jupiter's rapid-fire *cawing*. Bran sighed, turning toward the door. "She's getting impatient."

Cillian pulled on his backpack, then shouldered his rifle and followed Bran out of the cabin. Jupiter *cawed* again from her spot on the torn-up dirt path before dropping a sprig of blue-colored flowers at their feet. Cillian stared at it. "I've seen those before."

Bran shot him a sharp look as he knelt to retrieve the flowers. "Where?"

"By the cabin we found the surviving hiker in."

Bran stood with the flowers in his hand, turning them over between his fingers. "These are Otherworld flowers. I found one clutched in my mother's hand at the morgue, and the Fae lord had a garland of them wrapped around his antlers. Did you tell Mac about the flowers?"

"Why would Mac need to know?"

Bran shrugged and pocketed the flowers. "He's a guardian. They're families who patrol the forests and mark the encroachment of the wyrding when it arrives for a witch to handle. In the olden days, they also helped divert attention from covens so people wouldn't see we were witches."

"So he knows? About you and your family?"

Bran turned away and started walking. "He's always known."

A flash of anger hurtled through him, but Cillian stuffed it down. Secrets were meant to be kept, and he couldn't be mad that Mac had kept this. "What now?"

Jupiter *cawed* and flung herself into the air, flying through the trees. Cillian watched her go and wasn't surprised when Bran followed after her. "We find the wyrding."

Cillian didn't look back as they walked away from the cabin, the forest alive with the sound of insects and birds up with the sun. He gripped his rifle tight and kept an eye on their surroundings, looking deep into the trees that surrounded them. He'd always had a healthy wariness for the forest, but now he knew what horror called its shadows home. There was no unknowing what had happened last night. That Bran had lived his entire life knowing what clawed itself out of the woods however often would have given Cillian nightmares as a kid.

The rising sun chased the shadows away until it didn't. Jupiter flew toward a distant shadow between the trees that might have been mist on any other day, but Cillian knew better now. The fog drifting between the trees wasn't burning off, casting a pall over the hill they approached. Jupiter alighted on the leafy branch of a massive oak tree up ahead, its trunk split down the middle from what might have been a lightning strike. The cavity widened closer to the ground, like a black hole against a living trunk.

Flowers bloomed around it, but they weren't any flowers Cillian had ever seen in a field guide. Tiny, vibrant crimson blossoms attached to thin branches that curved outward from the hole seemed to beckon them inside. Ice-white tulip-shaped flowers clustered at the base of the trunk and the gnarled roots there that dug into the earth and the mound behind it. Dripping from the jagged edges was the same sort of black sap he'd seen on the tree from yesterday.

They came to a stop in front of the oak tree, the space they stood in cold and the area quiet. Cillian reflexively looked over his shoulder, squinting through the thin fog, but saw no lights floating through the trees. The lack of them didn't ease his worry any.

"This is the wyrding?" Cillian asked.

"The edge of it." Bran looked up at the branches and raised his arm over his head. Jupiter launched herself off the branch and flew to him. She flapped her wings hard to break the dive, her claws reaching for his forearm. Bran moved his arm to take her weight, bringing her up to his eye level. "Lead the way?"

Jupiter preened Bran's hair for a couple of seconds before he tossed her into the air again. Instead of flying up, she flew into the shadows within the tree, the tips of her wings brushing against some of the crimson flowers hanging down. It swallowed her whole, and Cillian worried about her crashing, but Bran didn't seem concerned about Jupiter. About this place, yes, but not her.

"Why not burn it?"

"We've tried. It always comes back. This isn't the first way into the Otherworld we've found over the years, just the newest. Jupiter tracked the lights here last night after they left the cabin. She couldn't the other night because she was helping me see straight while I made a potion to get rid of my concussion."

Cillian's hand twitched with the need to touch Bran. "I didn't know you were that hurt."

"It doesn't matter." Bran's expression was resolute in the dim sunlight coming through the lingering fog. "Ready?"

He didn't want to be, but Cillian still followed Bran through the strange flowers and into dark shadows held within the massive oak tree. His feet sank into something that clung like mud once inside that cavity, and Cillian could only hope it was just that and nothing else. He didn't need to crouch, the carved-out space large enough that he wouldn't be able to touch the sides if he stretched out his arms. Even with the flowers, it smelled...rotten.

The lip of the hole had hidden a large cluster of softly glowing mushrooms that protruded from the inside bark of the tree close to the ground. Bran crouched before them, hands already sinking deep into the mass. Cillian watched as he pried the mushrooms apart, clawing them free, revealing a pulsating hole beneath them, somehow edged with more flowers giving off an eerie blue light. Bran glanced back only once before he wedged himself into that hole that shouldn't exist. Cillian crouched behind him, snagging the back of Bran's T-shirt with his hand, not wanting to be separated.

Cillian ducked his head, gritted his teeth, and pitched himself into the impossible, following Bran the same way he'd done as a kid. Vertigo hit almost immediately. Through the swirling ache in that eerie blackness, he thought he heard a voice whisper at the farthest range of his hearing, distant and lyrical, calling to him with a terrifying sense of knowing.

Welcome home.

Chapter Nine

They came out in shadows that seemed to stick to Bran's skin, a chill in the air making him wish he hadn't lost his sweatshirt in the woods back home. His palms skidded against damp earth as he clawed his way free of the dark, gasping as he came into the Otherworld. A flail of his arm sent a bone shard skittering away, and he gagged. Bran stumbled to his feet, swallowing against the nausea from the passage through the wyrding and the sound of bone crunching underfoot. He steadied himself with a couple of deep breaths, stepping out of the way so Cillian had room to crawl through after him.

He looked around, taking in the area they had arrived in, the wyrding a strange place of shadows that lingered. The day seemed gray through the fog crawling over everything, muffling the Otherworld. The air was cold and damp when he breathed it in, tinged with that same scent of rot that had existed in and around the tree back home. Large gray standing stones shot through with brilliant blue lines jutted up in a circle around the low mound they'd crawled out of. Bran thought the lines might mean something—they seemed too purposeful to be of nature—but he couldn't be sure.

The Otherworld wasn't natural.

He stepped forward, and his heel came down on something that snapped beneath it. He looked down at the gray bone he'd broken in half, not recognizing the shape of it. He followed the curved length to a flared end, the spine it should have connected to nowhere to be seen. Bran swallowed, tasting bile at the back of his throat. Wrenching his gaze away from the bones, he looked back at the entrance surrounded by the same tiny crimson flowers. Bran wiped at the sticky black sap-like substance that had dripped from both entrances, hoping it wasn't poison. It smeared over his skin, leaving his fingers tacky.

Cillian came to stand beside him, staring in shock at the place they'd stepped into, voice hushed when he spoke. "I have to admit, I keep thinking this isn't real."

"It's real, and we'll be dead if we don't get moving. The wyrding let us out in a boneyard, and we should find some cover before whatever eats here comes back."

Jupiter flew through the fog toward them, startling Bran even though he'd sensed her approach through their bond. He stepped back out of reflex, running into Cillian, who steadied him with a warm hand against his hip. Bran had a split second of wanting to stay in Cillian's hands before hastily putting some distance between them.

Jupiter made no sound, no greeting, as she circled them overhead before flying off again. Bran followed her without reservation, hoping she knew a safe path away from the boneyard they'd arrived in. Cillian kept pace, still clutching his rifle, and Bran wasn't sure how useful it would be there in the Otherworld. Mortal technology didn't work here, and the loud sound of the rifle would surely make them targets.

"I wouldn't use your rifle right now. It'll draw too much attention," Bran said in a low voice.

Cillian gave him a disbelieving look. "I'm pretty sure a high-velocity bullet is better than me throwing rocks."

Bran waggled his fingers at Cillian. "I'll keep you safe."

"The lights hunt witches. What makes you think they won't find us because of your magic?"

He had a point. "Then let's keep moving."

"And go where? Have you ever even been here before?"

"No," Bran admitted. "But I know my coven's history."

"Well, I don't, so maybe you could share."

"Now? When we don't know what's around that could hear us?"

Cillian grimaced but tipped his head in agreement. "How do you plan to find Aisling?"

Bran fingered the beads on the bracelet wrapped around his wrist, his mother's magic embedded in them a cool wash of comfort. "It requires magic."

Cillian's earlier words haunted him, though, and for all the stories that had been passed down through the generations, Bran had never experienced crossing the wyrding to the Otherworld before now. But this was where Aisling had been brought, and he'd fight to get her back, even if it killed him, which was a distinct possibility.

"Jupiter seems to know where she's going," Cillian said.

"Yeah."

In a strange land filled with Fae who wouldn't think twice about murdering a witch, Bran didn't have the time to question why Jupiter seemed intent on the direction she was flying in. The sooner they found Aisling, the quicker they could leave. First, they had to survive, which was easier said than done.

They crept out of the boneyard, passing by skeletons of animals neither of them recognized, stripped clean down to bone, and a few half-buried kills that buzzed with clouds of insects. The stench coming off those corpses made Bran gag and cover his mouth, lengthening his stride to get clear of the dead.

"The bodies look like deer," Cillian said.

Bran thought of the monster that had battered down the Shoppe's door only to disappear, letting a Fae lord walk inside. He didn't know if they were one and the same, but both were dangerous. "I wouldn't trust any animal in this place."

They reached the edge of the clearing in the gray forest, passing the last standing stone with its strange blue lines that appeared carved into it. A faint vibration seemed to emanate from it, a thrum Bran felt in his teeth more than anything else. It made him hunch his shoulders, as if that would be enough to shield him from the sensation. Cillian didn't seem affected, or if he was, it didn't bother him.

Jupiter alighted on a branch up ahead, waiting for them. Bran and Cillian hurried to reach her, the dirt they walked on less muddy beneath the skeletal trees. He was glad neither of them wore any bright colors that might attract attention. Jupiter spread her wings a little and hopped on the branch. She didn't make a sound, but Bran heard her clear enough through the bond.

Danger comes.

He grabbed Cillian by the arm and dragged the other man with him over to a fallen tree trunk split in the middle by a boulder jutting out of the ground. When Cillian looked as if he might speak, Bran frantically shook his head. Cillian clamped his teeth together and didn't fight when Bran pulled him into a crouch behind the tree trunk. Bran looked up at Jupiter, his familiar having tucked herself tight against the spot where the branch met the tree, an unmoving statue that would look like a shadow from a distance.

Bran shrugged off his backpack and carefully lay down on the cold ground, shifting so that he was underneath the fallen tree trunk. He turned his head to the side so he could see through the narrow space between the tree trunk and the ground, face hopefully hidden enough by the scraggly weeds growing in the slimy moss. At first, he couldn't see what had made Jupiter give out her warning. Then, on the far side of the clearing, beyond the circle of standing stones and deep in the spindly trees, if he squinted, he could see a light.

Floating higher than the ones that had chased them through the forest, Bran watched it grow larger as it approached the clearing, casting an eerie brightness through the cold fog. It coalesced into something huge, fog peeling away from its terrifying form. The creature was tall, even though it was hunched over, dragging its arms along the ground as it walked. No, Bran realized as he lay there in the dirt, rigid and trying not to breathe.

It dragged prey.

The creature's skin was gray and wrinkled, sagging at its joints. Its face was an elongated nightmare with four eyes, two on each side of the mouth full of teeth bisecting its skull from jaw to top. The sound it made was a rasp like nails being scraped over metal. It gripped in its hands two massive deerlike creatures with deep russet hides, much larger in scale than any deer Bran had ever seen. Both bodies had broken antlers and ripped-open bellies, their intestines hanging from the death wounds and dragging behind them.

Bran thought the might-be-deer were too brightly colored to call the wyrding home. Nothing about this place screamed the living abided within it, but he was certain the animals hadn't come from the mortal world. He watched as the creature tossed first one and then the other into the boneyard. Then it reared back and roared, the sound making Bran wish he could cover his ears.

Cillian's hand gripped his leg right above the top of his hiking boot, fingers digging in hard. Bran didn't dare move, and he couldn't close his eyes, not if he wanted to make sure they weren't seen. So he lay there and watched the monstrous creature crouch over its kill and tear flesh from bone with its vicious teeth. Blood coated its body, shockingly red against its gray skin, even from a distance.

As the creature ate its fill, focused as it was on the bodies, Bran finally unclenched a hand from the dirt and weeds, carefully rolling to his side so he could reach for Cillian. Cool fingers gripped his, and Bran tugged at him, not needing to tell Cillian to move quietly and slowly. With great care, Cillian stretched out on the ground beside Bran, sliding beneath the broken tree trunk with him amid the sound of crunching bone.

There wasn't much room for them both, but they hunkered down together out of necessity. Cillian half lay on top of Bran, his head resting against Bran's shoulder blade, an arm hooked over his waist. The length of the other man's body pressed up against his was a weight he didn't want to leave. The ground leached all the warmth from his body, and the cold air wasn't much better. Cillian, though, he was warm, and Bran fought the urge to press closer—out of want or fear, Bran couldn't say right then. But Cillian was an anchor of sanity that Bran gladly clung to as the creature finished its meal, face covered in blood, and left the clearing.

Right in their direction.

Bran held his breath, heard the quietness from Cillian that told him the other man was doing the same thing. Cillian's fingers gripped Bran's hip tight enough to leave bruises. Both of them stayed still and quiet, hidden beneath the fallen tree trunk, as the creature passed them by mere yards away, its deep, raspy breathing almost like a laugh. Bran squeezed his eyes shut, silently praying to the Mother to keep them safe.

Neither of them moved until the sounds of the creature's passage were nothing but a lingering fear in the form of a rapid heartbeat. Jupiter sent *safe* through the bond, but Bran didn't immediately move, not until she flew down to them and hopped beneath the tree trunk. She pecked him lightly on the cheek, and Bran finally drew in a breath that wasn't tight in his lungs with fear. "Okay."

He nudged Cillian with his elbow, and the other man rolled away from him. Bran instantly missed having him close. They crawled out from beneath the tree trunk, muddy dirt and bits of moss sticking to the black sap already on their skin covering them on one side. Bran tried scraping it all off, but it was a lost cause.

"Where to now?" Cillian asked in a hushed voice.

Bran looked at Jupiter, who was now perched on the fallen tree trunk, staring back at them. She spread her wings and launched herself into the air, flying away, hopefully in a different direction from that creature. They picked up their backpacks, and Cillian carried his rifle in a position that would be easy to quickly bring it up and shoot, and they started walking.

They left the boneyard behind with its newly ravaged dead and walked into the fog. Jupiter led the way, the bond a warm weight in the back of Bran's mind. His mouth was dry, and he dug out a bottle of water, drinking half of it and passing the rest over to Cillian, who finished it off. Cillian put the empty plastic bottle into his own backpack, ever the ranger and refusing to leave trash behind, even here.

They walked for what felt like hours, Jupiter guiding the way through the fog on a winding path that saw them hide from the lights two more times before the chill began to abate. Each escape felt like a miracle, but Bran wasn't sure his nerves could take crossing the lights again. Eventually, though, the sun started breaking through the fog, the gray sky above showing slivers of blue. Trees with bits of green leaves began to appear between the spindly lifeless ones as the wyrding gave way to something else.

Something beautiful.

A forest like Bran had never seen before gradually appeared around them. The gray coldness of the wyrding faded away, revealing rich brown bark and deep green clover that covered the ground. The trees were *huge*, bigger even than the redwoods Bran had seen once in California when he was a child and his mother had taken him on a summer road trip. They rose above like giant sentinels, their canopies thick with green leaves, the sun glinting brilliantly through the branches.

The forest was old—far older than any in their world. Bran didn't trust it, no matter that it smelled earthy and rich, clean in a way that was refreshing after coming through the wyrding. The lingering scent of rot clung to both of them. He desperately wanted a shower, but more than that, he wanted to find Aisling.

The buzzing sound of a forest crept in, replacing the silence that had been suffocating in the wyrding. The bird song wasn't familiar, just slightly off to his ears, reinforcing the fact they weren't walking through the forest back home. That this land belonged to the Fae and they needed to be careful. All the warnings his mother had ever given him over the years tumbled through Bran's mind, keeping him company as they made their way through the forest, following where Jupiter led.

She took them through trees and across a bubbling creek, skirting a meadow that had a herd of those massive deer grazing. One stood apart, its antlered head held high, on alert for any threats. Bran didn't think it saw them as they passed by, but he wasn't keen on catching its attention. It might look like a deer—bigger, with the same sort of antlers—but looks could be deceiving in the Otherworld.

They were maybe an hour past the meadow and down another energy bar each when Jupiter *cawed* in three short bursts. Bran couldn't see her, but he could sense her up ahead.

"Trouble?" Cillian asked.

"No, but she found something."

They picked up the pace, Bran following his bond with Jupiter and taking the lead. As they walked between two trees, they stumbled onto something Bran could only call a road, the dirt worn down from use. He rocked to a stop at the edge of the forest, looking first one way, then the other.

Cillian walked a little farther into the wide road, spinning around in a slow circle, never letting go of his rifle. "What now?"

"Jupiter got us out of the wyrding," Bran said as he joined Cillian.

"And I'm glad for that, but how do we find Aisling in this place?"

Bran knew nothing about the Otherworld except for the stories kept alive by covens through the centuries. The important ones were shared, information gleaned by those witches who made it through the wyrding and to the Otherworld and back. Most of those were in his coven's grimoire, and while Bran had memorized witchmarks, he hadn't memorized the alchemist aspect of magic or the spells written down in dozens of handwritings from his ancestors.

Bran scratched at his tattoo, trying to rub off some of the black sap. The corded leather bracelet on his left wrist, with its iron and bone beads with witchmarks carved into them, remained surprisingly clean. He twisted it around until he found the bone bead that had Aisling's favorite flower carved on it in the form of a witchmark unique to his little sister. Their mother had planted Canada anemone around the Shoppe when Aisling first started kindergarten. The white petals nearly matched her hair, and Aisling had declared the flower her favorite for that reason alone.

He wanted her back. He wanted to take her out of this nightmare and get her home, where they could grieve, just the two of them, for what they had lost. It was all he wanted, and Bran realized, when Jupiter *cawed* out a frantic warning, he wasn't going to get it.

"Get back in the trees," Bran hissed, already turning to run into the forest.

They made it to the side of the road when horses came around the bend down the way. The animals mostly looked like their counterparts back home. Bran couldn't make out the three riders, but he knew they were Fae, and that made them the enemy. One of them raised an arm in their direction and shouted in a language he didn't understand. It sounded like it could be Gaelic, but he wasn't sure. The only Gaelic he knew were from rituals written down in his coven's grimoire, and his accent, he'd been told, was atrocious.

"Run," Cillian said, raising his rifle. "I'll hold them off."

Bran grabbed him by the back of his T-shirt and yanked him toward the trees. "We stay together, you asshole!"

No way was he letting Cillian run around the Otherworld without him. Bran didn't let go as Cillian got his feet under him, and they ran back into the forest, both of them looking for a place to hide. But hiding from the Fae was a whole different ballgame than hiding from the lights. Not to mention, they were in an unfamiliar place, and Bran didn't know where to go. Even Jupiter, when he tugged on their bond, couldn't give him better directions than *run*.

They jumped over roots and tore through shrubbery, trying to make it deeper into the forest before the Fae reached them. But they were the interlopers here, and Bran was acutely reminded of that fact when one of the Fae dropped down from the damn treetops right in front of them.

"Mortals," the Fae said in heavily accented English, his lips twisted in a smile on his too-beautiful face Bran didn't trust.

Cillian rocked to a halt, brought up the rifle, and pulled the trigger. The sound of the long gun going off echoed loudly in the forest, disrupting the quiet. Birds took to the air, chirping wildly from the disturbance. The Fae took the bullet right in the chest, staggering back with a look of surprise on his face before collapsing to the ground. Bran grabbed Cillian by the elbow, urging him on. "Let's go, let's *go!*"

Cillian didn't argue, matching his stride to Bran's as they left the Fae behind to die—and Bran wouldn't feel guilty about that—but they'd only gone so far before the pressure in the air changed. Bran recognized the force as magic, but even as his fingers bent to shape a witchmark, the spell slammed into them and sent them both flying. He landed in the dirt rather than against a tree, managing to not knock his head this time around. The impact forced all the air out of his lungs, leaving him gasping for breath, body aching.

He distantly heard Jupiter call out to him, and Bran dazedly pushed an order down the bond for her to *stay back*. He lifted his head, frantically looking for Cillian. The other man was sprawled at the base of a tree trunk, his rifle lying some distance away, and he wasn't moving.

Bran swore, heart beating fast as he shoved himself up from the ground, pain shooting through his ribs. He wrapped an arm around his chest, carefully taking a breath. His ribs hurt, but they didn't feel broken. Gritting his teeth, Bran got to his feet, looking around wildly for the Fae chasing them as he hurried to Cillian's side.

Please be alive, Bran thought desperately as he knelt by Cillian, touching two fingers to his throat. The pulse that beat against his fingertips made Bran sag in relief. He gripped Cillian's shoulder, shaking him, trying to wake him up. "Cillian?"

"What an interesting name to call your friend."

Bran twisted around on his knees, ignoring the pull in his ribs, and faced a pair of Fae who stood mere yards away, having not heard either of them approach. He raised his arm, drawing a witchmark in the air, knowing it would be the same as drawing a target on his back. "Back off."

The Fae who had spoken was beautiful in the way all the stories said the Fae were. Tall and lean, he wore a velvet moss-green coat and pants with intricate silvery-white embroidery that matched the waistcoat. The outfit wouldn't have been out of place in some 1700s European court, as if he were the gentry on an afternoon ride. His deep brown hair was straight and long, falling to his elbows and not tied back in any way. His companion was a lady dressed more like the Fae that Cillian had shot, garbed in duller colors and carrying a bow with an arrow nocked and aimed in their direction. Guards, maybe, or servants.

The courtly-looking Fae studied Bran with narrowed brown eyes, lips curling hatefully. "Witch."

His guard drew her arrow back a fraction more. She said something in the Fae's language that Bran didn't understand but which had the Fae in charge making a gesture with his hand. A root exploded from the ground, wrapping around Bran's wrist too quickly for him to process. His hand was yanked to the ground, along with the rest of him if he didn't want to break his wrist, the witchmark sputtering out. Another root wrapped itself around his other wrist, pinning him down further. He yanked at the hold, but the roots wouldn't budge.

"I think our lord would be interested to know what a witch and their companion are doing in Tír na nÓg where the Summer Court rules," the Fae said.

Bran dragged his fingertips through the earth, prepared to pour his magic into the barest of witchmarks he could eke out, when Cillian made a sound that had Bran snapping his head around. He stared in horror at the root wrapped around Cillian's throat, threatening to squeeze tighter than it already was, Cillian staring desperately back at him.

"Let's not do anything rash, shall we? I would hate for your companion to pay the price of your decisions."

Bran slowly flattened his fingers against the ground, never looking away from Cillian's face. If it was just him, he'd use all the magic at his fingertips to fight, but he wouldn't risk Cillian's life.

"You should have stayed behind," Bran said in a cracked voice as the Fae approached.

Even with the root wrapped around his throat, Cillian always had to have the last word between them. "Never."

Bran closed his eyes, drew in a shuddering breath, and tried to remember everything his mother had ever taught him about bargaining with the Fae.

Chapter Ten

Cillian flexed his wrists against the root tied around them like rope, knowing better than to touch the one wrapped around his throat like a collar. The other end of it was held by the dressed-up Fae on horseback who'd run them down in the woods. The horse was going at a pace that forced Cillian to walk quickly if he didn't want to choke.

His backpack hung from the Fae's saddle along with Bran's. His rifle was slung over the Fae's shoulder, his only real weapon so close but completely out of reach, the same way Bran's knives were, hidden away in his backpack on the Fae's orders. The guard rode behind them, leading the third horse with their compatriot's body draped over it.

Bran could have maybe gotten them free if Cillian wasn't at risk of dying the instant he tried anything. Cillian looked to his left over the horse's rear at where Bran walked on the other side with his hands tied behind his back and the threat of Cillian's broken neck keeping him from casting any magic. A tree root from the forest was wrapped around his torso, the other end of it tying him to the saddle.

Even now, walking through a different world, a part of Cillian couldn't believe Bran was truly a witch with actual magic. But he'd seen things in the last day or so that defied explanation, and the only option he had was to immerse himself in denial or believe in myth and magic.

Believe in Bran.

His mother's warnings rang in the back of his head, but Cillian rather thought, between a witch and a Fae, the Fae were the deadlier threat right then. "All right?"

"Yeah," Bran muttered.

Something cut across his shoulder, leaving a vicious sting behind. Cillian flinched, shoulder rising against the hit, and looked up. The Fae lazily waved the riding crop at him, those dark brown eyes staring right at him. "Did I say you could speak?"

Cillian clenched his jaw and swallowed a retort. As bruised and aching as he felt, he'd seen the way Bran had cradled his ribs on the walk out of the forest. The last thing he wanted to do was annoy the Fae who held them captive and cause them to walk at a faster pace, hurting both of them. He settled instead for glaring at the Fae, who stared back with a curious look in his eyes that Cillian didn't trust at all.

"How strange to see you like this," the Fae mused before facing forward again.

Cillian shared a disbelieving, worried look with Bran. He didn't know why the Fae spoke so familiarly with him, but he didn't like it one bit. Bran squinted back at him, some of his dark hair falling across his hazel eyes as he shook his head in silent confusion. Cillian looked ahead again, wondering when they'd reach wherever the Fae seemed to be heading.

He kept half his attention on the Fae and the rest on the forest the road cut through. It was nothing like the one back home. The trees here were massive things, the leaves on them unfamiliar shapes. Even the smell of the place was different—heady and rich, nothing tainted with exhaust or garbage. And it was *quiet*. He hadn't realized how loud the forest back home was until he was here and the absence of cars and planes was impossible to miss. The only noise around them was the sluggish wind rustling the leaves, the horses' hooves clopping against the dirt road, and their own footsteps.

Cillian hadn't seen Jupiter since the forest. He hadn't dared ask Bran where she was, not wanting to put either of them in danger. He wanted to believe she was alive because Bran wouldn't have been able to hide his devastation if she wasn't.

Eventually, the trees on either side began to thin out. Cillian could see the way the land stretched into a wider horizon. The road led them to the top of a hill overlooking a vibrant valley below and more rolling hills and fields in the distance. Settled at the bottom was a town sprawled near a river whose waters reflected the late-afternoon sunlight. It was stunningly beautiful, a striking view of greens and blues that Cillian wouldn't mind staring at for hours if it was anywhere but here.

The ropelike root around his throat tightened, and he was yanked forward, the Fae smirking back at him. "Not much longer now. We are almost to his lordship."

Whoever this Fae lord was, Cillian didn't want to meet him. "What is this place?"

The Fae turned his horse to the side so he could look at Cillian without twisting in the saddle. He tapped the riding crop against his thigh in an absent manner, staring at Cillian with a focus that made him want to take a step back. But something told him to dig in his heels, so he did, refusing to cower.

"Does it not look familiar?" the Fae asked, seemingly fine with Cillian talking for the moment.

Cillian arched an eyebrow, trying to put as much condescension into his voice as possible. "Why would it?"

"This is Baile Átha Luain, my lord's rightful seat, granted to him by the largess of the Dagda who rules the Summer Court."

"That doesn't mean anything to me."

The Fae's eyes narrowed thoughtfully for a second before he turned his horse back down the road. "Keep up."

Cillian put one foot in front of the other as they walked into the valley, the sun past its zenith. It was almost too warm, and his tongue was sandpaper dry in his mouth by the time they reached the entrance of the town. The road abruptly became cobblestones at the town's edge, and Cillian nearly tripped from a misstep, the root pulling tight around his neck.

The guards on duty at what passed for a gate or checkpoint didn't stop them, but Cillian could feel their eyes on him as the group walked by. More and more looks were cast their way as they walked down a street in a town that seemed so human if one ignored the eerily beautiful Fae who called it home.

Cillian didn't see anything with an engine on their walk through the streets, nothing but horses, carriages, and wagons. They passed through an intersection that had one street cordoned off, filled with sellers hawking produce, meat and food, like a farmer's market he'd find back home. The smell of roasting meat made his stomach grumble, and he was reminded that the last thing he'd eaten was a single energy bar after leaving the cabin. He could do with food and a drink but wasn't sure either would be safe to accept.

Gradually, the buildings went from small wooden structures to more grandiose ones. Their little group finally turned down a dead-end street. Ahead was a high stone wall and a set of golden gates Cillian doubted were made out of wrought iron. Rising over both was a massive estate at least three stories tall, built like a Victorian mansion, with gabled roofs and a couple of towers. The wooden walls were painted a rich green with gold trim, and the vines climbing up the sides were real rather than a mural.

The two Fae guards on duty pushed open the golden gate, allowing them all to enter a forecourt dominated by a marble fountain that had a trio of wolves rising from the center, water pouring from their mouths in a steady burble. Rather than a lawn, what looked like rosebushes bloomed on either side of the cobbled drive, creating a wild garden of color. The scent was so strong Cillian had to fight back a sneeze, knowing it would hurt with the root still wrapped around his neck.

The Fae dismounted, handing the reins over to a servant who seemed to appear out of thin air. He wasn't as tall as the other Fae, and his cracked nut-brown skin reminded Cillian of tree bark. The horses were led away, but not before their captor untied the roots from his saddle, holding both like leashes.

With the horse no longer separating them, Cillian stepped closer to Bran, pressing their arms together. He felt the way Bran sagged for a moment, leaning against him, seeking out a single second of comfort before they were both yanked unceremoniously forward.

"My lord awaits," the Fae said.

The guard from the forest walked behind them, her compatriot's body taken somewhere else. Cillian didn't know how the Fae handled their dead, but he still hadn't quite processed the fact that he'd killed a man. A Fae. That he'd taken a life. It might have been in self-defense, but that didn't change the fact he'd pulled the trigger and the result was death.

They climbed a wide set of stairs to a shaded porch. A servant already had the double doors open for them, and they followed the Fae inside to a grand foyer. The floor underfoot was marble but a different pattern and shade than the white of the porch steps. The foyer marble was onyx shot through with veins of gold, easily reflecting the shine from the massive crystal chandelier overhead. What lit the chandelier wasn't candles but glittering light that floated in different-shaped glass that Cillian saw in every sconce and lamp they passed on their way through the mansion.

They passed several servants as they walked down hallways filled with paintings depicting a land Cillian had never seen before. Each servant paused to dip their heads at the Fae who held their rootlike chains, but Cillian couldn't quite shake the weight of their curious gazes when they stared at him.

Finally, they reached a gilded door the Fae pushed open without knocking. Cillian and Bran were pulled into a room that could have doubled as a small library despite it apparently being used as an office. Rather than a single story, it was two, with a spiral wooden staircase leading up to a mezzanine that wrapped around each wall and overlooked the main space below. The walls were lined with bookshelves that sat between arched windows overlooking a swath of greenery Cillian assumed was a garden of some sort.

Even as he took in the space, most of his attention was focused on the pair of Fae before them whom their captor bowed to—no, Cillian thought, just the lord, because that was who sat at the grand wooden desk carved with a motif of wolves. He wore a soft gray coat embroidered with violet thread that matched a waistcoat of the same color. His black hair was cut much shorter than their captor's, and there was a streak of white running through it at an angle. A faint scar cutting toward his left eye marred the otherwise perfection of his face.

The Fae lord was handsome in a way that would have made Cillian look more than twice at a bar or a club back home. Here, when those silver-colored eyes stared at him and widened fractionally, Cillian only wanted to look away.

The lady standing next to the Fae lord's ornate chair wore a peach-colored gown that paired well with the soft pink of her pinned-up hair, showing off her pointed ears capped in gold. She held an open book in her arms, one finger frozen on a page, staring at them with pale yellow eyes, her lips parted slightly in surprise.

The Fae lord set down his pen and stood. "Damarus?"

The Fae who'd caught them in the forest and dragged them to this town gestured with the hand that still held both roots. He spoke in English rather than the Fae's own language, and Cillian wondered about the reasoning behind letting him and Bran know what was being said. "Lord Ainmire. I found mortals in the forest during my ride."

The Fae lord's gaze never left Cillian's face. "Mortals."

"A witch and their companion."

Ainmire wrenched his gaze from Cillian to Bran, and Cillian had the sudden urge to step between the two of them. "A witch? And you didn't kill him?"

"There were extenuating circumstances, as you can see."

Again, the Fae lord's attention snapped back to Cillian, the lingering silence in the room suffocating. After a moment, he turned to the lady with him. "Leave us."

So maybe not his lady, but *a* lady, someone who worked for him, because she made no argument to the order, merely dipped into a shallow curtsy, set the book on the desk, and left the room in a gliding sweep of her skirts. The guard from the forest went with her, closing the door behind them both. The latch caught with a quiet click, the sound overly loud in the silence.

Ainmire finally came out from behind his desk, approaching where they stood in the middle of the room with slow, measured steps. Light caught on the golden wolf pin attached to the lapel of his coat, making it glint. He stopped directly in front of Cillian, studying him with an intensity that made his skin crawl. They were of the same height, and

Cillian raised his chin a fraction of an inch, ignoring all his discomfort, refusing to show weakness in front of the Fae lord.

Ainmire lifted one ungloved hand and wrapped his fingers around the knot that kept the root tied around Cillian's throat. The pressure made Cillian swallow reflexively, throat hurting from how dry it was. He was pulled closer, forced to move so he didn't choke. Ainmire stared at him for a long minute, not blinking, before he finally released the root, letting Cillian rock back onto his heels.

"You say you found them in the forest?" Ainmire asked.

"Well past the boundaries of where the wyrding has encroached in the past," Damarus said.

"They certainly stink of that place."

"Your friend here didn't want to stop somewhere and let us clean up first, so you'll have to deal with the smell like we have," Bran said.

"Be quiet," Cillian said warningly.

Too late. Bran speaking up meant Ainmire's attention turned to him, a smile curving at his lips that Cillian didn't like.

"You must be the witch," Ainmire said, moving to stand in front of Bran, a look in his eyes that made Cillian stiffen. "We Fae have a standing law to kill your kind."

"Same for us witches," Bran gritted out.

Ainmire gripped Bran's chin, forcing his head up. The Fae lord was taller than Bran and seemed intent on using that fact to try to intimidate him. Cillian could have told him it would get him nowhere. "Is that so?"

"Get your hands *off* him," Cillian growled. He managed a single step toward Ainmire when something came to rest against his back, over his spine, blade so sharp it cut through the fabric of his shirt with no pressure at all. When it cut into his skin, he froze, warm blood trickling down his back.

"None of that," Damarus said in a low, amused voice. "Not if you wish to keep his spine intact."

It took Cillian a moment to realize that Damarus wasn't speaking to him and hadn't seen him as a threat. That it was *Bran* who'd been the one to cause the Fae to act—Bran, who had magic glowing in his clenched fists tied behind his back, chin still caught in Ainmire's grip.

Bran's eyes flicked toward Cillian for a second before he let out a heavy breath and unclenched his fingers, his magic fading to nothing.

Ainmire smiled at Bran, eyes gone half-lidded, thumb moving to drag over Bran's bottom lip. Cillian wanted to rip his fingers away bone by bone. "Good choice, pet."

"*Fuck* you," Bran spat out.

"I don't fuck pets. Not until they are housebroken, at least. You tend to bite until then."

The flash of revolted horror that crossed Bran's face had Cillian ignoring the knife at his back in his need to put himself in front of Bran. Before he could even lift his foot off the floor, the root around his throat went tight, cutting off his air. He was reeled backward, a boot hitting the back of his knees, taking his legs out from beneath him. Cillian crashed to his knees; the only thing saving them from something worse than bruises was the plush rug covering the hardwood floor.

That knife which rent skin so easily kissed the side of his throat beneath the root. A stinging pain heralded a tiny trickle of blood sliding down to stain his T-shirt. The pressure in Cillian's lungs grew and grew until the root around his throat finally loosened. He drew in a ragged gasp, mouth and throat so terribly dry. Bran stared at him with wide eyes, still held in the Fae lord's grip.

Ainmire finally let Bran go, his attention back on Cillian, where Cillian preferred it to be. On his knees, Cillian had no choice but to tilt his head back to meet the Fae lord's eyes in that beautiful face. Unlike with Bran, Ainmire didn't touch him. "You care for this witch."

It was a statement, not a question. Cillian didn't respond.

Ainmire studied him with an intensity he couldn't turn from, not with the knife at his throat. "Such skin you wear."

"My lord?" Damarus asked. "Your orders?"

"Take him to the cells. He'll live for now."

"And the witch?"

"The witch stays with me."

"No," Cillian snarled, pressing forward despite the knife at his throat. Surprisingly, Damarus shifted his grip and didn't cut Cillian's throat with it.

"If we're prisoners, then I'm staying with him," Bran said.

Ainmire laughed, sounding cruelly amused as he turned toward Bran. "You speak as if you have a say in what happens. You will stay, witch, and you will obey like a good little pet, or your companion will die on my say-so, at my whim, whatever it may be."

The root drew tighter around Cillian's throat, and he gagged. Bran stared at him with such a bleak expression that Cillian wanted to tell him it was okay, to not worry, but he couldn't find breath to shape those words.

"Fine," Bran said desperately. "Just don't hurt him."

"Pets don't give orders. You will do well to learn that." Ainmire approached Bran again, divesting him of the roots with casual touches that dragged over Bran's body. Bran went rigid, and an icy knot of anger bloomed in Cillian's chest. "I will show you where he will stay and what will happen if you disobey."

Cillian didn't like the sound of that, but he wasn't in any position to protest. Damarus slid the knife away and hauled him back to his feet by way of the root wrapped around his throat. Cillian could do nothing but follow where it pulled, and it pulled him back through that eerily beautiful mansion and down into a circular underground room that smelled of blood.

Six cells surrounded a center space cluttered with all manner of instruments and devices Cillian refused to let his mind linger on. Damarus led him to the third cell, and while the first one was empty, the second one was not. Cillian only got a brief glimpse of someone huddled in the corner, tucked as small as their body would allow, before the root around his neck and wrists was sliced clean through by that dangerously sharp knife Damarus wielded. Then, he was shoved rather unceremoniously into the cell.

Alone.

He caught himself before he fell, turning around and throwing himself at the bars as the door clanged shut. Cillian banged his fist against one of the bars, hand aching from the blow. "Let me out."

Ainmire only smiled at him. "I take no orders from you."

Cillian wrenched his gaze to where Bran stood, hands clenched into fists and face far too pale beneath the dirt and grime from their passage through the wyrding. "Are you all right?"

Ainmire stepped between them before he could answer, blocking Bran from Cillian's sight. He was apparently unconcerned with Cillian's desire for murder right about then. "Truly, you are a sight to behold. Such joy it brings me to see you like this."

Cillian wished the bars he was clutching so tightly were the Fae lord's neck. "Don't you dare hurt him."

"He only comes to harm if you try anything. The same rules apply to the witch. You are each other's salvation or damnation, so choose your path wisely, Cillian."

Ainmire turned from him and left the way they'd come, Bran following after him at the point of Damarus' knife. Bran looked back at Cillian with wild eyes as he was forced out of a room that was more in line with a dungeon.

"Hey!" Cillian shouted, trying to shake the cell bars loose in his fury, but they wouldn't budge. "*Hey*! Bring him back!"

The door closed behind Damarus with a squeak of hinges, and Cillian swore, slamming his fist against the bar once more. He shoved himself away from the cell door and had to flail his arms as his feet suddenly skated over something smooth and slick, providing no traction to his hiking boots. He looked down at the dirt floor, staring at the patch of cracked blue-white ice that covered the ground where he stood, the jagged edges of it extending farther into the cell, some of it crawling up the walls.

His breath came out in soft white puffs, the air in the basement suddenly exponentially chillier. Cillian carefully stepped off the ice in favor of solid dirt, cold in a way he rarely was, as he realized that no one had told Ainmire his name upon their arrival.

But the Fae lord had known it.

Chapter Eleven

Bran's fingers itched to draw a witchmark, but the memory of Cillian's face behind a cell door was burned into his mind. He let his magic lie fallow in this place for Cillian's sake. For now. He needed to find a way to free them both so they could locate Aisling, and the only way to do that would be to pry information out of the Fae lord. Bran wasn't looking forward to that, not after the way Ainmire had looked at him.

Had touched him.

Bran suppressed a shiver as they returned to the library, the elegant space exactly as they had left it. He was acutely aware of Damarus behind him, with that knife that had barely touched Cillian's skin and drawn blood. His own knives were in his backpack, and he had no idea where it'd been taken. The only thing with them from the mortal world was Cillian's rifle still slung over Damarus' shoulder, but he knew trying to take it back would result in Cillian being harmed, so he didn't even try.

Ainmire made a lazy gesture with his hand in midair, and a cut-crystal glass dropped into it, amber liquid sloshing against the edges. He turned around and leaned against his desk in a way Bran would find seductive in anyone else, but there was nothing about this Fae lord that Bran would ever trust. Not his looks, not his magic, not his words, and most definitely not his intentions.

Damarus stood some feet away, his knife nowhere to be seen. Bran was under no illusion the knife wouldn't make a reappearance if he tried anything, but the threat of Cillian coming to harm was enough to keep his fingers still. Bran stood before Ainmire, meeting those silver eyes with a bravado that tasted a little like fear in the back of his throat. He hoped Ainmire couldn't smell it.

"It has been some time since witches have come through the wyrding," Ainmire said. "Why are you here?"

Bran bit his tongue and refused to speak, defiantly keeping quiet as he stared at the Fae lord. Something like amusement flickered across that too-handsome face as Ainmire sipped his drink. Then, he set it down on his desk and walked toward Bran, who couldn't help the half step back he took. Belatedly, he steeled himself and kept his feet planted where they were.

Ainmire's gaze flicked up and down Bran's body in a way he didn't like. He'd been checked out plenty of times by guys in bars back in Boston, but the look in Ainmire's silver eyes wasn't enjoyable at all. "Did you come as part of an incursion?"

Bran stayed stubbornly silent, but his defense crumbled at Ainmire's next words.

"You will answer me, or I will have Damarus practice his knife-work on your friend's skin."

Bran swallowed thickly, wishing he had water, anything to wash away the dryness in his mouth. "No incursion. It's just us."

"Hm." Those warm fingers curled around his chin like before, the touch firm, forcing his head up in a way that made it impossible to look anywhere but at Ainmire's face. "You do not lie."

He made it a statement, and Bran wondered how he knew. But then, words had always been the purview of the Fae.

Ainmire studied him with unblinking eyes. "Your name, witch. You will give it to me, and you will not lie, for I will know if you do. If you refuse, your friend will pay the price of your silence."

Bran flinched, the fingers on his chin tightening. Ainmire wanted the one thing they weren't supposed to ever give willingly to the Fae, what witches were taught to never give up if only to save their minds. A Fae knowing their true name gave the Fae power over a mortal, witch or not.

His one consolation was the handful of iron beads on his bracelet that provided some semblance of protection against a Fae's power when it came to mental control. Magic kept the iron hidden, the spell so diffused it shouldn't be noticed. Iron was the Fae's weakness, and while they might have his knives, they hadn't taken his bracelet.

Yet.

He hoped Cillian still had his iron on him as well.

And Cillian was the reason he would give up his name.

"Bran."

Ainmire hummed thoughtfully, stroking his thumb over Bran's cheek, the touch far too intimate for his liking. "We Fae do revere our ravens."

Bran tried to jerk free, but Ainmire only tightened his grip. "I'm not yours to do anything with."

"That is where you are wrong, pet."

"I'm not your *pet*."

Ainmire's smirk deepened into something wholly unsettling. "You will learn otherwise. You mortals always do, especially you witches."

Bran didn't like the sound of that at all. "I thought you said you had a law to kill us on sight?"

"Would you like me to?" Ainmire forced Bran's head up before sliding his hand down to fit it around Bran's throat. "Perhaps I should crush your throat, or perhaps I should give you to Damarus to play with. My right hand is never kind with his pets and treats them rather poorly."

"I get my enjoyment from them," Damarus drawled.

Ainmire let go of Bran's throat in favor of gripping his wrist, lifting it to better study the tattoo on his forearm. Ainmire ran the fingers of his other hand over the design, tracing out the witchmarks in the trees with unerring fingertips. Bran felt like little more than cattle in that moment, poked and prodded for someone else's enjoyment.

He tried to pull his arm free, but Ainmire tightened his grip until the bones grated together. Bran grimaced as he was yanked forward, right up against Ainmire's body. His arm was drawn between them at an angle, Ainmire's other hand sliding through his dirty hair and getting a firm grip, holding him in place. Bran froze, breathing raggedly as Ainmire bent his head and dragged his lips over Bran's cheek to his mouth, hovering over it.

"Or perhaps I take my fun some other way," Ainmire murmured, the heated intent in his eyes something Bran couldn't look away from.

"No," he ground out, heart beating painfully fast, terror locking every joint in his body.

"That isn't a word pets are allowed to say." Ainmire turned his head, mouth moving to Bran's ear, his deep voice a rumble that sent an unwanted shiver down Bran's spine. "But it's so much more satisfying when your kind yields because I made you want to rather than to simply take. A challenge, you see. Such things amuse me so, and I think you will amuse me greatly, *pet*, if only for the hurt you can impart."

Bran wasn't prepared to be shoved away with a strength that sent him sprawling to the floor. He rolled to one elbow, staring up at Ainmire, stomach roiling from the Fae lord's words. Ainmire rubbed his fingers together, glancing down at whatever muck was on them now from touching Bran's dirty face. "Damarus."

"Yes, my lord?" the other Fae replied.

"See that he is washed and appropriately attired. He will have the evening meal with me."

"I'd rather be put in a cell," Bran said.

Ainmire laughed lightly, no amusement in his voice, in his eyes. "If you wish your friend to eat, then you will dine with me."

And Bran could do nothing but obey as much as he didn't want to. Cillian's safety was worth picking himself up off that rug and leaving the office under Damarus' sharp eyes. His fingers twitched with the need to cast a witchmark, but Bran didn't think about any of the ones that could help him. He let the intent die in his thoughts so that Cillian might live as Damarus led him to a tiled bathing room with a clawed tub and several Fae servants waiting for them.

"His lordship wants the pet cleaned up for the evening meal,"

Damarus said. The servants bowed their heads in understanding before bustling about the space to start the water. The room was lit by a glass globe overhead, sparkling light giving off illumination. Damarus turned toward Bran, arching an eyebrow. "Strip."

"Are you going to watch?" Bran asked warily.

Damarus' smile was a cruel curve. "Pets aren't left alone until they are housebroken."

Bran tried not to think about how mortals were treated in the Otherworld. Every use of *pet* was hinting at a life he wanted no part of and wasn't going to stay in. More and more, his coven's belief that the Fae were dangerous and cruel was hardening his heart with every second that passed. Bran turned his head and looked at the tub, now filling with warm water from a copper spigot, the servants eyeing him expectantly.

It's like the gym.

If the gym was full of people who didn't have the manners to look away.

Bran steeled himself and got undressed. He tried not to think about the eyes on him, focusing on a point on the blue-tiled walls instead. When his clothes were a pile next to his hiking boots, the servants gestured for him to get into the tub, and he went because he had no choice.

The water wasn't scalding, but it definitely was warmer than he preferred, making him hiss a little. He thought he'd get to wash himself, but the servants approached with soap and oil and cloths. He jerked his arm away from the first servant who reached for him but froze as Damarus' voice echoed in the bathing room.

"Let them wash you," Damarus said.

He said nothing else, the command clear in his tone, in his gaze when Bran chanced meeting it for a second. The Fae leaned against the tiled wall, arms crossed over his chest as he watched the proceedings with a slightly bored expression. At least it didn't look like he was getting off on the situation, but Bran would have preferred privacy over being made to feel like a child.

Or a pet.

He had no choice but to let the servants scrub him clean of the dirt and grime accumulated from trekking through a forest and dragging himself through the wyrding. Every time a sponge ran over his sore ribs, he winced. Bran made sure his bracelet didn't come into contact with any Fae's skin. The water in the tub became dirty, and he was made to stand so clean water could be poured over him by copper pitchers filled from the spigot until the Fae were satisfied he was clean.

He stood there beneath Damarus' gaze as the servants went about drying and clothing him in an outfit that was several centuries out of date from where he came from. The pants, buttoned-up shirt, and coat weren't as elaborately embroidered as Damarus', but neither were they the servants' drab clothing.

When the servants finally stepped aside, Damarus came forward, circling Bran like one would circle an animal for sale. The Fae reached out and adjusted the way the coat sat on his shoulders, poking and prodding until he was satisfied with the job the servants had done.

"Acceptable," Damarus said, turning on his heel. "For a pet. Follow me."

Bran had no choice but to obey, not if he wanted to keep Cillian safe. Not knowing what was happening in the cells left him to fill in the horrors of it on his own, his stomach roiling into knots. A faint tug on his bond with Jupiter came away with a vast silence of a kind he'd never felt before in all the years she'd been his familiar. She wasn't dead, only —far away. Bran didn't know if it was this place messing with their connection or something else, but her absence left him adrift in his mind when he couldn't afford to be distracted.

Damarus led him through the mansion with the expectation that Bran wouldn't try to kill him by way of magic. Funny how Bran wore no chains and yet was so incredibly bound.

He was taken to a drawing room on the first floor, where Damarus left him under the watchful eyes of the surviving guard from the forest for several hours. Sitting in silence, with only his thoughts for company as he watched the late-afternoon sunlight darken to twilight through a window, left him feeling anxious and out of his depth.

Damarus returned for him when the sun had fully set, and Bran's stomach felt as if it was trying to eat his spine. The Fae had changed clothes from the outfit he'd worn for his ride in the forest into a court suit of maroon satin. "Did the pet act out? Cast any magic? Soil the carpet?"

"I'm not a pet," Bran snapped.

"No," the guard replied, answering Damarus as if Bran hadn't even spoken.

"A pity. I'd be well within my rights to cut him if he had." Damarus gestured at Bran with a bored expression on his face. "My lord is ready for you now. But do tell me if you've decided to deny him your company."

"If it gets my friend and me fed, I'll sit at the table," Bran said, slowly rising to his feet.

"I know your companion's name. Refusing to speak it won't remove it from my tongue."

"How do you even know English?"

Damarus waved aside the question, as if it were beneath him. "Come with me."

Damarus led him out of the drawing room and to what felt like the other side of the mansion. They passed more servants on the way there, none of whom looked twice at Bran even as he stared at them. Most of them were Fae, but there was one who made Bran do a double-take and nearly miss a step because that was a *human* with rounded ears in a silver collar inlaid with tiny emeralds. Her black skirt fell to her ankles, and the wide corset belt she wore without a blouse put her bare breasts on display. Her hair was twisted into a knot at the base of her skull, so it was easy to see that the lacings of the corset were threaded through small silver hoops pierced through her skin and running the length of her spine.

Bran slowed his pace long enough to watch the human servant draw a witchmark and cast it into the empty glass sphere of a sconce. Magic flared brightly for an instant before falling into sparks that shimmered as they danced in the air. The witch who was a servant never acknowledged his presence, but that didn't stop Bran from turning on his feet, trying to engage with her. "Hey—"

Damarus grabbed him by the arm, the Fae's silkily amused voice filling his ear. "Pets know better than to get distracted from their work."

Bran tried to wrench free, but Damarus was stronger than him. "She's a *witch*. What did you do to her?"

Because no witch would willingly support the Fae like this. It had to be a trick—maybe it was a Fae glamoured to look like a mortal—but even as Bran desperately tried to think of a reason for that witch's existence here in the Otherworld, he knew it was a lie. Witchmarks were used solely by witches. The Fae didn't cast magic that way. Bile crept up Bran's throat as he realized whoever that witch was, they'd been broken and changed into this blank-eyed servant using their magic for the Fae's pleasure.

A *pet*.

Damarus hauled him around and dragged him the last bit of the hallway to the closed door at the end. Damarus opened it, leading Bran into a large dining room meant for grand parties, not the three place settings taking up space at the end of a long mahogany table. Grand paintings of beautiful Fae in all manner of dress and locations hung from the wooden wall on his left. A huge mirror was set over a long fireplace that wasn't lit, while chandeliers with those odd glass globes of illumination lined the ceiling. The wall to his right held windows instead of paintings, the curtains drawn shut for the evening meal.

"The witch is displeased with the tasks you give your pets, my lord," Damarus said as he shoved Bran toward the table.

"Is he now?" Ainmire replied, staring at Bran from the head of the table. The Fae lord wore in an all-black ensemble that should have made him appear washed out but didn't. The coat was tailored to emphasize the breadth of his shoulders. A gold ring with a large cabochon emerald was his only piece of jewelry. He looked powerful and alluring seated there, and some part of Bran was fascinated by Ainmire's unreal beauty.

The rest of him wanted to stab the Fae lord in the face.

"I thought you killed witches?" Bran asked through clenched teeth.

Ainmire arched an eyebrow. "Would you like me to kill you?"

Bran chose silence over answering, letting Damarus prod him into the empty seat to Ainmire's left. Both Fae seemed amused at his reluctance to open his mouth. Bran fisted his hands on his lap and stared at his gold-edged empty plate, water and wineglasses filled but no food on the table yet. That changed the moment Damarus took his seat. A different door was opened, and a line of servants entered, each carrying a serving dish.

A roast was set down first, with other dishes arrayed around it: glazed carrots, roasted potatoes, fresh bread, half a dozen different sauces, and a tureen filled with a cold soup in deference to the summer day that had ended. Bran's stomach growled at the smell that wafted up from the dishes as they were set on the table. Damarus chuckled at him, and Bran tried to ignore the flush that came to his face. He wouldn't apologize for being hungry when the Fae were the reason for it.

"I wonder," Damarus mused. "Do you believe in those silly stories that you mortals can't leave the Otherworld if you eat or drink our food?"

Bran's gaze snapped up at the question, flicking between the two Fae. "And if I do?"

Damarus' smile was as sharp as his knife. "Then I suppose you will never leave."

Bran watched the servants fill all their plates and bowls with servings of the food. Ainmire and Damarus began to eat after the servants stepped away from the table and retreated from the dining room, giving them privacy. Bran still hesitated, but it was the thought of Cillian going without that forced him to pick up the silver fork and knife to cut his slice of the roast into bite-sized pieces. He was starving, but he ate at a regular pace, savoring the taste of everything and hating that he liked it. Bran didn't want to like anything in the Otherworld, especially not something given by a Fae lord who kept calling him *pet*.

He ate what was on his plate, hoping none of it would trap him in any way, and didn't reach for seconds. He ignored the wineglass in favor of water. It tasted clean, and he finished the entire glass in a couple of swallows. When he set it down, he found Ainmire studying him in a way Bran didn't care for.

"I have questions that you will answer," Ainmire said.

"And if I don't?" Bran asked carefully.

Ainmire smiled slightly, as if he were amused by Bran's pushback. "Then I take it out of Cillian's skin."

Bran wondered if he'd be able to fight against a Fae lord and win, but even as he thought about the odds, he knew they wouldn't favor him. Bran was a strong witch, and his skill lay in the casting of witch-marks and building up intricate spells, but the more powerful spells were written in his coven's grimoire, and it was missing. Of the hundreds of witchmarks he'd memorized over the years, none could save them unless he first got Cillian out of what passed as a dungeon in a place like this.

Bran leaned back in his chair, putting his hands on his lap so he'd be less likely to give away his true feelings. He glanced at Damarus, who seemed as interested as Ainmire, but made no attempt to speak, leaving the interrogation to the Fae lord. And that's what this was—a deadly game of words.

"I had my guard check my borders for other witches. They found no sign of anyone else who might have crossed through the wyrding, but that does not mean more won't yet come. So tell me, who might try to rescue you?" Ainmire asked.

Despair was bitter in his mouth. "No one."

"Try again. A truthful answer and your friend will be given bedding for tonight. It gets cold below."

The funny thing was Cillian had never felt bothered by the cold when they were growing up. Bran wasn't sure if that was the case now, though if it was, the Fae lord's offer was a useless one. But Bran would bargain for Cillian's care and comfort before he'd ever bargain for himself. "I'm the last of my coven because you sent the lights to kill my mother."

He spat the words out, wishing they were bullets that might pierce Ainmire's heart and kill him the same way they had killed a part of Bran. The grief was still too raw, too new, for him to choke back behind an emotionless wall of stoicism. Bran didn't meet anyone's eyes, glaring instead at the detritus of food on his plate.

"I have sent none of my people to foray into the mortal world with the lights to lead the way."

Bran snorted his disbelief, picking through the statement. "Sure."

Someone *had*, but Bran wasn't going to give up the fact they had walked into the Shoppe and walked out with his little sister. The less he gave up, the more he'd get to keep.

"You are free with your words." Ainmire shifted on his chair, and

Bran flinched when fingers curled over his chin and forced his head up. He had no choice but to look at the Fae lord, fingernails digging into the palms of his hands as he met that dangerous gaze. "But I rule here, by the grace of the Dagda, and I'll rule more than the lands given to my House centuries ago when I bring Cillian to our king. You would do well to remember that."

Bran felt as if he'd been doused in ice water. "What do you mean?"

Ainmire smiled, nothing kind in his eyes. "Consider him a tithe, if you will. Another pet to add to the Dagda's collection who serve at the pleasure of the Summer Court."

Bran wrenched himself free of Ainmire's grip, leaning away. "Like the witch in the hall? How does she serve you?"

"However I like. She knows her place and bows to me gladly. You will learn yours."

The words *I'd rather die* were on the tip of his tongue, but Bran choked them back. "And what happens if I never do?"

"Then your bones will find a place in my mother's garden. Eventually." Ainmire settled back in his chair, and Damarus poured him another glass of wine. He never took his eyes off Bran. "One witch and a surprise, but no incursion that my people can find. Why did you come?"

"We got lost."

"A lie. You witches guard your forests the way a wild cat guards her kittens. You know those paths better than the mortals who no longer believe in your kind."

The truth in that statement made Bran swallow. "The same way they no longer believe in you?"

"You don't know your history."

"I know you Fae are the enemy and always have been. I know you want our world, and we'll never let you have it."

Ainmire laughed, low and rough, before getting to his feet. "Your world *was* ours. And it will belong to us once more in due time."

He reached for the table, coming up with a flat, square-shaped wooden box that hadn't been there at all during dinner. Bran tensed as Ainmire opened it and pulled out a metal collar. A silver crest with embossed wolves was set onto the front of it, bracketed by a cluster of tiny emeralds. Bran was on his feet in an instant, nearly knocking over his chair. "*No.* I won't wear that."

Ainmire smiled icily as he came toward Bran. "Do you think a witch can have permission to walk around without being claimed? Without being *owned*?"

"I did what you told me to."

"Do you think I trust your intent? You will wear the collar, or Cillian will suffer in your place. What will it be, witch?"

Panic clawed at his mind as his eyes locked on the collar held in Ainmire's hands. He didn't want to wear it—absolutely *did not* want to become what that other imprisoned witch had been broken down into —but he couldn't be defiant if it meant Cillian was hurt or worse. He dragged his gaze up to meet Ainmire's eyes, hating how the Fae lord smirked at him with such dark intent. Swallowing, Bran could only nod.

"Good choice, pet," Ainmire said in that silky voice of his.

Bran still took a half step back before steeling himself for the inevitable. Ainmire opened the collar, the tiny hinge making no sound as he fit it around Bran's neck. The metal was cold, the fit disquietingly perfect. The snap of the lock clicking into place rang loudly in his ears.

Ainmire touched his fingers to Bran's chin, forcing his head up. "You look better like this."

Magic sparked over his emerald ring, and the collar grew warm. Between one breath and the next, a barrier cut Bran off from Nature and seemed to suffocate him, emptying his lungs. Bran reached for the collar, gasping for air as he stumbled away from Ainmire, nearly falling over the chair. His fingers touched the collar, and an electric shock jolted from his fingertips all the way up his arms. He cried out and yanked his hands away, crashing to his knees. He pressed a hand to his chest, clawing at the shirt because he couldn't claw at the collar.

Shiny black boots walked into his vision, but he barely paid any attention to them. All his focus was on the way his magic felt tangled and out of reach, Nature missing from his fingertips, an emptiness inside him that hadn't ever been there before. Then a hand settled on his head, fingers gripping his hair tight. Bran had no choice but to look up at Ainmire's face, hating the satisfied glint in the Fae lord's eyes. "You will learn your place. Your kind always do. Damarus?"

"My lord?" Damarus replied.

"See the witch to his room."

"I'd rather have a cell," Bran croaked out, the collar around his throat impossible to ignore, but he refused to cower, even if that was all he wanted to do in that moment.

"Your room locks, and I hold the key, so consider your wish granted."

"And Cillian? You'll give him a meal like you promised? Something cooked and not rotten?" He went for specificity because he could see the way his words could be bent when the promise had been to just feed Cillian.

Ainmire seemed to find his attempts to navigate their dance of words amusing. "A meal will be brought to Cillian, as promised. If you want him fed in the morning, you will join me for breakfast."

Bran wanted to do anything but that, except he had no choice. "I want to see him."

"You may earn a visit if you behave."

Bran hated the cruelly amused look in the Fae lord's eye as he dangled the choice like bait between them. There was nothing Bran could say to him that wouldn't make his and Cillian's predicament worse.

Ainmire let him go, and Bran got dazedly to his feet. Damarus escorted Bran out of the dining room and back down the long hallway, to a small room on the first floor that didn't look like the cell it was until he stepped inside it. The door shut and locked behind him, leaving him alone without magic for the first time in his entire life. It wasn't gone—just out of reach. Muffled. Impossible to touch.

Living without it would drive him mad.

Bran stumbled toward the window, wanting fresh air, and found it wouldn't open. He banged his fist on the glass, yanking his hand back with a hiss when fluid lines curled across the pane, magic in their shape. He stared at it, hand throbbing from the fiery shock he'd experienced at the touch.

It was a witchmark, one meant to contain.

Placed there, most likely, by a witch on behalf of the Fae.

Shaking his head, Bran sank down against the wall beneath the window, gripping his hair and giving it a hard yank. The momentary pain helped him focus, to get himself centered again, but the fear didn't leave him. He curled a hand over one shoulder, breathing raggedly, hyperaware of how close his fingers got to the collar.

If this was how Ainmire and other Fae controlled witches, Bran could see the appeal of promising anything so they could feel their magic again.

Bran silently promised himself he wouldn't ever bargain like that.

It was going to take everything he had to keep it.

Cillian lifted his head at the sound of the door to the dungeon opening. He pushed himself to his feet, wincing at the stiffness in his body as the blanket he'd been given by a guard slid to the ground. He hurried to the cell door, glancing at the dirt floor, relieved to see the ice was gone. Whatever magic was in the cell, it existed to make his stay uncomfortable.

The fear that had kept him company all last night disappeared when he saw Bran step through the dungeon's door with a tray of food in his hands, escorted by Damarus. Bran hurried over to him, and Cillian did a double take at his appearance.

"What the hell is around your throat?" he growled. "And why are you wearing that outfit?"

Bran wasn't wearing the clothes he'd hiked in through the forest but the same sort of courtly outfit Damarus was in, only less bright and ornate. It looked like he was playing dress-up for a Renaissance Faire. But it was the collar wrapped around Bran's throat that had Cillian clutching the cell bars with a fury that made him wish he could punch something. He didn't like it and wanted to rip it off.

"What does it look like? I have to take my meals with the Fae lord so you get to eat," Bran said tiredly, making a face. "There's no accounting for taste when it comes to clothes, but the food is decent. Did you get dinner last night?"

"Yes." The bread and thin soup had arrived at some point last night, pushed through the narrow food delivery door in the cell by a bored-looking guard. He hadn't eaten it, and when he'd woken up after a fitful doze, the tray had disappeared.

"Good. I asked to bring you breakfast so I could see you." Bran stepped up to the cell door, his eyes searching Cillian's face. "Are you all right?"

"I feel like I should be asking you that. You're the one having to deal with the Fae."

Bran grimaced. "You're the one stuck down here. I have to keep you safe somehow."

Cillian shook his head. "You don't have to do that."

He didn't say that Bran should find a way to leave, even if it meant abandoning Cillian, because they'd come here to find Aisling. Cillian couldn't stand the thought of her trapped in the wyrding, hunted by the lights.

"I won't leave you behind."

He hadn't in the forest before the lights found them, and Cillian knew he wouldn't now. Which meant they had to find some way to get him out of this cell so that Bran would have a chance to escape. Cillian just didn't know how.

"You saw him. We're leaving," Damarus said.

Bran gave Cillian an apologetic look as he knelt to place the tray on the ground. He undid the latch on the flap and lifted it so he could slide the tray inside. Cillian knelt, wanting to reach for Bran's hand, but Damarus' attention made him reach for the tray of food instead. Cillian stared through the bars at Bran's pale face, the worry in his eyes making Cillian ache a little for being the reason it was there.

"I'm okay," he said in a low voice. What he meant was *I'll be okay if you leave*.

Bran shook his head and stood. "Eat. Is there anything else you need?"

"I don't want you selling off pieces of yourself for me."

"That isn't what I said."

Cillian picked up the tray and stood, still staring at Bran. "Just don't. Not for me."

Bran didn't respond, but the stubborn set to his jaw was familiar, even all these years later. It made something warm settle in Cillian's chest, and it was that warmth that kept him company after Bran and Damarus left. What passed for breakfast was a savory kind of porridge and dry toast, with a glass of water that Cillian sipped at rather than finish in gulps. He wasn't sure how many meals Bran would be able to bargain for, and at least water kept better than food.

Cillian retrieved the blanket and folded it up, using it to sit on at a spot close to the bars of his cell. The person locked up in the other one hadn't answered his attempts at conversation last night, and they still didn't when he tried to get their attention. He didn't know if it was due to them not knowing his language or fear or maybe a combination of both. Sitting in a cell by himself with nothing to do left him bored and anxious, wondering what Bran was being put through for the sake of making sure Cillian didn't starve.

It was difficult to track hours in that dimly lit space with no windows to see out of. He'd learned last night that his watch didn't work, probably hadn't since they'd gone through the wyrding. The battery had died, and it was useless now. There was little else for him to do but sit and wait, a task that made his skin crawl in a way he didn't like. Cillian wasn't one who got anxious all that often, but sitting there, in a different world, after having been chased by monsters through the forest and knowing that magic was real and so were the Fae, it was little wonder he started to spiral.

Bran didn't come that night, or what Cillian assumed was the night, but he received a tray of food that consisted of meat baked into a flaky pie and another glass of water. The spices were different yet familiar at the same time, as if the herbs used were a cousin plant rather than the ones he used when cooking. As before, the tray disappeared when he slept, no matter where he left it. Cillian never heard who came into his cell to retrieve it—whether it was the guard or some other Fae—and their ability to move without waking him was disconcerting.

Bran came the next day with the lunch tray rather than breakfast, dressed in a different ridiculous outfit and looking a little wild-eyed in a way that Cillian didn't like. Damarus escorted him again, the Fae avidly watching them.

Cillian stepped up to the bars but didn't touch them. "What's wrong?"

"Besides the obvious?" Bran asked.

"What are you giving up?"

"Nothing I'm not prepared to offer."

Cillian scowled, not wanting to argue in the precious few minutes they got to see each other, but neither did he want Bran to keep doing anything stupid. "I already told you to stop."

"And I don't want you to starve if I can help it. So just—take the food and eat it. Please."

"Then tell me what's going on. Are you okay?"

Bran let out a harsh breath, face screwing up in a tired, scared expression that Damarus couldn't see, not with his back to the Fae. "The collar blocks my magic. It's taking some getting used to."

Cillian didn't know anything about how Bran's magic worked, but if the stress he carried in the tense lines of his body was caused by not being able to use it, then Cillian wanted him out of that collar. "You don't need to get used to it."

Bran shook his head and set the tray on the ground before opening the metal flap to slide it into the cell. "I won't leave you here."

Cillian knelt, reaching for Bran's hand because it had been days since he'd last been close to the other man. He didn't care if Damarus saw them; all that mattered was the desperate grip of Bran's hand in his over the food Bran had bargained who knew what to give him. "I wouldn't blame you if you did."

Bran scowled at him, some hint of anger burning through the fear in his eyes. "Shut up. I'll see you tomorrow."

Cillian had to force himself to let Bran go, the loss of touch an ugly feeling that settled in his skin in a way that left him desperate for company he wouldn't get outside these brief moments. They both stood after the tray flap was locked again, looking at each other through the cell bars.

"He's been fed. It's time to go," Damarus said.

Cillian glanced at the Fae, frowning slightly at the contemplative look on his face. Cillian wasn't sure what to make of that focus, but it didn't matter once Bran stepped away from the cell, the other man schooling his expression into something not so emotional.

They left, and Cillian ate his meal because not doing so would be a slap in the face to Bran's efforts. The quiet got to him after a while, like it always did. To fill it, he hummed the tune of a lullaby his mother used to sing him as a boy. He couldn't quite remember the words, but the thought of her, somewhere on her cruise, alive and well, was a comfort to him.

Cillian got lunch that day, which meant he probably wouldn't get dinner, so he set aside the bread for later and ate the potatoes mixed with greens. He'd received two meals a day, at different intervals, with no way to know what time of day it could be based on what was on his plate.

What must have been hours after Bran's visit, Damarus returned, this time alone. The Fae approached the cell door with a smile on his face Cillian didn't trust.

"Get up," Damarus said. "My lord wishes to see you."

Cillian slowly picked himself off the ground, aware of the grime on his clothes and skin still and the faint scent of urine he refused to be embarrassed about. There wasn't anything resembling a toilet in the cell, and he'd been making do as best he could with a corner and scraps of his T-shirt.

"Why?" Cillian asked.

Damarus stepped up to the cell door, staring at him through the bars with curious eyes. "You truly do not know, do you?"

"Know what?" Damarus didn't answer, but the smile that came to his face stayed there as he unlocked the cell door and gestured for Cillian to step out. Cillian exited warily, keeping all his attention on the Fae. "Where's Bran?"

"You do not need to worry about the pet."

"Don't call him that."

"Your concern for a mortal is new and amusing, especially when that mortal is a witch." Damarus pointed at the door. "Walk. I won't keep my lord waiting."

Cillian headed for the door as ordered, Damarus right on his heels.

It was the first time out of his cell and that dungeon in days, and coming above into a brightly lit hallway had him squinting and ducking his head, eyes watering from the light.

"This way," Damarus said, taking the lead. The casual way he treated Cillian—as if he wasn't a threat—grated, but Cillian didn't know what he could do to fight the Fae. His rifle was gone, and he didn't have magic. All he had were his wits, and even then, he wasn't sure he could match them with the Fae.

Damarus took him to that same library as before, pushing open the door and waving him inside. "My Lord of Flames and Wolves, I bring your prize, as requested."

The title given to Ainmire had Cillian staring across the library at the Fae lord. Like Damarus, Ainmire wore a richly embroidered courtly outfit, the clothes pristine, making Cillian mindful of his own filthy state. He refused to be embarrassed by his appearance, though, not when the Fae were the cause of it.

"Bring him here," Ainmire said.

He wasn't sitting behind his desk this time, but standing by a long wooden table on one side of the library. Damarus arched an eyebrow at Cillian, who reluctantly walked toward the table, trying to stifle the curl of fear and unease settling in his gut. "Where's Bran?"

"You don't rule here. Demands such as that aren't yours to make," Ainmire said without looking up from the items he perused.

"I don't care. Where is he?"

"He's been with me. I took him on a stroll through town today. You weren't missed."

Damarus stood behind Cillian, and he swore he could feel the edge of that Fae's knife against his back again, even though it wasn't there. The cuts from before had scabbed over and thankfully were not deep enough to become infected while he sat in the cold cell.

Cillian glanced down at the table, frowning at what was laid out across the shiny cherry-red wood. The Fae had emptied everything from his and Bran's backpacks, spreading out their supplies. Bran's curved railroad spike knives were carefully laid out with fabric wrapped around the iron hilts. Cillian's rifle lay across the table as well, ammunition lined up near it. Cillian's fingers twitched as he thought about grabbing it, but he knew he wouldn't succeed. He'd seen how fast the Fae could move, and they'd stop him before he could even touch it.

Ainmire picked up the jar containing the healing ointment Cillian used with one gloved hand, turning it over in his fingers. He unscrewed it and took a quick sniff before turning to meet Cillian's gaze. Ainmire didn't speak for a few moments, and Cillian defiantly held his gaze, refusing to look away.

"This is a curious balm for you to have in your possession," Ainmire finally said.

"Why?" Cillian asked.

Ainmire smiled slightly, still holding the small jar. "Our healers make something quite similar."

"I doubt that."

"Do you? Witches know what iron does to us. It has long been their weapon of choice when they murder us."

Cillian thought of Ray's torn-up body and Juliana's damaged home he'd helped clean up, of Aisling's terror-stricken face when he'd found her in the forest. "You harm them first."

"They started this war between us when they forced us out of Éire and stole what belonged to us. Such a betrayal has never been forgotten or forgiven by our kind. And yet, here you are, caring about a witch when you shouldn't."

"I trust Bran more than I'll ever trust you."

Ainmire laughed, shaking his head as he set the jar down and reached for one of Bran's knives with his gloved hand. He held it up, and Cillian had to remind himself not to step back, not to show fear. If he was going to die, then he'd die, and at least his death would free Bran from the bargains he was making.

"How strange to hear those words out of your mouth." Ainmire studied the iron blade with narrowed eyes. "I wonder if this will burn you."

Cillian licked his lips. "It won't."

"Ah, there is the lie." Ainmire reached for his hand, and cool fingers wrapped around his wrist. Cillian kept his fingers curled in a fist, only straightening them out after Ainmire dug his fingers into the tendon of his wrist. "Does he know?"

Cillian's gaze snapped up from his hand, meeting those silver eyes. "What?"

"Your witch. Does he know your secret?"

Cillian opened his mouth to ask what the hell he was talking about when Ainmire pressed the flat of the knife against his palm,. Cillian tried to jerk his hand free, but Ainmire's grip was like a vise around his wrist, holding him in place. When he tried to shove Ainmire away, Damarus grabbed his other arm and yanked it behind his back, that dangerously sharp knife of his held threateningly close over Cillian's throat.

Cillian clenched his teeth against the growing heat and pain in his hand from the touch of iron, glaring at Ainmire as the Fae lord pressed the flat edge of the knife harder against his palm, as if he were waiting for something. Cillian's breathing came quicker as the seconds became a minute, became more. The burn forming beneath the railroad spike knife got hotter, like a brand was sitting on his palm, seeking to mark him. He tried to yank his hand away again, pain making him panic, but the Fae lord wouldn't let him. The scream torn out of Cillian felt like a surrender, even if he had no choice but to give in.

"Iron is our downfall," Ainmire said almost absently as he lifted Bran's knife off Cillian's hand. The skin beneath it was burned raw and red, blistered throughout, the reaction worse than it had ever been, even when he was a child. "I'm surprised you forgot our history. But then, you look nothing like you should with this skin of yours."

The knife at his throat slid away, Damarus letting him go even if Ainmire didn't. Cillian breathed through his clenched teeth, cold sweat prickling his brow, the throbbing in his hand impossible to ignore. "I don't know what you're talking about."

"Another lie." Ainmire set the knife down on the table and let Cillian go. "One you seem to believe as truth."

Cillian shook his head, holding his burned hand close to his chest. "You talk in riddles, and it's getting real fucking annoying."

"And here I thought I've been speaking plainly." Ainmire removed his gloves and reached for the jar of ointment, holding it out to Cillian like an offering or a bribe. He didn't know which. Cillian didn't take it. "The wound on your hand will become infected if you don't use this."

"Like you care."

"I care about making your witch trust me because they break so much better when they do it to please their masters."

Cillian didn't realize he was moving until he tried to introduce his fist to Ainmire's face. He got close before Damarus hauled him back, spinning him around and kicking his legs out from under him. Cillian crashed to the floor, knees taking the brunt of the hit, and he swore as fingers tangled in his hair, yanking his head back. He watched as Ainmire leisurely walked around to face him again, the jar still in his hand. He looked down at Cillian, a vicious glint of superiority in his eyes.

"You once promised you would never kneel to me, and yet, here you are."

Cillian's heart skipped a beat, anger warring with confusion in his mind, and the confusion won. "What?"

Damarus reached down and grabbed Cillian's sore wrist, yanking his hand up for Ainmire to take. The Fae lord dipped his fingers into the jar and proceeded to slather the ointment over the burn on Cillian's palm. The ointment was a cool relief, already starting to numb the pain and the itch crawling up his arm. When he finished, Ainmire set the jar aside, and Damarus let go of Cillian's wrist, if not his hair.

"The Dagda's right hand arrives tomorrow. You will show them and your witch the truth you so clearly do not believe, and my place in the Summer Court will be elevated above all others save the Dagda himself for my loyalty."

Cillian didn't know who or what the Dagda was. He wasn't about to put himself into any kind of debt by asking.

"You keep talking and not making sense," Cillian gritted out.

Ainmire bent over and touched Cillian's ear, tracing the shape of it with his fingertips. Cillian tried to jerk away, but Damarus' fingers tightened in his hair, keeping him in place. "I know what you have seemingly forgotten, and that will be your downfall. I will relish it, the same way I will relish breaking the witch you care about so much."

"Don't you *dare* touch him."

"Your witch won't want anything to do with you after tomorrow night, and the Dagda doesn't care for witches at all, so my new pet will stay with me once I present you to the Summer Court. I will enjoy breaking him immensely." Ainmire pulled his hand away and straightened, something like pleasure in his eyes. "Take him back to his cell."

Damarus hauled Cillian up to his feet and out of the library, smiling all the while, clearly pleased with that little show. Cillian was taken back down into that cold, dimly lit dungeon and tossed back into the cell. He stumbled from the shove, nearly falling to his knees again but managing to stay on his feet as the cell door shut with a clang behind him. He turned around, glaring at Damarus through the bars.

Damarus looked him up and down before raising an eyebrow. "I would advise you to shed your skin by tomorrow, or my lord will have it done for you."

He turned on his heel and left. Cillian stood there, breathing harshly, holding his wounded hand close against his body. He stepped back, foot sliding on ice, and he nearly fell before he regained his balance. He stared down at the ice streaking over the dirt floor once more, and he couldn't tell what made his skin prickle in that moment— fear or the cold.

Taking a deep breath, Cillian stepped off the ice, his hand throbbing, keenly aware of all the warnings his mother had ever given him about witches.

Chapter Thirteen

After delivering Cillian breakfast, Bran thought he'd be left to his own devices as he had been over the last few days, so he was surprised to find Ainmire waiting for him at the top of the stairs, a metal leash dangling from his hand. He nearly missed a step on his way up, wariness making him want to be out of arm's reach of the Fae lord. He stepped into the hallway, keeping his attention on Ainmire as Damarus closed and locked the door behind him.

"I thought I was free to do my own thing until lunch?" Bran asked. He'd been given surprisingly free rein of wandering the estate grounds, always with a guard, but he'd walked the area to know it. He'd never been allowed past the estate walls, though. He half wondered if it was some psychological test.

"I am taking a trip into town today. You will join me," Ainmire said, holding up the leash.

Bran's entire body recoiled at the implication. "I'm not wearing that."

"Oh, but you are. Damarus?"

"My lord?" Damarus said.

"Is the carriage ready?"

"Yes, my lord."

Bran glanced from one to the other, trying to come up with any excuse to stay. "What will your people think about a witch keeping you company?"

"That you are a pet who doesn't know their place and is in need of instruction," Ainmire said.

The flush of anger and humiliation that came to Bran's face was difficult to ignore. "I'm not your—"

"Oh, but you are, and a pet you will remain if you want to keep Cillian safe. That was the bargain we made." Bran snapped his teeth together, cutting off what he wanted to say in favor of silence. Ainmire smiled indulgently at him and stepped closer. "Good. You will enjoy this outing with me. I intend to show you that we Fae are not the monsters you think we are."

"And you think a trip through some Faerie town will get me to change my mind? Are you forgetting what the lights are? What the wyrding is? What your kind did to my mother?"

"We were not the ones who created the wyrding."

Bran snorted his disbelief. "And the lights? Are you going to say you didn't create those?"

Ainmire laughed, the sound richly amused as he reached for Bran's collar, clipping the leash to it. "Far be it for us to not take advantage of what you witches carved into being between our worlds."

Bran stared at him, trying to steady his breathing. "The wyrding is Fae doing."

"And history is always so terribly one-sided."

Ainmire tugged on the leash, forcing Bran to follow. Bran's face burned with every step as Ainmire led the way through the mansion to the front door. An enclosed green-and-gold carriage waited for them outside, a pair of chestnut-colored horses harnessed in place. A driver sat on the outside bench, long whip in hand, while another servant in uniform held the carriage door open for them. Ainmire entered first, and Bran was prodded by Damarus to follow after. He would have sat on the opposite cushioned bench if the Fae lord hadn't ordered him otherwise.

"You will sit beside me," Ainmire said, leash held in one gloved hand.

Bran grimaced and did as he was told, digging his fingers into his thighs. Damarus took the other bench, and the servant closed the carriage door behind him. The windows were slid down on either door, allowing for a breeze to blow through, which Bran appreciated. What he didn't appreciate was how bumpy the ride was on cobblestones. He had to brace his feet against the floor of the carriage to keep from sliding off the bench. Both Fae didn't seem bothered at all.

The discomfort soon became ignorable, mostly because of what he could see outside the carriage windows. The quiet street the mansion was located on opened up onto the bustling ones he remembered from their arrival. The wooden structures of houses and shops reminded him uncomfortably of human establishments.

While there weren't any motorized vehicles, there were plenty of other carriages and horses on the road. Bran stared at the Fae on the street, with their varicolored hair and skin tones and their clothing that ranged from coveralls to courtly outfits similar to what the Fae in the carriage with him wore. The only thing Bran knew for certain was that Ainmire and Damarus were probably the highest-ranked in town.

He had questions—so many questions—but Bran didn't want to ask them, even though he knew he should. The more knowledge he had of the area, the better, but neither did he want to seem too interested. He didn't want to give the Fae lord any more of an opening to engage than he had to.

He didn't want to owe them.

"Where are we going?" Bran finally asked.

"Pets don't question their lord," Damarus said, not looking up from the small book in his hand he was reading.

"Training takes time," Ainmire said.

"You've a soft hand with this one."

"Perhaps. I have my reasons."

Bran bit back a grimace, not wanting to know what sort of punishment he was dodging because the Fae lord thought he'd get more out of Bran with the carrot rather than the stick. He honestly didn't know why the bargain he'd made had worked, not when it seemed the Fae thought so little of mortals and witches alike.

He didn't expect an answer after that, so he was surprised when

Ainmire continued speaking. "We are heading to the town's library. The head archivist has been notified to expect us."

"Why?" Bran asked.

"Because your education has gaps that need to be filled."

Such a polite way to say the Fae lord thought he was stupid. "Fae history isn't mine."

"If that were true, then you witches wouldn't stand guard at the wyrding so attentively."

Bran was at a loss in their verbal dance and bit his tongue against all the words lodged in his throat. Playing word games with Fae never ended well. Instead, he turned his head to stare out the window, trying to brace himself against the motion of the carriage that was doing its damnedest to bruise his tailbone.

Damarus had called the town Baile Átha Luain. Bran wondered how much of the land surrounding the town by a river Ainmire ruled. It wasn't enclosed by any kind of wall, instead sprawling over the valley floor, as if the Fae who lived there didn't fear what could walk out of the wyrding. Maybe the lights didn't come this way.

No wall meant he and Cillian might have a chance to make a run for it if he could figure out a way to break Cillian out of the cell. That seemed like more and more an impossible dream with every day that passed. Bran was watched every second he was free of his room, a guard forever trailing in his shadow.

The town's streets were winding, not built on a grid in any meaningful way. It reminded him of any modern city, if all the buildings were made of wood and some kind of metal he doubted was iron. They passed shops for food and clothes, tailors and cobblers, and even what looked like a forge down an alleyway.

He wondered what had happened to Cillian's rifle and his pair of iron railroad spike knives. The only weapons he'd seen any Fae carry were the occasional bow from a hunter and swords or glaives for the guards on patrol. It felt, weirdly, like he'd stepped back in time somehow, even when he knew he'd just slipped sideways.

Eventually, the street widened a little, adding another lane. The buildings with shops and homes became buildings meant for a government. They were designed differently, with more elaborate facades and a slight uptick in guards. Carriages were parked in designated spots with their drivers chatting in small groups. Single horses were tied to posts that held both food and water buckets on either side. Their carriage eventually pulled in front of a three-story redbrick building with white trim and ivy growing up its side. The windows on each level appeared to be made of stained-glass images Bran couldn't quite make out.

Damarus opened the carriage door rather than wait for whatever servant had tagged along and got out. Ainmire exited next, and Bran was forced to follow, leash pulled taut between them. The sidewalk wasn't as crowded here as it had been in other parts of the town. Bran craned his head around, taking in all the buildings clustered around a wide green park. He'd guess they were in the civic heart of the town but wasn't going to ask for confirmation.

"This way," Damarus said, tilting his head at the library. "Pets follow their lords."

"Not a pet," Bran said through gritted teeth, but he still listened like he was one, led along like one, and it galled him.

For Cillian. I'm doing this for Cillian.

The thought was cold comfort as they entered through a pair of wooden double doors into a receiving hall where a Fae stood in a plain sort of gown, her daffodil-yellow hair swept up into a loose bun atop her head. She wore a gold brooch pinned over her left breast, the open book within a thin circle a device that probably meant something. She dipped into a shallow curtsy before speaking in the Fae language Bran was more and more certain was similar to Irish Gaelic. Ainmire conversed in the same language, and whatever they decided on, the lady nodded and turned on her heel, acting as escort.

They followed her through well-lit hallways that made Bran wonder if a witch was responsible for the glittering sparks floating in the glass sconces. He didn't see anyone who might be mortal amid the tall Fae they passed with their pointed ears and condescending regard if they even deigned to look at Bran. They looked at Ainmire, though, sometimes stopping him for a brief chat before moving on.

The lady took them to a doorway that led to a huge, three-story room filled with rows upon rows of books. Bran stared at the vast expanse of space built to house a library. Four spiral staircases, two on each side, were set equidistant from each other and the entrances on either end of the room. They connected each floor, the gilded wood matching the railings that encircled every upper floor.

Bran's gaze was drawn to the ceiling, where a mural was painted of a fierce-looking red-headed man with a harp strapped to his back leading the charge against an enemy painted in diluted color rising out of a gray-looking forest. The hero stood in front of a massive cauldron, with Fae soldiers climbing out of it.

"The Dagda," Ainmire said, noticing Bran's curiosity. "He rules the Summer Court out of Murias. You'll see him soon enough, after I meet with his right hand tomorrow."

Bran snapped his head around, shock jolting through him. "What?"

The librarian frowned at him, but Damarus said something to her that had her shaking her head. Bran didn't care what excuse the Fae had peddled—he was more interested in knowing about the Dagda's right hand, if the person held the same kind of rank that Damarus did for Ainmire. Some trusted sort of advisor, maybe, or something more.

Something worse.

"The Dagda will want to know I found you."

"Why? Because I'm a witch?"

"Among other reasons."

Before Bran could respond, Ainmire stepped forward, speaking to the librarian, who then turned on her heels and led the way once more. Other Fae sat at tables on the ground floor, studying books or writing on paper. Several glanced at them as they passed, murmured conversation following in their wake.

The librarian led them to one of the spiral staircases. They went up single file to the second floor, heading to a bay of bookshelves that surrounded a glass display case holding a three-dimensional map of a familiar island.

"That's Ireland and Northern Ireland," Bran said, staring at it.

"Éire," Ainmire corrected, stepping closer to the map. Damarus wandered toward one of the bookcases to peruse the titles there, but Bran had no doubt the other Fae's attention was on his lord. "We lived there first, and we named it."

Bran hesitantly approached the display case, staring down at the green rolling hills and darker forests, the glittering blue lines of rivers and pools of lakes, and brown peaks of mountains in the west and north. It looked exactly like the huge island that held Ireland and Northern Ireland back home, only this map was carved up with border markings that made no sense to him, with city and town names that didn't match the counterparts he knew.

Ainmire tapped a finger against the glass case, and Bran sucked in a breath as markings in the same style he'd seen on the standing stone in the wyrding glittered into being. It was, he realized with a sinking stomach, a language not unlike the witchmarks were. But where witchmarks held the language of intent, this appeared to be the Fae's own everyday form of communication.

The elegant whorls of words flowed over the case like a waterfall, taking the glass with them, as if it never even existed. Whatever magic was in the words seemed to animate the map inside, causing rivers to flow and an invisible wind to blow through the forests. Hints of clouds came and went above the island, casting faint shadows on the land below. Miniature waves crashed against the shores, as if the island truly sat in an ocean.

Ainmire moved along the length of the table as the librarian disappeared down another aisle, pulling Bran along with him by way of the leash even when Bran wanted to plant his feet. But thoughts of Cillian in that cell kept him moving, kept him compliant. Ainmire came to a stop on the eastern side of the map. "Look here."

Bran looked down at the map, seeing the markers depicting town and city names now glowed golden. The brightest were four cities in the north, south, east, and west, all held within boundaries marked with black lines.

"My domain lies here," Ainmire said, pointing at an area. Below, a swath of land and a town flashed gold. It was miles from what Bran assumed was the capital that sat in the exact location Dublin did back home. "The Dagda rules from Murias, and his Summer Court holds sway over Tír na nÓg."

The border surrounding the eastern portion of the map glowed brighter. Bran studied the area, trying to see where the wyrding was around the town the Fae lord claimed, but he couldn't find any gray spots that would depict it. "This doesn't mean anything to me. Why are you showing it to me?"

"I'm showing you the mirror of what we Fae lost when you witches forced us to the mounds after raising the wyrding against us. We made the Otherworld our home and filled the wyrding with lights because we had to, but we never forgot what we lost. We have never forgiven you witches for that, but we have found uses for you."

"Like the witch in your home? You broke her mind."

It was the only answer he had for the slavish submission that other witch had shown, the way they'd gone about their chore so happily in the enemy's home, barely clothed and collared like an animal.

"Your magic was ours once, but it has changed over our lifetimes. We must identify the changes somehow."

"By experimenting on us? By killing us?" Bran couldn't help the way his voice rose.

"You think your hypocrisy absolves you. It doesn't." Ainmire glanced at him, a slight, condescending smile on his face that Bran wanted to tear off. "You witches drove us out of Éire, but that was not enough for you. Your covens come through the wyrding to attack our towns and kill our people. Is it no wonder we do the same to you?"

"Because you attack first!"

Ainmire shrugged that accusation off. "I have buried enough of my people who died at the hands of a witch over the centuries to tire of it."

"And you what? Want to ally with me to try to stop it?"

"Pets can't be allies," Damarus mockingly said.

"Not a pet," Bran snapped over his shoulder.

"Your current predicament belies that. You'll become accustomed to such a role soon enough," Ainmire said. He reached out then, so quick Bran couldn't dodge, the Fae lord's hand wrapping around Bran's right wrist with a strength he couldn't break. He tried, but even digging in his heels wasn't enough to stop himself from being dragged closer to the table the map sat on. "Be still."

The order echoed in his ears as if he'd stuck his head in a large bell and rang it. Bran shook his head, the edges of his mind prickling with the sense of something trying to get *in* but couldn't.

Always keep iron close.

Habit turned into tradition was what saved him in that moment, the iron beads on his bracelet that no Fae had yet touched or been burned by, were an anchor for his stubbornness that kept a Fae lord's power out of his mind. Bran glared at Ainmire, body rigid, holding himself so tight he thought his bones might break if enough pressure was applied.

"You will be a challenge," Ainmire murmured, far too much pleasure in his tone. "Damarus?"

Bran bared his teeth at the Fae lord, not daring to punch him, even though he wanted to.

Damarus sidled up to the table, that too-sharp knife of his in hand. "My lord?"

Ainmire drew Bran's hand down toward the map, fingers angled over Baile Átha Luain. Ainmire caught Bran's gaze, pinning him with his words. "Do not move, or you know who will be punished."

Bran clenched his teeth together, his one free hand fisted at his side. His gaze cut to Damarus' knife as the other Fae angled it to touch the point to one of Bran's fingertips. It didn't feel like anything at first, the blade so sharp his body's reaction was delayed. Only when a drop of blood welled up did the pain set in, like a needle being stabbed under his fingernail. Bran winced as the drop of blood fell onto the map, next to the town's name marker. It sank into the forest there, turning the miniature treetops gray, a spot of darkness in all that green.

"Every city and town in the Four Lands has a map like this in a library, whether a grand one like here or a one-room dwelling in the farthest-flung reaches of a Court's rule," Ainmire murmured into Bran's ear, making him shiver involuntarily. "Every time a witch makes it through the wyrding, we take their blood to warn others the wyrding has its tendrils in our land once more and an incursion might be imminent. This mark will show on every map. Can you see them now?"

Bran stared at the map, and maybe it was because of his blood now connecting him to whatever magic lay in the construction of such a display, but shadows popped up across the island, some small, some large. All the dark stains broke up the sprawling greenery of a world that mirrored his own.

"All those areas are past and present incursions, a blight that never leaves, places where your kind have come to murder ours."

There were so many of them.

But so, too, Bran knew, plenty of covens had been killed by Fae.

A disquieting thought at the back of his mind whispered that it didn't make either side right.

Ainmire let his hand go, and Bran snatched it back, pressing the pricked finger and his thumb together to stop the bleeding. Bran stared at the map of Éire and a history he'd only been taught as a way to save his own people and the world witches had sworn to protect.

A part of him—the part saturated in grief—was glad the Fae had suffered for their attacks on witches.

But hate didn't make anyone a better person, and Bran wondered, as they left the library, if maybe that was the point of the trip, of the lesson that Ainmire wanted to impart.

That witches and Fae weren't so different after all.

Chapter Fourteen

He didn't want to wake up.

"Cillian."

Maybe it was a dream.

"Cillian."

"Go 'way," he mumbled.

"I need you to wake up so you can eat your breakfast."

The thought of food right then made Cillian's stomach churn badly, but making Bran worry would make him feel worse. Cillian opened his eyes and batted at the blanket around him, hissing when his still-healing hand caught against the coarse material. Once he was free, he sat up, rubbing at his face with his left hand, back still to the cell door.

"Cillian, what's wrong?"

Worry made Bran sound tense in a way Cillian didn't like. Sighing, he got to his feet, wincing at how stiff he felt. "I'm fine."

"No you're not. What are they doing to you?"

When Cillian turned around, his gaze zeroed in on where Damarus stood nearby. Damarus met his gaze, a mocking smile curving his lips, as if daring Cillian to tell Bran what had happened yesterday.

"Nothing," Cillian lied as he approached the cell door.

Bran was crouched by the metal flap, ready to slide the tray in. He wore another elaborate outfit, the maroon color warring with the dark circles underneath his eyes, collar still locked around his throat. Cillian hated the sight of it. He knelt, keeping his still-healing hand palm down against his thigh to hide the discolored skin. He studied Bran's face, not liking how drawn and tired he appeared. "What's wrong?"

"I asked first," Bran said.

The stubborn look in Bran's eyes was almost a comfort, something he remembered from when they were kids. "I'm fine. I promise. I just miss the sun."

Which was true. Being stuck in the cell was getting to him, with no chance to see the sky or a horizon. Cillian had spent his entire life running around and working outside. Being locked away underground wasn't easy, but he didn't want to dump that on Bran, not when the other man had his own precarious situation to deal with.

Bran let out a heavy breath before undoing the metal flap and pushing the tray inside. Today, it looked like Cillian was getting eggs and a side of potatoes, along with another glass of water. The smell of food should have been enticing, but it only made Cillian a bit nauseous. The reason for that stood nearby, the threat from yesterday and the warning hanging over him like a guillotine. Damarus didn't say anything, though, only watched with those eyes of his, listening in on every word they spoke because privacy wasn't something they got.

"I could ask to maybe get you time in the garden?" Bran asked.

Cillian jerked his gaze back to Bran. "Don't. I already told you not to bargain for me."

Bran frowned worriedly at him. "You'd be worth it."

"I'm not who you should be worrying about." Damarus would probably think Cillian meant Bran, not Aisling, but Bran knew who he spoke about. They hadn't spoken her name since they'd been captured, neither of them wanting to clue in the Fae she existed. But she was the reason they were in the Otherworld, and Bran needed to find her.

Bran's gaze dropped to the food tray now on Cillian's side of the cell. "I'll see what I can do."

"No," Cillian said sharply. "I don't want you putting yourself in danger for me."

He didn't say *you know why we came here*, but he hoped Bran could read it on his face.

"You're here because of me."

"I wasn't letting you go into the forest alone. That goes against everything we were taught."

"And what is it your town's witches taught you?" Damarus asked.

"Not to trust you Fae," Bran snapped.

Cillian clenched his teeth when Damarus laughed, not looking at Bran or the Fae. All he could think about was the conversation he'd had with Ainmire yesterday and the words that didn't make any sense—or maybe they did, and he just didn't want to believe them. His hand still ached, even with the healing ointment easing the burn, but one application wasn't enough to make it go away.

"They told me you went into town yesterday," Cillian said.

Bran wouldn't look at him. "Yeah, to some library. I was shown a map."

"He bled on a map," Damarus drawled.

Cold iced its way up Cillian's spine. "What did they do to you?"

Bran wiggled his fingers a little. "Just a finger prick. Nothing bad."

Cillian glared at Damarus, thinking he'd look nice spread across the torture devices in the center of the dungeon. Damarus stared back at him, that hint of a smile on his face slowly fading.

"Cillian."

He jerked his gaze away from the Fae, focusing on Bran. "You're okay?"

"I'm not hurt in any way that matters." Bran hesitated, touching Cillian's hand through the cell bars where it gripped the edge of the tray. Cillian wanted to wrap himself in the warmth of it. "They said the Dagda's right hand is arriving today. I don't know why or who they are."

Cillian turned his hand to hold Bran's, squeezing tight. He wanted to say *you should have left me behind*, but he couldn't. "When?"

"Later this afternoon. There's supposed to be some fancy dinner in their honor."

"Are you going?"

"I'd like you to eat."

Which was yes. "I could skip a meal."

Bran shot him a withering look. It almost—*almost*—made Cillian smile. "Don't be stupid."

"You like me stupid."

Bran's eyes softened a little, whatever animosity he'd held for Cillian when he first arrived in Pelham gone here in the Otherworld, where they only had each other to rely on. "Idiot."

It was like they were kids again, squabbling as friends did. It made Cillian want to ask what he couldn't in the cabin when they'd been hemmed in on all sides by monsters, wondering why Bran had refused to talk to him after the night they'd kissed years ago. But those were secrets Cillian would never speak of in front of the Fae. So he let Bran go, watched him walk out of that dark place, always looking back.

In those moments, it felt like some kind of love.

Cillian sighed and stared down at the tray of food, not hungry but not wanting Bran's sacrifice to go to waste. He ate what he could, keeping the glass of water for later, as always. Then he retreated to the far side of the cell and curled up with the blanket. He'd found that sleeping away the hours when he could made the time seemingly go by faster. He knew it probably wasn't a good habit to start, but he didn't have much else to do. Exercising as much as he could had gotten old and gross when he couldn't shower or change clothes.

He slept fitfully, dreams churning into nightmares that made no sense. He woke however long later to the cell door creaking open. Cillian's eyes snapped open, and he scrambled to his feet as Damarus entered the cell, backing him up against the wall with that knife at his throat. It didn't cut him, not yet, but Cillian was aware that it could, which was probably the point.

"My lord requires your presence," Damarus said, brown eyes looking almost black in the shadows of the cell. "I see you didn't heed my warning."

"I don't know what the hell you're talking about," Cillian gritted out. The wall at his back was as cold as the ground, the same sort of chill that had settled in his body while he slept.

"You will." Damarus stepped back only far enough to allow Cillian to sidle away from the wall. "Out."

Cillian had no choice but to obey, leaving the cell at the point of

Damarus' knife. Once above in the mansion proper, eyes watering from the lights in the lamps and sconces they passed, Cillian was taken to a great chamber lit by chandeliers that illuminated the many paintings hanging on the walls. Chaises and chairs were scattered in the corners, leaving the center space open for mingling.

A group of Fae stood there, and Cillian found himself presented to them like some kind of prize.

"The prisoner, as you requested, my lords, my ladies," Damarus said with a shallow bow.

Cillian warily eyed the Fae who were present, sizing them up. Ainmire was a mostly known threat, but the half dozen new Fae were a dangerous addition he didn't care for. The way they stared at him had Cillian wishing for his rifle. He forced himself to look away from them all, gaze searching out Bran, finding the other man standing next to Ainmire in another ridiculous outfit that wasn't even half as fancy as the ones the Fae wore. The gray color washed him out, or maybe that was the hint of fear Cillian could see in his eyes.

"Are you all right?" Cillian asked Bran, ignoring the Fae. Bran barely nodded, not convincing Cillian at all.

"You were correct, Lord Ainmire," a Fae lady said in English, sounding surprised. "He does appear mortal. The similarity is uncanny."

"A puzzle indeed, Lady Etain," Ainmire said.

Cillian dragged his gaze away from Bran and to the lady who had spoken. Etain was an inch shorter than Cillian, dressed in a shimmery, sleeveless rose-pink gown. She wore gold rings on every finger and a pair of gold armbands as well, along with a delicate golden harp pendant hanging from her throat. Her long blonde hair was half pinned up to show off her pointed ears and the gold caps covering them inlaid with pink sapphires the same color as her eyes. They held no kindness, those eyes, but Cillian forced himself to meet her gaze anyway.

Etain came forward, circling him slowly. Cillian fought not to turn his body to follow her steps, the hair rising on the back of his neck regardless when she passed behind him. Every instinct in him told him she was as dangerous as Ainmire, and he didn't like feeling small before either of them.

When she stopped in front of him, Cillian had to look down slightly to meet her eyes. She stared back, gaze searching, and whatever she saw in his face, in his eyes, amused her. "You do not remember me, do you?"

Cillian arched an eyebrow, trying to muster up the same disdainful tone. "I've never seen you before in my life."

She smirked, long-nailed fingers dragging up his arm. He would have pulled away, except Damarus was at his back, with that damned knife of his, and Cillian had no choice but to allow the touch. Etain's fingers reached his ear, tracing the shape of it, before cupping his jaw, studying his face. "Even in this mortal skin, you are the same in your eyes."

Cillian stared at her in confusion. "I'm not whatever it is you people think I am. I didn't grow up here. I grew up with Bran."

"With a witch, yes. It is astounding you consider him a friend. Perhaps even a lover?"

"They care for each other," Ainmire said. "The witch bargained his presence at my table for Cillian to eat."

"Pets do not eat at our tables," Etain tsked.

"I had my reasons."

"Yes, I stand before it on behalf of our king."

They were, Cillian realized, talking about him.

He didn't know why.

Etain finally released him, stepping back. She never looked away, though, her attention focused on him like everyone else. "Was there anyone else with them in the wyrding?"

"No, my lady," Damarus said. "My lord sent scouts to patrol the border with the wyrding, but it does not appear to be an incursion."

Etain pursed her lips, still looking at Cillian. "Our king will not be pleased."

"That we came alone?" Cillian asked.

"That you are here. Alive."

Considering what had chased them through the forest in Pelham and what they'd hidden from in the wyrding, Cillian rather thought that was a minor miracle.

"What do you mean?" Bran asked.

He shouldn't have spoken. Cillian realized that as Ainmire gripped

Bran by his hair and forced him to his knees with a show of strength that could have broken bone but didn't. A kindness, maybe, but Cillian didn't see it as such, not when Bran's face was twisted with pain.

"Ah," Etain said, interest in her voice, in her eyes, directed right at Cillian. "Perhaps it *is* love. And with a pet witch, of all atrocities."

"Bran isn't an atrocity, and he's not a *pet*," Cillian snarled.

Etain moved cat-quick, her sharp nails digging into Cillian's skin when she gripped his chin and dragged his face down close to hers. "*There* it is. Your rage that once brought winter, hidden in this mortal skin of yours. We thought we'd killed it."

"Cillian?" Bran gasped out.

Cillian glared at her. "I don't know what the hell you're talking about."

She smiled, her beauty nothing more than false advertising for the cruelty beneath. "You will."

Etain let him go and stepped back, her vicious gaze flicking up and down his body. Cillian looked past her at where Bran knelt, hair still gripped in Ainmire's hand, those wide hazel eyes looking right at him in a pale face. His fingers twitched as if to maybe use his magic, but Cillian didn't see any hint of it. He didn't know if Bran could fight against all the Fae around them, and Cillian didn't want to see him die for his efforts. He wouldn't survive that.

"What do you want?" Cillian asked, finally dragging his attention back to Etain. For all that this home was Ainmire's, she seemed to be in charge right now. What had Ainmire said these new Fae were? Sent from the Dagda? Their king?

"Hold him," Etain ordered.

"No!" Bran cried out as a pair of Fae stepped forward.

Etain turned, gesturing sharply with her left hand, glittering motes of pale pink light following her fingers. "I tire of your outbursts. You will be silent. Pets do not speak unless commanded to."

The scream Bran let out became muffled as his mouth was sewn shut, black thread conjured up from thin air cutting through his lips to seal them together. Blood trailed down his chin, dripping on the clothes Ainmire had put him in as he clawed at his face, horror in his eyes.

"Don't hurt him!" Cillian snarled, lunging at Etain, but her Fae reached him first with a speed he couldn't match.

Hands grabbed him, hauling him away from her. The pair of Fae forced his arms behind his back, Damarus' knife kissing the back of his neck, over his spine. The sting of a cut was negligible, as was the trickle of blood running down his back. Bran was more important, and he was still screaming, the sound ragged even through his sewn-shut lips.

"My Lady of Threads and Illusion, I would like the pet to live," Ainmire said in an offhand way, as if he didn't care one way or another what she decided. "He provides incentive."

Etain drew her arm back. "You gave it a long leash. Shorten it, or I will."

Ainmire inclined his head, expression impassive. Cillian jerked against the hands holding him, Damarus' knife cutting deeper, the sting turning into a burn. Cillian didn't care. "Leave Bran alone."

Etain turned to fully face him again, clearly amused, judging by her soft laugh. "Truly, I had never thought to see the day you worried over a witch. You never cared for them in the past."

"You keep talking like you know me. You *don't*."

"Oh, but I do. We thought you dead, yet here you are, exactly as you were, only wearing mortal skin and consorting with the enemy. Such traitorous actions will surely see you dead once more. Perhaps this time it will keep." Etain tilted her head a little, a lock of her long hair falling across one shoulder. "The Dagda will decide your grave, as he did before."

She raised her hands, fingers curled like claws, a glimmer in her eyes that was all magic. Cillian tried to lean away from her, but the hands holding him tight and Damarus' knife ensured he stayed within reach. "Don't touch me."

"I am the Dagda's trusted right hand, and I will see you delivered to the Summer Court as you are meant to be."

Her fingers touched his face, and an electric shock coursed through him, burrowing deep. Cillian opened his mouth to protest, but the words died in his throat as she sank her fingernails into his skin, tearing downward, a searing wave of magic eating through him like acid.

Cillian screamed, he knew he did, but he couldn't hear it over the wild pounding of his heart drumming in his ears, the world beginning and ending in his bones, in his skin. Etain unraveled him like one might a piece of cloth, one thread at a time, peeling him open, tearing him apart, and Cillian could do nothing to stop it.

Something wrenched free of him, something anchored deep in his being. The world fell out from beneath his feet, and he fell with it, down into a body that wasn't his.

Couldn't be his.

He tasted blood when clarity returned, his senses so much *more* than they had ever been before—sound and smell mingling like a migraine in his brain. He couldn't stop the whimper that escaped his mouth, hot face pressed to the cool wooden floor, the hem of Etain's gown fluttering inches from his nose. Cillian blinked slowly, voices distant and thick, like he was hearing underwater.

Hands gripped his arms, his hair, dragging him to his knees so he could look up at the Fae who'd flayed him down to the very center of his soul. Everyone's touch burned him like a brand he couldn't escape. Etain was blurry in his sight, but he still saw the smile she gave him, saw her reach for him, and he flinched.

It made her laugh.

"Welcome back, Winter Prince."

Whatever else she said, he didn't hear it through the pain gouging its way into his body. The Fae guards dragged him out of that room and to another, the wooden floor becoming cool tile. The hands on him were exchanged for others, but Cillian barely noticed, his wavering sight locked on the mirror in the bathing room he'd been taken to.

Cillian didn't recognize the Fae staring back at him with his own blue-gray eyes.

Chapter Fifteen

"Hands down," Ainmire said.

Bran blinked tears out of his eyes, head wrenched back, squinting against the light that haloed Ainmire. His fingers caught on the smooth thread *sewn through his lips*, blood coating his teeth and tongue. He wanted to gag but couldn't, not if he didn't want to choke. He swallowed blood, the metal taste saturating his mouth. Ainmire's eyes narrowed slightly, and the next thing Bran knew, he was being shaken the way someone might scruff and shake an animal out of anger.

Because that's what the Fae thought he was.

A pet.

Cillian never had, and he was—

He was—

Bran dropped his bloody hands to the floor, clawing at the hardwood instead of clawing at his mouth. Pain throbbed through his lips and across his cheeks from the effort of trying to open his mouth. Focusing on the pain was better than focusing on the horror rattling through his brain, the realization of what Cillian was.

The lie of it all.

Unbidden, his gaze went to the spot Cillian had collapsed on the floor before being dragged out by Etain's Fae. Cillian had sounded like he was dying from whatever magic Etain had performed. Bran had yelled futilely with his sewn-shut mouth, kept in place by Ainmire's hand while Etain peeled off Cillian's skin one strip at a time.

Peeled off his glamour until he'd looked—like a Fae.

Like those Bran had grown up believing were the enemy, except this was *Cillian*. This was his childhood best friend, his first love and first kiss and first broken heart all rolled into years of memories he'd never been able to let go, haunting him like a ghost. Years of growing up with him in Pelham, where he'd been *human*.

Mortal.

But when he'd fallen to Etain's feet, Cillian had looked like all the other Fae in the room with them—an otherworldly, eerie beauty that had been hidden from view gilding his body, blazing blue-gray eyes, and pointed ears.

Bran didn't want to believe it, but the truth had been peeled open— literally—right before his eyes. Even knowing Etain's title and the games Fae played, Bran had no doubt what was done was real and not a trick. What use would they have for tricking him? Bran was one witch, the last in the Gallagher coven, guarding some backwater way into the wyrding. His wasn't a coven with ties to the Council of Witches; he didn't have any connections that would be of note. There should be no reason he shouldn't be dead, save for one.

Cillian.

Bran swallowed more blood, flinching from Ainmire's grip or Etain's attention; he figured it didn't matter which. Not while he was on his knees, collared and bowing to the whims of whatever the Fae wanted.

All the teachings he had learned over the years, all the warnings he'd grown up with, had said to never trust the Fae. That they were the enemy and always would be. If Cillian was Fae, and if Bran was worth his coven's witchmarks tattooed on his body, he'd find a way to escape and leave Cillian behind, exactly how Cillian kept asking him to. He'd leave and hope Jupiter found him so he could track down Aisling.

But this was Cillian, and despite the betrayal, Bran couldn't leave him here to some unknown fate.

Every other witch would, Bran knew.

Etain walked over to him, looking down her nose at where Bran knelt. He stared up at her through the tears and the pain. If this was the only way he could be defiant—to look them in the eye—then he would. His heart rate felt too fast, chest aching with the need to gasp for air and being denied. He tongued at the thread pierced through his lips, no gap between them.

"If you wish to keep Cillian in check, the pet needs to live," Ainmire said in a bored voice.

Etain waved off his words. "He has no memory of us, which means he has no memory of his power. As for this one, you give it too much liberty."

"As you deduced, they care for each other."

"And I suppose you want it out of revenge for what Cillian did to your face? You still have not forgiven him for the scar you carry."

"If the Dagda allows it, I want Cillian to know what I took from him when I brand his pet with the mark of my House right in front of him."

Bran tried to still his breathing into something that was less panicky, hating how the Fae talked over him, as if he weren't worth their time.

As if he were an object to be used and bartered.

Etain hummed, staring at Bran, before dismissing him with an elegant little shrug. "We leave for Murias tomorrow. Your pet may come with us."

"And your threads?"

Etain snapped her fingers, and Bran couldn't stop himself from screaming as the threads tying his lips together were practically torn free, leaving numerous tiny bleeding holes in his lips. He cupped a hand over his mouth, blood smearing over his palm and chin, saliva welling up around his tongue.

Ainmire's grip on his hair tightened, and Bran was dragged to his feet by the Fae lord. Head tipped back, pressed up close against a body he didn't want to touch, all Bran could see was Ainmire's eyes.

So he spat in them.

Whatever smirking triumph Ainmire hoped to have over him was reduced to a backhand punch that crashed into Bran's face. Bran took it in the eye with a smile, pain spiderwebbing through his head from the blow. He collapsed to the floor, catching himself on his hands, spitting out blood around a hoarse laugh.

"Would you like me to sew its mouth shut again?" Etain asked with an amused little laugh.

Bran turned his head so he could look up out of the corners of his eyes at Ainmire, watching the Fae lord wipe the spit and blood off his face with a handkerchief. The fury in his gaze was worth the throbbing black eye Bran knew would swell up by morning.

"Damarus," Ainmire snapped.

"My lord?" Damarus said.

"Take my pet to his room."

Hands dragged Bran back to his feet and spun him around, the other Fae's hold as bruising as Ainmire's as Damarus escorted him out of the great chamber.

"That was quite stupid of you," Damarus said flatly.

"Not housebroken, remember?" Bran rasped. Talking hurt, his lips still bleeding and swelling up, but he wasn't going to take their words like barbs when he didn't have to.

"You will be."

The threat made Bran want to close his eyes, but he still needed to watch where he was going and what Damarus was doing. It was a matter of minutes for Damarus to bring him to the door of that horrible little room with its false sense of comfort. Bran couldn't help the way he dug in his heels, just for a second, the weakness something he couldn't help after everything.

But Damarus was stronger, and it was no great effort for the Fae to shove Bran through the doorway and slam the door behind him. Bran stumbled over his feet, and here, at last, he let himself sink to his knees on his own accord, pressing his forehead to the thin area rug, gasping for air and wishing betrayal didn't hurt so badly.

Cillian was Fae.

Bran was a witch.

He couldn't reconcile the two just then, not after a lifetime of knowing what he stood against, what he stood *for*.

Bran wanted to scream out his horror and shame and anger, but he refused to give the Fae the satisfaction of hearing him break down.

Sniffling through a swelling nose, Bran lifted his head and crawled across the floor to the bed. He leaned his back against it and stretched out his legs, shaking hands resting on his thighs. He stared blankly up at the wooden ceiling, aching and hurting, but his heart was the worst of everything.

After all these years, this wasn't the answer Bran was looking for when it came to Cillian.

But even knowing what Cillian was, Bran couldn't leave him behind.

Didn't even want to.

He laughed, the sound ugly and bitter-tasting, before it turned into a choked sob. Bran scrubbed at his face, flinching when he pressed too hard on the wounds there.

He was losing everyone in his life who had ever mattered.

He might even lose himself.

"Mother, guide me true," Bran whispered, praying to the deity his coven had followed and the one he hadn't yet had a chance to bury.

Bran stayed there on the floor through the night, unable to sleep, staring out the window at the darkness that slowly lightened as day approached. For once, he didn't want to see a sunrise, but it came anyway, inevitable in its breaking dawn.

Sometime later, when the light outside was clear and bright, the bedroom door was unlocked and opened. Damarus stood in the doorway, long hair falling loose to his elbows. He was dressed how he had been for the forest, the outfit meant for a day of riding.

"We are leaving," Damarus said.

"What?" Bran asked, voice raspy and coming out of swollen lips. His entire face felt hot and sore from what he'd endured yesterday. "No breakfast?"

"You haven't earned it."

Bran slowly got to his feet, still in yesterday's clothes. The blood-stains down the front of his shirt and coat had dried during the night. The sleeves were stained as well from when he'd tried to wipe his face before giving up. He knew he looked a mess, and he knew no one would care. Witches weren't worth such compassion, not here in the Otherworld.

"Where's Cillian?"

Damarus laughed at the question, gesturing for Bran to leave the bedroom. "Here I thought you would want nothing to do with him now that you know the truth of his skin."

Damarus led the way to the front of the house, the forecourt with its burbling fountain crowded with carriages that had travel trunks lashed to the tops. Farther down the drive, Bran could see a group of riders on horses in different uniforms, armed with bows and swords. Servants darted about with additional supplies, and Fae were already situated in two of the four carriages.

"Your pet, my lord," Damarus said, pushing Bran down the porch steps to the cobblestones.

Ainmire stood near the second carriage, dressed far more grandly than all the long days Bran had been the Fae lord's prisoner. He was beautifully handsome in the black pants, silk shirt, and coat edged in silver embroidery, the color matching the waistcoat, cravat, and his eyes. Bran's attention was drawn to him in a magnetic sort of way he chalked up to fear.

"You didn't clean him up," Ainmire said.

"Was I supposed to? I'm sure Lady Etain wouldn't appreciate the delay."

"Where's Cillian?" Bran asked again, not seeing him or Etain anywhere in the flurry around them. Their absence didn't put him at ease.

"She is securing the prisoner. You would do well not to speak in her presence," Ainmire said, looking at him with half-lidded silver eyes.

Bran touched his fingers to his swollen lips, the holes from the thread forced through them stingingly tender. He knew the cost of speaking, but he also knew he couldn't stand by silently and watch Cillian be hurt, even after knowing the truth of what he was.

Ainmire's gaze flicked up and down Bran's body. "Curious that you care for him, even now after he has lied to you and caused you pain."

"I grew up with him. He was mortal."

"Was he?" Ainmire asked, cryptic in the way Fae loved to be.

There had always been stories of changelings in their history, of children snatched away in the dead of night and replaced with someone else —some*thing* else. Parents of changelings might not know the truth of their child's existence, but witches always would, and Cillian had never seemed like one.

What's more, Cillian's mother had loved him. She had raised him and worried over him, and if she knew of his true origins, she'd never said. Cillian had appeared human in all the years Bran had known him, with rounded ears and no hint of magic in him.

But Fae were masters of lies. Maybe even to themselves.

A commotion at the front door had Bran looking over, taking a step toward it as he saw who came through. Ainmire grabbed him by the arm, hauling him close against the Fae. Cool lips brushed over his ear, making Bran jerk his head away. "When we get to Murias, you will never see him again. I can't wait to see his eyes when he realizes that you will remain with me."

"I want to ride with Cillian," Bran said, gaze locked on Cillian as he was half carried out of the mansion between two Fae, Etain sweeping down the steps ahead of them like a blazing star in the gold gown and glittering diamond tiara she wore. "Please."

"If you dream of escape, it will not happen. There is no place for you to run and not be hunted down and killed for it."

Bran swallowed, half-formed, hysterical plans shredding themselves in his thoughts. Still, he had to try. "I want to say goodbye. Give us that time."

Ainmire touched his fingers to Bran's bruised cheek, turning his face so he had to look up at the Fae lord. "You think me kind to ask for that?"

"I think you'll enjoy it."

A slow smile spread across Ainmire's face. "Get on your knees and beg me for the chance."

Maybe it was meant to be a humiliating request, but Bran didn't think twice about kneeling before the Fae lord, those cool fingers cupping his chin, forcing his head up. He stared up at Ainmire and the covetous look on his face, as if Bran was some prize to be won and owned for reasons that still weren't clear.

"Let me stay with Cillian," Bran said, not needing to fake his desperation. "I want to say goodbye. *Please.*"

Ainmire's thumb touched his bottom lip, pressing down hard, pain singing through Bran's jaw. "Please what, pet?"

And oh, *there* was the humiliation, the sick fear that made bile crawl up Bran's throat. He choked it back with the same determination he choked out the words that put such a pleased glint in Ainmire's eyes. "Please, master."

Ainmire slid his thumb past Bran's lips and teeth to stroke his tongue, making him want to gag, but he didn't. He held Ainmire's gaze, let him touch so Bran could get what he wanted while he knelt on the cobblestones, quiet and still.

Submissive because he had to be.

"I see you shortened its leash," Etain said as she approached.

"He will break in time. They always do." Ainmire slipped his thumb free of Bran's mouth and pulled his hand back, but Bran stayed put, trying not to hunch his shoulders. "I would ask that Cillian ride with us."

"I intend to deliver him alive to our king."

"And you shall." Ainmire's fingers ran through Bran's hair before getting a fistful and turning Bran's head around. Bran stared past Etain at where Cillian stood, slung between two Fae guards, in a new ice-blue courtly outfit, barely aware of what was happening around them. "But I want Cillian to know what he has lost."

Bran held his breath, knowing that even though he'd begged Ainmire for the chance, it was Etain who would decide their fate that morning. It wasn't benevolence that made her eventually agree, Bran knew, but cruelty.

"Very well. Put them both in your carriage."

Bran let out a breath that was buried beneath the sound of Cillian's groan as the Fae guards hauled him toward Ainmire's carriage. Bran winced as he was dragged to his feet by his hair, skull throbbing. He was hauled aside before Ainmire let his hair go. Bran kept his eyes on Cillian, hoping not to catch Etain's attention. He'd had enough of it to last him a lifetime.

Once Cillian was deposited into the carriage, Ainmire allowed Bran to climb in. He found Cillian sprawled across one cushioned bench, legs dangling off the side and one arm trailing to the floor. Bran scrambled to his side, bracing himself over the bench so he could look down at Cillian, staring at a face he'd thought he'd known well.

It was like looking through a dirty window that was suddenly wiped clean. This close and Bran could see the way Cillian's Fae blood made his features a little sharper, more beautiful, how his ears tapered to a point that Bran's fingers hovered over. Someone had shaved off the stubble that had been growing over the days he'd spent in that cell, leaving his skin smooth to the touch. Cillian's eyes fluttered open, gaze slowly focusing on Bran, but recognition was slow to come.

"Bran?" Cillian rasped. "You're...hurt."

Bran closed his eyes, stomach twisting at the worry and care in Cillian's ruined voice. It made him ache in the back of his lungs, chest tight with everything he couldn't say. "I'm fine."

It took some maneuvering, but Bran managed to lift Cillian's upper body and slide onto the bench beneath him, hauling the taller, heavier man up against his chest to hold Cillian in his arms for the first time in years. Cillian clumsily reached for Bran's hand, fingers shaking, strange silver cuffs embedded with pink sapphires clasped around his wrists. Bran tangled their fingers together over Cillian's chest, the embroidery on the coat soft against his palm.

Bran bent his head and hesitated only a second before brushing a soft kiss over the top of Cillian's head, breathing in the clean scent of the other man. "I'm sorry."

They should never have met, not on the same side—their side. But they had, growing up together in Pelham for years. Cillian had been his best friend, and it was no wonder Bran had fallen in love with him when they were teenagers—with his kindness and the way he looked at the world, like it was something to save rather than conquer. Bran could admit now that seven years hadn't been enough to kill that love, even as it had cultivated a hurtful anger that could so easily become hate now that Bran knew Cillian was Fae.

But in that moment, the only thing Bran wanted was to never let Cillian go again.

"I see begging was worth it," Damarus said as he finally entered the carriage, settling on the other bench.

Bran raised his head, glaring in defiance, refusing to be shamed. "Yes."

"Such sentiment for one who wouldn't think twice about gutting you in the past."

Bran tightened his hold on Cillian, the other man not making a sound, eyes closed as if he slept. "You don't know Cillian."

"Perhaps not now, but I knew him then." Damarus smirked lazily at Bran. "You are a witch. Even his Court kept pets, the same way Ainmire will keep you."

"His Court?" Bran echoed. "What do you mean?"

"You'll find out soon enough."

Damarus looked away from him, the dismissal impossible to ignore. Bran followed his gaze, watching as Ainmire climbed into the carriage and took the seat beside Damarus. A servant closed the carriage door, and Bran flinched at the sound it made.

"Bran?" Cillian murmured, twitching in Bran's arms.

"Here," Bran said. "I'm right here."

"Not for much longer," Ainmire said as the carriage lurched into motion.

Bran swallowed, staring at his and Cillian's hands where they were clasped together over Cillian's heart. "How long of a ride do we have?"

"We will reach Murias by nightfall."

Not even a day to say his goodbyes. Bran breathed around the ache in his chest, words a jumbled knot in his throat. He had so much he wanted to say to Cillian, to ask, but none of it deserved an audience. He wouldn't give Ainmire that kind of ammunition to further hurt Cillian wherever they ended up. And maybe that was cowardice on his part because then Bran wouldn't have to know what Cillian would say to him when they were like this.

So Bran held him, bracing them both against the jolt of the carriage as it rolled through and out of the town, onto a road that would deliver them to a king who had no love for either of them.

They never made it.

Hours after their departure, when Bran's stomach was protesting the missed morning meal and Cillian was sleeping fitfully in his arms, the wind picked up with a howl that sounded like a roaring freight train. A line of fast-moving clouds blotted out the sun, thunder rumbling in the distance and growing louder.

The Fae outside started shouting, Bran unable to understand them, but Ainmire and Damarus certainly did. Damarus swore and flicked his knife free as the carriage jerked to a halt. "They know he has returned."

"Impossible," Ainmire snapped. "No one would breathe a word that we have him."

Damarus grimaced at his lord, one hand reaching for the handle that would open the carriage door nearest him. "My lord, the Wild Hunt—"

Terror at knowing what was outside slammed into Bran the way the wind slammed against the carriage, rocking it hard, tipping it onto two wheels. Bran fell off the bench to the floor, unable to brace himself, dragging Cillian down with him. His bruised ribs throbbed, and he couldn't stop his head from smacking against the door on his way down, tangled up as he was with the other man. The windows shattered from the force of the howling wind.

Too late did Bran realize it wasn't the wind but the spirits riding it.

The carriage door he half leaned against was yanked open. Bran cried out as he and Cillian fell out of the carriage, slamming to the ground. All the air was driven out of his lungs as fire erupted inside the carriage, wielded by Ainmire's gloved hand.

"They are *mine*!" Ainmire snarled, staring right at Bran as the carriage was picked up by a horde of hideous specters that started tearing it apart. Ainmire was forced to defend himself and his right hand against the dead with magic that burned wildfire hot.

A spirit riding a macabre ghostly horse with missing flesh exposing its ribs settled to the ground by Bran, face vacillating between that of a lady's visage and the skull beneath it. Bran wriggled out from beneath Cillian's deadweight as the spirit dismounted, stalking toward them with lethal intent. Heat from the burning carriage made the air waver like a mirage as he got one knee beneath him, holding on tight to Cillian.

Then the spirit was suddenly *right there*, ghostly, clawlike hands reaching for them. Its touch burned worse than the fire, and Bran yelled in shock, jerking back—right into the hands of another spirit. He was wrenched off the ground, taking Cillian with him, refusing to let the other man go. The spirit rider helped lift them into the hold of another spirit that pulled them into the sky with a thunderous scream as lightning forked to the ground.

Bran got a glimpse of a horde of the ghostly dead swarming the carriages and horses on the road beneath them before they hit the low-lying storm clouds, what had to be the Wild Hunt spiriting them away to some new and unknown terror.

He didn't know how long they flew, how far the storm reached, only that when they finally descended, Bran couldn't feel his fingers, and he was soaked through from rain, teeth chattering painfully.

The clouds started to thin until they left the sky behind. Bran got a glimpse of a river and a tall-masted ship before he had to close his eyes against the nausea welling up in his gut as the Wild Hunt spiraled down to earth. The ghostly, clawed hands that had carried them away from Ainmire's clutches deposited them on the deck of the ship, into the hands of a Fae whose arms were outstretched to the ceiling of storm clouds, eyes burning like molten gold in her beautiful face, the long braid of her blonde hair lashing around her body.

Bran collapsed with Cillian in his arms, heaving for air, trying to stop the world from spinning around him. The roar of the wind died down, its absence ringing in Bran's ears. He watched the Fae with lightning at her fingertips and golden eyes approach, something like reverence in her raw voice.

"My prince," she said, staring at Cillian as she knelt beside them, reaching for his slack face with one shaking hand. "It is truly you."

"Don't hurt him," Bran got out, already resorting to begging because it had worked before, and maybe it would work again. "Please."

She looked at him, this beautiful Fae, and the incandescent joy in her teary golden eyes changed to something harder, something full of bitter distaste when her gaze dropped down to the collar he still wore. "Witch."

Before Bran could respond, a familiar *caw* from above made his entire body jerk, head snapping up. He stared in disbelief as Jupiter dived to meet him on the deck of that ship, bond flaring open between them despite the collar locked around his neck. His familiar landed on the deck beside them and hopped onto Cillian's lap, spreading her wings in hello.

"Jupiter?" Bran said, voice cracking.

She *cawed* at him again, pushing *safe, safe, safe* through the bond.

After everything they'd gone through, he wanted to believe her—he *did*—but he couldn't, not when they were surrounded once more by Fae who all looked at Cillian like Ainmire had.

Like they knew him, when Bran was beginning to think he hadn't known Cillian at all.

Chapter Sixteen

Awareness came back to Cillian slowly, like a dream.

"He doesn't know you."

"He is my prince."

"You're Fae, and your kind have been torturing us all week. He won't trust you, but he'll trust me."

"If you harm him—"

A short, sharp laugh had Cillian wanting to soothe the edges of Bran's fear through the migraine pounding through his head. "I traded myself to keep him alive when Ainmire had us. Do you think I'd hurt him now?"

Bran's words penetrated the fog wrapped around his mind better than an alarm. Cillian groaned, forcing his eyes open, staring up at a wooden ceiling, the bed beneath him swaying with a motion that wasn't him but wherever they were. "Bran?"

The other man's familiar face appeared above him, and the state of it had Cillian moving before he realized that was probably not a good idea. Pain stabbed through his entire body when he got an elbow underneath him, and he hissed, resisting the urge to flop back down on the bed. His head ached, pain spiking through his skull.

"Lie down," Bran said, grabbing him gently by the shoulders and easing him back anyway. "Apparently, being skinned by Etain takes it out of people."

Cillian gripped Bran's arms, blinking up at the other man's bruised and swollen face, everything coming back to him in jagged segments. Ainmire and the cell. Etain and whatever her magic had done to him. And Bran—

"What did that bastard do to you?" Cillian rasped.

Bran blinked down at him, his dark brown hair falling over his forehead, one eye half-swollen shut above a bruised cheek. His lips were swollen as well, the holes from thread cutting through them barely scabbed over. "Besides be a creep? Not what you're thinking."

Cillian tightened his hold as best he could on Bran, searching his eyes. "You're sure?"

"You were worth everything I gave up."

"Bran. What did you trade?"

"I got on my knees and begged to ride with you in that carriage, but that's it. Ainmire said yes."

Bran wouldn't quite meet his eyes, and Cillian knew there was probably more to that interaction than Bran was letting on, but he decided not to push. "You're okay?"

"Other than my face and our current situation? Yeah. I'm okay."

Cillian tensed. "Current situation?"

Bran moved to sit on the edge of the bed. Cillian didn't want to let him go but reluctantly did so. Bran turned his head, and Cillian followed his gaze. "Niamh helped take us from the carriage. You were unconscious when it happened. She took off Ainmire's collar for me, too, along with the shackles they had on your wrists."

The Fae in question stood nearby, dressed in knee-high boots and skintight pants, a white blouse, and a black corset, making her look not unlike a pirate. A bandolier was slung over one shoulder, small throwing knives attached in a neat line over the front. A gold necklace hung from her throat, the round pendant embossed with a crest depicting a sword pointed downward through the image of a crown framed on either side by a bird of prey. Her long blonde hair was tied back in a single braid, pointed ears devoid of any jewelry. Her golden eyes more than made up for the lack, their brilliance impossible to look away from as she stared at him.

Cillian's eyes widened when she dipped into an elaborate curtsy, her gaze never leaving his. "My prince."

He jerked his gaze to Bran, sucking in a breath as he remembered what he'd glimpsed in the mirror of that bathing room. He'd thought it was a dream. "Bran?"

Bran's jaw twitched before he leaned over and grabbed something off the small shelf nailed to the wall beside the bed. It turned out to be a handheld mirror, and when he held it up, Cillian didn't want to look at it.

"Etain removed the glamour you'd been living in," Bran said quietly, not meeting his eyes. "You're Fae, Cillian."

"No," Cillian said, but the truth was staring back at him, the face in that mirror all features that were his but not quite and pointed ears he'd never seen before. "That's not me."

Bran set the mirror down on the bed, still not looking at him. "It is. I'm sorry. I don't know how or why, but—everyone here seems to know you."

Cillian stared at him in disbelief before glancing over at Niamh, the Fae still looking at him as if he was about to disappear any second. "I don't know *them*. Bran, I grew up with *you*. In Pelham. I'm *human*."

He said it desperately, as if maybe that would make it true and the mirror a liar.

"I know. I didn't imagine you." Bran swallowed, shoulders hunching a little. "Maybe you were a changeling."

"He is not," Niamh said sharply. She stepped closer, going to one knee before the bed. She kept her hands to herself, though, for which Cillian was grateful. "You are no changeling, Cillian. You are the Winter Prince returned to us by the Cauldron's blessing."

"I'm not," Cillian said raggedly. "I'm not who you think I am. I can't be."

But he remembered, just then, that eerie voice when he and Bran had passed through the wyrding, the way it had called to him.

Welcomed him.

And his thoughts felt broken and sore deep in his mind, like something had cracked open inside of him. Something he'd never noticed before.

"I'm going to be sick," he decided, rolling to his side because his stomach was doing its damnedest right then to crawl out his mouth.

Bran swore and leaned over, coming up with a metal pail that he shoved beneath Cillian's face. He held back Cillian's hair as he vomited up bile, nothing worthwhile left in his stomach to expel. Cillian spat out the last of it, the taste in his mouth worse now. Groaning, he sat up, gritting his teeth against the way the room spun briefly. He dragged a hand through his hair, freezing when his fingers grazed the tip of his ear, shivering at how the nerves in the point there registered the touch in his body.

He fisted his other hand against the bed, looking at Bran, remembering what Bran had said about witches and the Fae in the cabin after outrunning the lights. How they had only ever been enemies. "Tell me it's an illusion like Etain's magic."

Bran shook his head. "It's no illusion. I'm sorry."

"I don't want us to be enemies. Seven years was enough, and they were terrible." He couldn't live his life without Bran in it. Not again.

Bran's gaze softened, hand twitching like he wanted to reach for Cillian but didn't. "That wasn't us being enemies."

"What was it, then?"

"Us giving each other the silent treatment."

Cillian barked out a harsh laugh, shaking his head. "That's what you want to call it?"

"I don't think now is the time or place to talk about it." Bran's gaze flicked to Niamh, then back to Cillian. "We have other things to worry about."

"Right." Cillian swallowed, nearly gagging at the taste of vomit in his mouth. "Are we prisoners?"

"No," Niamh said immediately, rising to her feet.

"Okay. Then where are we?"

"On my ship, the *Bone Breaker*."

Cillian stared at her. "That would make a terrible cruise line."

Niamh didn't seem to know what he was talking about. "One of the Mórrígan's own guided me to you."

"A raven," Bran said at Cillian's questioning glance. "Jupiter. I don't know how she found Niamh and her people, but she did."

"Did she find Aisling?" Cillian asked.

Bran shook his head, fiddling with the bracelet on his wrist. "No."

"We need to."

"I've been saying that, but no one here will listen to me."

"I take no orders from a witch," Niamh said coldly.

"Don't talk to him like that," Cillian snapped.

Niamh pursed her lips, gaze darting between the two. "He is the enemy."

"He's my *friend*." He bit back that he wanted Bran to be more because the Fae didn't need to know that.

She looked like she'd swallowed something terribly sour. "You used to never care for witches."

"You and everyone else keep talking like you know me, but you *don't*. I grew up with Bran. We were kids together back home. I can't be this prince of yours." His head throbbed as he spoke, pain skittering through his thoughts. He swallowed against the nausea in his gut, trying to keep it at bay.

Her shoulders slumped as she crossed her arms over her chest, staring at him with a pained expression in her eyes. She murmured something in her own language under her breath that he didn't understand before shaking her head. "When the witch told me Etain had unraveled your mortal skin, I had hoped that meant she had made you whole, but it seems she left your mind alone."

"That's not a bad thing," Bran said testily.

"It is when what was stolen is still gone," Niamh retorted. "Cillian is our Winter Prince, heir to the crown and throne of the Winter Court, and *he does not remember*."

Cillian shook his head, which was probably not the best thing to do since it made his vision swim a little and his migraine worse. "It has to be an illusion. Maybe Etain didn't remove anything but put something on me. What did you call it, Bran? Glamour?"

"There's no glamour on you. At least, not anymore. This is the real you," Bran said reluctantly.

"No." Cillian reached for Bran's hand. "No, I'm not Fae. I'm not one of *them*. I won't be."

Bran flexed his fingers but didn't try to pull away. "I guess we both had something to hide over the years."

Cillian growled in frustration. "I didn't lie as a kid, and you did for a damned good reason."

Bran looked up in surprise, shoulders loosening. "I didn't want to, not with you. But Mom always said to never talk about my magic."

"And mine said never to trust a witch."

"She did?"

Cillian looked down at his right hand, palm still sore and red from being burned by iron. And wasn't that some bit of proof of everything the Fae were telling him? "I thought it was because she didn't like your religion."

"What happened to your hand?" Bran asked sharply, reaching for it.

"Ainmire."

"It looks like an iron burn," Niamh said.

Cillian flinched at her words, not at Bran's touch. Bran cradled Cillian's hand in both of his, thumbs carefully framing the length of the still-healing wound stretched across his palm. "Ainmire used your knives on me."

Bran swore. "I hate that bastard. If we were home, I could mix something up to speed up the healing."

"I had an ointment your mother made in my backpack." At Bran's questioning look, Cillian shrugged stiffly. "I have an allergy."

"Iron?"

Cillian closed his eyes, feeling like all his excuses were slipping away. "Yeah. I always forgot about it."

"It makes sense, even if neither of us knew why before now." Bran slipped Cillian's hand between both of his, holding it with a carefulness that Cillian wanted to burrow into. "But I think we need to know how you could grow up with me and still be this prince of theirs."

"Because he was supposed to die," Niamh said. They both stared at her, but her attention was on their joined hands. "Three of our years ago, the Dagda attacked the Winter Court, accusing the Cailleach of conspiring with witches against the Summer Court. He said he had proof."

"Who is the Cailleach?" Cillian asked, stumbling over the name.

"Your grandmother, once the Winter Queen before she stepped aside so your father could rule."

"Oh." Cillian had no memory of her or his father, drawing a complete blank.

Bran jumped back into the conversation when Cillian faltered, for which he was thankful. "Did the Dagda have proof?"

"Such an accusation is not given lightly, and all witches look the same to me. The one the Dagda put forth before the Spring and Autumn Courts to gain their support for him to attack the Winter Court was said to be from their Council. The witch produced a contract—a bargain—and such a terrible alliance would be the only thing that could ruin a Court."

"Bran?" Cillian asked, not liking how Bran went stiff.

Bran exhaled shakily. "Covens take their orders from the Council of Witches in Salem. There are thirteen separate covens who claim a seat. I don't know the politics of how a seat changes hands, but the last time it happened, the First Seat stepped down, giving it to his daughter, and he wasn't seen again."

"When was that?"

"Almost twenty-six years ago in the mortal world. It could have been him who was with the Dagda."

"How does that even work if it was only a couple years here?"

"Time moves different in the Otherworld than back home."

"Okay." Cillian would figure that strangeness out later. "I thought witches and Fae were at war?"

"We are."

Cillian looked at Niamh. "If that's the case, then what was the proof?"

"The Cailleach would not consort with witches," Niamh said flatly.

"They said she did or made it seem like she would. And who knows if that witch was a pet or there of his own free will. So why would the Dagda make that accusation?"

Niamh's fingers dug into her arms, knuckles going white. "Because the Dagda could not stomach that his wife found enjoyment in someone else's bed."

"An affair?" Bran scoffed in disbelief. "He destroyed your Winter Court because he was having marital problems?"

"The Mórrígan was hand-fasted to the Dagda, though they are not mates. They made a vow to each other for political reasons between their Houses. She broke it in secret when she found her mate in the Cailleach's son, Finn, and had a babe, who grew up in the Winter Court." Niamh's gaze slid to Cillian, the intensity of it making her eyes burn. "The Cailleach was the Winter Court's queen, even after she stepped aside. Your House was royal. When the Dagda finally discovered you were also of the Mórrígan's blood after five hundred and thirteen years, he wanted you dead to hurt her."

Cillian stared at her. "I'm not half a millennium old. I'm twenty-five. I'll be twenty-six on—"

"Winter Solstice," Niamh cut in. Cillian snapped his teeth together, rattled that she knew. "That was when the Dagda attacked the Winter Court, during your celebration. We were not prepared for the purge that followed. He slew the royal family, most of the loyal courtiers, and trapped the Cailleach in stone. I was forced to *watch* as he—as he—"

Niamh sucked in a breath that filled her entire lungs, letting it out through her clenched teeth. "He bade the witch use Chaos to steal your years and your memories. You became a babe—mortal, I thought— when he gave you to his right hand and had you taken to the wyrding to be left for dead."

"Etain," Bran murmured, his hands tightening around Cillian's. "He gave you to Etain."

Niamh nodded slowly. "The Mórrígan arrived too late to save you. She had been tasked with putting down an incursion of witches within the Summer Court's borders. A diversion, in the end. When she saw the ruin of the Winter Court and discovered what the Dagda had done to her mate and you, she swore he would never have her heart and she would have her revenge. The Mórrígan fled before he could stop her. We all thought she went after you, to try to save you, but that the wyrding or the witches killed you both, for neither of you have been seen since. Until now."

"You said the Dagda killed everyone?" Cillian asked, struggling to comprehend what she'd dropped on him like a bomb.

"Everyone royal. He left some courtiers alive. Myself. Your right hand. Others."

"Wait. Cillian has one of these right hands? What exactly are they? Other than creepy fucks," Bran said.

"They are a noble High Fae's most trusted companion, their proxy when needed, their protector, shadows even unto death," Niamh said. "It is a great honor to be chosen as one."

Cillian arched an eyebrow. "And the Dagda left mine alive? That sounds incredibly stupid."

"He gave Verlin to Medb when he gave the Queen of Air and Whispers your crown and throne in an attempt to authenticate her rule. Verlin had no choice but to agree because you were dead, and it kept his House alive and everyone else in Tech Duinn unharmed." The strain on her face eased, lips curving into a faint smile. "He will be so pleased you have returned."

"I don't remember him, the same way I don't remember you."

She looked away, expression pinching, but didn't argue his point. "If you were in the mortal world all this time, what made you return to the Otherworld?"

Cillian didn't answer her, looking to Bran, because the whole reason they had gone into the forest in the first place was his to talk about. Bran finally let Cillian's hand go with a sigh. "The lights in the wyrding came to Pelham and murdered my mother and stepfather. My little sister survived the attack but was kidnapped by a Fae lord soon after. I couldn't stop him."

"You must not be all that powerful for a witch."

"I know my limits, and I know my strengths," Bran snapped. "I'm not strong enough to go up against a Fae lord who was like a god with just witchmarks."

Niamh narrowed her eyes at him. "There are no gods in the Other-world. They left us long ago."

"Yeah? Whoever that Fae lord was, he was powerful."

"Then how did you survive?"

"I don't know."

"A lie."

"You people would be the worst to play poker with."

"Bran?" Cillian asked. "How did you survive the attack at the Shoppe?"

Bran grimaced. "Jupiter came with dozens of ravens and crows to distract the lights. But the Fae lord left, I think, because he got what he wanted. He got Aisling."

"And why would he want your sister?" Niamh asked.

"She's part of my coven. You Fae seem pretty insistent on eradicating us whether we have magic or not."

"The same can be said of you witches when it comes to us Fae" was Niamh's cool response. "If a Fae took your sister, then she is most likely dead."

"Hey," Cillian snapped. "Until we know for sure, we're still going to search for her. That's why we came here."

Niamh stared at him for a long moment before shaking her head. "You came for a witch and not for your people."

"I think we'll all be a lot better off if you and everyone else quit acting like you know me when you don't."

"But I do. Or I did." Niamh smiled, the twist to her lips this time almost mournful. "You should rest. I will fetch you something to eat."

She inclined her head to him and left the small room, closing the door behind her. Cillian sighed and leaned his head back, closing his eyes, still so tired and sick to his stomach. "Please tell me this is some terrible dream and I'll wake up."

"I wish I could," Bran said, pushing himself off the bed. Cillian opened his eyes, watching as the other man stretched his arms over his head, the coat riding up even if his shirt didn't. A pity. "I can't get us off this ship."

"Where are we heading?"

"To Tech Duinn, the Winter Court's land. It holds territory in the northern part of the country. Niamh said she wasn't taking us to the capital there, though."

"How did we even get here?"

Bran tilted his head a little, bruised face difficult to look away from. Cillian had the furious, riotous urge to rend Ainmire limb from limb for touching Bran. "The Wild Hunt stole us from the carriage. Ainmire couldn't stop the spirits. Apparently, you're their master."

"What?" Cillian shook his head. "I don't even know what that is."

"They're spirits. They hunt wayward travelers, and I guess they found us. Niamh says they obey you. I was surprised about that." His gaze lingered on Cillian. "I was surprised about a lot of things."

Cillian's hands curled into fists as he held Bran's gaze. "I'm still me. You have to believe that."

"I do," Bran said after a moment. "You may look Fae, but at least you don't call me pet."

Maybe he meant it as a joke, but it fell flat between them. Cillian grimaced, lifting a hand and waving for Bran to come closer. He did, sitting back down on the bed, letting Cillian hold his hand like a lifeline. "I won't be like them. I refuse."

"You got your body back. What happens if you get your memories back and you lose the person you are now?" Bran's eyes stared at him intently, something like fear in them. "Would you even want me alive? Ainmire said the Winter Court kept witches as pets like he did."

"They what?"

Bran looked away, fingernails digging into Cillian's skin before he realized what he was doing and stopped. Cillian hadn't minded the prick of pain. "The Fae keep witches and mortals as pets. Servants. Slaves. Take your pick. There was this witch in Ainmire's home, tending to the lamps with magic. She never acknowledged me, was just...this blank shell of a person. I don't ever want to be that."

Cillian leaned forward, all his discomfort falling away amid a cold-burning fury. "Is that what that bastard wanted to do with you?"

Bran's eyes widened, and Cillian followed his gaze, startling badly at the appearance of ice on the floor beneath the other man's boots. It radiated a coolness the same way the ice in the cell had. He let Bran go, slumping against the pillow, and stared at Bran.

"Well." Bran swallowed loudly, still looking at the ice. "I can definitely say that was you and not me."

"I don't—I didn't—"

He cut off as Niamh came back into the room, a tray of food in hand. She paused in the doorway, eyeing the ice on the floor. Her gaze brightened at the sight, and she shot Cillian a pleased look. "Your magic wasn't damaged after all."

"I don't have any magic," Cillian automatically said.

Niamh walked across the ice with an ease Cillian was a little wary of. She set the tray down on his blanket-covered lap, gesturing at it. "Eat. We still have a ways to sail."

The food was simple fare: slices of bread, dried fruit, a hard cheese, and a bowl of seafood soup that was more broth than anything else. There was enough for two, but Cillian wasn't sure how easy it would be for Bran to chew right now.

"Can you bring something to help with Bran's wounds?" Cillian asked. "And then get us to shore. We need to find Aisling."

Niamh frowned at him, one hand on her hip. "Why? You must know she is dead."

"I'm not going to believe that unless I see her body," Bran bit out, pale-faced with anger around his bruises.

"And where do you think to look for her after all this time?"

"I can find her." Cillian's eye was drawn to the way Bran touched the bracelet around his wrist and how areas of his tattoos seemed to shine bright for a second. "I just need to be on land to do it."

"We're going even if we have to dive overboard," Cillian warned.

Niamh shot him an exasperated look. "You are still so stubborn. Like an unmovable glacier."

"Then take us to shore."

He stared at her expectantly, wondering if she would listen. And maybe there was something to being this Winter Prince after all because Niamh's shoulders fell when she sighed, giving in. "Very well, my prince."

She left, presumably to give her crew their new orders and hopefully bring something back that would take away Bran's pain. Cillian looked down at the tray of food, wondering if he could even choke any of it down with the way his stomach felt. He set the tray aside, meeting

Bran's gaze as the ice on the floor started to fade, the same way it had back in that cell. "We'll find your sister, and then we'll get back home."

Because Cillian didn't care what anyone said about him or this place. Home was Pelham and the forest he patrolled as a ranger. Home was the people he knew and had grown up with.

Cillian would get them back there to make a life with Bran, even if it killed him.

Chapter Seventeen

Bran followed Cillian up the narrow stairs to the deck above hours later, ducking his head against the wind filling the sails. The sound of the crew calling to each other momentarily paused as they came onto the deck. Bran shielded his eyes with one hand, squinting against the sunlight at the shore some distance away. In the middle of the day, with clear skies, the pitch of the ship wasn't as terrible as it had been last night when motion sickness had been a constant companion. Right now, the waves didn't look too bad, but he wasn't a sailor, so he couldn't say.

The crew stared at them—well, they stared at Cillian. They glared at Bran if they even bothered to look his way. Cillian noticed, judging by the way his mouth firmed and he stepped closer to Bran, still a little wobbly on his feet. Bran put a hand on his arm to steady him, and he swore several of the Fae started reaching for some hidden weapons.

"I'm all right," Cillian said.

"If you face-plant on the deck, everyone is going to blame me," Bran muttered.

Cillian tossed a smile his way, and Bran found himself wanting to stare into Cillian's eyes and look away in equal parts. He was so different yet exactly the same—still tall, still the same stormy blue-gray eyes, but there was a presence around him now that was impossible to ignore. A kind of magnetism every Fae seemed to possess, but Bran noticed Cillian more than anyone. He always had.

"My prince," Niamh called out, clattering down the stairs from the wheelhouse and coming over to them. "You should not be up."

"I'm fine," Cillian said. "I wanted to see where we were heading."

Niamh ignored Bran, which shouldn't have bothered him. All the Fae in the Otherworld treated witches and mortals like servants or worse. The only reason Bran wasn't dead or forced into servitude on the ship was because of Cillian.

A *caw* from above had Bran looking up, automatically raising his arm to give Jupiter something to land on. The raven flew toward him between the sails, wings flapping for balance as she angled her taloned feet to grip his forearm with a gentleness few people realized she had. He hefted her close, smoothing two fingers over the feathers on her head as she *cawed* at him in greeting. She blinked her starry black eyes at him before leaning close to preen his dirty hair.

"Yes, yes, I know. I need a shower," Bran said.

He smoothed his hand down her back, scratching between the feathers there, before lifting his arm a little higher so she could hop to his shoulder. Jupiter's weight was familiar after so many years of carrying her, as was the way she kept preening his hair. When he finally looked away from his familiar, he found Niamh studying him through narrowed eyes, and she wasn't the only Fae doing so.

"She's not hurt?" Cillian asked, reaching around to pet Jupiter.

Bran tugged at the bond, the connection soft and open between him and his familiar. "No, she's fine."

"How did she even know who to go to for help?"

"I don't know. She kept her distance when we were with Ainmire, and the collar didn't help any."

"She is one of the Mórrígan's own and came to us when we were at sea. We answered her call and sailed south, into the river," Niamh said.

"And no one noticed your ship?" He found that difficult to believe. The prow was decorated with the actual skull of what might have been a sea serpent. Bran had noticed it when he'd been taken above by Niamh for what amounted to an interrogation while Cillian had slept after they first arrived.

"Trade exists between the Four Lands. We sailed under that regard."

Bran furrowed his brow, dragging up the memory of that map he'd bled on in the library. "Which river? The one north or south of Murias?"

Niamh tilted her head, one brow arching in a surprised manner. "The northern one. How do you know of either?"

"Ainmire showed me a map. He said the same kind exists in every city and town to depict the reflection of the wyrding inside your borders." He touched his thumb to the spot his finger had been pricked, the wound there gone like the ones on his face. One of Niamh's crew members had reluctantly healed him after Cillian had woken up and requested such aid. Bran had only flinched a little at their touch. "The northern river was far from where I think we were traveling."

"It is. I was relieved the Wild Hunt chose to help us."

Bran eyed her. "Can anyone summon those spirits?"

"I did not summon them. I sent a prayer into the wind, and the Wild Hunt chose to answer. Only my prince may summon them."

"That didn't answer my question. Are you High Fae?" Bran had observed there were social classes while in Ainmire's custody, and if Niamh purported to know Cillian, she had to be pretty high socially. He turned out to be right.

"Yes. I am the Lady of Sky and Lightning, a trusted member of my prince's inner circle," Niamh said, inclining her head in Cillian's direction. "There are others who hold the same trust."

"Do any of them know I'm here?" Cillian asked.

Niamh hesitated before nodding slightly, touching the medallion that hung from her throat. "I scried Verlin and informed him of the situation. He sent Carrick and Seamus south on the fastest ship he could give them without Medb noticing. We were to meet them halfway before you demanded we go to shore."

"Who are they?"

"Carrick is a loyal friend. You granted him the title of Lord of Blood and Earth when you took him into your Court."

"That's not concerning at all," Bran muttered, having realized the High Fae's titles reflected the magic they wielded. "And Seamus?"

"A knight and captain of the personal guard to the royal family of the Winter Court."

"And he survived the purge?"

"He was the only knight to do so."

Bran could read between the lines of that answer. "He was left alive as punishment, wasn't he?"

"As an example, a warning, and a hostage," Niamh corrected.

"A hostage for who?" Cillian asked.

"Medb holds Seamus' leash to keep Verlin in line. Seamus is Verlin's mate, and Verlin will not act against Medb so long as she controls whether Seamus lives or dies. All the rest of us who would rise up against Medb's rule on behalf of Verlin cannot do so because we won't risk either of them dying. Verlin's House is not royal, but he has our loyalty. That is why the Dagda did not bid a bean sí cry when he crowned Medb and heralded her rule. We do not rebel to keep them both safe."

"I thought a bean sí heralded death?" Bran asked.

"That is not all they can do."

More and more, Bran realized that for all the knowledge his coven and others had gained over the centuries about the Fae, they still knew so little about their culture. Their power, yes, but not the intricate connections that tied them together between House and Court. "Does Medb let Seamus and Verlin stay together?"

Niamh smiled bitterly. "Medb has Seamus on a long leash. She shortens it when it amuses her."

Bran knew all about how Fae found their amusements. "Then isn't it a risk to send Seamus to us? Won't she find out?"

"There is no order that any of us could give that would keep Seamus from our prince's side now that we know he is alive."

A pained look crossed Cillian's face. "I don't want to be responsible for anyone's death."

"We choose to serve," Niamh said, as if that was the end-all and be-all of the argument.

Cillian shook his head. "We need to find Aisling."

"How long until we get to shore?" Bran asked, looking past Niamh at the cliffs. He didn't see any feasible way up them.

"We will reach the cove soon enough." Niamh eyed them critically. "But you both must change. The clothes you are in are too noticeable for the village we will be passing through. And I will bring another healing draught for my prince to take."

"Isn't there any way we can bypass the village?" He just needed to be on shore to activate the locating spell in his bracelet. From there, they could travel to wherever Aisling was.

"To do so would draw more attention. We have wares to trade, and some of my crew will handle that while we see what your magic can do."

Her tone said she didn't believe it would amount to much, and it stung. Bran held his tongue, though, not keen on arguing around so many Fae.

Bran tapped Jupiter on the beak, then held out his arm again. She hopped onto his forearm, and he launched her into the air, watching her fly up to perch on top of the highest mast. Then they were ushered back to the room Cillian had been recuperating in below deck. Niamh wasn't long in returning, her arms laden down with clothes, a cavalier-style hat, and a small box. "Your boots you can keep. Please change into these. The hat is for you, my prince. And you, witch, must wear this."

"*No*," Bran said, the word wrenching itself from his mouth as he stared at the collar and leash in the box she held up after placing the clothes on the bed. "I won't."

"All mortals wear such items in the Otherworld, whether witch or not. You are not one of us, and you must be owned," she said flatly.

"No one owns Bran, and he isn't wearing that," Cillian growled.

Niamh set the box with the collar and leash on the bed and stared them both down. "Witches have no rights in our world. They are the enemy and always have been since our world was cleaved from theirs. If he walks around with freedom, that will draw attention more than anything else we do. Attention that will get him killed. You say he is your friend. If you wish to keep him safe, you must leash him. He is far too willful to pass as a servant."

"You mean broken," Bran spat out. "Your kind doesn't keep willful witches. You break them into pets."

Niamh shrugged, as if it didn't bother her one bit that their society allowed such horror.

"What would happen if he didn't wear it?" Cillian asked.

"It is not done for pets," she said.

"I'm not—" Bran said.

"You are such a thing here," Niamh hissed, taking a single step forward, though she didn't reach for any of the throwing knives on her person. "Here, you are a witch, and if you are that, then you are one of two things—dead or owned. If you do not wear my prince's collar, then you are fair game for any Fae to claim."

Bran stepped back, one hand going to his bare throat as he stared at her. The idea of being a prisoner to someone like Ainmire again sent a jagged bolt of fear through him.

"Can you give us a minute?" Cillian asked quietly.

She sighed before passing over the last thing in her hand to Cillian. "Drink this. It will ease your lingering aches."

Niamh left, closing the door behind her. Bran sucked in a breath and stepped away from the bed, glaring at the collar and leash. "I'm not wearing it."

"Bran," Cillian said. "I don't want you to become a target."

Bran spun around, gesturing sharply at the collar and leash. "So you want me to wear *that*? Want me to willingly put it on and suffer through not being able to use my magic again?"

"Niamh didn't say it would do that."

"She didn't say what it would do at all. That's how Fae speak, Cillian. You have to listen to what is and isn't said when they talk. It's all word games to trap you in a corner."

"Is that what Ainmire did to you?"

Bran looked away from him, glaring at the wall. "You wouldn't have been fed if I hadn't agreed to what he wanted."

Neither of them had been able to attempt an escape for fear of the other one coming to harm. Leashed by words, if not by a physical one, at the time. It still pulled the same way. And now, Cillian was contemplating what Ainmire had done, and the idea of it had Bran sick to his stomach.

"I hated Ainmire's collar on you," Cillian said in a low voice. "And I'll hate any Fae who tries to put one on you."

"So you'll end up hating yourself?"

"Not if it will keep you safe."

Bran met his gaze, the steadiness of it like the calm eye of a hurricane. There wasn't any of the sick satisfaction that had been in Ainmire's eyes there in Cillian's, only a depth of worry and care he couldn't look away from. "I don't want to."

"I know. But if it keeps other Fae from hurting you so we can find Aisling, then I will ask you to please wear it. You can take it off as soon as it's safe."

Bran laughed harshly. "Safe? We aren't safe so long as we stay in the Otherworld."

"We'll get out. We'll get back home. But we need to make you as safe as we can in order to do that." Bran watched as Cillian picked up the collar and leash, holding it out to him. "So, please. Would you wear it?"

Bran clenched his teeth so hard he thought he might crack one. He couldn't help the way his breathing sped up at the thought of having that physical form of ownership locked around his throat again. He remembered what it had felt like when Nature was taken from him and his magic had been blocked—the horrible emptiness it had left him with. It would drive him mad if he had to suffer through that again.

But he'd suffered through that indignity once before to keep Cillian safe. He could do nothing less to find Aisling.

"I couldn't touch Ainmire's collar without it hurting," Bran said stiffly.

A hot rage flashed across Cillian's eyes and the air in the room went sharply cold. "I think Niamh knows I wouldn't stand for that. If it does, I'll let my displeasure be known."

"I don't know if I can."

"Please. For me. I want to know you're safe."

Bran ran a hand through his hair, trying to stifle his nerves and failing. Mostly because—because it was Cillian asking, and Bran had never been good at telling the other man no when they were kids. It seemed that habit was still alive.

He slowly reached for the collar, fingertips grazing the metal, steeling himself for pain, but none came. It was made out of silver and hinged to open, cool to the touch. The same crest on Niamh's pendant was welded to one spot, the crown protruding like a ring for a leash to attach to. Delicate filigree was etched into the metal around it, none of which flared with magic when Bran's fingers brushed against the design, ready to snatch his hand back at the first touch of pain. Tiny sapphires and diamonds framed the base of the crest, whatever magic was in those jewels quiet.

Grimacing, Bran took the collar from Cillian and thumbed at the small latch, opening it. With a shaky breath, he lifted it to his neck and closed it around his throat, locking it in place. It wasn't constricting, not how Ainmire's had felt, resting at the base of his throat, but it still felt as if it were choking him.

Cool hands cupped his face. "Hey, look at me. I need you to breathe."

Bran stared up into Cillian's eyes, breath hitching in his throat as he realized how close the other man was. His skin buzzed from the touch on his face, and Bran wanted desperately to pull Cillian closer, like he once had the right to. Only a few inches separated them, but it felt like a chasm in that moment. Cillian's gaze dropped down to Bran's mouth for a split second before jerking back up again to meet his eyes. A jagged bolt of heat shot through Bran as he held Cillian's gaze, wondering for a fleeting moment what Cillian would taste like if they kissed.

He immediately strangled that thought.

Cillian cleared his throat and dropped his hands, stepping back, which was the last thing Bran wanted, but he couldn't make himself reach for the other man. He swallowed hard. "I'm okay."

"Let's get dressed," Cillian said roughly.

Bran was more than happy to get out of the clothes Ainmire had put him in, still stained with blood from Etain's cruelty. The clothes Niamh had brought fit him well enough, though Cillian's looked like they fit perfectly. Bran's pants were a dark brown, and the shirt felt like linen, a dull cream color with long sleeves that covered his tattoo. No cravat or tie was anywhere to be seen, and the shirt didn't have a dress collar that would cover the one around his throat. Bran scowled down at the leash coiled in the box, and the disgust he felt at picking up the thin metal chain made him want to throw it across the room.

"Do you want me to put it on you now or when we're on the shore?" Cillian asked.

"Shore," Bran said immediately, handing it to him. The longer he could stave off the inevitable, the better he'd feel.

"Okay." Cillian picked up the hat and put it on, the angle of it giving him a rakish look. "Let's find Niamh."

They left the room, making their way back up to the deck. The ship swayed a bit beneath his feet, and Bran had to brace himself against the pitch of it. Niamh caught sight of them from her spot up on the steering deck. She waved to acknowledge them but kept talking to the Fae who stood at the ship's wheelhouse. Crew up in the rigging shouted to each other as the sails were repositioned a little to catch the wind, angling the ship toward a break in the cliffs.

Niamh finally made her way across the deck to them after a few minutes. "We'll anchor in the cove and take a boat to shore."

Bran peered past Cillian at the cove in question. "Are we in Summer Court territory?"

"Unfortunately, yes. We're still within Tír na nÓg." She eyed him, sizing him up. "I do not know where your magic will lead us."

"Ainmire said every city and town had a map to mark the wyrding. Would the village have one?"

"They will have one. Why do you need it?"

"Because I can use it to pinpoint Aisling's location."

"We have maps on the ship."

"Ones that show the wyrding?"

Niamh frowned. "No."

"I need accuracy." He didn't know where Aisling was—in one of the Four Lands or the wyrding—but he needed a map that would show everything.

"If the village has what Bran needs, then we'll use it," Cillian said, heading off the argument Bran could feel building.

Niamh sighed. "If we must travel inland, I will instruct my first mate to sail north after some of the crew have traded at the market. I don't want the Dagda's hunters to detain them."

"Will he know where we are?"

"Ainmire and Etain would have made it to Murias by now and given their report to the Summer Court. I am doubtful the Dagda will let the situation be known publicly."

"Why not?"

"Because there are Fae in the Four Lands who believe he went too far with what happened in the Winter Court. If it is known you survived? That would complicate things. He will not want to advertise his failure."

Bran didn't know what to believe, and he hoped Cillian wouldn't take what Niamh said at face value. Fae weren't to be trusted. Bran had grown up believing that, internalizing it, but now, everything he'd learned beside his mother was thrown into question when it came to Cillian. His mind and heart were jumping through hoops to separate Cillian from every other Fae in existence.

"You gave Cillian a hat. I don't know if that will be enough to hide him," Bran said.

Niamh eyed them both critically. "The skin you say he wore made him appear mortal. I do not want to cast glamour on him to try to change his appearance. That is not my strength."

"Can you keep people from noticing him?"

"They will notice him because of you."

"I already said I'd keep my mouth shut."

"Niamh," Cillian said quietly. "Please. Do what you have to."

She grimaced but still raised her hands. "Very well. I will make it so others notice those around you who are not the witch first."

Bran tensed, wanting to protest. They didn't have the greatest track record with Fae magic. Cillian braced himself, but Niamh's magic, when she cast it, was a soft glow that spun around his wrists and head before disappearing.

"How do you feel?" Bran asked.

Cillian tilted his head a bit. "It doesn't hurt."

"I would never harm you," Niamh said stiffly.

Neither of them said anything to that, and Niamh left with a sigh to take charge of her crew. The *Bone Breaker* sailed into the cove, and the crew laid anchor, winching a pair of boats into the water filled with crates. Bran gripped the edge of the bench he and Cillian sat in as the boat finally splashed into the sea. The crew rowed them to shore with a skill he could appreciate more once the hull of the boat dug into wet sand. Bran scrambled onto the beach, staring up at the rocky cliff. This close, he could see the stone steps carved like a switchback road into the cliffside.

He didn't see any railings.

"I guess it's a good thing I'm not afraid of heights," Bran muttered.

Cillian laughed, but he still looked concerned, staring at the cliffside. "Yeah. Me too."

The other Fae in the two boats hauled crates and trunks to the shore. Niamh checked in with everyone, speaking in their language, so Bran didn't know what her orders were. She approached them after a few minutes, nodding in the direction of the cliffside. "The trade village is up there. My crew will set up in the market square while we check their records for a map so you can do what you need to, witch."

"He has a name," Cillian said testily.

Niamh shook her head, pointing at the collar Bran wore. "Not here. Not like this. Remember what I said. If you want him to survive, he must be silent, and he must be owned. Do you have the leash?"

Cillian clenched his jaw but nodded. Bran wanted to protest, but he knew following Niamh's orders would keep him safe, no matter how much he hated them.

"Good," Niamh said.

She led the way up the beach to the cliffside. The sand became a little rockier the farther they got from the waves. The steps leading up were carved out of stone, large enough for a single person to walk up safely if one ignored the sheer drop on one side. Bran readied himself for the climb and followed Cillian up, only making it to the top by not looking down. He joined Cillian on green grass, the land sloping down to a sprawling little trade village. Bran stared at it, uncomfortable with the part he was about to play but knowing he had no choice.

"Ready?" Cillian asked quietly, drawing the leash from his pocket.

"No, but I'll have to be," Bran said.

He didn't think he'd ever get used to being collared and leashed like an animal, but at least Cillian's touch was kind when he tilted Bran's head back to clip the leash into place. Cillian gave him an apologetic look before stepping back, leash in hand, leaving no choice but for Bran to follow where he led.

Chapter Eighteen

The village Fae seemed happy enough to see the crew. Niamh took charge, making sure Cillian and Bran were pushed to the back of the group, attention on the crew and not them. Bran didn't understand anything being said, wishing he had his coven's grimoire at hand. He knew translation spells were somewhere in the history of it, and that would have come in handy the entire time they'd been in the Otherworld.

The village leader was a Fae who clearly didn't come from wealth, but his tunic and pants appeared decently made. Bran and Cillian made sure to stay at the back of their group as Niamh's crew set up their wares in the village square at permanent stalls, the wood weathered from past storms.

Cillian never let go of the leash, and Bran was hyperaware of the thin metal chain that linked them together. The collar was a weight he had to fight from touching. Ainmire's collar had only brought pain when he touched it. Even though this one was nominally Cillian's, Bran knew Fae would expect it to hurt him if he tried to touch it.

"Are you all right?" Cillian asked in a low voice.

"I have to be, don't I?" Bran muttered back.

"Just hold on a little longer."

He reminded himself he was doing this for Aisling. Bran could bow his head and not look any Fae in the eye, could follow behind Cillian like an obedient, mindless puppet if it meant he could find his little sister.

Bran would have liked to see what it was the crew planned to sell, but Niamh nodded at the village leader, accepted a sip of some drink from a wooden cup he offered her, and then retreated to their group. She made a discreet gesture in their direction, which prompted Cillian and Bran to follow after her, along with a few other crew members. A different villager led them to a one-room stone building down a dirt road on the outskirts of the village. Their guide cast Bran a wary look but didn't even glance at Cillian before leaving.

The two crew members with them posted themselves outside by the door while Niamh entered. Bran dug in his heels at the tug on the bond, looking up at the sky. A black dot far above resolved itself into Jupiter seconds later. He raised his arm, allowing his familiar to land. She made no sound as she did so, well aware of the need for quiet and secrecy.

"Ready?" Cillian asked.

Bran nodded and followed him inside a space empty of any furniture, the air so hot it made him sweat. The building had no windows, but it had four lanterns hanging from the wall, all of which flickered to life with the same sort of light that had illuminated Ainmire's home.

"What's in them?" Bran asked, staring at one of the lanterns. "Ainmire had a witch tending to his."

"Fire elementals," Niamh said, glancing at him. "They are drawn to Nature."

"You Fae can't light your own fires?"

She shot him a withering look.

"Let's look at the map," Cillian hastily said, handing Bran the leash now that they were out of sight of prying eyes.

Bran shoved the end into his trouser pocket and hefted Jupiter up to his shoulder. "Where's the map?"

Niamh pointed at the floor. "We are standing on it."

He'd been expecting the grand reproduction like he'd seen in the library in Ainmire's town. What he had to work with was faded paint that offered little depth, but the map was still the same outline he remembered from the library. "This is it?"

"You say you can find your sister? Then find her."

Bran tried not to take the faint derision in her voice personally, but it was hard to ignore. Niamh's attitude when she addressed Cillian was kinder, more deferential. Bran knew he'd never earn that from any Fae, but the hostility was stress-inducing.

He rolled up his sleeves and held his hand over the bracelet tied around his left wrist. Taking a deep breath, he sketched a witchmark in the air, the golden lines bright, his intent to *locate* drawing out the spell in one of the beads. The shape of his mother's magic made him blink back a sudden wetness in his eyes. The witchmark that represented Aisling expanded outward, floating in the air to dance around his own.

He flexed his hands before making a sharp swiping motion from elbow to wrist. Brilliant golden sparks twisted around his forearm and into the palm of his hand. He tipped it, magic falling to the floor like a firefall, golden and bright.

The intent of the spell flowed down the connection tying it to the witchmark anchored on the bead of the bracelet his sister wore. Bran's stomach twisted, lurched, as his awareness was stretched thin, his ability to orient himself difficult in the Otherworld. Jupiter steadied him, anchoring him in that maelstrom as Nature washed through him.

His magic poured out of him and flooded the floor, following the lines of the map. It snaked to a spot on the eastern side of the painted island, pooling in a gray area. The bead on his bracelet with the witchmark of Aisling's name pulsed brightly, and Jupiter *cawed*, the gold flecks in her eyes shining like stars. Bran fell into it, fell into their bond, letting Nature drag his awareness over the face of a world he'd never walked until it slammed into a grayness he couldn't see through—but he knew that beyond it was his sister.

Bran came back to himself with a wrench, staggering forward. An arm wrapped around his waist, drawing him up against a warm, firm body, and Bran couldn't help but lean into the touch. Cillian's voice was a low reverberation in his ear that made him shiver. "I got you."

Bran swallowed audibly, trying to steady his breathing and ignore the hot spike of *want* that cut through him. "There. She's there."

Niamh walked over to where Bran's magic glowed brightest, her steps slow, tracing a route inland from the coast. When she stopped, the toes of her boots almost brushed against Bran's magic. "This is the wyrding."

Bran's stomach sank, fear latching onto him like a wild animal. They'd been in the Otherworld for what passed for a week or longer. "How do we get there?"

Niamh tilted her head. "The wyrding appears where it likes. The passages between the mounds that connect the Otherworld to yours are different than the shadow paths that link each spot of blight. For those, you enter the wyrding in one location and arrive somewhere else, but you have to follow the lights to find them."

"Those monstrous creatures?" Cillian asked dubiously. "They tried to kill Bran."

Niamh looked as if she was sad they hadn't succeeded. "I know the shadow paths there. I've traveled them before on your behalf and Verlin's. If the witch can use his magic to locate his sister, I can lead him and you to her."

"Bran?"

He stared at the glow of his magic on that map whose paint had to be imbued with its own kind of power. So different yet so similar to that grand map in Ainmire's library, all of it meant as a warning. "I'm not leaving Aisling behind."

He was all she had, and she was all he had. He refused to look at Cillian, forcing himself to pull away from the other man's hold, even though it was the last thing he wanted to do right then. He would save Aisling from whoever or whatever had her, even if it killed him, but he would *not* leave her in this place.

"That wasn't in doubt," Cillian said, as if agreeing to Bran's crazy ideas was nothing new. And it wasn't, if he let himself think of their past. "How do you get us to one of these shadow paths?"

Niamh sighed, stepping back from the dying embers of Bran's magic as he drew it all back into himself. "We must head into the wyrding."

"Is it close to here?"

Niamh smiled bitterly, taking measured steps to a spot on the map that looked like their position, scuffing the toe of her boot over a smear of black paint close to a village marker. "It is always close when witches are around."

Bran bristled at that but held his tongue. She was his way to Aisling, and he'd take any insults she tossed at him if it meant she could get them to his little sister. "Then let's go."

"Hold his leash," Niamh said to Cillian, the biting words a reminder and warning all in one.

Bran grimaced but pulled the leash out of his pocket and handed the end to Cillian. Their fingers brushed in the handover, and he suppressed a shiver at the way Cillian looked, holding his leash, in total control. Cillian eyed him carefully, gaze searching. "All right?"

"Just don't let go," Bran muttered as Niamh headed for the door, yanking it open.

"I won't." Sunlight spilled into the room, haloing Cillian in a way that made it impossible to look away from him. "They'll have to fight me for you."

It shouldn't have made him ache, but it did, some part of him wanting Cillian to mean it in a way he had no right to want, not after how he'd left seven years ago. Bran dropped his gaze, licking his lips, cognizant of the thin metal that connected them as Cillian led him out of the room, aware, too, of the collar around his throat with Cillian's emblem on it. A claim that somehow felt right despite his initial trepidation.

He blamed the sun for the heat in his cheeks as they left the stone building. Jupiter flew out behind them and back into the sky. Niamh took the lead when they reached the village square again, making nice with the Fae in charge. It wasn't long before she split her people up, leaving some behind to trade and the rest going with them. They left the village, starting down the dirt road that curved between low hills, a forest dotting the horizon in the distance.

"What was the excuse you gave them?" Cillian asked once they were out of earshot.

"Hunting," Niamh said. "I never said what."

Fae and their word games. Bran hated both. "How appropriate."

"I told my second-in-command to scry Carrick and Seamus and send them through the wyrding to us at the coordinates you gave.

They've traveled the shadow paths before. They'll know where to find us."

"Is the wyrding that easy for you Fae to traverse?"

"Yes and no."

They passed Fae working the field and a few travelers on the road with laden-down carts. Cillian held tight to the leash, and Bran didn't fight him on it. The sun overhead heated the air to a summer warmth that had Bran sweating by the time they reached the forest, the tree line like the other they'd run through after leaving the wyrding behind— filled with massive trees, the flowers and plants shaped differently from the ones back home. The shade beneath the branches was a little cooler, sunlight dappling the ground where they walked.

Niamh hopped onto a large root, pressing a hand to the massive tree trunk to steady herself. She peered deeper into the forest before gesturing at one of her crew. She gave an order that had the other Fae bounding forward, disappearing between the trees.

"Where are they going?" Cillian asked.

"To scout ahead. The forest is getting colder when it shouldn't be," Niamh said.

"It's *hot*," Bran muttered.

She cast him a withering glance. "The wyrding is always cold. Tev knows the signs better than even I do. He was a border guard before he joined my crew."

"You said we had to follow the lights," Cillian said.

"Yes, but the lights will not harm us."

"No, they just harm mortals," Bran said sharply, thinking of how the horror of them had attacked the Shoppe.

"You witches raised the wyrding first." Her gaze swept up and down him, lip curling slightly. "We are here by the grace of my prince for your sister. So you will find her."

He hooked a thumb around the chain of his leash, the end still clutched in Cillian's hand. "I want this off."

"No." Niamh turned on her heel and strode away, the handful of her crew with them following after her. Bran ground his teeth but was startled out of his anger by Cillian stepping close, tucking the end of the leash into Bran's pocket like he had the right to be so close. Bran's breath strangled itself in his throat, gaze snapping up to meet Cillian's.

"Let's find Aisling," Cillian murmured.

They pushed on, the forest cooler than the road had been, but not by much. Sweat dried on his skin, his shirt unsticking itself from his back. Bran stayed close to Cillian as they followed Niamh. What might have been an hour later, Tev returned, darting between trees on sure feet. He flung himself over a root and landed lightly beside Niamh, speaking in a low voice that Bran could barely make out, not that he understood a word the Fae said. Niamh nodded before looking over her shoulder at them. "The forest is dead up ahead. Stay close."

Bran tensed at her words. He knew what to expect now, but it was still a shock when the trees started to lose their color the deeper they went, brown leaves carpeting the dirt where nothing else grew. Niamh's crew didn't spread out as much, staying close with weapons near at hand. Bran's shoulders knotted with tension as he walked beside Cillian, Jupiter flying from tree branch to tree branch ahead of them, a silent, shadowy companion.

Fog crept through the air, blocking out the sunlight. The temperature plummeted, and Bran didn't know he could miss the summer heat so much, but he did. He stepped closer to Cillian, fingers flexing, the power of Nature a witchmark away. The buzz of living things in the forest faded until their breathing and the crunch of footsteps on brittle leaves was the only sound around them.

Niamh seemed to know where she was going, leading them through spindly, dead trees that offered nowhere to hide. The smell of rot lingered in the air, and the lifeless trees they passed sometimes dripped with that sticky black sap. He didn't know how long they'd been walking before Niamh pulled up short, gesturing in a way that had her crew scattering for what limited cover the trees could provide. Bran and Cillian belatedly followed suit, ducking together behind a dead tree.

Bran found himself pressed up against decaying bark by Cillian, that black sap seeping into the back of his shirt. Cillian was warm in front of him, bracketing him in, and Bran tried not to curl into that warmth. To distract himself from the way Cillian's close proximity made his heart beat faster, he closed his eyes and reached for his bond with Jupiter so he could stare through his familiar's eyes. She was perched high above them, motionless in the cold wind. Her vision wasn't like his, but it was impossible to miss the monster stalking through the woods, its path taking it right to them.

Niamh hadn't bothered to hide, standing alone in the dirt, arms loose at her sides and hands empty. But he'd seen her magic on the ship when the Wild Hunt had carried them to her. Bran knew what devastation she could cause and knew the monster that approached wouldn't survive if Niamh didn't want it to.

Through Jupiter's eyes, Bran watched the monster halt between two trees, wishing he could forget what it looked like—all exposed bone jutting through rotten flesh along its spine, its legs ending in cloven hooves while its arms ended in three-fingered hands. Its head had eyes, but its mouth was located in its chest, the vertical slit there prying apart and revealing a fanged maw that screeched a terrible sound that made the hair on the back of Bran's neck stand on end.

Niamh spoke, and the monster screeched again before it turned around and staggered off. Niamh stayed put, not moving, her eyes on its departure. Jupiter stared at it until she could no longer see through the fog, and Bran slipped free of his familiar's eyes.

Niamh appeared around their tree, eyeing them. Cillian didn't pull away from where he had Bran pressed against the tree, and Bran was acutely aware of the lack of space between their bodies. "The shadow path is ahead. We must follow the light to it. Keep your witch leashed."

"Those things tried to kill me before," Bran hissed.

"If you are leashed by a Fae, the lights will not attack you here."

Bran highly doubted that, but it didn't stop Cillian from stepping back to give Bran room to turn around. Cillian dug the end of the leash out from Bran's pocket, fingers warm through the cloth against his thigh. He sucked in a breath, gaze snapping up to Cillian's face. The other man stared back, mouth pressed into a grim line, his hair straggling free of the ponytail around his pointed ears, cavalier hat still firmly on his head. "Sorry about this."

"Let's go," Bran muttered. It was humiliating, being led around on a leash, but there was a part of him that didn't mind when Cillian did it, and Bran refused to think about why.

The last thing he wanted to do was follow a light into the dark of the wyrding, but that was what Bran and the others did. Niamh led the way, tracking the monster's direction with a skill he'd appreciate if it wasn't a nightmare they were following.

He never saw it after that first appearance. Still, it led them to a shadow path that Bran would've walked right on by if Niamh hadn't stopped. No mound this time, only a cracked-open tree that must have been hit with lightning once upon a time. It still stood but was hollowed out from some long-ago fire. It reminded him of the tree at the foot of the mound in the forest back home.

"Whatever you do, don't stop walking," Niamh said, ducking into the crack in the tree. The shadows swallowed her whole, and her crew didn't hesitate to follow her, even when Bran wanted to.

He raised his arm, and Jupiter flew to him, alighting on his forearm. He let her hop to his shoulders, feathers brushing against his ear and cheek as she found her balance. Then he followed Cillian into that dark space, unsurprised to find it led somewhere else.

Shadow paths, Niamh had called them. The name fit, for Bran couldn't see anything once they'd entered the inside of that tree and the hidden way through. Niamh's words rang in his mind, and Bran took them as the warning they were. He couldn't see Cillian, but he could feel the leash between them, the metal pulled taut, and that soothed him somehow. He walked through darkness, feeling as if he were falling, stomach twisting uncomfortably like he was in free fall, until a flicker of light in the far distance became a way out.

They crawled out of a gap between two boulders, back into the wyrding, and found Niamh waiting for them with her crew in a clearing that was empty of bones this time. Bran didn't know how cold he was until he left the shadow path behind, teeth chattering, grateful for even the weak daylight filtering through the fog. Cillian didn't appear bothered by the chill at all, but he eyed Bran with concern.

"I'm fine," Bran said. "Where are we?"

"Where your magic said your sister would be," Niamh said.

The wyrding looked the same as it had before. He wanted to believe she hadn't led them astray. "You're sure?"

"I know how to bend the shadow paths to my will."

That sounded a lot like *intent*, and Bran decided he wasn't going to think about that. Instead, he focused on Aisling's witchmark on his bracelet, pulling it free with a twist of his fingers and a tiny pulse of magic. The sparkling ball of magic was the size of a grape, and he fed it to Jupiter with cold fingers. "Find her."

Jupiter launched herself from his shoulder, flying silently away, the urge to follow singing through their bond. Bran didn't think twice about running after her, Cillian keeping pace so the leash wouldn't hold him back. He wanted desperately to call out Aisling's name but didn't dare, not wanting to draw any attention from the lights. All he could do was go where Jupiter bade him, the wyrding a blur of gray as he ran.

His lungs burned by the time he skidded to a stop on a hillside, Jupiter circling overhead, silent when she'd be *cawing* loudly if they were back home. Magic coursed through him, eradicating the chill from the shadow paths. Bran stared around frantically, forgetting, in that moment, to be quiet.

"Aisling?" he cried out. "Aisling, it's me!"

Nothing but silence met his ears over the sound of his harsh breathing. Bran called out for her again and again, sliding down the hill with Cillian right beside him. He didn't care about Niamh or her crew, didn't care about the lights, didn't care about anything when he caught sight of movement at the base of a tree. A dirty, pale head peeked over a gnarled root, and Bran let out a choking gasp that somehow became a name. "*Aisling!*"

Bran raced toward her, the leash flying free behind him as Cillian let him go. Aisling scrambled over the root in jerky motions, mouth open on a silent yell, her voice still gone, still stolen, but she wasn't anymore. Then he had her in his arms, squeezing his little sister tight, Jupiter sending *found, found, found* through their bond as Bran cried into Aisling's dirty white-blonde hair. She clutched at him, shaking in his arms, getting the front of his shirt wet from her tears as she sobbed so hard her entire body shook. She barely made a sound, breath coming out in ragged little gasps.

He didn't know she was trying to warn him until it was too late.

"Bran!" Cillian yelled behind him.

He jerked his head up, Jupiter *cawing* a sudden warning as around them, the fog peeled away from Fae soldiers marching between dead trees, an emblem of a deer head with horns etched into their armor chest plates. They were led by a Fae riding one of the massive deer they'd seen in that meadow days ago. The sight of him made all the blood drain from Bran's face.

"So Lord Ainmire's words were true. The Winter Prince lives after all," the Fae lord who had stolen Aisling said.

Chapter Nineteen

"B ran!" Cillian cried out, hell-bent on pitching himself down the remainder of the hill to get to the other man's side, but a vise-like grip grabbed him by the arm, holding him back.

"*No*," Niamh said through gritted teeth. "You cannot stand against Cernunnos as you are now."

Mortal in every way that mattered save the skin he now wore. Cillian couldn't even control the magic Bran swore was his. "Let go."

If anything, Niamh's grip tightened, her voice coming out low and harsh. "That is Cernunnos who speaks your title and knows your face. He is old, even amongst our kind, and one of the most powerful High Fae in the Four Lands."

Cillian stared at the Fae lord in question, taking in that too-beautiful face and long brown hair, the antlers that protruded from his head, and the richly tailored and embroidered courtly outfit he wore. He sat straight and proud on the deer he rode, exuding a sense of power that even Cillian could feel, the way it made the air crackle, pricking at his skin.

Cernunnos and his Fae soldiers ringed the area at the bottom of the hill where Bran and Aisling stood, cutting off any chance of escape except the way they'd come. But to move would risk dying from the arrows nocked to bowstrings or the magic that curled around Cernunnos' hands like some brightly glowing living thing.

"I don't care who he is. He's not taking Bran," Cillian ground out.

He was tired of Fae threatening them both, of speaking as if they knew him when they didn't. Bran was his best friend, had always been that—a permanent presence etched into his bones that not even seven years of silence could erase. Knowing Bran was a witch would never change that. In this strange and dangerous world, the only person Cillian knew he could trust was Bran.

The last thing Cillian was going to do was give him up again.

Cernunnos stared at Cillian, and he met the Fae lord's eyes with a glare of his own, finally yanking his arm free of Niamh's grip with a strength he was still getting used to. He took a step forward, then froze as half the Fae archers at the bottom of the small hill aimed their arrows in his direction. Niamh hissed something in the Fae language, forgetting that Cillian couldn't understand a word she said.

"Back off," Cillian growled.

"You are in no position to give orders," Cernunnos said, nudging his deer forward. The massive animal trotted closer to where Bran and Aisling stood.

Cillian groped desperately for an argument that was the only one he thought the Fae lord would acknowledge. "I collared Bran. That makes him *mine*, not yours. Don't you dare touch him or Aisling."

Cernunnos chuckled, tugging on the reins to bring the deer to a stop. "You think highly of your pet."

Anger was a cold, cold thing coursing through Cillian's veins, nearly choking him. "I think I'm not going to let you kill him or Aisling."

"I have no intention of killing the herald."

The way Niamh sucked in her breath couldn't be a good thing. Cillian didn't know what Cernunnos meant by that, but he didn't care about word games right then. All he cared about was dragging Bran and Aisling back to his side and never letting go. He took another step forward but rocked to a halt from the arrow that lodged itself in the ground mere inches from the toe of his boot. He stared at it, at the warning it likely represented, and weighed it against the fact the archer hadn't aimed for his heart.

"I have no intention of giving up what's mine," Cillian replied. He lifted his gaze from the ground to meet Bran's wide-eyed one, the other man staring back at him from the bottom of the hill, Aisling wrapped up tight in his arms. From what he'd seen, Bran would need his hands free to cast his magic using a witchmark, but he couldn't do it if he was holding on to his sister.

Thunder rumbled in the distance, deep and threatening. Niamh came to stand by his side, the air crackling around her from the scattered bits of lightning crawling over her hands. "You heard my prince. The witch and the girl do not belong to you. They have been claimed."

"Only one wears a collar, and pets die as easily as the next," Cernunnos drawled dismissively.

"You would not risk the herald."

"Neither would you. Do not bring your storms, Lady of Sky and Lightning. I will ruin you if you try."

"You aren't touching Niamh either," Cillian snapped.

"Your possessiveness has not changed at all. Perhaps I shall take you all to the Summer Court and let the Dagda deal with each of you for my amusement."

"You despise the Dagda," Niamh said.

"One can despise a king and still play politics."

"Is that what you want to do here?" Cillian asked. "You want us to bargain for our lives?"

Cillian had no desire to do that. He was tired of being someone else's pawn, and he wasn't about to let this asshole use Bran and Aisling against him. He dug his fingernails into the palms of his hand, the cold rage inside him scratching at his skin, itching to be released. The ground cracked underfoot, his bootheel catching on a divot. He glanced down and saw they stood on iced-over dirt, the edges crawling down the hill in fits and spurts. His breath came out in soft white puffs, the temperature dropping substantially.

Niamh tackled him to the ground, arrows whistling through the air where he had stood. They hit ice, sliding down the hill. Bran screamed his name as the Fae soldiers lunged toward the siblings, everything drowned out by the crackling strike of lightning bolts all around them.

The lightning didn't melt the ice, winter kept alive by the rage pouring out of Cillian.

Niamh kept hold of him, covering his body with her own as the stink of ozone filled the air. Magic erupted around them, bright and golden, a witchmark conjuring up a barrier that kept the arrows that made it through the lightning storm from reaching them. Cillian's heart clenched at the feel of Bran's magic all around them, keeping them safe as they slid to the bottom of the hill.

His feet hit ice, the ground leveling out. They skidded to a stop, Fae shouting all around them. Niamh wrenched herself to her knees, thrusting one arm toward the gray sky above and the roiling storm clouds that seemed to obey her every command.

Cernunnos was a pillar of brightness in the descending gloom, haloed by magic, the antlers on his head burning with it. The garland of blue flowers tangled there lashed about his head. But it was the bits of brightness in the dead forest beyond the Fae lord that made a quiet sort of terror crawl up Cillian's spine.

Lights.

It didn't matter that Niamh had said the lights wouldn't harm Fae. Bran and Aisling weren't Fae, and Cillian wasn't about to risk their lives to the monsters in the wyrding.

He staggered to his feet, slamming a fist against the wall of Bran's magic he couldn't get past. "*Bran!* Get over here!"

"I'm trying!" Bran shouted back. He had Aisling pressed up against his side, one arm wrapped around her shoulders to hold her close. His other arm was thrust outward, fingers moving as he drew witchmarks in the air, casting magic that pushed back the few Fae managing to get close to them.

Cernunnos rode his deer forward through the lightning storm and wasn't touched at all by any of it, flanked by some of his soldiers. His own magic seemed to bat the lightning bolts aside, all his attention on Bran and Aisling, and like hell was Cillian going to give them up.

"Don't you fucking touch them!" Cillian yelled.

A Fae lunged toward Bran, sword cleaving through the air when his momentum abruptly stopped. Blood sprayed from the Fae's throat, pouring out of a thin cut that didn't look like it had gone that deep. The

Fae clawed at the wound, skin going gray and pale behind their helm as they crashed to their knees, bleeding out in seconds. A shadowy blur moved to the next soldier, magic heavy and thick in the air, tasting like metal in the back of his throat as Cillian breathed.

Niamh let out a huff as she got to her feet. "*Finally.*"

"What?" Cillian asked dumbly.

"Carrick found us."

Another cut, another waterfall of blood, staining the dirt and ice all around them crimson. Niamh's lightning disappeared, thunder a mere echo in his ears as Cernunnos' deer reared on its hind legs, kicking at the person who danced close. Cernunnos snarled something in the Fae language, his magic calling up roots from the earth that couldn't pin down Carrick dancing through the soldiers like an angel of death, if Fae even believed in that sort of thing.

A blade flashed bright silver, slicing across the deer's ribs. Blood exploded from the shallow-looking cut, and the deer let out a horrific sound that made Cillian want to cover his ears. Cernunnos vaulted from the jeweled saddle as the deer ran off, leaving a blood trail behind.

The shadow darted their way, sliding to a halt between them and where Bran and Aisling stood. The new Fae was garbed all in black, cloth and leather alike, half a dozen knives and stilettos attached to his body. Even the bits of armor Cillian could see were painted a matte black, all of it matching the Fae's short black hair. He held a blood-coated stiletto in one gloved hand, his other glowing with magic. Sloe-colored eyes looked right at him in a face that carried a thin scar curving between both eyes and over the bridge of his nose, ending on his left cheek.

Cernunnos straightened, eyes snapping with fury. "So the Lord of Blood and Earth has abandoned his loyalty to the Winter Court."

"My loyalty has always been to my prince," the new Fae said in a low, dangerous voice, looking away from Cillian. "*He* is the Winter Court."

"Medb will shorten your leash for this folly."

"She can try."

"Carrick," Niamh said in a tense voice. "We can't leave without the witch and the herald."

"I saw the collar," Carrick said, never taking his eyes off Cernunnos. "Seamus is dealing with the lights."

Cernunnos raised a hand, magic spinning like a small green vortex at his fingertips. The roots all around them ripped free of the earth, straining against magic Cillian couldn't see. "Is this the side you choose?"

"We certainly aren't going to side with *you*," a new voice spat.

Some of Cernunnos' remaining soldiers spun to face the Fae that stepped out from behind a tree, black blood covering the blade of the sword he carried. He was dressed much like Carrick, though he was a little taller and broader, and wielded his sword as if he wasn't bothered by the weight of it. His hair was a strange, dark moss green, though Cillian couldn't see the color of his eyes. A pair of thick silver cuffs embedded with labradorites were sealed around his wrists, reminding Cillian of the ones Ainmire had made him wear.

"Ah, the fallen knight," Cernunnos mocked. "Here to fail at your duty again?"

"No," the Fae who could only be Seamus ground out.

Cernunnos eyed them all, not looking the least bit concerned at being partially hemmed in after losing more than half his soldiers and his ride. Part of that reason came from the way he had Bran and Aisling dead in his sights. "You children cannot best me."

"We don't need to. We just have to outrun you."

Cernunnos smiled as he laughed, and Cillian didn't realize he was screaming until his throat shredded from the sound. Molten magic tore through the air toward Bran and Aisling with a strength he knew—somehow—that Bran wouldn't be able to counter. That it would kill them, and the last thing Cillian wanted to do again was live his life without Bran in it.

Bitterly cold power exploded from the center of his soul, wind howling through the trees as a wave of ice and cold erupted outward. The concussive force of winter iced over almost everything it touched, turning the Fae soldiers into frozen statues. Trees became solid ice, and the ground looked as if it had become a frozen river. Snow flurries spun through the air, falling across everyone. Cernunnos was forced back, feet sliding over ice as the fury of winter lashed at him, driven by Cillian's rage.

He didn't know where the magic came from—how it worked—only that it was his. That this power cutting through his skin and spilling out of him was a season that could last forever if he so wished it.

Blue-white lines of magic ran up his arms from fingertips to shoulders like ice fissures. His fingertips were painted blue from it, all the power of winter cascading out of him, and there was no standing one's ground in the face of a blizzard like that.

So Cernunnos—sly as he was—didn't.

The Fae lord wrapped himself up in the roots of the dead trees, disappearing into the earth. The Fae soldiers left behind died as a group, frozen into statues that would never breathe again. Cillian staggered forward, knees wanting to give out, but before they could, Bran was there, arms wrapping around his torso to hold him up.

"I got you," Bran said through chattering teeth. "I'm here. Pull it all back. You have to."

"I can't," Cillian gasped. "I don't know how."

"It's instinct. It's intent. Make Nature bend to your will. You're so stubborn. I *know* you can do it."

Cillian closed his eyes, trying to do what Bran said, floundering in the wake of magic that had brought winter to their small little area in the wyrding. He struggled to grasp it all, to understand the wealth of power that pulled at him, begging to be used, to be set free, as if it were some living thing. And maybe it was. Maybe that was what Nature had always been.

Bit by bit, Cillian wrangled his magic into some semblance of control, feeding it back into himself in a way that felt right, until nothing was left of it outside his skin. He wrenched his eyes open, wavering on his feet, the frozen statues of the Fae soldiers around them like something out of a fairy tale.

The only Fae still standing were Niamh, her crew, and the two new arrivals, as if his magic had known not to touch them. Aisling was tucked in close, he realized, her arms wrapped around Bran and her face buried against his shoulder. She was dirtier than she had been when he'd found her in Pelham's forest, shivering from the cold, and Cillian wanted nothing more in that moment than to get her somewhere warm.

Niamh seemed to read his mind when she said, "We need to leave."

Seamus came closer, his eyes never straying from Cillian. That same, almost worshipful look in them that still shined in Niamh's filled his gaze, making Cillian look away. "Verlin is expecting us."

"We put him in danger if Cernunnos reports of our transgression to the Dagda."

"Cernunnos won't. He conspires against the Dagda. Why else seek out a herald? He will not confess to going behind his king's back in order to steal his crown."

"What herald?" Cillian croaked.

Carrick frowned, gaze dropping to Aisling, who still wasn't looking at any of them. "The bean sí. Is that not why you wanted to rescue her?"

"I wanted to rescue her because she's my *sister*," Bran rasped, eyes wide with shock. "She's not Fae."

Carrick gave him a scornful look. "For a witch, you truly are blind."

Aisling squeezed Bran tighter, shaking her head in silent denial. Cillian forced himself upright, resting a hand on her head. "It's all right. If you're like me, Bran will still love you."

He felt Bran jerk at that, but the other man didn't pull away. Bran stared at him, mouth pressed into a hard line, but it was telling he didn't argue. All he did was hold Aisling closer, refusing to let her go, the same way he'd refused to leave Cillian behind in Ainmire's estate.

And Bran called *him* stubborn.

"The shadow paths await," Niamh said pointedly.

They left that pocket of winter and retraced the way back through the wyrding. Bran and Aisling walked beside him, all three of them huddled close, surrounded by Fae that Cillian wasn't sure they could trust, no matter the kindness shown so far.

Chapter Twenty

They came out of the wyrding not in a forest this time but a valley between two mountains, stumbling between large rocks and boulders as the afternoon sun overhead burned away the fog. The cold from the wyrding disappeared the farther they got from that blight in the countryside.

"Where are we?" Cillian asked, squinting as he shielded his eyes against the sunlight with one hand. He could see a lake in the distance and mountains beyond, the land a riot of lush greens and rich browns, trees scattered in thick clusters. The air smelled of living things, and after hours in the wyrding and the shadow paths that only smelled of rot, he breathed it in gratefully.

"Gleann Bheatha," Niamh said. "The country home of Verlin's House. He is expecting us."

She pointed ahead of them as they walked, and Cillian could see a smudge on the other side of the valley that rapidly grew into individual horses. The Fae in their group didn't seem afraid, no one reaching for weapons, but Cillian wasn't one to trust them completely. He dug out the end of the leash from Bran's pocket, ignoring the tired but annoyed glance the other man tossed his way.

"When we get to wherever we are going, you're taking this damn thing off," Bran said, gesturing at the collar around his throat with one hand.

Cillian tried not to look at it, rubbing his thumb against the thin metal chain wrapped around his fingers. He did his damnedest to ignore the hot feeling in his gut that came from the sight of Bran collared and leashed, telling himself it was wrong to wonder what Bran would look like on his knees. "If it's safe."

Bran huffed at him but didn't argue, turning his head to mutter something to Aisling, who had yet to stop clinging to her brother. Dried tear tracks streaked over her dirty cheeks, and her long white-blonde hair was a knotted mess, bits of leaves and twigs tangled in it. Cillian was so incredibly glad they had found her, but they didn't know what she had endured. She still couldn't talk—Bran had told them about the geas on her throat on the walk out of the wyrding—and her forced silence made Cillian want to inflict the same sort of terror on Cernunnos.

Everyone seemed to think she was Fae, though her ears were rounded like Bran's. If she wore mortal skin like Cillian once had, he didn't want her to experience the pain of having it ripped from her. Bran wasn't treating her any differently, though, even if the other Fae were. They looked at Aisling with equal parts wonder and calculation in their eyes, and Cillian didn't trust what that might mean. Aisling was barely a teenager. He wouldn't let her or her brother be harmed, not if he had anything to say about it.

And he would, it seemed, far sooner than he thought as that group of Fae soldiers thundered closer on their horses, dust kicking up behind them. They were all armored and armed, the crests painted on their chest plates that of a fox within a circle of flowering vines. The lead rider let out a shout in the Fae language that Niamh responded to in kind. Bran stepped closer to Cillian, bringing Aisling with him. Cillian pressed his free hand to Bran's back, keeping the leash clenched tight in his other.

Niamh turned away from the rider and tilted her head in Cillian's direction. "They'll escort us to the castle. It is perhaps an hour's walk from here along the shore of the lake."

"A castle?" Cillian asked dubiously.

"It belongs to Verlin's House and is far from the viper's nest that is Gorias these days with Medb on the throne."

"Is it safe?" Bran asked.

The Fae on the horse said something sharp, his tone not one Cillian cared for. Niamh didn't react other than to speak over her shoulder at him. The deep frown the Fae sent Bran's way didn't sit well with Cillian. "What is he saying?"

"He wonders why the witch speaks out of turn. I explained you have him on a long leash."

"It's actually pretty short, but I know that's not what you meant. Tell everyone that Bran isn't to be treated like a servant or a pet. I won't stand for that."

It was Niamh's turn to frown at him, but Cillian stared her down until she complied. He couldn't understand what she told the newly arrived Fae but could only hope it was the exact order he'd given her.

"Thanks," Bran muttered, jaw tight when Cillian glanced at him.

"Don't thank me for that." Cillian still held Bran's leash, and that was a cultural aspect of the Otherworld he didn't think he'd ever get over.

They started walking, the sun well past its zenith as they made their way through the valley toward the lake, escorted by the Fae on horseback. They paused briefly at one point to allow Aisling to climb onto Cillian's back so he could carry her piggyback-style when she stumbled one too many times, looking dead on her feet. For all that she was tall, she didn't weigh that much. Cillian couldn't tell if that was because of his body or hers. He hadn't yet had a chance to process the strangeness of the face that stared back at him in mirrors or the new strength in his hands.

"She could ride," Niamh said. "Any of us would gladly give up a horse."

"No, it's fine," Cillian said, not wanting Aisling out of reach. He knew Bran would feel the same way and didn't bother to ask the other man's opinion.

She fell asleep before they reached the lake, and Cillian didn't have the heart to wake her to point out how beautiful and ethereal it was.

The lake was so clear and blue, surrounded by large rolling green hills and dotted with trees along the shore. The road that wound past it was shaded in some areas, the dirt path leading them toward a castle that grew larger on the horizon with every step they took.

Cillian hadn't traveled anywhere back home that had castles, so he didn't have anything to compare this one to. It sat on top of a small mound beside the lakeshore, its gray stone walls and towers not taking away from the surrounding countryside. The roofs he could see were a dark blue, with pennants flying from the top of the two towers. They were too far away for him to make out the crest on them.

The dirt road turned into a stone drive once they got close. The horses' hooves sounded louder on stone as their group was escorted up to the castle. Aisling was still asleep on his back, and Cillian was weirdly not tired yet from carrying her. He still held Bran's leash, and he was glad for it when he saw the person waiting for them in the courtyard once they passed through the guarded gate.

The Fae lord stood alone, with no retinue to attend him. He was tall like all Fae seemed to be, with brown skin and dark hair twisted into locs that fell past his shoulders. He wore a deep green court coat elaborately decorated with gold embroidery over a fancier outfit than anyone in their party currently wore. He was more on the lean side than Carrick and Seamus, and he might have been weaponless, but Cillian wouldn't believe he was helpless. His piercing amber eyes stared right at Cillian, the expression on his ridiculously handsome face something like relief.

"Cillian," the Fae lord, who could only be Verlin, said. He spoke English with what Cillian would call an Irish accent if they were back home. "When Niamh scried to let me know of your return, I had thought she'd gone mad."

"I am not the one haunted by ghosts," Niamh retorted. She waved her crew on across the courtyard, and Seamus signaled the same for the Fae on horseback, who left through a different door that Cillian assumed led to stables. Soon, it was just their small group standing in the courtyard, Aisling's soft, sleepy little snores echoing in Cillian's ear. Seamus and Carrick moved to flank Verlin, but Niamh remained beside Cillian.

"I'm not who you think I am," Cillian said into the silence that settled between them.

"Niamh told me that, too," Verlin said. He still bowed deeply, locs spilling over his shoulder from the motion, one fist resting over his heart. Seamus and Carrick bowed as well, and Cillian didn't know what to do in the face of that show of respect he didn't think was owed him. "Your memories might be missing, but you look exactly as I remember you."

"I don't know my own face right now."

Verlin straightened, gaze meeting Cillian's. "Perhaps with time, you will."

"I don't want to." Cillian shook his head. "Look. I'm grateful to Niamh for getting us out of Ainmire's hands, but we only came into the Otherworld to find Aisling. We have her now. We just want to go home."

Verlin's gaze flicked briefly to Aisling. "Yes, the herald."

"She's not a herald," Bran said testily. "She's my sister."

"And it speaks."

The condescending words and dismissive tone had ice forming beneath Cillian's feet without him realizing it, sliding underneath everyone's boots. The sun was still bright overhead, but the temperature dropped by at least twenty degrees. "Don't talk about Bran like he's a *thing*. I'm tired of that shit."

Verlin stared down at the ice covering half the courtyard, expression impossible to read. Then, he raised his gaze to meet Cillian's eyes once more. "You used to not care about witches."

"He cares for this one," Niamh said quietly.

Verlin looked at Bran for the first time since they arrived, with none of the covetous want Cillian had seen in Ainmire's eyes back in Tír na nÓg. "You have forgotten your history, my prince."

"I've lived almost twenty-six years in Pelham. That's the only history I know, and Bran is part of it," Cillian snapped. Aisling stirred on his back, and Cillian winced as he realized his raised voice must have woken her. She lifted her head, nearly overbalancing before she remembered he was carrying her. She flailed for a second before her hands grabbed his shoulders again. Bran stepped closer, reaching for Aisling and helping her slide off Cillian's back. She flinched at the ice beneath her bare feet, and Cillian had half a thought to swing her up in his arms to keep her comfortable.

"Let's go inside and talk. I instructed the servants to provide an early evening meal for us, and it should be ready," Verlin said. He made an elegant gesture with his arm, entreating them to follow. Cillian still kept hold of Bran's leash, not trusting the Fae even if they purported to be his allies. They clearly weren't Bran's.

Jupiter *cawed* overhead before finding a perch on the roof. Cillian eyed her for a moment. "How's she doing?"

"Hungry," Bran said. "She'll find something to eat while we're inside."

They crossed the courtyard and passed through an ornate wooden door. Cillian expected the inside of the castle to match the outside with gray stone walls and flooring, but it didn't. The floor underfoot was green-and-gold marble, the tall entryway flanked by gold pillars stretching down the long hallway. The walls and ceilings were covered in gilded wood with interspersed panels of richly colored wallpaper. It was such a startling juxtaposition from the bland exterior that for a moment, all Cillian could do was stare.

"This way," Niamh prompted, getting him moving again.

Cillian didn't see any servants on their way through the castle, which he thought was odd. A structure this size should have had people around to keep it clean and running, but they passed no one on their way to a large drawing room decorated in white, gold leaf, and a blue that reminded him of the lake beyond the castle walls. The elaborately designed furniture looked uncomfortable, but when he gingerly sat on a couch, the cushion was soft.

A side table practically overflowed with food laid out on trays and other serving dishes. Aisling craned her neck around to stare at it, and no one missed the way her stomach growled. Cillian didn't know the last time she'd eaten, but he wasn't about to deny her anything. He handed the leash back to Bran, tilting his head toward the side table. "Get her something to eat, but make sure she eats it slowly and in small amounts. We don't want her getting sick from it."

Bran nodded. "You want anything?"

"Whatever you're eating, if it looks safe." It already looked better than the food Ainmire had fed him.

Bran took a wide berth around the Fae, escorting Aisling to the side table. Cillian watched them start to fill their plates with food before returning his attention back to the other four. Niamh had taken a seat in a chair next to the couch he sat on, while Verlin perched on the opposite couch, a rectangular wooden table with gold trim between them. Verlin folded his hands together over his lap, staring at Cillian without blinking. The weight of his attention was more than a little disconcerting.

The pair came back a few minutes later with two plates filled with food, Bran's having more than his sister. Bread, various cheeses, savory sausage rolls, and tiny berry tarts covered their plates. Aisling already had crumbs on her lips, chewing fast.

"Take it slow," Cillian reminded her.

Aisling scrunched her nose at him and nodded, then proceeded to ignore him by shoving a berry tart into her mouth like any normal teenager would. Bran sighed and passed Cillian his plate before taking Aisling's, holding it hostage in the face of her pout. "Sit."

She took the far spot on the couch, leaving Bran to sit between her and Cillian. The end of Bran's leash was tucked into his pocket again, the metal chain out of the way as he started to eat. Cillian kept the plate steady, popping a triangle of soft cheese into his mouth. It tasted like a garlicky brie, rich in a way he liked. The Fae let them eat for a couple of minutes before Verlin cleared his throat.

"Niamh said you have no memory of your life in Tech Duinn," Verlin said.

"None," Cillian agreed, looking at the Fae lord.

"You truly don't remember me?"

"She said you were my right hand, but I still don't know what that means. If you're like Etain, then I don't want to know you."

Verlin reared back a little. "I was—*am*—your most trusted companion. My House has been allied with yours for centuries."

"But you weren't there when the Dagda took him," Bran said.

Cillian couldn't tell if the flash of anger that crossed Verlin's face was because Bran spoke or his words. "I don't need to explain myself to you."

"No, you don't. But you have to explain yourself to Cillian," Bran said before taking a bite of the sausage roll. He looked down at it in surprise. "This is good."

"Is it?" Cillian reached for the other sausage roll. He sank his teeth into the flaky crust and the spicy meat inside, thinking Bran was right. It *was* good. "Better than anything Ainmire gave me."

Bran grimaced. "Sorry."

Cillian shifted so he could press his thigh against Bran's in a comforting way. "You have nothing to apologize for. You kept me fed even when I told you to go find Aisling."

Bran shot him a withering look. "I wasn't leaving you with that bastard."

"You bargained for Cillian's safety?" Verlin asked sharply.

"Ainmire knew who Cillian was before we did. He kept me in line by threatening Cillian. I think he was only humoring me when I bargained to keep Cillian fed." Bran touched the collar, a troubled look in his eyes. "He could have killed me anytime he liked."

"If he had, then he would not have needed Etain to break through Cillian's glamour to reveal his skin and regain his magic. Your death would have been enough of a catalyst, and I think Ainmire knew that," Niamh said.

"Yes, I can see that," Verlin said, eyeing the plate Cillian and Bran were sharing.

Cillian passed a berry tart to Bran. "Do all Fae talk in riddles?"

"You were one of the best when it mattered."

"I'm not that person."

"Yes, I see that, too." Verlin sounded wistful, almost mournful, as he met Cillian's gaze. "But you came back to us, and I will not be regretful of that, even if you have no memory of your life before. If there is a way to reverse that part of the spell, then we must try."

"Whoa, wait," Bran said. "Messing with someone's mind is powerful magic. Cillian says he doesn't remember. Maybe you should accept and respect that and back off."

"The glamour hid that he was Fae. There must be some other

element in play if it took his memories as well. If one can be reversed, then so can the other. It needs to be if he is to survive."

"I *have* memories," Cillian snapped. "Of my life growing up in Pelham. Of going to school with Bran. Of being *human*."

"But you aren't."

The words were like a slap, making Cillian rear back a little, the plate wavering on his thigh. Bran grabbed for it, keeping it from falling, and set it on the table. "Just because Cillian looks Fae doesn't mean he's one of you."

Verlin cast him a derisive look. "You know nothing of our ways."

"I know you keep witches as pets and little more than slaves. I know you break my people. I know Cillian isn't like that."

"You purport to know him for a handful of decades when we have known him for centuries."

"But he doesn't remember, and I won't let you rip apart his mind like Etain ripped apart his body to get to something that might not even exist anymore."

"Bran is right," Cillian cut in before the argument got any more heated. "I don't know any of you, and from what I've seen of the Other-world, I'm not sure I want to."

Verlin flinched, those amber eyes snapping back to meet his. "You cannot mean that."

Cillian shrugged. "My home isn't here. I don't know your politics or your culture. You want me to play the part of your prince, and I think that's the best way for you to lose. For all intents and purposes, I'm human. I didn't even know witches with real magic existed until a few days ago."

"Yet you are...friends with one."

Cillian glanced at Bran, who stared back at him with a fierceness he remembered when they were children and facing off against other kids on the playground. "I grew up with Bran. I know him, and he knows me, better than anyone. You Fae think of witches as pets, and he's not that."

"He wears your collar."

"Yes, because Niamh said that was the only way to keep him safe. But Bran can do what he likes when he's with me, and Fae are going to have to just deal with that." It didn't matter that they hadn't spoken for seven years. The moment they'd been reunited, they'd stumbled back into standing side by side against the world again. That gaping hole in his heart had filled up, and it was like he could finally breathe again. Cillian had missed his best friend, but he had Bran back now, and he wasn't about to let the other man go again. The thought of doing so was ruinous.

Verlin turned his head to meet Carrick's eye, a silent conversation passed along in that glance. Carrick arched an eyebrow, the motion tugging at the scar between his eyes, before shrugging. "Ainmire and Etain know he's alive, and that means the Dagda will know as well. But the Wild Hunt stole them from Tír na nÓg, and no one will trace that back to us."

"Cernunnos can."

"He won't. He had a herald and hid her in the wyrding. He had no intention of handing her over to the Dagda." Carrick looked over at Aisling, his eyes narrowing. "She carries a geas of silence on her."

Aisling paused with a berry tart halfway to her mouth. She shot Bran and Cillian a frantic look before Bran wrapped his arm around her thin shoulders. "You can see it?"

"Yes."

"Cernunnos killed our mother and Aisling's father." Bran's voice cracked a little, and Cillian touched a hand to his lower back as a form of comfort. "Aisling got away, but Cernunnos attacked us at home later on and kidnapped her."

Verlin stood, coming around the table to them. He gestured at Aisling, eyes on Cillian. "May I check her over?"

Cillian raised an eyebrow. "I'm not the one you should be asking."

"The answer is no," Bran said before Verlin could ask again.

"I mean her no harm," Verlin said.

"I don't believe you."

"Would you have her suffer? If you had the power to lift the geas, you would have done so already."

Bran glared at the Fae, still holding Aisling close. "That doesn't mean I'm going to let you touch her."

"I won't harm her. I swear by my House."

"That doesn't mean anything to me."

Verlin shot Cillian an exasperated look, clearly biting back words he knew would only piss Cillian off. "You say you want to return to the mortal world? How will she fare without her voice?"

"Mutism exists," Cillian said.

"She had a voice. Would you not want to give it back to her?"

Cillian hated that Verlin made a good point with that argument. He sighed, gently nudging Bran in the side. "You said it was Fae magic that put the geas on? Maybe he can tell you how to undo it."

"Are you seriously taking his side right now?" Bran asked in aggravation.

"I'm taking Aisling's."

That seemed to deflate some of Bran's anger. With a sigh, he tilted his head in Verlin's direction. "Get me a notepad and a pen or pencil, something she can write on. We're not doing anything unless *she* wants to do it."

Niamh stood. "I'll retrieve one."

They sat in awkward silence until she returned, holding a small leather notebook and a slim fountain pen that must have been self-inking since there wasn't a pot of ink to go along with it. She offered both to Aisling, who hesitantly took them. Aisling scooted farther back onto the couch so she could sit cross-legged, still barefoot and still in need of a warm bath and clean clothes. She scribbled for a minute in the notebook before lifting it and holding it open so he and Bran could both read it.

"She wants her voice back, but not if what you're doing is going to hurt. It hurt when Cernunnos took her voice," Bran dutifully read for Verlin's sake.

Cillian ground his teeth, unaware that his magic had reacted to his anger until Seamus looked askance at the tall windows in the drawing room. "You've frosted the windows."

Cillian contained a wince, a little embarrassed at the ice coating every single pane of glass. "Sorry."

"It will melt." Verlin knelt in front of Aisling, wisely not reaching for her. "If your...brother allows it, I would like to check you over. I promise you, it will not hurt."

"If it does, tell me, and I'll hex him," Bran told her. Aisling bit her lip, staring at them both with her wide, deep blue eyes. She scribbled something into the notebook before showing them again. Bran pursed his lips before nodding. "All right. She says you can try."

Verlin lifted a hand, talking through every motion and every step he took in his spellcasting, even if they didn't understand it. Aisling held herself stiff beneath the barest touch of his fingers against her throat, flinching when the geas appeared on her skin, the magic terrible to look at. Cillian hadn't ever seen something like it before, but the ugly black lines of it were horrific to look at against her pale skin.

"Does it hurt?" Bran asked, hands twitching as if he were ready to haul Aisling out of reach.

She shook her head. A few minutes later, Verlin pulled his hand away, frowning thoughtfully. "Her voice isn't suppressed. It's gone."

"What do you mean gone?"

"A bean sí's magic is in their voice. To remove it is to deprive them of their power. But stealing a voice is meaningless without the body to carry it."

"So you're saying Cernunnos is still going to come after her?"

Verlin nodded. "He most likely killed your mother to get to Aisling."

"Why? What's so special about a bean sí? Aisling is just a kid."

"A bean sí is rare, even amongst Fae. They are known to herald the crowning of kings and queens for our people in all Four Lands as much as they herald death." Verlin looked over at Cillian, catching his gaze. "For what is a reign if not the burying of one era in favor of a new one?"

"That's what the Dagda did, isn't it?" Cillian asked into the silence. "With the Winter Court."

"He tried, but you came back."

Cillian didn't know what to say to that and could only look away from the hope in Verlin's eyes.

"Aisling is tired. I'd like to get her washed up and in a bed to rest," Bran said stiffly.

Verlin stood and gestured at the door. "The servants have set aside rooms for each of you."

"The rooms better be together. I'm not leaving Aisling."

"I'll take a room next to theirs," Cillian said.

Verlin pursed his lips slightly, which told Cillian that Bran had prob-ably been given a room somewhere not in the vicinity of Cillian's and Aisling's. "Of course. Whatever you wish."

Cillian shared a look with Bran, relieved that this time, they wouldn't be separated how they had been at Ainmire's estate. The last thing he wanted was Bran out of his sight.

CHAPTER TWENTY-ONE

"How is she?" Cillian asked when Bran slipped into his borrowed bedroom.

Bran closed the door behind him with a quiet click, leaning against it with a sigh. "Sleeping now. Jupiter is watching over her, and I set witchmarks on the door and windows. I'll know if anyone tries to get in while we talk."

Cillian nodded, taking a seat on the cushioned bench at the foot of the bed. "I think we're overdue for that."

He'd tried in that cabin in the woods, both of them distracted by the monsters attempting to claw their way inside. Then there'd been no time while they suffered as Ainmire's prisoners, their every move watched over by the Fae. Privacy had been a laughable dream, but they had it here in this castle. Bran had done something with his magic to make sure the room was free of any spells the Fae might have put in it, his witchmarks hidden in the corners now. That small act of protection had left Cillian feeling safe, and he knew he'd sleep better whenever he did crawl into the huge bed Verlin had given him.

All three of them had taken time to wash up, getting rid of the rotten scent of the wyrding. The servants had left out an elaborate set of clothes for Cillian that he'd tossed to the floor in favor of a pair of plain brown pants and a linen shirt he'd convinced them to find for him.

Bran fiddled with the end of the leash, the metal glinting in the light from the wall sconces. The same glass spheres from Ainmire's estate were used in this one. Cillian had relied on Bran to get the fire elementals to burn when they'd entered the room, still having no idea how to use his magic.

"Are you mad that I'm Fae?" Cillian asked, gesturing at his face. The dresser had a mirror over it, and he'd tried not to look into its reflective glass, still finding a stranger staring back at him.

Bran slowly shook his head. "Your heart is still human. You'd hate me if it weren't."

"But you should hate me, right? Isn't that what you and everyone have been saying? That witches and Fae are at war with each other?"

"I don't hate you."

"You left."

Bran let the leash go so he could cross his arms over his chest, glaring at Cillian in a way that was so familiar, even after years of absence. "You pushed me away."

Cillian slowly got to his feet again. "And I told you I didn't mean to."

There weren't any monsters clawing at the door and walls of the bedroom, fighting to get in—just the two of them and a past that had haunted them both for years.

Bran had been a ghost in Cillian's memories, haunting him since graduation, lingering in the empty spaces of his life. Bran was both regret and want to the foundations of the man Cillian had become before he knew he was Fae underneath the skin he'd lived in for almost twenty-six years. But Bran hadn't walked away after that reveal, so here they stood, in some impossible land, told to be enemies by habit and culture, and both of them only reaching for each other.

"You were my first kiss," Cillian confessed. "And you literally burned me."

Like iron, he didn't say, but Bran's flinch told him the other man made the connection anyway. "Maybe your glamour reacted to me because I was a witch?"

"I don't know. I remember it hurt, and I wasn't expecting it. So I pushed you away, but I never meant for you to *leave*." He couldn't keep the ache out of his voice, expression twisting as he tried to suppress the hurt. "I dated other people, you know? But none of them were you."

"We never dated."

"They weren't you," Cillian repeated, staring at Bran. "I never wanted them to be. I only wanted you. I *want* you."

Bran closed his eyes, tilting his head back. "I didn't think you did back then. Pelham is a small town, and I couldn't stand the thought of living there if you hated me."

Cillian took a step forward. "I could never hate you."

Bran opened his eyes, meeting Cillian's gaze with a wealth of emotion writ plain across his face. "Everyone here wants you to."

"Fuck them. If I'm their prince, then they can't tell me what to do."

"You realize that if I didn't know you, I'd want to kill you?"

"The same way you'd kill your sister?"

Bran took a half step back at that, hunching his shoulders as if Cillian had punched him. "That's not fair."

"Isn't it? Everyone here thinks she's a Fae, too."

"She's my sister."

"Exactly. And I'm your best friend. It doesn't matter that we're Fae."

Bran dragged a hand down his face, swearing quietly. "It should. Any other witch would want you both dead."

"You don't."

"Because I know you!" Bran burst out, shaking his head rapidly, causing the leash to swing back and forth. "You may look like one of them, but you *aren't*."

"And you might be a witch, but you don't hate me."

At that, Bran let out a little ragged laugh, hazel eyes watery when he looked at Cillian. "How could I? I think I've loved you in one way or another since we were kids, even when I didn't have you by my side. I can't just turn it off now that I know what you are. It'd be like asking me to give up my magic. I won't do that. I *won't*."

The words had Cillian closing the distance between them, heart pounding hard. He stopped in front of Bran, mere inches between them that didn't feel so far anymore. He caught the end of the leash in one hand, rolling his wrist to wind it around his hand until his fingers touched the silver collar around Bran's throat. Bran hadn't taken it off, its presence a claim and mark of ownership that kept him safe from every other Fae around them because the crest on it told everyone that Bran belonged to *him*.

Cillian lifted his other hand to Bran's face, using his thumb to gently wipe at the corner of one eye, brushing away the faint hint of a tear. "I might look like the prince they lost, but I don't have his memories. If regaining those means I would see you as the enemy, then I don't want them."

He didn't speak of the terrifying cracks at the back of his mind. He chose instead to focus on Bran, who sucked in a harsh breath, lips parting. Cillian did what he should have done seven years ago, what he'd dreamed about doing ever since he'd lost the man now standing in front of him.

He kissed Bran, and this time, it didn't burn.

Cillian was taller than Bran now and had to lean down to kiss him, tilting the other man's chin up for their mouths to meet. Their lips brushed, soft and gentle for a single second, before Cillian deepened it, slipping his tongue past Bran's teeth to taste him. He groaned when Bran hesitantly kissed back, the other man's fingers gripping the front of Cillian's shirt to tug him closer. Cillian kissed him fiercely, backing Bran up until he had the other man pressed against the door, heat pooling in his gut.

Bran gasped against his mouth, sliding one hand up Cillian's chest to hook around the back of his neck, holding him close. He kissed Bran again, over and over, still holding on to the leash, his hand splayed over Bran's shoulder, thumb pressed into the hollow between Bran's collarbones. His skin felt on fire when all he'd felt was cold over the last few days, cock slowly hardening in his pants, body pressed against Bran's.

It took effort to tear his mouth away from Bran's, resting their foreheads together as he breathed raggedly, eyes closed as he tried to get himself under control when all he wanted to do was let go. "Tell me you want this. That you still want me."

Bran choked out a laugh, his fingernails digging into the back of

Cillian's neck. "I couldn't forget you for seven years. If I left again, I'd still think about you."

Cillian opened his eyes and raised his head, staring down at Bran. He tugged lightly on the leash, arching an eyebrow. "You can't run while wearing this, but if you tried, this time, I would follow."

"I know," Bran whispered.

Cillian's gaze dropped down to the collar Bran wore, the jewels glinting in the low light. "Do you want me to take it off? I can when we're alone."

Bran licked his lips, eyes full of desire when Cillian met his gaze again. "I hate what the Fae do to witches, but...I feel safer wearing your collar, knowing that it makes me yours and no one else can touch me."

Cillian would be lying if he said his cock didn't get harder at those words. "Then we'll leave the collar on."

Bran shuddered, falling back down on his heels, pupils blown wide in his eyes. He swallowed thickly. "You're the only one who can take it off."

A dark thought coiled its way through Cillian's lust-addled mind—that if he had his way, he never would.

Bran couldn't leave if he was collared and leashed, after all.

Cillian stole another kiss. "I'm going to find something to fuck you with. Finish getting undressed."

The way Bran whimpered made his cock *throb*, and he only wanted to hear more of that sound.

Tearing himself away from Bran took effort, but Cillian succeeded in prying his hands off Bran and making his feet move, practically running into the attached washroom. The open shelves above the porcelain basin sink held all manner of vials and tins containing supplies for washing. One of the glass vials had an oil that didn't smell too strongly, and Cillian carried it back to the bedroom, coming to an abrupt stop past the door.

Bran was half-undressed, standing barefoot in his pants, the leash dangling from the collar. He looked up at Cillian's arrival, pausing in the motions of undoing the buttons at his waistband. A flush came to his cheeks, gaze skittering away. Cillian drew in a steadying breath, approaching the bed to set the vial on the side table there. When he turned around, Bran had managed to get out of the rest of his clothes, standing naked save for the collar, fiddling with the end of the leash. He'd even removed his bracelet. The only mark on his skin was the tattoo on his right forearm, and Cillian wanted desperately to get his mouth on Bran's skin, to mark him up.

"Come here," Cillian said hoarsely as he yanked off his shirt. Something hot curled in Cillian's gut when Bran obeyed. He grabbed the leash once Bran was within arm's reach, holding it while he let his gaze rove over Bran's body. He reached out with his free hand to hook a finger around the collar, feeling the way Bran swallowed against it. "Is it wrong that I like how you look wearing my collar?"

Bran licked his lips, staring at him. "I don't mind that it's yours."

His was the only one he ever wanted to see locked around Bran's throat. Something primal in him was pleased at the sight and had hated when it'd been Ainmire's. Cillian knew owning people was wrong, but something in him said Bran was *his* and always had been.

Bran would never belong to anyone else.

Cillian let go of the collar and slid his hand down Bran's chest, fingers ghosting over twitching muscles before they closed around Bran's half-hard cock. Bran rocked into the touch with a whimper, and Cillian reflexively tugged on the leash at the sound. "Get on the bed."

Cillian let him go and got out of the rest of his clothes. Then he crawled onto the bed after Bran, the mattress sinking a little beneath his hands and knees. Bran watched him crawl closer, fingers gripping the blanket underneath them, the leash draped over his chest and the end coiled near his hip. Cillian slid his fingers around the metal before dragging it along to grip Bran's hand. He tangled their fingers together, the leash caught between them, before raising Bran's hand to his lips, pressing a lingering kiss over his knuckles. "I won't ever lead you astray."

Bran let his hand go, leaving the leash with him, and palmed Cillian's face with shaking fingers. "I should have stayed."

"We were teenagers. We didn't know any better."

"It's not like we know any better now."

Cillian turned his face into Bran's touch. "I know you, the same way you know me. Seven years doesn't change that. What we are doesn't change that."

Other people might say it did, but Bran was still the same person in his heart that Cillian had befriended as a kid and fallen in love with as a teenager, magic or not, and that was all that mattered.

They were all that mattered.

Bran pushed himself up on his other elbow, kissing Cillian so tenderly it left him ravenous. "I think I always belonged to you."

Cillian groaned, kissing Bran with a possessiveness he'd never felt with anyone else before. It was like winning a battle he hadn't known he'd been fighting, a sense of vicious relief and wondrous victory coursing through him.

He pressed Bran back onto the bed, settling over him, his hard cock sliding against Bran's. A shudder racked its way through his body as they touched, Bran's skin almost burning hot beneath his hands. Bran gasped when Cillian rocked their hips together, spreading his legs so Cillian could settle more easily against him. Cillian kissed his way over Bran's jaw, down his throat, his lips catching on the edge of the collar. He licked the skin under it, humming at the way Bran jerked beneath him, the taste of sweat and metal on his tongue, leash gripped tight in his hand.

Fingers touched his pointed ears before tangling in his hair, holding on. Touching Bran didn't burn like iron, didn't leave Cillian hurting how he once had. If anything, it settled something in him to have Bran like this—collared, leashed, and under him with no other option but to *stay*. He kissed his way down Bran's chest, licking over a nipple on the way to his cock. Bran seemed to be one of those people who kept himself groomed, which was fine by Cillian. When he took Bran's cock into his mouth, the sound that left Bran's lips was something Cillian knew he wanted to hear again.

It'd been a while since he'd had another man's cock in his mouth, and he savored the weight and taste of it on his tongue, sucking on it lazily. Bran jerked beneath him, an aborted twitch of his hips telling Cillian he was trying not to thrust into his mouth. It was easy to pin Bran's hips to the bed, and Cillian didn't question the strength in his hands that kept Bran where he wanted him.

He sucked Bran's cock until it sounded like Bran was about to come, finally pulling away without an ache in his jaw. That was new and something he didn't mind. Bran was panting harshly beneath him, one hand over his eyes, his cock hard and red, curving toward his stomach. Prying himself away from Bran took a herculean effort, but Cillian managed to do so, letting the leash go long enough to grab the vial from the side table.

Cillian poured oil over his fingers, some of it dripping down his palm. He trailed his fingers down Bran's cock and over his balls, teasing the sensitive skin behind them until Bran bucked against him with a soft moan. "*Cillian.*"

Cillian shifted on his knees, pulling Bran's legs over his thighs to spread him open while his other hand, slick with oil, slipped farther down, fingers stroking over his entrance. Bran tossed his head back at the first press of Cillian's finger inside, collar straining against his throat as he swallowed convulsively. Cillian pulled his finger back out and pushed it back in slow, relishing the clench of Bran's body around it, thinking about how it was going to feel when he sank his cock into Bran.

"I never thought I'd get to see you like this," Cillian said, words coming out in a deep rasp. Bran blinked his eyes open, a thin ring of hazel the only bit of color showing around a black pupil. Cillian leaned over and kissed him, bracketing him in, swallowing the whine Bran let out when Cillian's finger brushed over that sensitive spot inside him. The way Bran shuddered in his arms had Cillian groaning, adding a second finger to the first, oil easing the way.

He kept kissing Bran as he worked him open, finally getting three fingers in him and loving the way it made Bran writhe. Cillian ignored the way Bran yanked at his hair and smacked a hand against his shoulder, gasping when he stroked Bran's cock with his other hand.

"In me," Bran choked out. "Get *in* me."

Cillian groaned, his cock throbbing at the demand, and he pulled his fingers free. He grabbed the vial again, pouring oil over his fingers and his cock, stroking himself lightly. He tossed it aside after that and didn't know where it landed, nor did he care. All he cared about was doing what Bran asked.

He pressed the blunt head of his cock against Bran's entrance, pushing inside with a groan. His cock was thicker and longer than

Bran's, and he'd tried to ease the way with his fingers, but the hot clutch of Bran's body was still tight, drawing him in. Cillian stared hungrily at the way his cock slid into Bran inch by inch, fingers digging bruises into Bran's hips as he held the other man in place at the perfect angle that would give them both pleasure.

Bran cried out at the intrusion, legs shaking as he dug his heels against the bed. One of his hands gripped the blanket over his head, the other clawing at Cillian's forearm. It took all of Cillian's fraying control not to thrust in hard like he wanted to—to claim, to *own*. Some dark little thought crept through his mind, promising that next time he'd do what he liked.

Take what he liked.

Gritting his teeth, Cillian swore and sank in a little deeper, forcing himself to go slow and let Bran adjust to the thickness of his cock. By the time he sank all the way in, Cillian was breathing as if he'd run for miles, Bran hot all around him and beneath his hands.

Cillian leaned over him, kissing away the gasp from Bran's mouth as the motion changed the angle of Cillian's cock inside him. Bran's fingernails scraped down his back in a way Cillian didn't mind. He snagged the end of the leash with his hand and hooked an arm under one of Bran's knees, hiking his leg up higher to open him up more. He rolled his hips, grinding in with intent. Bran moaned, burying his face against Cillian's shoulder.

"You feel so good," Bran gasped, body clenching tightly around Cillian's cock.

It was Cillian's turn to groan, lips dragging over warm skin as he planted a hand on the mattress, the metal chain of the leash tangled around his fingers. He pulled out, cock dragging almost free, before thrusting back in, panting harshly. Bran cried out, arching into his next thrust, and Cillian couldn't stop himself from giving in to the desire to see Bran come undone beneath him.

It was almost like a dream, the way Bran opened up for him, held him close, and begged him for more. The way he tossed his head back and tried to breathe through his cries of pleasure, the collar shining from the light burning in the sconce near the bed, sapphires and diamonds glittering softly. Cillian dragged his hand over Bran's chest up to his throat, fitting the curve of his fingers beneath the collar there, holding on as he stared into Bran's eyes while fucking him so hard the bed creaked beneath them.

"You're mine," Cillian growled, something clawing through his skin from deep within him, a truth to his words that felt *right*, splintering through his chest. This was want, and this was love, a need that could only be soothed by the witch beneath him. "You always have been. I won't let you go again."

Bran yelled his name when he came, shuddering through an orgasm that slowed Cillian's pace for a handful of heartbeats. Cillian pulled out almost all the way against the clench of Bran's body before snapping his hips forward, cock sinking in deep again, throbbing with his own need to come. His breath rasped loud in his ears, the sound overlaid with the ones of their bodies coming together, of Bran urging him on with hands and mouth, eyes sparking gold from magic.

Cillian came with a shout, grinding in deep with a few short thrusts as he spilled his cum inside Bran. He stared down at where Bran lay sprawled beneath him, collared and leashed, their breath puffing between them in soft white clouds. Cillian blinked in surprise at the snow falling around them, over them, melting on their overheated skin.

"Come here," Bran croaked, his magic still bright in his eyes, flecks of gold in a sea of hazel.

Cillian slid his hand up from Bran's throat to his cheek, cradling his face close for a lingering kiss. The bedroom was full of winter, but Bran was warm beneath him, like a fire on the coldest night of the year.

Chapter Twenty-Two

Bran woke with a pleasurable ache in his body he hadn't felt since his last one-night stand months ago. He cracked open one eye, the sconces long since dimmed, but the weak light trying to peek through the edges of the curtain told him it must be morning.

He blinked both eyes open, breath catching in his throat a little as his vision parsed the shadows, making out Cillian sleeping beside him in the large bed they'd shared last night. They had gone to sleep wrapped up around each other but had drifted apart sometime during the night. Bran tried not to think of that as a reflection of their past. He hadn't left for Aisling's room to sleep on her floor last night only because Jupiter had promised to keep watch.

He tugged on their bond, getting an immediate query back from his familiar that felt like *awake*. Satisfied that Jupiter had Aisling's well-being in hand, he shifted a little closer to Cillian, listening to the other man breathe slow and deep in sleep. His hair was tangled on the pillow and draped over his shoulders, longer than Bran remembered him ever wearing it when they were kids. Just another difference grown in the years they'd not spoken, but he couldn't say he minded the style. It suited Cillian, especially now.

Bran lifted a hand and reached out to gently stroke the pointed tip of Cillian's ear, tracing the shape of it. Cillian as a Fae wasn't much different than Cillian as a human—just more beautiful. Bran couldn't find it in his heart to hate the other man the way the Council of Witches bade every coven to feel toward the Fae. Bran couldn't think of Cillian as his enemy if his life depended on it. He'd always loved Cillian in some way, even through hurt and anger.

"Mm." Cillian shifted on the bed, turning his head in Bran's direction. Bran shifted his hand to cup Cillian's jaw, gently stroking his thumb over the sharpness of a cheekbone. "What time is it?"

"I don't know."

Bran watched Cillian open his eyes, the color gray in the soft morning shadows. He dragged a hand up from the blankets tangled around their hips to press it over Bran's, shifting onto his side. "Come here."

Bran scooted closer, slotting their legs together and trying to ignore the interested twitch of his cock. Cillian fit his hand over Bran's hip, stroking over the shadow of bruises he'd pressed into Bran's skin last night. Bran sighed, curling closer. "We should get up. We need to figure out how to get back home."

"Can I even go home looking like this?"

"Fae can look human when they're in the mortal world. I don't know how to cast glamour, but someone here should know."

"I'm not sure I trust any help they'd give us."

"Well, they're certainly not out to kill you like Ainmire was."

Cillian's hand tightened on Bran's hip. "They'd kill you without a second thought for being a witch."

"You won't let them." The collar around Bran's throat was proof enough of that resolve. He'd hated the one Ainmire had made him wear, that horrible thing cutting him off from Nature and his magic. Cillian's was a claim he found he didn't mind, only because it meant he belonged to Cillian, and Bran knew he'd always be safe with him. Any other collar would leave him in a panic, but Cillian's only provided relief in the Otherworld.

"No, I won't," Cillian said with a fierceness that made Bran shiver.

"We'll figure out how to make you look human, and then we'll go home."

"How do we get there? Through the wyrding again?"

"Unfortunately, yes."

Cillian sighed. "We're going to need a shower after we get back."

Bran hummed agreement before leaning forward to kiss Cillian on the cheek. "We should get up."

Cillian wrapped his arms around Bran and rolled him onto his back with a suddenness that had him gasping. The weight of the other man on top of him made him shiver, made him think of the way Cillian had so expertly taken him apart last night. It made him jealous of the people Cillian must have learned it from over the years, hating each and every one of them with a churlishness he wouldn't apologize for.

"I love you," Cillian said in a low voice. "That isn't going to change when we get back home."

Bran swallowed, aware of the collar around his throat and the way he'd never been able to let Cillian and the memory of him go over the years. Aware, too, of the duty every witch was meant to keep when it came to the Fae. "I love you, too."

Cillian leaned down to kiss him, lips cool against Bran's. It could have been a dream, but when Bran touched him, Cillian was solid and real, there after being only a memory for so long. He let Cillian press him against the bed, lazily kissing him, feeling his cock stir with interest, but any chance of repeating what they'd done last night was interrupted by a timid knock on the bedroom door.

Cillian tore his mouth away from Bran's with a quiet curse, rolling off him. "Right. Let's see who that is."

He left Bran on the bed with the sheets, taking the blanket with him to wrap around his waist. He cracked the door open, then pushed it wider, and Aisling ducked under his arm, coming inside the room. Bran frantically made sure he was covered up. "Hey, Aisling. We were just getting up."

She went over to the sconce on the wall and poked at it. The fire elemental inside brightened, providing enough illumination they could all make out the mess of clothing strewn across the floor. Aisling stared at the clothes before looking at Bran, wrinkling her nose.

"Nope, we're not talking about this when I'm not even dressed,"

Bran hastily said, trying not to feel embarrassed. "I'm up. Go get dressed, and we'll come get you when we're ready."

She couldn't speak, but she gave him a thumbs-up before darting back out of the bedroom to hers right across the hall. Cillian closed the door behind her, looking a little red in the face. At least Bran wasn't the only one feeling judged by a thirteen-year-old.

He got out of bed, and they both hastily dressed in the set of clothes servants had set aside. Bran put his bracelet back on, absently touching a finger to one of the beads. Cillian's outfit was far more elaborate this time around than even the sort Verlin had worn to greet them. The glacial blue court coat, matching pants, and crisp white shirt made Cillian's eyes stand out. His pale gray boots were knee-high and matched the style Bran had been given, even if his own outfit was far duller than Cillian's. The brown and cream clothing clearly put him in the category of servant.

Once dressed, Cillian turned toward the side table to retrieve the leash. Bran swallowed a sigh and tilted his head back, giving Cillian room to clip it to the collar. He sighed a little at the sound of the click, knowing he should hate the intended degradation of both, but he couldn't, not when Cillian held the leash.

Cillian bent his head and kissed him softly. "I won't let anyone hurt you."

"Don't make promises you can't keep."

"I'll keep this one the same way I'll keep you." Bran shivered at his words and let Cillian tuck the end of the leash into Bran's pocket before taking his hand. "Let's get some food and then go home."

They left the bedroom, finding Aisling waiting for them in the hallway, hopping around with Jupiter in a game that made no sense to Bran. The dress she wore had a high collar and puffy short sleeves, falling to her ankles in gauzy layers from an empire waist. She looked up at their arrival and frowned at Bran. She gestured at her own throat, then pointed at him.

"Ah." Bran touched the leash dangling from the collar. "You know how we always said Fae and witches are enemies? Well, it's true. They don't like witches all that much in the Otherworld."

"The collar is mine. It's to keep Bran safe. As soon as we're back home, he can take it off," Cillian said.

The momentary visceral rejection Bran felt at those words startled him. Ducking his head, he hid his discomfort by kneeling and holding his arm out to Jupiter. The familiar hopped over to him, and he lifted her up to his shoulder. She preened his hair as he stood, her presence a soothing thing in the back of his mind.

Aisling picked up her notebook and pen from the floor and pointed down the hallway with a questioning look on her face. Bran shrugged. "Let's see where it leads."

They realized fairly quickly they had no idea where to go. Luckily, a servant saw them a few minutes later, curtsying deeply to Cillian, nodding at Aisling, and completely ignoring Bran. He tried not to feel annoyed about that and kept silent as Cillian asked for directions. The servant took it upon herself to lead them to a grand dining hall decked out in reds and oranges and gold, looking like autumn had thrown up in the space.

The table was already set, with three empty place settings on one side of the long dining table. Verlin sat at the head, with Seamus to his right and Carrick to his left. Niamh sat next to Carrick and greeted them with a small smile, the only one to do so.

"I hope you all feel refreshed and the rooms were to your liking last night," Verlin said.

"It was nice to sleep in a real bed," Cillian said after a moment.

Verlin gestured at the seats meant for them. "Please, join us for the morning meal."

Cillian took the chair next to Niamh, and Bran sat beside him. Aisling hopped onto the one next to Bran, setting her notebook and pen on the table. She used both hands to tuck her long hair behind her ears before reaching for her water glass. Bran leaned over to speak softly into her ear. "I know you're hungry, but eat slow."

He still didn't know all that she had gone through since being kidnapped from the Shoppe. She'd been too tired yesterday to write much after her bath, and Bran had wanted her to get some rest. He'd stayed with her until she fell asleep and had meant to go back to her room after speaking with Cillian, but, well. He'd been distracted.

He still was, if he was being honest. The faint ache in his ass was a reminder of last night he couldn't ignore, and Bran shifted discreetly on the cushioned chair.

Aisling reached for the serving utensil and started poking around the plates and platters in the middle of the table. It was definitely a hearty spread, with pan-fried sausages, small pastries that could have been filled with savory or sweet fillings, fried potatoes and onions, a tureen of porridge, and fresh sliced fruit. Tiny rolled omelets were piled on a plate, and Bran went for those first. Cillian passed him a teapot, and Bran poured out a nice-smelling amber-colored tea for himself and Aisling. It tasted like toasted nuts and honey when he sipped it.

The Fae were nice enough to wait until the three of them had served themselves and eaten a little of the food before initiating conversation. Verlin took the lead, clearly the one in charge of their group. He was dressed just as elegantly as Cillian, in a shade of darker blue that complemented Cillian's outfit. Some of his locs had been tied back with glittering strands of thin silver chains.

"I researched the geas last night," Verlin said as he cut apart a sausage. "It is an older one and rarely used."

Bran looked up from his plate and stared at the Fae lord. "Can it be reversed?"

Verlin's eyes flicked to Cillian before he answered, and Bran tamped down his annoyance. He had a feeling the Fae were including him at the table only because of Cillian's wishes. "The only way to reverse it is to return her voice, which means we must locate it first."

"We believe her voice is in Cernunnos' possession," Niamh said.

Bran abruptly lost his appetite. He set his fork down and rested his elbows against the edge of the table, dragging a hand through his hair. "If he has her voice, he won't stop looking for her."

"Will he come here?" Cillian asked.

Verlin tipped his head in Cillian's direction. "He might try, but Cernunnos is of the Summer Court. He would need to find a reason to visit the Winter Court, and Medb has always been wary of his aspirations."

"What if he travels through the shadow paths in the wyrding?

Wouldn't the wyrding hide his comings and goings? He was keeping Aisling prisoner there," Bran said.

"There is a chance he will be on the lookout for you in the wyrding. I think it highly more likely he will return to where your coven is, still following the gist of the Dagda's order to exterminate you."

Bran's stomach sank somewhere to his feet. "He's going to Pelham?"

Verlin arched a dark eyebrow. "You are going there, so Cernunnos will likely follow if he is not already in the mortal world."

Bran closed his eyes at the thought of Pelham being ravaged by lights in his absence. If he was here, that meant no witches were left to defend the town, and that failure would surely make it back to the Council of Witches if the Fae managed to gain a foothold in the mortal world. "We have to go back."

"That was the plan," Cillian reminded him.

"No, I mean, we need to go back today. Remember how time flows different here than it does back home? It's slower, but weeks would have passed back in the mortal world while we were here in the Otherworld." Bran shoved his chair back and stood, looking at Verlin. "How do we get back?"

Verlin's lip curled faintly, unable to hide his distaste at being ordered around by a witch. Whatever he would have said died on his lips as a commotion at the entrance to the dining room had Verlin rising to his feet. Bran turned and watched as an almost too-thin Fae lady stepped into the room, servants hovering behind her worriedly, though they didn't try to stop her.

She was tall like every other Fae Bran had crossed paths with. Her deep purple gown hung loosely on her, the belt around her waist doing more to highlight the starved look of her body than anything else. Her hair was a mass of black curls cascading over her shoulders, streaks of white cutting through the dark ringlets. The shade of her skin was as dark as Verlin's, and the resemblance was impossible to miss.

Verlin greeted her in the Fae language before hurrying around the table to her. He offered her his arm, which she gamely took with a shaking, bejeweled hand. Her dark-eyed gaze darted around the room, and she said something that Bran couldn't understand.

Cillian stood, discreetly tugging the end of the leash out of Bran's pocket to hold it. The tension didn't leave Bran's body as the lady zeroed in on Cillian, paling a little. Verlin had to brace her before Seamus reached them, helping to guide the lady to an empty chair at the other end of the table. Verlin spoke low and quick in their language before finally switching over to English. Bran knew it wasn't for his benefit but for Cillian's.

"He does not remember, Mother," Verlin said, looking down the table at them.

The lady drew in a breath, one thin hand clutching at the collar of her gown. "He looks exactly the same."

Her words were spoken in heavily accented English, that same, almost Irish lilt to her words. Bran wondered how it was the Fae could speak the language so well, thinking it had to be magic of some sort. Maybe a translation spell or something similar.

"My mother, Lady Fiadh," Verlin said by way of introduction, speaking mostly to Cillian.

"A pleasure to meet you?" Cillian said, sounding unsure. Bran kept quiet, resting one hand on Aisling's shoulder in a comforting way as she leaned toward him.

"Welcome back, my prince," Lady Fiadh said, ignoring Bran. "Our home is yours, as is our House."

"Thank you." Cillian cleared his throat. "But we were just leaving."

She blinked at him, as if his words didn't make any sense. "Why?"

"Because the Otherworld isn't our home."

"Our," she echoed, finally dragging her gaze away from Cillian to meet Bran's. "You include a pet in your words?"

Bran raised an arm and held Cillian back when the other man would have headed toward the other end of the table out of anger. "I'm not a pet."

"You are collared and leashed like one."

The temperature in the room plummeted when Cillian growled, "Don't speak to him like that."

Verlin eyed the windows, which Bran assumed were covered in frost again. He didn't look to check. "Like we told your son, Cillian grew up with me in Pelham. We met as children. He doesn't remember who he was before that."

"Then we can help him regain his memories," Lady Fiadh said shakily, raising a hand toward Cillian in entreaty. "My mate may not have been so lucky, but you are *here*. We can help you."

"I don't want to recover them," Cillian said flatly. "I don't know who I would be if I did, and I like who I am now."

Cillian stepped closer to Bran, making his side known. Lady Fiadh leaned forward to brace herself against the table. "You cannot mean that. You cannot give your allegiance to a *witch*. You are the Winter Prince."

"I'm a ranger back home, and I'd rather be that than someone cruel."

"You think us Fae cruel when you stand beside a witch? Their cruelty is what banished us to the Otherworld in the first place."

"Mother," Verlin said in a tight voice. "Please stop."

"Banished?" Bran echoed. "We never banished you. You Fae have been murdering witches for centuries while trying to take over our world. We've been trying to stop you."

"Your history is ill-informed," Lady Fiadh said coldly. "But I expect such revisionist thinking from traitors."

"We can't be traitors if we were never on the same side."

"Ignorance keeps you blind, I see. Our prince would not stand by you if he remembered the truth of his past and the war your side started."

"I won't fight Bran," Cillian said in a low voice. "And I won't stand for anyone else harming him either."

"He is the enemy," Verlin said, glaring at Bran. "His kind always has been. They slaughter us—"

"And the Fae slaughter witches right back. I saw what the lights do to them. I saw his stepfather's body in the woods. The wrong done to you doesn't absolve you of the terror you inflict on others, whether they are witches or innocent bystanders."

Aisling whimpered, turning to burrow her face against Bran's shoulder. He curled his arm around her, holding her close. He might not have liked Ray, but Ray had loved Aisling in his own way, and she didn't need to be reminded of his murder by someone who clearly didn't care.

"So you think we should let the wyrding spread like the blight it is, let it poison the land left to us?"

"That's not what I said."

"That is *exactly* what you said." Verlin straightened up and raised his chin. "Do you know why witches have magic? Because long ago, they were Fae who betrayed their brethren by allying with mortals to banish us from Éire. They called themselves Fomorians, and the battles waged lasted decades. It was the Fomorians who called upon Chaos to exile us to the Otherworld and raise the wyrding between us, denying us our homeland and poisoning the one we were left with."

"You're lying," Bran blurted out, sick to his stomach at the accusation that some distant ancestor might be Fae.

Verlin shot him a scathing look. "Fae do not *lie*. I speak the truth, one you witches used to know. The wyrding is your kind's doing, and the only way to slow its encroachment in the Otherworld was to kill the Fomorians and the witches they eventually became. Chaos is not Fae magic and never has been. Nature dies in the wyrding, and we cannot live there either. But we needed a way to stop you witches from constantly attacking us in the Otherworld, so we carved out paths back to the mortal world and attacked you."

"You *enslave* us when you don't outright kill us."

"Your magic helps keep the wyrding at bay. The witches Fae don't kill as a sacrifice, we keep for experiments, for entertainment. You pets have your uses until you don't, and then we send you into the wyrding." Verlin smiled then, baring his teeth, the glitter in his amber eyes hot and furious and cruel. "You witches have magic still, so there is some bit of Fae blood left in you. The Chaos in the wyrding changes you into monsters that know us, that obey us, because pets remember their masters and always will. And it is they who murder your kind on our say-so to keep our own people safe from your bloody incursions."

What little breakfast Bran had eaten threatened to crawl up his throat. He swallowed hard, trying to keep from vomiting as saliva filled his mouth. "That's not true."

"Fae do not lie." Verlin spat the words out before drawing in a steadying breath and closing his eyes, working to get himself under control. "If Cillian goes back with you, what do you think will happen when your masters find out he is Fae?"

"I don't have any masters."

Verlin opened his eyes, lips curling back over his teeth. "What do you call that Council of yours?"

Bran had no good response to that. "Cillian hid beneath a glamour until he came here. He can hide again."

"He cannot control his magic like this, and you think he can hold up such a thing against any witch who comes around asking questions?"

"Do you have so little faith in your own magic?" Bran shot back.

Lady Fiadh raised her hand to press it over her son's hand that rested on her shoulder. "So you would keep him as a pet?"

Bran reared back at that accusation, feeling the blood drain from his face. "I don't own Cillian."

"No. You would only have him deny everything about himself. You would have him bury who he was in favor of a human veneer that is a lie. How long do you think it will take until he resents you?"

"I could never resent Bran," Cillian said fiercely.

Lady Fiadh stared at Cillian with unblinking eyes. "And when you outlive your pet? What then?"

"*Stop*," Bran snapped raggedly. "Stop trying to guilt Cillian into staying. We came here for Aisling, and we found her, so we're leaving. Just let us go."

"We are Fae. We are his people. None of you can deny that."

The truth rang between them, quiet and chilling, and Bran had no defense against it. He knew what Cillian was—what Aisling probably was—and what he wasn't, no matter what Verlin had said. Witches weren't Fae.

They couldn't be.

Bran glared at Verlin, at Cillian's supposed right hand, and refused to back down. "We're going home. I won't let Cernunnos raze our town, and I'm getting my sister's voice back."

"You call her sister, yet she is Fae," Verlin said.

"I don't care what she is, the same way I don't care what Cillian is."

He loved them both in different ways but no less deeply. He

wouldn't apologize for that, and he'd fight for them until his dying breath—against the Fae, against fellow witches. It didn't matter who stood against them; Bran would not back down if it meant he could keep them safe.

Aisling pulled away, and he let her, staring down into her wide-eyed, upturned face. Then she grabbed her notebook and pen, writing quickly. What she showed him seconds later made Bran's heart hurt.

REALLY? YOU LOVE ME?

"Hey," Bran said, sinking back down into his seat so he could be at her level. He reached for her hands, giving them a gentle squeeze. "I mean it. You're my little sister. I'm always going to love you. I'm not letting you go into foster care or anything like that. I was working with a lawyer to make myself your guardian before Cernunnos took you."

Aisling's expression crumpled, and she lunged for him, crying almost silently as she hugged him. Bran hugged her back, wishing he could take her grief, ball it up, and set it aside so she wouldn't have to feel it. "I know. I'm sorry. I wish Mom was still with us, too."

Their mother would know what to do. She'd have answers. But she wasn't here, and she never would be again, and Bran had to learn to be the leader of their coven and carry the mantle on his own now.

A warm hand settled on his shoulder, and Bran looked back at Cillian, who gave him a crooked little smile. "Let's go home."

Bran nodded, more than ready to leave the Otherworld behind.

Chapter Twenty-Three

None of the Fae were happy with his decision to return to Pelham. Cillian told himself he didn't care, but some small part felt a little guilty. Niamh had made it possible for him and Bran to escape Ainmire's clutches. Verlin had provided his home as a place to hide, but Cillian didn't trust the Fae lord. Kindness wasn't kind when there was an ulterior motive behind the smiles.

"You would go with him?" Verlin asked, looking at Cillian. "You would leave your people to Medb's terror? Your kingdom? You would let the Dagda ruin the Winter Court?"

Cillian squinted against the sunlight in the castle's courtyard, watching Niamh and Seamus call out orders to the Fae who had been chosen to escort them to the wyrding. Cillian refused to show how Verlin's words worried him. "This isn't my home."

"It *was*."

The argument from the dining room had followed them outside and would most likely follow them home since Niamh had declared she would be staying with them in Pelham. Seamus would join them only long enough to help fight Cernunnos before reluctantly returning to the Otherworld. Cillian was glad because that meant they only had one Fae to deal with in Pelham, but it also meant Verlin wouldn't be targeted by Medb for Seamus' absence. Cillian didn't want to be the cause of someone else's agony.

"I don't know what you want me to say," Cillian said in a low voice, turning his head so he could meet Verlin's gaze. "I told you I have no memory of this place."

"We can give your memories back to you."

Cillian shook his head, glancing over at where Bran and Aisling stood by the horses so that Aisling could pet one under the watchful eyes of one of Niamh's crew. "I don't want them. Not if it means losing Bran."

Gaining what everyone said he'd lost would make Cillian lose the one person he loved, and he couldn't do that. He couldn't promise Bran he'd be the same man who'd grown up in Pelham if he took back the memories of a Fae who had lived centuries. The Fae wanted him to be their Winter Prince, but all Cillian wanted to be was someone Bran wouldn't look at in horror.

"You truly love him," Verlin said, sounding aggravated. "This witch whose people would see ours destroyed."

"He's not like that."

"They are *all* like that."

Cillian clenched his jaw. "I won't leave him."

Verlin stared at him, expression impossible to decipher. Then those amber eyes closed, and something like pain crossed his face. "Is he your mate?"

"What?"

Verlin opened his eyes, pinning Cillian with a look he couldn't turn away from. "Your mate. You didn't have one before the purge of the Winter Court. You had hoped for one, taken countless lovers, but none were your mate."

"I don't—"

"Could you live without him? Could you let him walk away? Or would you do anything in your power to keep him safe? Would your heart wither and die without him in your life? Do you feel a bond between you both even when he is not there?" Verlin turned his head, staring at Seamus, something warm coming to his eyes, features gentling. "I knew Seamus was my mate the moment I saw him centuries ago. He was one of your personal knights, long before he became captain of them all. He was in the throne room when I was presented to you at the Winter Court."

Cillian winced. "Please tell me we weren't—"

Verlin laughed, none of the cruelty that Ainmire had possessed in the sound. "Betrothed? No. We were not suited, especially not after I found my mate. I was sent to the Winter Court to be a companion, to learn to be your right hand. You trusted me above all others, and I followed you everywhere. I would have followed you into death itself if my mother hadn't convinced me to live for our people, to care for them in your stead amid Medb's atrocities. And I could not do to Seamus what had been done to my mother when she lost her mate."

"Your father?" Cillian asked carefully.

"He died in the purge. Medb made an example of him in exchange for my life. My mother...she wasn't at the Winter Court. She was here. She has been here ever since."

Grieving with the entirety of her being. Verlin didn't have to say it, not when it was so easy to see in the fragile lines of Lady Fiadh's figure.

"My father's body rots in his armor in the Great Hall of the Winter Court, as do others who tried to stand against the Dagda and his lies," Verlin said, anger and grief riding his voice.

"I'm sorry." Cillian meant it. No one should experience the loss of a parent in such a way.

Verlin pressed his lips together for a moment, skin paling at the seam of them. "Are you sorry for leaving us?"

"This isn't my home."

"So you keep saying." Verlin sighed, turning at the sound of the door behind them opening. "Mother, what are you doing? You should be resting."

Lady Fiadh stepped into the courtyard, a servant hovering behind her. Verlin reached for her, letting her lean her weight on his arm. "I am fine, my dear. I could not miss Cillian's departure."

"You wouldn't have to if he stayed."

"He has always been stubborn." Lady Fiadh looked at Cillian, a gravity to her gaze he couldn't escape. "You take after your mother in that way."

"The Mórrígan would stay. She would fight."

"Hush," Lady Fiadh said before Cillian could argue that he didn't know a Mórrígan. "You cannot be angry that Cillian leaves to keep his heart intact. Your father begged and bargained for such an escape for you once upon a time."

Verlin's jaw twitched. "And he died because of it, half killing you."

"And that is why I do not want Cillian to ever experience the despair and emptiness I live with. But I have survived to see the Dagda's downfall stand before me once again, and I do not regret that." Lady Fiadh patted Verlin's arm before letting him go to stand in front of Cillian. They were nearly of height, making it easy to look her in the eye, to see the faint crow's feet at the far corners of hers and the shadows that stained the hollows of her cheeks, even in sunlight. "Every word you have spoken, every action you have done, has been for the benefit of that witch. It is anathema among our kind to care for the enemy, but there is no reasoning with the heart when a mate is involved."

"I don't know if Bran is my mate," Cillian said slowly, reeling a little from her words.

"Sometimes the only lie a Fae can tell is one of the heart because we believe it to be true." Lady Fiadh raised her hands, and Cillian stiffened as she framed his face, her gaze boring deep. "The witch is your mate, and as much as I loathe that, I can't ignore the truth of it. There is no Fae who will ever accept it, and they will use him to ruin you."

"I won't let anyone hurt him."

"I thought the same for my mate, and he for me, and now I live without him for all days. I mean this as a warning and nothing else, my prince. You get to decide what kind of love this is, but I will tell you what kind of loss it could be—one you never recover from."

Cillian had to look away from her, searching out Bran where he stood across the courtyard with Aisling, the other man staring back at him. He remembered how it had felt last night, when they'd been tangled up in each other. The way Bran had drawn him close, drawn him in, how kissing Bran had wiped away seven years of uncertainty and regrets and loneliness, settling some inner clawing need he'd done his best to ignore for years.

The idea of letting Bran go was an impossibility he would not fathom.

The thought of turning his back on the Fae forever didn't sit well with him.

"We have to get Aisling's voice back," Cillian said, meeting Lady Fiadh's eyes again. It wasn't a promise in any way, but the faint, satisfied smile Lady Fiadh gave him told him she heard what was left unspoken, even if Cillian couldn't.

"You cannot appear as you are in the mortal world. You will need to use your magic to glamour yourself again."

"The glamour Etain tore apart wasn't mine."

"You still need to use your own magic. Now, close your eyes and listen to my voice."

Cillian hesitated before doing what she asked, closing his eyes and letting her words wash over him. It was difficult for him, at first, to turn his awareness inward, to actively search for a power that had so far only exploded out of him without his conscious control. Remembering Bran's words in the wyrding was what ultimately enabled him to grab hold of his magic and draw it out of him.

Bending Nature to his will meant wrapping his magic around his body, holding it tight until *something* wove together and stuck. Willing himself to not appear as he truly was took effort, but he did it. Cillian didn't need to look in a mirror to know he now appeared human because it felt as if his skin didn't fit over his bones anymore, like clothes that were a size too small, constricting all his limbs.

He opened his eyes, finding Bran and Aisling standing next to him, Jupiter perched on Bran's shoulder. Bran stared at him worriedly. "Are you okay?"

Cillian stepped away from Lady Fiadh's hands. "Yeah."

"You look like you again."

He raised a hand to touch his ears, tracing the point there that he knew no one else could see. "I don't feel like it."

"Niamh says we're ready to leave. She has our horses saddled."

"Our legs are going to hurt."

"I'll take that discomfort if it means we get home."

Cillian turned to look at Lady Fiadh. "We appreciate your hospitality."

"It was my pleasure to help my prince," Lady Fiadh said easily enough.

She didn't beg him to stay; no argument left her lips. Verlin didn't seem happy about any of their choices, but he, too, held his tongue as they crossed the courtyard for the horses. Cillian watched Verlin approach Seamus, reaching up to cover the other Fae's mouth with his hand. He then kissed the back of it before pulling away, murmuring something in the Fae language Cillian didn't understand.

"I thought they were mates?" Cillian said, curious at the strange way they said goodbye.

"Verlin is the Lord of Breath and Bone. His magic can steal the air from a person's lungs with a single kiss. His mate is not exempt from that," Niamh said.

Seamus pressed his and Verlin's foreheads together with an intimacy that made Cillian feel as if he was spying on something sacred. He turned away, busying himself with Niamh's instructions on how to swing himself onto the gray horse they'd given him. He was glad to see the animal wasn't as large as the deer they'd seen before. Its tack was fairly elaborate, all black leather inset with jewels at the connecting points. The saddle was similar to an English one in style, and when Cillian swung himself up onto it, he was surprised that it fit him exactly and was comfortable. How long that comfort would last remained to be seen.

The Fae had also found horses sized for Bran and Aisling. While Bran looked a little uncomfortable in his, Aisling was excited, leaning forward to happily rub the horse's neck. Her horse tossed its head and whickered happily, keeping its hooves planted on the flagstone. The Fae holding those reins spoke gently with Aisling, explaining how to issue orders to the horse using the reins and her knees. She'd changed out of her gown into soft gray pants and a pale, rose-pink blouse. Her knee-high dark brown boots would be good for riding.

"I will see you again, my prince," Verlin said when he returned to Cillian's side, a defiance in his tone that Cillian didn't know how to address.

"Bran said time runs faster in our world than it does here. I'll send Seamus back to you as quickly as we can. I don't want either of you to be harmed by his absence," Cillian said.

"Feel free to bring yourself with him."

Verlin stepped back, bowed deeply, and retreated to where his mother stood across the courtyard. Niamh called out an order, and everyone on horseback clattered toward the exit. Once outside the castle, everyone ranged themselves down the road. Seamus rode beside Aisling, with Bran trailing behind her. Cillian was behind them both, and he wasn't blind to the fact the three of them had been put in the middle of the group of armed Fae. He couldn't find it comforting.

The ride to the forest was beautiful, at least. No pollution meant everything felt so much brighter, the color deeper everywhere he looked. The flowers they passed were more vibrant and the trees larger than anything found in the forest he patrolled back in Pelham. Cillian loved the outdoors, and part of him loved how the valley looked stretched out around them.

All that color faded when, hours later, the edges of the wyrding crept through the trees they rode through. The temperature dropped, sunlight growing weaker as white fog drifted through the air. Niamh whistled, drawing the attention of the lead rider. Cillian recognized Tev from before. The Fae tossed his reins to the rider closest to him before dismounting and jogging away between trees, a dagger clutched in one hand. The fog swallowed Tev up, and Cillian pulled on the reins to bring his horse to a stop.

"Will we need to follow the lights this time?" Cillian asked.

"No," Niamh said.

"We didn't come out here when we crossed over. Will we even end up back home?"

"There are only so many ways into the mortal world. We'll take a shadow path back to the wyrding near Ainmire's estate and slip through there."

The last thing Cillian wanted to do was let Bran anywhere near Ainmire. "Will he know we're in the wyrding?"

Niamh shook her head. "He shouldn't unless he has scouts

patrolling the wyrding, but the last thing he should think is we would return to where you first came through."

Cillian could only hope that was true. When Tev returned with confirmation he'd found a shadow path in the wyrding, Niamh dismounted and gestured for Cillian to do the same. Not everyone did so, and the small group who huddled with Tev at the front of the escort consisted of Cillian, Bran, Aisling, Niamh, and Seamus.

"The entrance is ahead, but there isn't much coverage halfway to it. The light has moved on, but we should leave the horses behind," Tev told Niamh.

"We'll make the rest of the way on foot." She turned and gave out an order Cillian didn't understand, but the gist of it was clear enough when all but two of their escort turned their horses back around. At his curious look, Niamh nodded in their direction. "They'll return to the castle. A few will stay behind for when Tev returns."

"What about Seamus?" Cillian asked.

"I will stay with you until we retrieve the young lady's voice," Seamus said.

"Seamus knows his way through the shadow paths. He'll be able to make his way home," Niamh promised.

"You could always go with him," Bran said as he raised an arm so Jupiter could fly down and land on it. He guided her to his shoulder and stroked her beak.

Niamh ignored him. "Let's go."

They trekked deeper into the wyrding, leaving behind all the warmth of the forested valley. Cillian missed it with a depth that surprised him as the world became endlessly gray around them. Bran kept Aisling close, holding her hand and never letting her go. Cillian was never more than an arm's length away from them both, always keeping them in his sights. No one spoke in the hushed quiet of the eerie border between the Otherworld and the mortal world. It was depressing, the way the wyrding sucked the life out of everything.

He thought about the argument in the dining room that morning and the accusations that made too much sense not to be true. If the Fae and witches had been at war for centuries—maybe millennia—Cillian could see how they'd each fight to use such a horrible place against each other. That didn't make either side right, though.

This time, they steered clear of the lights as Tev led them to that first shadow path. They left him behind and continued clawing their way through pitch-black holes buried in rot. Niamh led them through shadow paths and the fog of the wyrding until they stumbled into a boneyard Cillian knew he'd never forget.

"Here," he said into the eerie quiet. "We came through here."

The standing stones were still present, bones scattered about and snapping underfoot as they walked toward the center. Cillian breathed through his mouth from the stench of half-eaten, rotting bodies tossed around the clearing. Niamh led the way, pausing outside the hole in the stone. She crouched, picking something up from the ground. Bran made a startled sound at the sight of the brilliant blue flower resting in the palm of her hands, the color shocking against the surrounding gray. "Those were twined around Cernunnos' antlers."

"It's a sign he might have come through this way," Niamh said, letting the flower fall back to the ground. She straightened, frowning at the way that would take them home.

"He may have left a trap on the other side," Seamus said, unsheathing the sword from his back. He wasn't in full armor, but the cuirass and shoulder pauldrons he wore were matte black, making it easier to go unnoticed. Cillian didn't know if the knight had any magic or a title that would hint at a particular skill, but Niamh seemed to have no problem stepping aside.

Seamus went first through that nightmarish hole, and the rest of them had no choice but to follow. Cillian reached for Bran's hand rather than the leash, holding on tight. Bran gave him a grimace of a smile, holding on to Aisling with his other hand. "Let's go home."

Cillian nodded. "Yeah."

Clawing his way through the terrible dark of the shadow path connecting the Otherworld to the mortal world was just as stomach-churning as the first time. Vertigo hit hard, making it impossible to find his center in that pitch-black space. But Cillian kept moving, kept driving himself forward, never letting Bran go.

He didn't know how long they were there until he stumbled over a rock, his hand sinking into bioluminescence. Something soft gave beneath it, and he kept pushing, prying those weird mushrooms away. He shoved his way forward into that hollowed-out tree they'd passed through what felt like a lifetime ago.

Cillian gasped, breathing in air that still smelled like rot, black sap smeared over his hand and arm, but beyond the broken-up tree trunk was a place he recognized. He pitched his way toward it, dragging Bran and Aisling with him as they stumbled into a forest that looked like home. The summer heat and humidity felt hotter than when they'd left for the Otherworld, and he wondered how much time had passed. His stomach clenched with nausea, and it took a couple of hard swallows to steady it.

Seamus stood off to the side at the base of the hill, keeping an eye out as they all staggered away from the tree. Cillian strained his hearing, wincing when he accidentally set the pitch higher than a normal human's would be. He shook his head, hoping his senses would settle, glad when they did.

"It's safe enough for now," Seamus said, not taking his eyes off the surrounding forest. He didn't seem bothered by the heat that was such a jarring change from the chill of the wyrding.

"Where are we?" Niamh wanted to know, frowning at the trees around them. "This forest feels sick."

"Pelham," Cillian said. "I can get us home."

He finally let go of Bran's hand, dredging up the direction they'd originally approached this location however many days ago. Once he was oriented, Cillian started walking, and the rest followed after him. The sounds of the forest slowly crept over them as they walked, and the familiar noise settled Cillian somewhat. The sunlight slanting through the branches had an angle to it that spoke of midday sun.

Cillian mentally calculated the best route home and angled them west, thinking they could maybe find the kayak again and cross the reservoir or, at the very least, hike along the shore rather than over hills. They passed witchmarks on the way through the forest, spots of magic that drew Niamh's and Seamus' curiosity, but no one stopped, and no one questioned when Bran slapped his hand over each one, magic sparking gold beneath his palm as he walked past.

They'd brought supplies with them, pouches of dried fruit and meat and leather canteens of water. They ate and drank while on the move, finally making it to the reservoir, breaking through the trees to stand on the shore. Unease settled in his gut as Cillian eyed the sun's trajectory.

"If we try going north, we'll be stuck in the forest by the time nightfall hits," he said. They had a better chance of crossing to the other side and hiking to State Route 202, but only if they could remember where they'd stashed the canoe.

"Freeze the water," Seamus said. "We can cross it that way."

Cillian stared at him. "What?"

"You've done it before when we needed to cross rivers and lakes. Build us an ice bridge."

"It's summer."

Seamus shot him a droll look, amusement in his pale blue eyes, some of his moss-green hair falling across his forehead. "And you are the Winter Prince."

Like that was an answer.

And maybe it was.

Bran was crouched beside where Aisling sat on the damp rocky shore, clearly tired. He looked up at that statement, chewing on his bottom lip. The collar he still wore glinted in the sunlight. "There's no one around who would see if you did."

Cillian nodded slowly. The Quabbin Reservoir had more restrictions than most other natural wilderness places simply because of the lake's designation as drinking water for Boston. There wouldn't be any boats or swimmers or people fishing. Hikers were restricted to approved paths, and not many of those made it to the water.

The only problem was he didn't know how to call upon his magic and do what Seamus suggested. He knew he had the ability to do it—all the ice he'd unconsciously summoned was proof of that—but he didn't know *how*. Bran did, though, and Cillian was forever grateful for the younger man's support.

Bran came to stand in front of him, taking Cillian's hands in his. "You remember what I said before? How it's your intent that will drive your magic? That's never going to change, no matter what spell you're performing. I don't know how Fae cast their magic, but for me, it's bending Nature to my will. If you want to build an ice bridge to get us across? Then build one. Make the water do what you want."

It sounded so simple, so easy, when Bran said it. Doing it was another matter entirely.

Cillian still tried.

He walked up to the water's edge, bootheels sinking into the gravelly shore, staring across the water that didn't seem as blue as the lake by the castle. But this wasn't the Otherworld; this was Pelham. This was home, and if Cillian was going to help protect it, he needed to use his magic.

He closed his eyes, thinking about how strange his body still felt, the glamour wrapped around it tight like a prison, and that core of power burning in the center of his chest he'd done his damnedest to pretend didn't exist. But he couldn't stay ignorant of what he was, not when Bran's and Aisling's and everyone else's life in Pelham was at stake.

Winter was the dark time of the year, where snow turned everything white, and the cold could and did kill. But it was also beautiful, those months where people remembered that technology and the modern world couldn't always stand against the natural one and so hunkered down, leaving Nature to exist as it once had. Maybe that's how magic had died out over the years, left in the clutches of witches who had once been Fae, hidden away and lost. Humanity had spread across the globe, and there was no giving back a world of iron to the Fae who wanted so badly to return.

But they could command pieces of it.

And somehow, Cillian knew winter would always bow to his demands.

It spilled out of him in an icy wave of power, ripping across the water with a crackling snap, freezing over in an instant. Not the entire lake or even its entire depth, but a bridge that cut straight across, thick enough to take their weight. Cillian felt the power of it pull at him as he opened his eyes, staring at the ice that had formed beneath his feet, digging into the rocky shore. It stretched across the water, glinting pale blue-white beneath the sunlight. Cold wafted up from the ice, but not even the summer heat could melt it.

"Will it hold us?" Bran asked from behind him.

"Yes," Cillian said without hesitation.

"Then let's get across."

Bran called out to Aisling, who huffed and slowly got to her feet. She was a trooper, though, and didn't balk about following her brother onto the ice bridge. Seamus went first, and Niamh took up the rear. The ice bridge swayed a little underfoot from the slight motion of the water, but the wind was sluggish, and there weren't many waves. Once they made it to the other side, the ice started to melt, no longer held by Cillian's need or intent.

Cillian took point then, heading west, leading everyone through trees and around shrubs. The land wasn't as steep on this side of the reservoir, which meant they could move a little faster. No one complained about the pace, not with the threat of lights out there.

Eventually, however long later, they stumbled out of the tree line onto the side of the road, State Route 202 stretching north and south in front of them. The sun was lower in the sky than any of them would have liked, the deepening blue in the east something that made Cillian's heartbeat pick up. "Where do we go from here?"

"The Shoppe," Bran said without hesitation. "We can—"

The sound of an engine rumbled in the distance, growing louder. Niamh said something in the Fae language, and when Cillian looked over at her, he was startled to see both Niamh and Seamus appeared human. Their glamour had changed their faces, even their clothes, and hidden their weapons. Which was fortunate because the black ranger truck coming down the road was familiar.

The truck slowed down, pulling over to the shoulder and braking hard. Its hazard lights went on before Mac stepped out, disbelief on his face. "Cillian? Bran? *Aisling*? You found her? Why are you all dressed like you're going to a Renaissance Faire?"

"Hey, Mac," Bran said tiredly, giving an awkward little wave. "What day is it?"

"We're at the end of August. You've all been gone for almost two months." The older ranger jogged over to them, eyeing Niamh and Seamus. "Who are these people? Are you—is that a *collar*?"

Cillian winced, turned toward Bran. "We should take that off."

Bran gestured at it as he rolled his eyes. "Have at it."

Cillian had to fight back the desire to leave the collar where it was—

wrapped around Bran's throat to show ownership despite Bran being his own person—and reluctantly removed it. He wound the leash around the metal, gripping it in his hand since they had nowhere to put it. Mac stared at them in silence for a few moments before shaking his head hard.

"Town is under a curfew. You're lucky I was heading back home and saw you," Mac said.

"Curfew?" Cillian asked sharply. "Is it the lights?"

Mac nodded grimly. "Two more hikers have died since you left, and no one goes out at night right now."

"Can you take us to the Shoppe?" Bran asked, holding tightly to Aisling's hand.

Mac eyed their group. "I don't have room in the cab for everyone, but yeah, I can drive you there."

"Don't worry. No one will notice anyone in the truck bed."

Wariness filled Mac's eyes beneath the brim of his wide hat, but he didn't demand an explanation for that statement, merely waved at his truck. "Get in. Sunset is in less than an hour."

The urgency in Mac's voice had everyone scrambling toward the truck. Cillian, Bran, and Aisling squeezed into the truck's cab while Niamh and Seamus hauled themselves into the truck bed. Mac stared at them in the rearview mirror, his grip on the steering wheel white-knuckled.

"Are you going to tell me what those people are?" Mac asked. Cillian thought he might already know, judging by the use of *what* rather than *who*.

"Just drive," Bran said, and Cillian nodded in silent agreement.

Mac, for his part, didn't argue. He just pressed on the gas and headed south, back to Pelham.

Chapter Twenty-Four

Bran expected the Shoppe to be boarded up from the attack, his car dusty from sitting outside for a couple of months. He figured Mac would have transferred Cillian's ranger truck back to headquarters with the help of another ranger. What he didn't expect to see was a convertible Porsche parked next to his Honda Civic and a woman who didn't know what *closed* meant standing on the porch.

"What's she doing here?" Cillian asked from the back seat.

"Being a problem," Bran said. Before Mac had even pulled into grassy dirt out front that doubled as the Shoppe's parking lot, Seamus and Niamh had flung themselves out of the truck bed. They still appeared human to his eyes, but the standoff wasn't something he liked. Cillian got out as well, and Aisling went after him. Bran glanced at the clock on the truck's dash. "Go home, Mac."

Mac scowled at him. "What the hell are you doing with Fae? Your mother never would have—"

"Well, she's dead, and I'm not," Bran cut in harshly. "And I'm doing what I have to so that Aisling and this whole town stays safe."

The silence in the truck rang loudly in his ears. Mac finally let out a heavy sigh. "The Fae are the enemy. They need to die. That's what your coven has always said."

Bran worked his jaw, needing to force himself from reflexively looking at Cillian. "Turns out if you want to kill a Fae, sometimes another Fae can do the job better."

"This isn't how your coven has ever done things."

"That's not your concern," Bran said in a low voice, not looking at the guardian. "There's still time for you to make it home. So go. We'll talk in the morning."

He didn't say they might not see the morning, but Mac was always good at hearing what wasn't said. Bran was the last of his group out of the truck, and Mac wasted no time in driving off once he shut the door, taillights bright in the encroaching darkness. Bran approached the Shoppe with Cillian and Aisling by his side, eyeing the woman on the porch. "Meghan, isn't it? What are you doing here?"

"That's not her name," Seamus said flatly, hand curled as if he were gripping something. Probably his sword. His glamour was good because Bran knew he was Fae, knew he was in armor and carried a bladed weapon, but he couldn't see a damn thing in the plain T-shirt and jeans Seamus presently appeared to wear. The modern clothes had no defects to the outfits. It made Bran wonder if Seamus had ever crossed the wyrding into the mortal world before.

Wondered if he'd ever killed any witches.

Bran shook that thought away as Jupiter *cawed* overhead before landing on the roof. Meghan was dressed in a casual outfit this time, looking fashionable in white wide-legged linen pants and a sleeveless white blouse. Her red hair was tied back in a fishtail braid while a large leather tote bag hung from her elbow.

"You never contacted me," Meghan said coolly.

"The Shoppe is closed for repairs. The boarded-up windows and door should have clued you in to that fact," Bran said, halting in front of the porch. Cillian came to a stop beside him, both of them standing in front of Aisling. Seamus and Niamh flanked their little group, looking ready to fight.

"You should have reached out." Meghan ignored them all in favor of digging through her tote bag, coming up with something that made Bran's heart nearly stop. "I believe your coven will have use of this."

In her hand was the Gallagher coven's grimoire.

"How did you get that?" Bran asked hoarsely, fingernails biting into the palms of his hands.

Meghan arched one perfect eyebrow. "Your mother asked for my help."

"I don't believe you."

"I wasn't talking about *your* mother, witch."

Her gaze settled on Cillian, and Bran drew in a sharp breath, glancing at the other man. Cillian's expression was cold and unreadable when he confronted Meghan. "How do you know my mother?"

"We're old friends."

"That's not all you are," Niamh said flatly.

Meghan studied the grimoire in her hand, the weight of the thick, leather-bound book seemingly not bothering her at all. "No, it isn't."

Her dark eyes filled with a power that made the air heavy around them. The skin over her joints seemed to split, peeling open and fading away, revealing the truth of her existence beneath it all. What her glamour had hidden was pale, freckled skin, brilliant sky-blue eyes, fiery red hair, and a face that was unmistakably Fae.

Niamh rocked back on her heels, sucking in a breath. "*Scáthach?*"

Bran's hearing washed in and out for a couple of seconds. "The Fae warrior?"

Scáthach smirked. "Ah, so you *do* know of me."

"Every witch knows your story."

Scáthach held the grimoire higher, eyeing the worn and peeling spine. "Nothing in here will return your sister's voice."

Bran put one foot on the porch step. "That doesn't belong to you. Give it back."

She smiled at him, cold and vicious. "Beg nicely."

Ice licked up the walls of the Shoppe, coating the porch and the ground beneath their feet. Cillian's voice was like the bitterest temperature in Siberia when he spoke. "Bran isn't yours to order around."

Scáthach eyed him with not a small amount of judgment in her gaze. "And I suppose you think that collar of yours belongs around the witch's throat?"

Cillian didn't immediately respond, and Bran couldn't decide what he wanted Cillian's answer to be. Because he liked his freedom, but some cracked-open need deep inside of him wanted to be owned by the other man. Bran rocked back on his heels a little, careful of the ice. "You could have saved my sister, maybe even saved our mother, and instead, you stole our coven's grimoire?"

Scáthach tucked the grimoire under her arm, tipping her head at Cillian. "Control your witch."

Then she turned and walked into the Shoppe before Cillian or Bran could reply, the plywood covering the door disappearing like it had never been there. The Shoppe inside was dark, and Bran knew the utilities bill hadn't been paid while he was gone, but the lights switched on anyway with a glitter around the bulbs that spoke of magic.

A warm hand settled on his lower back, making him stiffen, but Cillian didn't move away. "Who is she?"

The question wasn't for Bran but for the Fae who had traveled with them. When Seamus spoke, he sounded tired. "A brutal taskmaster and teacher, but one who is decidedly against the Dagda."

"That doesn't make her an ally," Bran said tightly.

Cillian pressed his hand a little harder against Bran's body. "You need the grimoire back, so let's talk with her. If she had wanted to kill us, she could have done that last month."

It was a chilling thought. The last thing Bran wanted to do was bargain with a Fae, but sunset wasn't far off, and they were running out of time. He reached behind him for Aisling, curling his fingers around her hand when she slipped hers into his a second later. They climbed the steps to the porch and went inside.

Mac had kept his word. The Shoppe had been put to rights—mostly. The wreckage of destroyed display tables and furniture was piled against one wall, next to a second pile that contained broken or damaged items. Everything else that had survived intact had been clustered together on other tables and shelves. Bran was glad to see nothing had been thrown out, but he internally winced at the headache doing an inventory of everything was going to give him.

Scáthach stood in the center of the Shoppe, grimoire still tucked under her arm. She'd set the tote bag down on the floor beside a table. In her other hand, she held a glaive, and the clothes she'd worn to look human were gone. In their place was a meticulous set of armor pieces that covered her chest, back, forearms, and shoulders. She wore greaves over knee-high leather boots, and daggers were strapped to each thigh. When she turned to fully look at them, Bran could see blue whorls tattooed around her eyes, creeping onto her cheeks and forehead.

Bran glared at her. "When did you steal my coven's grimoire?"

"What makes you think I stole it? Cernunnos' way is not mine, and he was focused on the bean sí," Scáthach said. Aisling made a hitching sort of breath, and Bran seriously thought about punching the Fae.

"Don't speak of their mother with such disrespect," Cillian snapped. "Juliana is dead because of your kind."

"Our blood runs through your veins. You don't get to absolve yourself of your history simply because you do not remember it."

A chill worked its way down Bran's spine. "How do you know that?"

Scáthach pulled the grimoire from beneath her arm and opened it up, the old pages crackling from the motion. "We Fae know each other, and he did not know me."

"But you know his mother."

"Everyone knows of the Mórrígan."

"She's been missing for years," Niamh said.

"Has she? Or have you all been looking in the wrong place?" Scáthach closed the grimoire and held it out to Bran. "Your familiar is of war's calling, and you are the mate of the Winter Prince. The Courts of the Four Lands will consider Cillian a traitor because of that and claim the Dagda was right in punishing the Winter Court."

Bran slowly reached for the grimoire, wondering if it was a trick. "Then why are you here?"

Scáthach smiled coolly. "To see Cillian survive."

That sounded more like a threat than a promise of aid. Bran yanked the grimoire out of Scáthach's hands, clutching it to his chest. Relief flowed through him, making him light-headed for a few seconds. He drew in a shaky breath, holding on to the grimoire and the countless memories he had of his mother flipping through its pages to teach him their history and the magic found within.

"If the lights have been hunting in the forest, then Cernunnos must have been here in Pelham for weeks. We need to let him know we're here somehow," Cillian said.

"The only way to do that is with bait."

Bran followed Scáthach's gaze to Aisling, and fury slammed through him like a storm. He stepped in front of his sister, pushing her back. "No."

Scáthach stared down her nose at him. "Yes. He will know she has returned."

"You are not putting my sister at risk. She's been through *enough*."

"Do you want to get her voice back?"

"How do you even know it was missing?"

"Small-town gossip is quaint but useful." Scáthach's gaze cut to Cillian. "If you want any hope of regaining your rightful place in the Winter Court, then you will need the bean sí's ability to herald your reign."

"And if I don't want it?" Cillian asked warily.

Scáthach snorted. "What will you do when the mortal ages and dies and you do not? Will you stay here and let the witches kill you? No, child. The Otherworld is your home, not this place of iron, and you know it."

"I don't remember it."

"One may not remember and still yearn for a home."

Bran didn't like the troubled look in Cillian's eyes, and his heart clenched at the thought of Cillian leaving him. He shoved that thought aside, needing to focus on the present and not some ephemeral possible future. "You're not using my sister to lure Cernunnos to us. Find another way."

Aisling tugged on his sleeve, and he looked at her. She held up the notebook, pages pressed open by her fingers, and read the note she'd written there. *I WANT TO HELP. YOU'LL KEEP ME SAFE.*

"*No.* Aisling—"

"Let her," Scáthach cut in. "Or do you doubt your magic is enough?"

Bran rounded on her, furious at the accusation but unwilling to bend. "Aisling is *thirteen*. She's my sister and the last family I have. I *won't* put her at risk."

"She already is. We Fae know what she is, and there are those who would do anything to claim rights to a bean sí and the crown such Fae can offer. Houses have been destroyed over such desires." Scáthach glanced at Niamh, who said nothing.

"She has a goddamn *name*. Aisling isn't a thing. Stop treating her like one."

"If you care for her, then treat her like she is worth protecting."

"What would you have us do?" Seamus asked like he had the right to.

"Cernunnos will come. He will not have left her voice behind, so he will have it with him. It must be freed and returned." Scáthach glanced up at the sharp tip of her glaive. "We must fight."

Before Bran could argue against that, Aisling tugged on his arm again. He read her newest note as she stared stubbornly at him. *I WANT MY VOICE BACK.*

His heart cracked at those words—written out and unvoiced. Bran stared at his little sister, seeing her and not the bean sí everyone was fighting over. He knew their mother would have done anything and everything to keep them both safe, but that job now fell to him, and putting Aisling in harm's way wasn't something he wanted to do.

It was something he had no choice but to do.

Because the forest wasn't safe, not when the lights hunted.

Bran swallowed thickly before resting his hand on her thin shoulder, looking into her deep blue eyes. "You don't leave my side."

Aisling nodded slowly and closed her notebook. She mouthed *thank you* at him before kissing him on his cheek. He hugged her tight with one arm, and she hugged him back, and Bran hoped it wasn't the last time he'd ever get to hold his little sister.

"So what's the plan?" Cillian asked.

Scáthach eyed him with something that might be regret. "You used to be one of the best swordsmen in the Four Lands."

"I know how to shoot a gun, not wield a sword, and something tells me bullets won't stop Cernunnos."

"He'll use the lights to attack us. It's what he did when he kidnapped Aisling in the first place," Bran said slowly. "So one of us will need to engage Cernunnos while the rest hold back the lights."

"Will the lights even fight against Fae?" Cillian asked.

"They can be commanded to," Niamh said reluctantly.

"Then that makes us all targets, including the town." Bran looked up at the sky and the fading sunlight, the eastern horizon smudged dark with the encroaching twilight. "I'll make sure the lights can only come to us."

Cillian frowned at him. "How?"

Bran looked down at the grimoire, stroking his fingers over the leather cover. "My coven has lived here for centuries. Our magic knows the forest."

Recollection crossed Cillian's face. "The witchmarks."

Bran nodded. "I'll keep the lights out of the town, but that means when they come to us, it'll be all of them, and I don't know how many that will be."

"We'll handle them and Cernunnos," Niamh promised grimly.

"Children," Scáthach drawled, gaining their attention. "You will deal with the lights. Leave Cernunnos to me."

"What about us?" Bran asked.

She flicked them a dismissive look. "Stay out of the way."

If Bran had hackles, they would've risen. He didn't like Scáthach— for many reasons—but her condescension was right near the top of the list. But the sooner they got through the night and survived, the sooner the Fae would leave.

Hopefully.

Bran turned toward the damaged display case. "I'm going to call the witchmarks."

He handed the grimoire to Aisling and assessed the debris piled on top of the door that led to the basement. Mac had piled and swept a lot of the debris behind the counter, where it was out of the way of foot traffic but made it impossible to access the door.

Bran sighed and raised a hand, tracing a witchmark in the air with a twist of his fingers, focusing on the debris to *move*. Magic glittered in the air, golden sparks that swirled around the debris and shifted them across the floor with a clatter. Bran stepped into the space and knelt, searching out the latch and prying the door open.

Aisling handed the grimoire back and followed him down into the basement, glittering magic lighting the way. Cillian joined them below, looking around curiously at the space that made up their mother's—*Bran's*—stillroom. The space was meant for their coven only, and Bran should have sent Cillian back upstairs.

He didn't.

"I never knew this place existed," Cillian said.

Bran set the grimoire on the table, the mess of herbs and vials there needing to be thrown away. Whatever potency they could have had would've been lost in the months they'd lain on the table, untended and unused. "It's not meant for outsiders."

"Do you want me to leave?"

Bran looked over at him, seeing Cillian staring back. He hesitated a moment before shaking his head. "No. You should stay."

Bran wasn't letting Cillian go again, and he already knew about Bran's magic. Besides, letting him inside their coven's circle didn't feel wrong, only right. The Council of Witches would probably call him a heretic for everything going on, but Bran didn't care.

He reached for a small metal box and opened it, digging through the iron bits inside it until he found three tiny iron disks the size of a quarter. He pocketed one, slipped one into Aisling's pocket, then went over to Cillian. He reached for Cillian's pants, tucking the iron disk into his pocket as well. "I know it burns your skin, but I'll feel better if you keep iron close tonight."

Cillian raised his hand to cup the side of Bran's face, thumb stroking gently over his cheek. "Thank you."

Bran nodded and returned to the worktable and the grimoire there. He opened it up with a flick of his fingers and a touch of magic. The grimoire's leather cover snapped open, the pages fluttering to the one he'd requested. It was closer to the beginning of the grimoire than the end, faded, spidery handwriting scrawled across the parchment. Drawings filled the page on the right: witchmarks still in use by his coven, carved into trees in the forest to guide the lost to safety.

This time, he needed to guide the lights to them.

Bran made sure the witchmarks on the page were how he remembered them before stepping away from the table. He settled himself in the center of the pentagram's circle, facing east. Aisling stepped into the center with him and held her hand out to Cillian, wriggling it. Cillian hesitated before joining them inside every line of the pentagram and circle.

"What are you going to do?" Cillian asked in a hushed voice.

Bran raised his hands, fingertips glittering gold with magic, Nature washing through him. "Keep the lights out of Pelham."

He drew the witchmarks in the air, focusing on the intent of what he wanted—*guidance*, only this time, not toward the safety of a cabin in the woods. He wanted the paths the witchmarks lined in the forest to lead to the Shoppe.

To them.

He framed the witchmarks with his hands and focused on his magic, letting it spill out of him and into the pentagram, lighting up the circle. Cillian gasped in surprise but didn't speak. Bran was concentrating too hard to be able to answer any questions anyway. He closed his eyes and centered himself, sinking into an awareness of Nature that pulled him along like a river into the surrounding land.

Bran's magic flowed outward in a wave that washed through the surrounding forest for miles. Amid the countless trees, carved where only the lost would find them, witchmarks burned in his inner sight, like guiding stars fallen to earth. He used his magic to dim some and brighten others, creating a path that snaked through the forest and ended in the trees outside the Shoppe. They would be impossible to miss, spread as they were across the forest, pointing the way for the lights to find them rather than go through town and put people at risk.

And at the edge of his awareness, far across the forest, something cold began to spread.

Began to hunt.

Bran extricated himself from the net of magic tangled over the forest through the witchmarks, opening his eyes. The witchmarks that hovered between his hands and anchored the spell had faded so much he could barely see them. The spell they powered clawed at the forest beyond the Shoppe, buried in all the witchmarks that had been carved into trees long before he'd been born.

Aisling tugged on his arm to get his attention, looking at him with a silent question in her wide, deep blue eyes. Bran tucked some of her hair behind her ear, the round curve of it like his—for now, at least.

"The lights are coming," Bran said.

There would be no outrunning them this time.

Chapter Twenty-Five

Cillian took the stairs up from the basement two at a time, finding the Fae had left the Shoppe and were back outside. Niamh heard them, looking over her shoulder as they exited the building. Her gaze flicked to Bran, who had brought his coven's grimoire with him. "Your magic touched the entire forest."

Bran scowled at her. "How else was I supposed to find the lights?"

"Most witches wouldn't have that reach."

The contemplative look she gave Bran had Cillian stepping between the two. "What now?"

"We wait," Scáthach said, the metal-shod butt of her glaive ground into the dirt. She faced the trees, not them, her fierce focus on the surrounding dark. "The lights will come to us, and so will Cernunnos."

"You seem real certain you can beat him when lots of people in this world consider him some kind of god," Bran said.

"Do you?"

"No. Witches who know better don't pray to Fae."

"Our gods left us so long ago they are nameless to us. We were told to make our own way, and we did, until we were banished. This world is not how it was when we ruled."

"Probably for the better."

"You poison the land. There is no pride in that."

Cillian winced, knowing she was right but not up to refereeing an argument. "So what's the plan when they do arrive?"

"You'd be safer in the building since you don't remember how to fight," Seamus said, sounding almost apologetic, like Cillian's supposed memory loss was his fault.

"Cernunnos will need to see we have the bean sí," Scáthach said.

"Aisling stays with me," Bran said.

Cillian nodded. "And I'll stay with them."

Scáthach shrugged, as if their decisions didn't matter. "Just stay out of our way."

Niamh approached, the light spilling out of the doorway behind them making the edge of her sword shine a little. Cillian didn't know anything about bladed weapons, but thought he must have, in some other life. He thought, in some far, distant, fractured corner of his mind, he knew what it felt like to pick up a sword. "Scáthach asked me to use lightning in the fight."

Summer was always so hot and dry, everything brittle and ready to burn with just one spark. The people who called Pelham home would be barricaded behind their doors with iron nailed to the frames, hiding from the lights. They'd have to leave to outrun a wildfire, and Cillian didn't know if any of them would. Not with the threat of lights haunting the woods.

"Maybe not the best idea. If you set the forest on fire, we'd have to deal with that on top of the lights," Cillian said.

"I could put out any fire with rain."

Bran snorted. "There's a whole damn reservoir to the east of us. It won't flood, and there's no waterways nearby you have to worry about, but wouldn't fighting in a storm make it harder?"

Cillian nodded. "He's right."

Niamh took them at their word. "Then I will call a storm as a last resort. The lightning I will call if it is safe."

They lapsed into silence, continuing to stare into the dark all around them. Seamus did slow circuits around the Shoppe, getting eyes on the forest behind them. The night breeze was warm, even with the sun long since set. Cillian's nerves were strung tight, and he nearly jumped out of his skin when Bran touched his lower back.

"Sorry," Bran said, staring straight ahead, a soft golden glow lining the pages of the open grimoire he held in his other arm. "Look."

Cillian followed Bran's gaze, squinting into the darkness for a moment before something caught his eye deep in the woods across the road. The flickering glow he thought he'd seen appeared again, almost like the warning flash from a lighthouse.

The lights were out there.

"You should head into the basement where the circle is," Bran said to Aisling. She immediately shook her head, pointing furiously at him and then the ground, making her choice known. Bran let out a frustrated noise that had Cillian grabbing Bran's free hand and squeezing it. "I need to know you're safe."

Aisling shook her head again and stared at him stubbornly. She crossed her arms over her chest and stayed where she was.

"I'd feel better at having her within sight," Cillian admitted.

Bran shot him a pained look. "I can't worry about you both."

"Then we'll compromise. Come on, let's stand on the porch." He didn't know how safe they'd be if the lights surrounded them, but if they had to run for the basement, they'd already be halfway there if they were on the porch.

They retreated to a spot in front of the door. Jupiter *cawed* a warning from the roof, and Cillian looked at the road, a chill crawling through him at what he saw.

In the distance, the forest was full of lights floating between trees, brightening the dark in a way the unsuspecting might think was safe when, in reality, it was nothing but a nightmare.

It made him wish for his rifle. He didn't trust the magic that was inherently his, despite the instances of subconsciously using it. With no control, he risked hurting bystanders and the people he loved, and that wasn't what he wanted. He had a sinking feeling he wouldn't have a choice.

The scent of rot grew in the air, and they couldn't even blame what clung to their clothes from the wyrding. The leaves rustled louder, the movement clearly not from the wind. Cillian froze as the lights came out of the woods, the soft illumination flowing back into the bodies of the monstrous creatures who used to be human, used to be witches. Now, they were nothing more than a vicious nightmare, and Cillian couldn't stop the rush of fear that coursed through him, pricking at instincts that told him to run.

The monsters that had chased them through the woods before were there, along with more than a dozen other horrific-looking creatures, all led by Cernunnos, the smile on the Fae lord's too-beautiful face one Cillian would never trust.

Scáthach lifted her glaive, spinning it to adjust her grip, holding it level to the ground so the bladed end pointed at the forest. "Cernunnos."

"Scáthach," Cernunnos said, not slowing his stride. "Here I thought you would never leave the Otherworld."

"I have my duty."

"And I have mine."

Scáthach stepped forward. "Betraying your king?"

Cernunnos laughed, the sound echoing in the night between the rasping breaths of the lights. "Soon, I will have no king."

Niamh and Seamus spread out on either side of Scáthach, swords in hand. All three had their backs to the Shoppe, so they didn't see how the witchmarks Bran drew in the air created a glowing circle on the ground. Bran's magic was soft and golden, a stark contrast to the coldness of the lights now ranged on the road.

"We will not let you take the bean sí," Niamh said flatly.

Cernunnos reached up to touch the glowing sphere that hung around his neck. "I have her voice. You have the child. One of us will have both before the night is over."

"I won't let you take my sister again," Bran snapped.

"A Fae can never call a witch family."

Scáthach held her ground. "If the Dagda knows about the bean sí—"

"He knows nothing of her," Cernunnos cut in. "He only knew a coven had been whittled down in this area, and I was sent to finish the job. Imagine my surprise when I discovered the bean sí and a supposedly dead dream."

Cillian didn't miss the way Cernunnos looked at him, the Fae lord's attention something he couldn't hide from. "And what do you want with me?"

Cernunnos' smile stretched wider. "Your death would do nicely."

One of the monsters threw back its head and howled, its neck splitting down the middle to its chest, multiple tongues flicking out of the cavity like tentacles. Others clawed at the road, damaging the asphalt, ready for the kill. They surged forward with howling voices, feet thundering against the ground.

Jupiter *cawed* furiously above them, the raven's cries drowned out by Bran's startled shout. Cillian stepped closer to the other man, putting himself between the oncoming lights and the Gallagher siblings on instinct, hand clenching in the air for a weapon he didn't have.

Scáthach moved, becoming a shadow that was difficult for him to track as she ran for Cernunnos. Niamh and Seamus met the lights halfway, swords flashing as they dodged grasping claws and terrible maws full of teeth. The sounds the monsters made were hair-raising, but worse than that was the way Cernunnos laughed as he blocked Scáthach's strike with his own glaive conjured up out of thin air. The garland of blue flowers tangled around his antlers swayed in the air as he met Scáthach blow for blow.

She had him as an adversary, but the lights were also a threat she had to be aware of. Niamh and Seamus were busy with their own targets and couldn't come to her rescue. Cillian couldn't worry about Scáthach, not when one of the monsters got past Niamh and charged at them.

It was the same creature he'd seen in the forest when he'd ran after Bran. Its thin form gleamed white in the moonlight, that crescent moon horn on its head like a crown. It screamed at them, the sound horrendous, but its speed was no match for the unmoving force of Bran's magic.

It crashed into the circle around the Shoppe, gold light flaring in the air where it clawed furiously. Cillian rocked back on his heels, looking over his shoulder at Bran. The other man had the grimoire open in his left arm, his other outstretched toward the fight. Witchmarks glowed in the ink of the tattoo on his arm. Golden magic sparked in his eyes, and the weight to the air had its source from him. Aisling clung to him, her face as pale as her hair, eyes wide as she watched the nightmarish fight happening beyond the protective circle of Bran's magic.

"How long can you keep your magic up?" Cillian asked.

Bran's jaw was clenched, muscles in his neck tight with the strain. "Hopefully long enough for Scáthach to get Aisling's voice back. But we have a bigger problem. Cernunnos is ripping up the forest from its roots."

Cillian thought about the roots Damarus had summoned to wrap around their throats back in the Otherworld. If Cernunnos did the same here, he knew the Fae lord wouldn't hesitate to break their necks.

The monster in front of them screamed its fury before it staggered away from the golden barrier. Behind it, Seamus rose into view, sword dripping with black blood, his armor spattered with it. His eyes snapped with fury when they met Cillian's for an instant before the knight turned to attack the monster again. Seamus drove it back, clearing the area around the front of the Shoppe.

The ground rumbled, moving in a way it never had before. For a split second, Cillian thought it was an earthquake. Then Bran swore, and when Cillian looked back, the grimoire's pages were flipping over on their own, his fingers drawing another witchmark in the air over it.

"Can you keep the forest at bay?" Cillian asked.

"I'll try."

Cillian jerked back around, staring at the fight. Niamh was easy to make out now, the lightning crackling around her arms illuminating her like a target. Her magic was a threat that had fried one of the monsters, its smoking, burned corpse lying on the road. She'd done it to watch Scáthach's back as the other warrior fought in lockstep with Cernunnos, the both of them limned with magic.

Cillian's eyes caught on the glowing sphere hanging from Cernunnos' neck. Scáthach had been right. Cernunnos had brought Aisling's voice with him, covetous like how Ainmire had been, always wanting to hold on to what they thought belonged to them.

The lights regrouped, and Seamus shouted at Niamh, who let loose another bolt of lightning at a monster with skin hanging off its ribs like tassels. The lightning only made it stagger but didn't kill it, and the snarl it let out made the hair on the back of Cillian's neck stand on end.

The monster lunged for Niamh, and she dodged, scrambling out of range, nearly into the jaws of another creature. She ducked and rolled, her sword flashing with the motion, and barely missed the swipe of a claw. Seamus was just as hemmed in, while Scáthach was still locked in her fight with Cernunnos.

Beyond them, in the trees, dozens of lights drifted their way, growing brighter.

Cillian wanted his rifle or sidearm but had neither. He couldn't join the Fae in their fight against the lights with a sword even if he had one, having no memory of ever holding one. Bran was caught up in his magic to keep Cernunnos from using the forest itself against them. Cillian had nothing other than the magic he had no idea how to consciously use and control in a fight. Building an ice bridge was different than fighting against a Fae lord who had millennia of skill behind him while Cillian had nothing.

But Bran had said it was about intent, about bending Nature to his will, when Cillian had always believed something like that was impossible. The natural world wasn't meant to be tamed, no matter how hard humanity tried. Eventually, the elements came calling.

And winter, it seemed, would always answer to him.

Cillian looked down at his hands, thinking of the ice that had appeared in moments of high emotion in his cell, on the *Bone Breaker*, and in that castle by the lake. It was proof he couldn't deny of his origins, even with a lie wrapped around his skin, so he let it go. The tightness eased over his bones, and he drew in a breath, ribs not feeling so constricted anymore.

"Cillian?" Bran rasped behind him.

He flexed his hands, not needing a mirror this time to know he didn't look human anymore. "They need help. Let me past the barrier."

Fingers grabbed the back of his court coat, twisting the fabric. "*No.* Don't go. You don't know how to fight."

He turned around, forcing Bran to let go. He met those gold-flecked hazel eyes and didn't look away, didn't try to hide. "You said it's about intent, and I intend to get Aisling's voice back."

"Cillian—"

"Bran. Trust me."

Bran worked his jaw, the hand gripping his grimoire white-knuckled. "The lights will try to kill you."

"So don't let them."

Bran swallowed loudly. "Okay. I'll open the circle."

Aisling still clung to her brother, fear in her eyes, lips trembling with it. The geas on her throat had come to the surface, a hideous, malevolent black thing that didn't belong on her skin.

Cillian turned his back on them and strode toward the edge of the circle. Bran's magic was a warm presence in the air that cleaved a narrow way open for him. Cillian steeled himself and stepped out of the safety of the circle, keeping his eyes open even as he turned his focus inward.

One of the lights caught sight of him, twisting away from where Seamus was cutting through one of its brethren. Its head was that of a bull, bleeding out of its eye sockets as it lumbered toward him, mouth splitting open to let out a pair of curved fangs as thick as his forearm.

"Cillian!" Seamus yelled. "Get back!"

Cillian reached for that river of power inside him, drawing it forth. And maybe he couldn't remember being the Winter Prince the Fae all thought he was, but he couldn't deny how *right* it felt to let Nature in all its fury burst out of him.

Ice exploded away from his feet, covering the ground in seconds. Chunks of it rose up to encase the monster, halting its forward charge mere feet from Cillian. It hacked at the ice with clawed hands that couldn't dislodge any of it. Blue-white ice covered its body before finally wrapping around its head, freezing the monster in its place, turning it into an ice statue like those Fae soldiers in the wyrding, the light that limned it dying out.

The air lost its sluggish heat, temperature dropping. Cillian's breath puffed out in soft clouds as he reached for one of the monster's iced-over arms. He wrapped his hand around the limb and used his newfound strength to break it off at the elbow, finding the ice had gone all the way through, leaving no rotten flesh behind.

He couldn't think about how he'd killed it, how he'd intended to stop it and his magic had interpreted that into a permanent end. All Cillian could do was direct his magic to the next monster lunging at him, winter pouring out of him with a ferocity he couldn't deny. Blue-white lines of magic opened up on his hands, cutting up his arms all the way to his shoulders. It didn't hurt, even though he thought it should, fingertips darkening to blue.

The ground jerked again beneath his feet, and Bran shouted a warning Cillian barely heard. He kept his balance on the ice instinctively, magic humming through him, cold power at his fingertips. Some of the trees across the road upended and crashed to the ground, roots rising. Whether called by Cernunnos or Bran, Cillian couldn't focus on them.

The only thing that mattered was getting Aisling's voice back.

Scáthach wrenched herself back from Cernunnos' reach, the sound of their glaives separating ringing in the air. She settled into a defensive crouch, not taking her eyes off Cernunnos, but her words were for Cillian. "You foolish child. This is not your fight."

"Cernunnos came to my town, to my forest. He killed people I knew and stole Aisling's voice," Cillian growled. "How could it not be my fight?"

He flung his arms outward to the side, magic rushing away from him in a wave of winter cold and ice that bent to his will. It coated the ground and the road around them, lashing at the lights until all the monsters became ice. The ones in the forest were still a problem, but for now, Bran could focus on those while Cillian dealt with the Fae lord.

Cernunnos straightened to his full height, the reach of his antlers making him taller than Cillian. Magic danced in the air around the Fae lord, his glaive glowing with it. "You are not the prince you once were."

"I don't remember who I was, but I'm still me."

"You are far too human now to survive."

Cernunnos wrenched the earth apart beneath their feet, ice cracking as a fissure opened up. Cillian lurched backward, somehow keeping his balance even as the heat of summer warred with winter all around them. He willed the cold to stay, for the ice to not melt, the air around him crackling with magic that made him glow. The glaive arcing through the air toward him was smacked away by Seamus' sword as the knight threw himself between them.

"Don't you *dare*," Seamus snarled.

Ozone burned in the air as lightning streaked through every single ice statue left of the lights around them, shattering them all. Niamh lowered her arm, hand clenched in a tight fist around flickering lightning. Scáthach had put herself between Cernunnos and the forest, glaive held at the ready. Cillian glanced over his shoulder, seeing Bran standing on the Shoppe's porch, aglow with golden magic, the ground unmoving beneath their feet, the lights in the forest held at bay.

Cernunnos didn't seem worried, merely amused. "You think you can win? Against me? The forest obeys *me*, not your witch. I will kill him the same way I killed his mother and take the bean sí for my own use."

Cillian's rage was fierce and cold, rising like snow drifts in a blizzard. The air went frigid, but he wasn't affected by the cold. "You won't touch Bran."

Because Bran was his—had *always* been his—and Cillian knew in that moment he would kill anyone who tried to take Bran away from him.

The smile slipped a little on Cernunnos' face. In the forest, the lights screamed a warning or a protest, Cillian couldn't tell which. But there was ice everywhere, their area in the world covered by his magic, winter a living thing he commanded. It burned through him, a wealth of power he'd never known existed before—in this life, at least.

If he thought about it too long, it might start to feel familiar, and he didn't know if he wanted that.

Cillian stepped around Seamus, who didn't try to hold him back, merely slotted into a spot on his left, guarding his back. Cernunnos stood his ground, summer fighting against winter, clawing out a patch of clear ground against the ice covering everything. It wasn't much, and that realization settled Cillian somehow. Like maybe, despite Cernunnos' power and intent, Cillian's determination could outlast the Fae lord's.

"You think because you know the truth now that you can best me?"

Cernunnos asked silkily, hand raised, magic pooling in his palm. He was haloed with it, the glass sphere hanging from his neck pulsating softly.

"I think you're in my world, and you don't belong here."

It was, perhaps, the cruelest thing he could say to a Fae—that their historical homeland was no longer theirs and never would be. Pelham might not be any town in Ireland, but the land was the same, cleaved apart geological ages ago, a long-lost memory of what the Fae would never live upon again.

And maybe Cernunnos wanted Aisling to take the Dagda's crown, but maybe—just maybe—he wanted it for the world here. Because the Fae lord hadn't said *where* he wanted to rule, just that he'd have no king. And the Fae couldn't lie but that didn't mean their words were ever true.

"This isn't your home anymore. It never will be again," Cillian said, utterly truthful, utterly cruel. "It's forgotten you and your kind, but I've walked this forest for years, and it knows *me*."

Cillian called to Nature, and it answered, ice breaking through Cernunnos' defenses there on the road with savage intensity. Moonlight reflected off the white landscape spreading all around them and the piles of ice that were all that remained of the lights from the initial attack. Pelham was always beautiful in winter, even when facing off against a nightmare.

Summer heat burned where his magic and Cernunnos' met, the air shimmering with it. Ice melted, then reformed in a vicious unending cycle, powered by Cillian's will and intent. Cillian let his magic wash through him, let it buoy him as he dragged himself forward against air that was suddenly so heavy, the ground shaking once more beneath his feet. Ice cracked around them, loud like a crescendo, and the lights in the forest screamed in an unholy way, their monstrous forms outlined between the trees.

Cernunnos tossed his head back, one arm thrust forward, fingers more like claws in that moment and glowing with magic. His beautiful face twisted with rage, with disdain, but he hadn't yet learned to fear Cillian. Roots broke through the asphalt, and somewhere in the forest, another tree fell. Behind Cillian, Bran started speaking in a language that might have been Irish once upon a time—so, *so* similar to the Fae language—but the words were full of magic that cut through the roots that would have strangled them on Cernunnos' command.

The bit of earth around Cernunnos shrank, winter clawing ever closer. Cillian forced the ice to bend to his will, lashing at Cernunnos with blue-white shards that could have pierced skin if they'd found their target. The wind picked up suddenly, howling over the forest like a mad thing, bringing with it enough snow to blanket every leaf in the surrounding trees, pulled from the very air itself. Through the twisting flurries, he could see the lights growing brighter, coming closer, fighting back against Bran's magic.

Cernunnos snarled, lips peeled back, teeth bared in a way that made him look like an animal now. But he wasn't the predator here, only the prey, and Cillian didn't let himself think about what he was doing, to second-guess himself, as he lunged forward into the circle of summer.

Heat crashed into him, a shock to his system, but he didn't let it distract him from his goal. Cillian reached through the ice shards keeping summer at bay to wrap his blue-tipped fingers around that tiny, delicate sphere hanging from Cernunnos' neck right as an explosion of magic sent him flying backward.

He didn't care how much it hurt.

He got what he wanted.

Cillian slammed into a body instead of the ground, Seamus breaking his fall with a loud grunt. They slid over ice, and it only took a thought from Cillian for it to rise up like a wall, stopping their motion. Niamh slid in front of them, sword raised and lightning crackling in her other fist to guard them.

Cernunnos threw back his head and roared, his body twisting, bulging, expanding outward. His clothes and boots melted away from his body, as if they hadn't been real. His skin split, the bones in his face breaking into something new.

What rose out of the human form was something taller than the two-story Shoppe, a macabre deer-shaped head in place of Cernunnos' other visage. His antlers had grown, protruding high over the three glowing eyes lined up across his face. Leaves grew from the antlers, blue flowers tangled in them, as the green of his magic dripped down his furred skin, burning in the air. The Fae lord stepped forward, his legs ending in cloven hooves now, and the ice beneath them shattered, the sound like bullets releasing from a gun.

Scáthach planted herself by Niamh, glaive pointed at Cernunnos' hulking form. "Leave this place. The forest does not want you."

Cernunnos laughed, a raspy thing that sounded like an animal. "I will take what is owed to me and leave you all to rot."

Cillian rolled off Seamus, and they both scrambled to their feet. He looked back at Bran and Aisling on the Shoppe's porch, both of them staring at him with equal parts fear and horror on their faces, the geas for silence a toxic shadow on Aisling's throat.

She needed her voice.

He was going to give it to her.

Cillian dropped the glass sphere to the ground and slammed his foot over it, shattering the glass.

Light flashed, golden and bright, before streaking away from the broken prison through the air and back to Aisling. She swallowed her voice with a loud, indrawn breath, the geas disintegrating in her throat. Then she doubled over, nearly falling, and would have if Bran hadn't caught her as her skin split with magic, peeling back in the same way it had for Cillian to reveal the Fae beneath the human veneer.

Aisling opened her mouth and *screamed*.

Cillian slapped his hands over his ears as the high-pitched, furiously haunting sound reverberated through the night air, drowning out the world. It tore through everyone and everything, magic in its own right, clawing at his skin. A bean sí's scream was meant to herald the dead and dying, but in this instance, it killed as well.

All the lights in the forest flickered before going out, leaving only shadows behind.

The scream faded, tapering off, until only silence reigned. Cillian's ears rang with it, and while it was difficult to hear anything over the pulse of his own heartbeat, he heard Cernunnos easily enough.

"I will kill you, son of winter," Cernunnos said in that terrible, monstrous voice of his.

"He is a son of *war*," another voice replied, making Cillian freeze. "And you will not touch him."

Cillian lurched around, staring wide-eyed at where his mother stood on the iced-over road, Jupiter perched proudly on her shoulder. She was in sneakers and scrubs, as if she'd left the emergency room in Amherst in a rush and hadn't bothered to find time to change. Her long black hair fell loose down her back, drifting a bit in the now sluggish wind, her entire being haloed in soft, bone-white light.

"Mom?" Cillian croaked.

His mother took a step forward, and Cernunnos—Cernunnos took a step back, that spot of summer drawing in tight around him. He raised himself to his full height, but Cillian's mother didn't seem cowed in the least.

"Mórrígan," Cernunnos said after a moment of tense silence. "Is this where you have hidden yourself all these years? Amongst the iron and the enemy?"

"You seem to have forgotten your place, Cernunnos. It is not here," his mother said in a cold, cold voice that echoed oddly between them.

Cillian thought, for a moment, that Cernunnos would try to strike his mother down. The Fae lord seemed to want to. Instead, he bowed his head, antlers dipping, the leaves and flowers there swaying with the motion. "My queen."

Then he straightened and walked into the forest without looking back, letting the trees and the darkness swallow him up.

Cillian didn't move—couldn't move—just kept staring at his mother. Scáthach spun her glaive around, digging the metal-shod butt into the ice, her voice breaking the eerie silence. "It's about time you showed up."

Niamh made a strangled sort of sound that eventually became words. "We thought you lost to the wyrding years ago, Mórrígan."

"One cannot be lost if you willingly leave," his mother said. Jupiter *cawed* and launched herself into the air, flying toward the Shoppe. His mother came to him then, striding across the ice with an otherworldly ease, never sliding once. When she reached him, her dark gray eyes searched his for a second before she drew him into a tight hug. "I have missed seeing you like this."

Cillian squeezed his eyes shut, questions tumbling through his mind, but they would have to wait. He let out a ragged breath, sinking into the comfort she'd always given him as a child and as a man. "How did you know we were back?"

"I came into town after my shift ended early to speak with Mac. I was at his home when he called me after he dropped you off here. I came as fast as I could." She pulled back, cupping his face. "You are all right?"

He let out a tired sort of laugh. "I don't know."

"Hm." She looked over his shoulder before letting him go. "Hello, Bran."

"Hello," Bran said, sounding wary.

Cillian turned toward him, drawn like a magnet to the other man. Bran's grimoire was closed and tucked under one arm, Aisling held close with the other. Her face had a more delicate look to it now, sharply pointed ears poking up through her white-blonde hair. She was clearly Fae, had probably always been so, wrapped up in a glamour the same way he'd been. And like him, she was loved by a witch.

Bran didn't pull away when Cillian stepped close to kiss him, and Cillian didn't want to ever let him go. "You're okay?"

"I have a raging headache, but yeah, I'm okay. I'm more worried about Aisling," Bran said.

"My throat hurts," Aisling piped up, wrinkling her nose at him. "I want ice cream."

Her voice startled Cillian, but then he smiled at her. "You can talk again."

"Yeah, it worked. I don't need to write everything down anymore."

"That's great."

Bran rubbed at her upper arm. "What now?"

Cillian took in the ice and snow that covered the land all around and the Shoppe with its boarded-up windows. The light from magic still spilling out of it was a warm and welcoming glow. "Let's get inside. I think we all need to talk."

He looked over at his mother when he spoke, and she didn't seem surprised or unhappy about his request. She merely nodded, a faint, sad smile curving across her mouth. "Yes, I think it's about time we did that."

She strode toward the Shoppe, the other Fae following her. A knot of complicated emotion settled in Cillian's chest as he watched her go, but the one thread cutting through it all that made sense and always would was his love for Bran. "You're staying?"

A soft look came to Bran's eyes, the gold flecks from his magic gone. "It's my Shoppe. Of course I'm staying. I'm not going anywhere. Not without you."

After everything they'd gone through over the last week or so in the Otherworld and the two whole months that had seemingly passed here at home, that was all the promise Cillian needed.

That Bran would stay.

Chapter Twenty-Six

Cillian's hands shook slightly from leftover adrenaline as they stepped into the Shoppe. The thrum running through his body would take a bit to dissipate. Everyone's attention was on his mother, who studied the wreckage with an unreadable look on her face.

"I am sorry about Juliana," his mother finally said.

"Did you lead Cernunnos to her?" Bran asked.

"No. He found his own way here to a border most Fae had forgotten about."

"You didn't forget it existed," Cillian said slowly.

"I have guarded the Four Lands against the wyrding since it was raised." His mother turned to face him, a weariness in her gray eyes that he hadn't ever seen before, even when she'd pulled double shifts at the emergency room when he was a kid. "You have questions."

He laughed. He couldn't help it. "You could say that."

"Let's go upstairs. We can talk in the apartment," Bran said, already prodding Aisling in that direction. She looked like she was about to pass out from exhaustion, and so Cillian didn't argue the suggestion.

They all trudged upstairs on creaking steps. The magic followed them in a golden glow, brightening the apartment. Bran saw Aisling to her room despite her protests of wanting to stay up. Niamh and Seamus peered around curiously, while Seamus went into the kitchen to poke at the stove and refrigerator. Cillian sat on the couch with his mother while Scáthach stood guard by the door.

Bran returned about ten minutes later, just when the silence was starting to get suffocating. He came to the couch and perched on the armrest rather than take the spot between Cillian and his mother. "Aisling is sleeping. Jupiter is with her. Will any more lights come for us?"

"No. The bean sí killed them all," Cillian's mother said.

"And Cernunnos?" Cillian asked.

"He knows you are here. That I am here. I do not know what he will do with that information, but there is the risk he will inform the Dagda."

"He called you the Mórrígan."

His mother nodded, her gray eyes never leaving his face. She was beautiful, even in her scrubs, holding herself straight-backed and regally. Her pointed ears were impossible to miss, as was the power that seemed to emanate from her, a wealth of magic that had been strong enough to force Cernunnos to retreat. "I am that which the warrior dead cry to. I am the raven of war. But I am also your mother. That is a truth the Dagda could never stand."

Cillian swallowed tightly, mouth suddenly dry. "So what Niamh said is true. You've been Fae all this time."

"So have you."

"You didn't raise me here like that."

"No, I didn't, and that kept you safe." Her gaze flicked to Bran, impossible to read. "As safe as one could be in land guarded by witches."

"You let us be friends." Cillian reached for Bran's hand, gripping it tightly, like the other man was an anchor in a storm. "You always said to never trust a witch, but you still let us be friends."

"This world of iron poisons us. Nothing could heal you but what the witch could brew, and I knew then the root of what had been done to you. I risked Juliana knowing the truth to keep you safe because I could not undo what Chaos had wrought without risking the Dagda finding you again. He'd taken you from me once before. I would not allow that to happen again. Not when you were so young and powerless."

"Did my mom ever find out what you were?" Bran asked.

The Mórrígan shook her head. "No. She never knew about Cillian. I made sure of it."

"Did she know about Aisling?"

"Juliana was a witch, but in all the time I watched her, she never went into the wyrding. She never called for your Council. She only kept the lights at bay and kept her son safe. That was a restraint I did not think a witch would ever have, but she did."

"That's not an answer."

"Isn't it?"

Bran hunched his shoulders. "She always stressed our job as witches was to protect Pelham."

"There are many ways one can twist an order." The Mórrígan glanced at Scáthach, the pair sharing a look Cillian couldn't read. "Bean sí are rare. When they are born, they belong to the Court of the land they are found in. Scáthach brought the infant bean sí to me instead, and I ordered her to give the babe to the witch."

"Why?"

"I belong to no Court. My life is meant for my students. But I did not care for the Dagda's ruination of the Winter Court. When I found the bean sí in Tech Duinn, her parents refused to send her to the Winter Court and solidify Medb's rule. They gave their child and their lives to me, and I knew the only place to keep her out of the Dagda's hands was in the mortal world," Scáthach said.

"Their lives," Cillian echoed, tensing. "You killed them?"

"They wanted their daughter safe. They could not ensure her safety if they were alive for Medb to break."

A queasiness settled in his gut, and Cillian swallowed against it. He looked at Bran, who appeared just as nauseated at the thought of what Scáthach had done.

"The bean sí would have been used to enshrine Medb in the Winter Court, forever removing Cillian's claim to it," the Mórrígan said.

"Aisling has a name," Bran said hoarsely.

"Yes. The witch gave it to her," Scáthach said.

Bran stood and stepped away from the couch and out of reach. Cillian wanted to pull him back and hold him tight, but the antsy way Bran paced told him it was probably best to let the other man move around. "So you gave Aisling to my mother. You had to know it could have ended wrong."

The Mórrígan arched an eyebrow. "You think your mother so cruel?"

"My mother is *dead*."

"Juliana knew what Aisling was, and yet, she still took Aisling in and loved her as she loved you. She didn't blame a babe for someone else's supposed crimes."

"She never told me." Bran halted in the middle of the living room, staring at a point in the distance. "I don't remember her being pregnant."

"She was raising you to be a witch. She couldn't risk a child spilling the secret of her transgression."

"What did you do?"

The Mórrígan hummed, staring at Bran, and Cillian had the strange urge to stand between them. "What makes you think I did anything?"

"You're Fae—"

"And your mother was a witch. Pelham was her town to guard. What makes you think I was the one who altered your memories? That I would risk mine and Cillian's cover in such a way as to use magic on a witch's child?"

The disbelief and horror that crossed Bran's face had Cillian finally rising to his feet. He closed the distance between them, putting his hands on Bran's shoulders. "Hey. Look at me. Your mom wouldn't ever hurt you."

Bran's hazel eyes were watery with unshed tears. Cillian wished, right then, that he could take Bran's grief and bury it where it wouldn't hurt. "She used magic to make me believe she'd given birth to Aisling."

"She's still your sister."

"I *know* that." Bran dragged a hand over his eyes, lashes clumping wetly together. "I'm not going to stop loving Aisling just because my mother lied about what she was."

Cillian couldn't help the way his fingers dug into Bran's shoulders. "And me?"

Bran rolled his eyes, but he didn't try to pull away. "Don't be an idiot."

Cillian tugged Bran forward, wrapping his arms around the shorter man. Bran tucked his head beneath Cillian's chin, his breath hot against the hollow of Cillian's throat. He wanted nothing more than to keep Bran safe from all the hurt in his heart but knew that was an impossible task.

"I warned you this would be a problem," Scáthach said, staring at the Mórrígan with a disappointed glare.

"I know," the Mórrígan said, soft and resigned, staring at them with something like regret in her eyes. "I knew then when they first met what the witch would be to my son."

Cillian tightened his arms around Bran, refusing to let go, even as Bran raised his head. "What are you talking about?"

Scáthach sighed. "A weakness."

Cillian frowned, staring at his mother. He thought about everything that had been cracked open in his life, all the secrets that had been revealed, and the history of a past he'd barely scratched the surface of. "Verlin thinks Bran is my mate."

The Mórrígan smiled tightly. "Verlin is not wrong. I knew you would love Bran, and he you, and that you would be bound to each other. I thought—if I had to let you grow up a second time, why not do so here, in this town, where a witch could maybe see you for yourself before he saw you as the enemy?"

Bran's fingers twisted in the back of Cillian's shirt before he sighed and let go, shifting so they could both face everyone else. "You didn't want me to hate Cillian."

"I know what it is like to lose a mate, to feel the other half of one's soul be ripped away forever. I did not want that for my son. So yes, I let you be friends. I gave you Jupiter. I gave Aisling to Juliana when Scáthach would have preferred I raise her. I tied you as best I could to the core of my son, hoping you wouldn't hate him when it mattered."

"I don't," Bran said after a moment, voice a rasp in Cillian's ears. "I couldn't."

"I know."

Cillian felt a little sick at the thought he might not have had a choice of who he loved, but whatever anger he had for his mother's machinations didn't burn hotter than embers. Because Cillian had lived his life without Bran for seven years, and he never wanted to suffer through that ache again.

He couldn't hate his mother for making sure he never did.

"And my coven's grimoire?" Bran asked, looking at Scáthach. "How did you come into possession of it?"

"Your mother gave it to me," Scáthach said with a careless shrug.

"She'd never willingly give our history and power to the Fae."

Scáthach smiled, the curve of her mouth sharp like a knife. "She would if it would keep her children safe. I heard rumors an incursion into a witch's territory was imminent, and when I learned the location was here, I came to warn the Mórrígan, only I couldn't find her. So I warned the witch, and she remembered me. She gave me the grimoire of her own free will to keep it safe."

"But not Aisling?"

"Your mother would give up her magic, but she would never give up her daughter."

Bran made a wounded sound that had Cillian wrapping his arm around Bran's waist and pulling him close. He looked at his mother, exhaustion tugging at his limbs. "What now? Ainmire and Etain know I'm alive, which means the Dagda has to know. They might not know where I am, but Cernunnos does. And I don't—I'm not who everyone thinks I am."

The Mórrígan smiled sadly at him, but there was love in her eyes, and that wasn't a lie. "I know. Chaos bound your body and your mind. But you're older now than you were. You can fight."

The problem was Cillian didn't know if he wanted to.

"I think it's been a long day. A long week," Cillian said after a moment, reluctantly pulling away from Bran. "I think we all need some sleep."

His mother nodded and got to her feet. "I'll take Niamh and Seamus home with me. We can talk more in the morning."

"Seamus needs to return to Verlin."

"I wish I did not have to return alone," Seamus said quietly.

Cillian said nothing to that, and Seamus didn't press the issue about staying. He'd already promised he would return to the Otherworld, and so he left with the others. The Mórrígan was the last out the door, but not before she paused by Cillian to tuck some of his hair behind his ear and press a kiss to his cheek.

"My ravens will guard the Shoppe," she promised. "Get some rest."

Then she was gone, and Cillian and Bran were alone in the living room while Aisling slept in her room under Jupiter's watchful eye. Cillian reached for Bran's hand. "Let's clean up."

The shower wasn't big enough for two people, so they took turns scrubbing off the remnants of the wyrding in the glow of candles Bran found in the hall closet. More candles burned in the bedroom where Bran waited for him after Cillian finished cleaning up, casting a soft glow over Bran's bare skin and damp hair, making him look almost ethereal.

"I've never hated you," Bran said into the quiet. "Even when I left, I could never hate you."

"I know," Cillian said, clutching at the towel wrapped around his waist.

Bran slid off the bed and padded over to Cillian. He raised a hand, resting his fingertips over Cillian's heart. The way Bran looked up at Cillian through his lashes made heat shoot through every nerve in his body. "I love you."

Bran kissed his way down Cillian's body, licking after water droplets, whispering those same words into his skin. The heat of his mouth was like a brand that Cillian wanted all over him, a burn like iron he'd gladly suffer. When Bran settled onto his knees, dragging the towel free and tossing it aside, Cillian could only think that he'd grown up with no religion in his home, but when Bran took his cock into his mouth, it felt like a prayer to some deity he couldn't name.

Bran sucked him down with more skill than Cillian had in that area, deep-throating him with an ease that made him moan. He dragged his hands through Bran's dark hair, grabbing a fistful and swearing when Bran swallowed around his cock. The constriction made his hips thrust forward, intentionally pushing his cock deeper into Bran's mouth, down his throat, Bran's nose pressed against his stomach.

"Fuck," Cillian swore, hastily pulling back, Bran's whine making his cock throb. "You're all I ever wanted."

Bran pushed at his thighs, against his hand, and Cillian slid his cock out of that tempting mouth, watching as Bran kissed the tip. "You don't need a collar to keep me. You always had me."

Cillian couldn't help the way his grip tightened in Bran's hair, the way his eyes went to Bran's bare throat. He swallowed, want carving its way into his body, the desire to claim rooted deep. The only thing he could do was push his cock back into Bran's mouth, watch those plush lips wrap around it greedily. Cillian touched Bran's jaw, fingers trailing up his hollowed-out cheek as he slowly thrust in and out, cock sliding over Bran's tongue, going a little deeper each time. Bran's fingers curled around the back of Cillian's thighs, biting into his skin, urging him on, and Cillian could only take what was his gladly.

He thrust in all the way, cock sliding down Bran's throat, choking him, watching as Bran's eyes fluttered shut, something like bliss settling in his face as he kept his mouth open for Cillian to fuck. Drool slicked his chin, his reddened lips, breath coming ragged as Cillian fucked his mouth, cock hard and aching in that wet, willing heat. Bran's hips hitched in small circles, his own cock hard and dripping precum, abandoned in the face of Cillian's pleasure. And wasn't that a revelation, to know that Bran wanted to give Cillian this—his mouth, his body, his heart—and always would.

Cillian groaned, loosening his hold on Bran's hair, palming the back of his head to hold him steady. He chased his pleasure in Bran's mouth, cock hard and aching, a tension at the base of his spine winding tighter and tighter until it snapped. Cillian came with a bitten-off shout, grinding his cock deep in Bran's mouth, spilling so far down his throat Cillian knew he wouldn't be able to taste it. He held Bran there for a moment, tilting his head back and closing his eyes as he caught his breath, Bran still mouthing at his cock.

When he finally pulled out, Bran's ragged breathing was something Cillian would apologize for if Bran didn't look so debauched on his knees, lips swollen and looking up at Cillian like he wanted to be nowhere else. Groaning, Cillian pulled Bran to his feet and spun them around, shoving him up against the wall by the door. He hooked an arm under one of Bran's knees, hiking his leg up, then got a hand between them to grasp Bran's cock.

"Look at me," Cillian rasped, staring down at the witch who loved him, fingers sliding through precum over Bran's cock. It wasn't enough to ease the friction, but the way Bran arched into his touch told him the other man didn't mind.

Bran tipped his head back, panting loudly as he clawed at Cillian's shoulders. "Don't stop."

"What do you see?" Cillian kept stroking him, keeping him pinned to the wall as he gave Bran what he wanted, what he needed. "When you look at me, what do you see?"

Bran tongued at his swollen bottom lip, never looking away. "I only see you."

Cillian shuddered at the truth in those words, a groan tearing free of his mouth. It was easy to kiss Bran, to claim him, to hold him and make him come, relishing the way Bran had to bite down on his shoulder to muffle his cry as he spilled over Cillian's hand. He shivered through his orgasm, arching into Cillian's touch like he couldn't help himself. Cillian carefully lowered his leg, waiting for Bran to get his feet back under him, before he curved his hand over the side of Bran's face and kissed him, slow and deep and wanting.

In that moment, Bran was the beginning and the end and everything in between for Cillian—nothing more, nothing less.

Just everything.

"I love you," Cillian whispered fiercely against Bran's lips. "No matter what, I will always love you."

Bran kissed him back, holding on. "I know. I love you, too."

Witch and Fae.

They should have been enemies, not mates—not everything they'd grown into being—but whatever happened from here on out, Cillian knew wherever he stood, he would always have Bran by his side.

Chapter Twenty-Seven

"Bran!" Aisling shouted from outside. "Something came for you!"

Bran looked up from sweeping as Aisling barreled into the Shoppe, clutching a stack of mail in one hand and shopping bags in the other. He didn't bother telling her to quiet down. Hearing her voice was the best thing these days, better than a quiet grief. "Hopefully, not more bills."

"No. Looks official, though."

The town's tiny post office had held their mother's mail, both for the home they hadn't set foot into since returning from the Otherworld a week ago and for the Shoppe. Bran hadn't yet revoked the hold, and Aisling had offered to pick it up on the way back from her shopping trip. Any other summer and she would have ridden her bike there, but after everything they'd experienced and survived, Bran wasn't allowing her to go alone anywhere. If Bran wasn't with her, then Cillian was when he was off duty, or Niamh was when Cillian could convince the Fae lady to pry herself away from him.

Bran didn't trust Niamh, and the feeling was mutual, but she'd do whatever Cillian wanted, and Bran trusted him. So, Aisling had a minder every hour of every day since they had returned. He'd figure out what to do when she started school up again, but until then, she was always in someone's sight.

The Mórrígan had returned to Amherst, but not before asking Bran's permission to place a glamour over Aisling to ensure her safety. Aisling was still young and didn't have control of her magic. The last thing Bran wanted was for his sister to be revealed as a Fae child in the middle of class since school started that week. As a witch, he should have said no, but he'd reluctantly let the Mórrígan help, hoping he wouldn't regret it someday in the future.

Bran was keeping Aisling out of school for the first few days so she could recover. They still needed to have a ceremony to lay their mother to rest, even though Juliana was already in her grave, courtesy of Mac's care, while Ray's body had been claimed by his family. It didn't matter that Juliana wasn't related to Aisling by blood; their mother had still raised her, and it was past time she found peace.

Bran took the letter from Aisling, looking at Cillian as he entered the Shoppe. He wasn't in his ranger uniform, Thursday being his day off this week, and he'd taken Aisling into Amherst to do some school shopping with cash from the safe. They must have stopped by the post office on the way home.

The windows and furniture in the Shoppe still needed to be replaced, and Bran had a call into the insurance company about that. For now, the windows were boarded up, but he'd bought a new door from a hardware store in Amherst the day after the standoff. Cillian had fitted it to the doorframe for him, and Bran had spent an afternoon carving witchmarks into it and hammering in iron nails at the corners. The handmade sign was still turned to *closed*.

"I'm hungry," Aisling said right before heading upstairs to the apartment.

"We're going to Red's for dinner," Bran called after her.

"Okay!"

Her muffled shout didn't hurt his ears, not like it had last week during the standoff against Cernunnos. Aisling's magic was visceral and haunting, something the entire town had heard that night if gossip was anything to go by. It was powerful, and she was so young, and the Fae would only ever see her as a weapon to be used. It was Bran's job to keep her safe now. To love her, but that would never be a hardship. Aisling was his little sister. Knowing she was Fae didn't change that.

The letter in his hand told him he would be expected to hate her.

To kill her.

Bran frowned down at the letter, carefully leaning the broom against one of the remaining display tables. The debris had all been piled up outside, ready to be hauled to the landfill tomorrow. The Shoppe was closed for the foreseeable future, at least until he could figure out the inventory. His mother's lawyer and the one he'd hired for the guardianship papers had been haranguing him since he'd gotten back in touch with them. Bran had lied about a cross-country road trip to get away from everything and had been unapologetic for the radio silence. Things were moving forward again, though, and his legal, rightful claim to Aisling was winding its way through the court.

"You don't look too happy about whatever that is," Cillian said as he approached. He hooked a finger underneath Bran's chin, tilting his head up for a kiss that Bran would never run away from again.

"It's from the Council of Witches," Bran said.

Cillian frowned down at the letter as well, brows knitting together. Like Aisling, he looked human, thanks to the glamour hiding his Fae skin. The otherworldly beauty of his ancestry was buried in human features, but even when it wasn't, his blue-gray eyes were the same as they always were. Cillian still looked at Bran with a depth of love and affection that made him feel unworthy after seven years of silence. But that was the past, as Cillian liked to remind him, and they were living in the present. The future would be what they'd make of it together.

"What does the Council want?"

They'd talked a lot in the days after making it home—all the secrets of their hidden lives laid bare between them. Bran had spoken of his coven and their history while Cillian had wondered about some other life he didn't remember but which they both knew had been real once.

Was still real past the wyrding, far away in the Otherworld.

A place they both knew they would have to return to someday because neither Cillian nor Aisling could deny what they were, and they would have to face the truth of that. When they did, Bran would not let them face it alone.

Bran hooked his finger beneath the flap of the envelope, tearing it open. The letter inside was written out on beige bond paper, done with a fountain pen rather than a computer. The person's penmanship was pristine, and Bran read through the words with a tight feeling in his gut. "They heard about my mother's death."

"How?"

He didn't think it'd been Mac, even if the guardian was wary of Bran's decisions when it came to the Fae who'd been with them in the woods. Niamh had stayed, taking up a part-time waitressing gig at Red's to learn how to act human, which had been surprising. Seamus had—reluctantly—returned to the Otherworld as promised, having done his duty to stand with Cillian against Cernunnos and gone back to Verlin's side and the leashes that held them both.

Bran's collar and leash were hidden away in Cillian's home, and its absence around his throat was something Bran tried not to think about too much. He would never approve of the way Fae treated witches, but he could be truthful to himself and admit he'd liked wearing Cillian's collar, liked the feeling of ownership when it was Cillian holding his leash.

Liked knowing he belonged to the other man.

"I don't know," Bran said slowly. "But they want to schedule a formal meeting sometime before Samhain."

"What does that mean?"

Bran sighed and folded the letter up again, tucking it back into the envelope. "Something to worry about for another day. Are you ready for dinner?"

"We can take my truck."

Bran headed for the stairs to the apartment and stuck his head through the doorway, calling for his sister. "Aisling! We're leaving!"

She came downstairs half a minute later, all coltish limbs and long hair, a fleeting smile for Bran on her lips and shadows in her eyes. She still grieved, still had nightmares, was still so quiet despite the magic in her voice. Bran wasn't pushing her to talk about any of it, only ever letting her know he was there for her. That he would always be there for her.

Just like their mother would have been.

They left the Shoppe, Bran locking up behind them. Jupiter *cawed* a greeting from the top of Cillian's truck—his personal one, not his work-issued ranger truck. Aisling climbed into the back of the cab while he and Cillian took the front seats. The drive into town was easy, Pelham in that late-summer slowdown where the tourists passing through were mostly gone and only the locals remained.

Niamh wasn't local, but she smiled at them like she was when they pushed open the door to Red's Diner. They weren't the only ones not wanting to cook tonight, judging by how full the place was. It was early to eat, but everyone was still mostly abiding by the old curfew. No one stayed out late these days, not wanting to be in the forest after dark.

"Sit wherever you like," Niamh said, shoving some menus into Cillian's hands. "I will bring you coffee."

"Uh, it's a little late for coffee. A beer would be better," Cillian said as Aisling went to pick out a booth.

Niamh frowned, muttering something under her breath Bran couldn't understand. "Fine. A beer. Go sit."

She was still beautiful, and probably made a killing in tips, but Bran would always know what skin lived beneath her glamour. She stayed for Cillian because Verlin, Seamus, and Carrick couldn't, but that didn't mean Bran would ever trust her.

Cillian took his hand, and Bran followed him to the booth Aisling had picked out, a milkshake already poured and sitting in front of her, courtesy of Lottie. The older woman must have seen them pull up and had it ready for Aisling. Every time they'd come to Red's Diner, Aisling had been given whatever milkshake or dessert she wanted for free. It put a smile on her face, so Bran had bitten back his protest and settled for stuffing twenty-dollar bills into the tip jar on the way out.

Cillian handed Aisling a menu but shared his with Bran. Niamh came back a few minutes later to take their order, better at it now than she had been on her first day earlier in the week. They'd passed her off as a friend of Bran's from Boston, looking to escape the city for a time. She slept in Cillian's extra bedroom while Cillian slept in Bran's bed, and all anyone in town could say was "You boys make such a cute couple. It's about time."

Lottie beamed at them as she set their beer on the table, her eyes on their clasped hands. Cillian smiled and chatted gamely with her for a minute while Aisling slurped at her milkshake.

"We got some fresh strawberry-and-rhubarb pie for dessert. Don't let me forget to cut you some slices," Lottie said before bustling off.

Dinner was a low-key affair, and everyone was kind enough to leave them alone. Small-town manners won out against curiosity, and Bran was able to eat his hamburger and chili cheese fries in peace. They lingered over pie after their meal, letting Aisling play some arcade games while they each finished their beer, Cillian's thigh pressed up against Bran's, his hand on Bran's knee under the table, present in a way the ghosts in his memory never had been.

It was addicting.

He didn't know how he had lived without this for seven years.

He'd label that stupid decision as temporary insanity.

But that was in the past, and when they left Red's Diner, they went back to the Shoppe together. Aisling tumbled out of the truck, using her own key to open up the front door. Bran watched her go, a faint smile on his face, the ache of loss in his chest still new, but at least he still had her.

"Hey," Cillian said as he came around the truck. "I promised Aisling on the way back into town we'd watch a movie together."

"Can't wait," Bran said, closing the truck door. Then he paused, turning his head, staring into the woods across the road.

Cillian came up beside him, wrapping an arm around his waist, the line of his body a tense thing. "What is it?"

"I thought I saw something." They stayed there, listening to the wind whistle through the trees, rustling countless leaves as the shadows grew ever longer. After a moment, Bran shook his head. "Must have been nothing. Come on. Let's get inside."

Cillian kissed him, soft and slow, the hands sliding beneath Bran's T-shirt warm and possessive. "All right."

They headed into the Shoppe, and if Bran looked back over his shoulder at the woods before closing the door, well, no one could blame him. He knew what the forest hid in its shadowy depths, but whatever he thought he'd seen, it wasn't anything to worry about right then.

It was just a trick of the light.

———

Do you want more Bran and Cillian?
Visit bit.ly/BDT-bonus for a bonus short story about their first date.
To stay updated on all Hailey Turner book news, join my newsletter. If
you like urban fantasy and mythology, check out Hailey Turner's
Soulbound series, starting with *A Ferry of Bones & Gold*.

Glossary

Short descriptions of words, acronyms, and phrases used in the story that weren't readily explained in text. Included as well are character names.

Ainmire: (AHN-meera) Fae. Lord of Flame and Wolves. Aligned with the Summer Court.

Autumn Court: Government. Ruling Fae Court of Emain Ablach.

Baile Átha Luain: (Balya Aw-ha Loo-in) Town. Country seat of Ainmire's House.

Bean sí: (ban-shee) Fae. One with the power to herald a new era or death.

Cailleach: (KAI-lach) Fae. Former Winter Queen.

Carrick: (KAIR-ihk) Fae. Lord of Blood and Earth. Aligned with the Winter Court.

Carroll, Ray: Human. Aisling's father and Bran's stepfather. Deceased.

Cernunnos: Fae. Lord. Aligned with the Summer Court.

Chaos: Power. The opposite of Nature and another source of magic.

Council of Witches: Ruling council that oversees all covens. Comprised of Thirteen Seats.

Coven: A family consisting of witches and sometimes humans.

Dagda, the: Fae. Summer King of the Summer Court. Married to the Mórrígan.

Damarus: Fae. Right hand to Ainmire.

Dunne, Cillian: Fae. Winter Prince of the Winter Court. A park ranger in the mortal world. Bran's mate.

Dunne, Shannon: *See* the Mórrígan.

Emain Ablach: (ee-main a-BLACH) Country. One of the Fae countries comprising the Four Lands of the Otherworld. Located in the south.

Éire: (ey-rah) What was once the Four Lands in the mortal world.

Etain: (ee-tane) Fae. Lady of Threads and Illusions. Right hand to the Dagda.

Falias: (FAL-us) City. Capital of Mag Mell where the Spring Court resides.

Familiar: Animal. Companion to a witch. Bound by magic.

Fiadh: (fee-ah) Fae. Lady of a House. Verlin's mother.

Findias: (fin-dus) City. Capital of Emain Ablach, where the Autumn Court resides.

Fomorian(s): (fo-mo-ri-an) Fae. A sect of Fae in the Otherworld who betrayed the others by partnering with mortals to banish the Fae from the mortal world. Their bloodlines and ability to cast magic were absorbed by successive generations of mortals who became witches.

Four Lands, the: Descriptor of the four countries comprising the Otherworld.

Gallagher, Aisling: (ash-lin) Fae. Bean sí. Bran's little sister.

Gallagher, Juliana: Witch. Bran and Aisling's mother. Deceased.

Gallagher, Bran: Witch. Head of the Gallagher coven. Cillian's mate.

Geas: (gee-yas) Magic. A Fae binding.

Glamour: Magic. Exclusively used by Fae, typically to hide their appearance.

Gleann Bheatha: (GLA-oon va-ha) Town. Country seat of Verlin's House.

Gorias: (gor-us) City. Capital of Tech Duinn, where the Winter Court resides.

Grimoire: (grim-waar) Object. A book containing each coven's history of spellwork and witchmarks.

Guardian: Rank. A human tasked by a witch to be a protector of their coven against those who would learn their secrets.

Jupiter: Raven. Bran's familiar.

Lights: Creatures. Remnants of witches broken by the Fae and turned by way of Chaos into monsters that haunt the wyrding and attack the mortal world.

MacIntyre, Henry: Human. A park ranger in the mortal world. A guardian beholden to the Gallagher coven.

Mag Mell: (mag mell) Country. One of the Fae countries comprising the Four Lands of the Otherworld. Located in the west.

Magic: Power. The use of Nature or Chaos by witches and Fae.

Mate: Descriptor of a relationship where two or more people are intrinsically bound together.

Medb: (may-ve) Fae. Winter Queen. Ruler of the Winter Court.

Mórrígan, the: Fae. Summer Queen of the Summer Court. Married to the Dagda. Cillian's mother. She lived under the identity of Shannon Dunne in the mortal world.

Murias: (mu-rus) City. Capital of Tír na nÓg, where the Summer Court resides.

Nature: Power. Source of magic.

Niamh: (neeve) Fae. Lady of Sky and Lightning. Formally of the Summer Court. Presently aligned with the Winter Court.

Otherworld: A mirror world of the mortal world where the Four Lands of Faerie were banished to.

Right hand: Rank. Proxy for a ruler when required. Most trusted advisor and supporter.

Scáthach: (SCAW-hach) Fae. Warrior. Aligned with no Court.

Seamus: (SHAY-mus) Fae. Knight. Aligned with the Winter Court. Mate to Verlin.

Shadow paths: Trails within the wyrding carved out by the Fae between locations within the Otherworld.

Spring Court: Government. Ruling Fae Court of the Mag Mell.

Summer Court: Government. Ruling Fae Court of Tír na nÓg.

Tech Duinn: (chawk do-in) Country. One of the Fae countries comprising the Four Lands of the Otherworld. Located in the north.

Tír na nÓg: (TEER-na-nog) Country. One of the Fae countries comprising the Four Lands of the Otherworld. Located in the east.

Verlin: (vur-LIN) Fae. Lord of Breath and Bone. Aligned with the Winter Court. Mate to Seamus.

Wild Hunt: Spirits. Ghostly beings who hunt the living and are commanded by the Winter Prince.

Winter Court: Government. Ruling Fae Court of Tech Duinn.

Witch: A human who can use magic. They are tasked with guarding the mortal world against the encroachment of the wyrding and attacks from the Fae.

Witchmarks: Power. The focus through how a witch casts their magic.

Wyrding: (weird-ing) The barrier between the mortal world and the Otherworld.

Author's Notes

This book wanted to pour out of me, and I have Lily Morton to thank for that. Lily held my hand and alpha read the chapters as I finished them and assured me it didn't suck when I second-guessed myself. I first told her about this story when we were together in York, England, a couple of years ago, and I'm so happy she loved it now as much as she did back then when she was so excited as I described it. She is honestly one of the best cheerleaders and one of my best friends.

May Archer, Aimee Nicole Walker, and Lucy Lennox kept me company while I wrote this book and never minded the cat videos I sent when I should have been writing.

Gary Furlong is an awesome narrator but also helped me out with the Irish phonetics. Any mistakes with the Irish language belong to me.

Sandra is forever keeping my commas in line. I honestly don't know what I would do without her keen eye.

I would be thrilled and grateful if you would consider reviewing *Bright Dead Things* on Amazon or Goodreads. I appreciate all honest reviews, positive or negative.

Connect with Hailey

Keep up with book news by joining Hailey Turner's newsletter and get several free short stories.
Join the reader group on Facebook: Hailey's Hellions
Follow Hailey on Instagram.
Follow Hailey's author page on Facebook.
Follow Hailey on Facebook.
Follow Hailey on BlueSky.
Follow Hailey on Goodreads.
Follow Hailey on Pinterest.
Follow Hailey on BookBub.
Visit Hailey's website for more information on her books and merch.

Other Works By Hailey Turner

M/M Science Fiction Military Romance

Captain Jamie Callahan, son of a wealthy senator and socialite mother, is a survivor.

Staff Sergeant Kyle Brannigan, a Special Forces operative, is a man with secrets.

Alpha Team, the Metahuman Defense Force's top-ranked field team, is where the two collide and their lives will never be the same.

<ins>Metahuman Files</ins>

In the Wreckage

In the Ruins

In the Shadows

In The Blood

In The Requiem

In the Solace

<ins>A Metahuman Files: Classified Novella</ins>

Out of the Ashes

New Horizons

Fire In The Heart

M/M Urban Fantasy

Patrick Collins is a broken mage running from his past.

Jonothon de Vere is a god pack alpha werewolf searching for a home.

In a world where magic is real, myths and legends exist, and gods walk the earth, Patrick and Jono are thrown together by the Fates themselves to fight against an enemy that threatens to consume the world. For if the gods fall and demons from every hell rise up, humanity won't stand a chance.

<u>Soulbound</u>

A Ferry of Bones & Gold

All Souls Near & Nigh

A Crown of Iron & Silver

A Vigil in the Mourning

On the Wings of War

An Echo in the Sorrow

A Veiled & Hallowed Eve

<u>Soulbound Universe Standalones</u>

Resurrection Reprise

Secondhand Skin

LGBTQ+ Epic steampunk-inspired fantasy

Welcome to Maricol, where the land will kill you, kinship turns the gears of war, and burning the dead lest they come back to life is the only way to survive.

Infernal War Saga

The Prince's Poisoned Vow

The Emperor's Bone Palace

The Queen's Starfire Throne

Infernal War Saga Novella

An Emporium of Hearts

M/M Romantasy

Caught up in a political game between Fae Courts, Cillian and Bran realize the most dangerous thing they can do is fall in love.

Bitter Legacies

Bright Dead Things

Twisted Iron Marks

* 9 7 9 8 9 9 0 0 2 7 1 2 1 *